"You're perfect."

Giselle let the words settle over her for an instant, enjoying their flash of warmth. She didn't hear compliments very often, particularly from her ex, who had looked at her as if she were simply part of the furniture for the last several years. But then she noted another of Fin's skittish glances and reminded herself he was probably up to something.

"You must know a million other women."

"Not old enough."

Her extraordinary reserve allowed her to keep perfectly still. One didn't get through excruciating high-school beauty pageants by letting hurt feelings show. Her eyes, however, must have given her away.

"I don't mean—" Fin lifted his hand. "I just mean I need someone my own age."

Clearly, he'd missed the mark on this one. "How old *are* you?" she asked.

"Twenty-nine . . . soon."

Giselle looked at him skeptically. "When's soon?"

"Next weekend."

She raised her eyebrow. Twenty-eight? She had about seven years on him. Although at least he was older than she'd thought. He'd looked boyish from a distance, but up close he had all the strength that brings a man over the threshold from boyish to sexy. He was definitely already there.

THE
Red Bikini

Lauren Christopher

BERKLEY SENSATION, NEW YORK

THE BERKLEY PUBLISHING GROUP
Published by the Penguin Group
Penguin Group (USA) LLC
375 Hudson Street, New York, New York 10014

USA • Canada • UK • Ireland • Australia • New Zealand • India • South Africa • China

penguin.com

A Penguin Random House Company

THE RED BIKINI

A Berkley Sensation Book / published by arrangement with the author

Berkley Sensation Books are published by The Berkley Publishing Group.
BERKLEY SENSATION® is a registered trademark of Penguin Group (USA) LLC.
The "B" design is a trademark of Penguin Group (USA) LLC.

For information, address: The Berkley Publishing Group,
a division of Penguin Group (USA) LLC,
375 Hudson Street, New York, New York 10014.

ISBN: 978-0-425-27441-5

PUBLISHING HISTORY
Berkley Sensation mass-market edition / July 2014

PRINTED IN THE UNITED STATES OF AMERICA

10 9 8 7 6 5 4 3 2 1

For Chris:
Some people say that romance heroes don't really exist.
But they're wrong.
Thank you for always being mine.

ACKNOWLEDGMENTS

There are so many people who made this book possible, I'm not even sure where to start.

So let me start at the beginning: I want to thank historical author Tricia Lynne, whom I met in a critique group in 2007. She read a *very* early draft of *The Red Bikini* and was Fin's very first fan. She asked for Chapters 7, 8, 9, 10 . . . and begged me to finish the book. She made me believe in this story and my ability to get it published. Tricia has offered so much support and encouragement over the years as the world's best critique partner—I truly couldn't have written this book without her brilliant help.

Next I want to thank my amazing and generous beta readers—Debi Skubic, Michelle Proud, Crystal Posey, Kristi Davis, Mary Ann Perdue—as well as my early-version readers, authors Nancy Freund and Michelle Bailat-Jones. All of you provided generous feedback that helped shape this story, and your support and unwavering encouragement helped spur me along.

Thanks to my friend Grace Todd for meeting with me and encouraging me, and helping with the surf culture.

Thanks to my fabulous Firebird sisters—the Golden Heart class of 2012. They've been there for me every step of the way, with e-mails of encouragement (thanks, Tammy!), hope, help, inspiration, and sometimes just a funny line to get me through the day. Such a wonderful group of women, always with our virtual arms around each other.

Thanks to my agent, Jill Marsal, who saw something in me and gave me the nudges I needed to get my writing out into the real world.

Thanks to editor Wendy McCurdy and to the staff at Berkley for great editing, copywriting, copyediting, and cover design, making this little idea I had in my head into a real-life book.

I can't forget all my family and friends, too, who never rolled their eyes or looked at me skeptically when I said I was writing . . . *again*. They never questioned my dream when I had to forego yet another weekend activity or book-club dinner or family event. They all believed in me until I finally believed in myself. Thank you—all of you!

Thanks especially to my parents, who were there clapping and offering encouragement for every writing award as far back as kindergarten, when my very first yarn-bound, crayon-printed book was on display at the Huntington Beach Mall.

And thanks to my kids, who went without clean socks many a Monday, and who left me to my own devices to write in quietude whenever a deadline loomed.

And last, but certainly not least, thanks to my amazing husband (and biggest fan) Chris, to whom this book is dedicated. This book would certainly not be possible if I didn't believe in true love. And, thanks to him, I do.

CHAPTER

One

Giselle flung the suitcase on her sister's tropical-patterned bedspread and let out the sigh she'd been holding since sometime over the air space of Kansas. Or maybe as far back as Illinois. Or maybe even since they'd been in the airport in Indiana.

She stared at a bright red cloth napkin Lia had left on the bed, next to a note in her sister's loopy handwriting: *"It's okay. Relax."*

Giselle frowned and lifted the napkin, then felt four strings slip through her fingers.

It was a bikini. How very Lia. How very *not* Giselle.

It's okay.

Relax.

She folded the triangles and tucked the package deep into the corner of Lia's dresser drawer, amid some tissue-wrapped lingerie and a lavender drawer sachet.

"Mommy," came a breathless voice from behind her, "there's *sand*!"

Her daughter flung herself onto the bed, sending the suitcase and all their clothes bouncing and squeaking. "And Aunt

Lia left me *sandals*! Can we go to the water now? Can I put on my suit?" Little hands gripped the edge of Giselle's suitcase.

"In a minute." Giselle closed the drawer. "Why don't you help me unpack?"

Giselle's fake enthusiasm—held in a false falsetto since Indiana—sounded too breathless, but Coco seemed to buy it, and her little pale legs whisked her to the front room.

Giselle tried to take her twenty cleansing breaths while Coco was gone, but, as usual, she only got to about the seventh. Coco came bumping back through the doorway with a pink Barbie suitcase.

"I wonder how Aunt Lia knew I liked *pink* sandals."

Giselle eyed Coco's sparkly shoes and the tutu she'd worn on the plane. "Probably a good guess." She lifted Coco's suitcase onto the bed beside hers.

Lia's beachside apartment was small—not much more than a box, really—but Giselle felt a wave of appreciation that her sister had opened it to them, and on such short notice. Sandy Cove was the perfect place to escape to for two weeks. But California would have been much too expensive without being able to use Lia's apartment. Giselle couldn't use up what was left of her cash reserves.

"What was that song Aunt Lia taught you?" Giselle asked over her shoulder as she yanked closed the bedroom's palm-colored curtains.

Coco flung one of her blond braids over her shoulder and began swaying her hips. *"Stir it up . . ."* she began singing. Her toothlessness lent a lispy charm to the Bob Marley song.

Giselle smiled. *". . . Little darlin' . . . stir it up . . ."*

Their hips moved in exaggerated sways, and soon most of Giselle's worries were tucked away with their T-shirts, shorts, Giselle's tailored slacks, Coco's sleep toy Ninja Kitty, and their sensible bathing suits.

While Giselle was sad she wouldn't get to see Lia, who was tied up with a business trip in New York, she was sort of relieved. The pitying platitudes were exhausting. Especially when coupled with the hushed tones from friends and family in Indiana: *Omygod, what will she do? And what will she do without Roy?* Giselle knew the way to make the hushed voices stop was to show everyone what she was made of—lift her chin, showcase her strength, saunter into a room with a confidence she might dredge up from somewhere. But she hadn't quite been able to do that. Maybe she just needed time. . . .

As Sandy Cove's afternoon light began calming her through the mango-colored shades, Giselle felt relaxed enough to get into Lia's tiny kitchen and bake. She'd picked up a few staples at the beach corner market to make her raisin cookies. Counting strokes and measuring ingredients always did her wonders.

While she measured and poured, Coco sat at the dining table and told knock-knock jokes until a sharp rap sounded at the door.

"Someone's here," Coco whispered.

The tightening began in her neck as Giselle wiped her hands on a towel and made her way to the entryway.

She peeked through the peephole and saw a totem pole of a boy standing on the porch.

He was young—maybe twenty—with a black rubber item folded like a tablecloth in his right hand. Sable brown hair coiled into quarter-sized curls all over his head, and a brown tuft of hair sprouted from his chin in a hippie "soul patch" style. His toast-colored eyes were close together, giving him a comical air. He brought them closer to the peephole, his face distorting in the funny glass.

Giselle opened the door a crack.

"Heeeeey," he said. His eyes took in as much of her as he could see from behind the door, but the gesture didn't feel insolent, or even flirtatious—which was good, since he seemed at least fifteen years younger than she was.

Giselle flung the dish towel over her shoulder and tucked a strand of hair back into her chignon as she pulled the door wider. He wore bright orange-and-brown knee-length swim trunks that hung low on his waist, as if there wasn't quite enough body to hold them up. He stood the same height as Giselle, but was reedier, the outline of his ribs pressing through his tanned skin. His knobby feet were covered in sand.

"You must be Lia's sister," he said lazily.

"Yes."

"You look just like her." A note of wonder hung on his words.

"Thank you." Giselle smoothed her skirt.

She was flattered—she thought of Lia as beautiful in every way—but Giselle didn't see a resemblance. She felt much older, although their age difference was only six years. But she also felt duller, and at least a dress size bigger. Despite the fact Giselle had won beauty contests throughout her teens, her confidence had plummeted when Roy had had his first affair.

"This is for your daughter." The rubber item unfurled from his fingers. It was a small wet suit. "I'm Rabbit."

Rabbit? Giselle blinked back her surprise. So this was who Lia had told her about? Somehow she'd had the image differently in her mind: She'd pictured maybe a grizzled old guru who lived on a sand dune with parrots. Or at least someone out of junior college.

Clutching the wet suit against her chest, she held out her other hand in default hostess mode: "I'm Giselle."

He regarded her hand with amusement, then shook it briefly. "Sweet. You have something cooking in there?" He tried to peek around the door.

"Oh—raisin cookies." She stepped back, and Coco popped her head around, able to stand it no longer.

Rabbit studied her as she pushed her way through the doorway. "And you must be Coco." He crouched to the ground, rubbing the tuft of hair on his chin. "I've heard all about you from your aunt. How do you feel about being a little grommet this week?"

"A grommet?"

"A young surfer. Lia signed you up for my camp. I have twelve new groms coming."

Coco's short, jilting bounces expressed everything.

Thank goodness Lia had arranged this. It would be good for Coco to escape the drama that had become their lives. All Giselle had to do in return was take pictures for Rabbit's brochure. And go out on one date with a guy Lia knew named Dave or Don or something.

Although it was a pretty close toss-up, the brochure made her the most nervous. Marketing-minded Lia had coordinated it, even though Giselle had insisted she had no brochure experience. In fact, she had no work experience at all, unless you counted posing as the perfect doctor's wife at charity balls. But Lia had insisted that the photos Giselle took of

Coco were excellent. *Your photos capture such truth and beauty,* her sister had said. Giselle had continued to protest, but Lia reminded her that Rabbit wasn't exactly a Fortune 500 company. He couldn't even pay. Except in trade. Which was where Coco benefited.

"I have a surfboard for you," Rabbit whispered to Coco. He glanced up at Giselle. "Can you come see it?"

Giselle hesitated. The unpacking wasn't done. She hadn't taken her twenty cleansing breaths. The raisin cookies had four minutes left. She needed to organize, prioritize, get their lives in order.

But she caught the expression on Coco's face—one of hopefulness, a trust in adventure—and decided she could take a few cues from her daughter. Giselle did need to learn to relax. She did need to straighten her backbone and garner some strength. She did need to learn how to grasp adventure.

"Sure," she said, shrugging as if she made impromptu decisions all the time. "But I have a few more minutes for the cookies."

"I'll wait." Rabbit grinned.

When the buzzer finally went off, Giselle loaded the entire batch onto a plate to bring to his apartment. She tucked a strand of hair behind her ear and took Coco's hand. "Then let's go."

She tried not to think of the clothing still on the bed, or the blind date with the man whose name she couldn't remember, or the twenty cleansing breaths, while she followed Rabbit next door.

Let their new life begin. . . .

A waist-high gate divided the halves of the second-story patio Rabbit and Lia shared.

When her sister had said that Rabbit lived "next door," Giselle hadn't realized how close that would be. No wonder their mother wouldn't stay here. Having their coiffed, French-manicured mother staying within shouting distance of a barely clad boy like Rabbit, who probably got stoned to the Doors and tracked sand across the patio on a regular basis, would be their mother's undoing. Eve McCabe typically chose to stay at a Hilton in posh Newport Beach several miles up.

Rabbit strode toward his wide-open door in that rubbery way lanky boys move. Music tumbled out: some kind of folk singer with a mellow, seaside sound. Soon the music swallowed him.

Giselle stalled. She peered around the doorway, but he'd already disappeared.

His place was entirely white and beige, with an empty expanse of stained carpeting. A lone card table was set up where a dining table would normally be, a smattering of potato chips and empty beer bottles littered across its torn top. Beanbag chairs were tossed about the living area, filled with boys with shaggy hair and sandy feet. One was playing a guitar to a song on the speaker.

Along the living room wall were four bright surfboards, each more colorful than the last. One showed off brilliant stripes and flames, two teemed with plant shapes, and the last was in swirls of yellows, oranges, and reds. A fifth, with a bright turquoise stripe down the center, lay across the mottled carpet. One of the boys sat on top, his legs crossed into a suntanned X.

"Hey," said the one on the board.

Giselle thought perhaps it was meant to be a greeting and gave an uncertain nod.

"C'min, Giselle," yelled Rabbit from around the corner.

She took a few tentative steps onto the linoleum patch that served as an entryway, her espadrilles crunching in the scattered sand grains.

A boy in the kitchen drew a bottle of beer out of a cooler and held it toward her.

"No, thanks," she said, wrapping her arm around Coco's neck and looking toward the doorway where Rabbit had disappeared.

"Are those for us?" he asked, eyeing the plate of cookies.

"Yes." She thrust the plate forward.

He took a cookie off the top and bit into it as he surveyed Coco. "You must be one of Rabbit's groms."

"I am." Coco nodded. "He's bringing me a surfboard."

"Step aside!" Rabbit's voice emerged from a back bedroom. In both hands, he gripped an enormous turquoise board. He dipped it so it didn't hit the doorway, then gingerly laid it across the carpet. The boys moved to make space.

"This was my sister's when she started," Rabbit said.

Coco bounced around it. A wood-grain pattern ran down the center, with two bamboo shoots on either side. A row of yellow hibiscus flowers entwined through the bamboo. The artwork was faded where the hibiscus flowers began, and there were plenty of scratches and dings, but Coco's face lit up like a Christmas tree.

"My sis was a little grommet like you once," Rabbit drawled. "Now she's on the Women's World Tour and rides for Roxy."

Coco turned wide eyes toward Giselle. She clearly didn't understand any of that, but she could tell it sounded impressive.

Rabbit walked around the board. "So you can use this when you practice, but in my class we're going to use blue foam boards like the other kids, okay?"

Coco nodded.

He patted the center hibiscus. "Kick off your shoes."

Coco mounted the board with great seriousness. Rabbit's finger outlined elements of the design that would give her cues—her left toe should line up with the wood grain, while her right heel should round the curve of the bottom hibiscus.

He sat back on his haunches and frowned at her feet. "Are you left-handed, little dudette?"

Coco nodded hesitantly.

"Ah, a goofy-foot," he said. "I thought so. This doesn't look natural for you. Kino surfs goofy, too." He motioned with his thumb to a guy sitting behind him. "Let's switch feet."

Rabbit continued in his rhythmic drone while Giselle breathed in the scent of the ocean that wafted through the nearby dining-room window. The boys' chatter went on in the background—some argument about something called onshore swells. The mellow seaside singer continued to encourage love and sunshine. Giselle closed her eyes and inhaled cocoa butter and salty air, feeling a strange, sudden peace in the room full of strangers with whom she shared very little except being part of the human race.

"Now!" shouted Rabbit.

Coco pushed up with her arms to bring her feet to the cues.

"Excellent," he drawled, grinning. "That was a beautiful pop-up. Let's try it again."

Coco giggled, and he went on while Giselle noticed a beer bong in the corner of the room. Over her shoulder, two of the boys began swearing. One shoved the other, and a third threw a bottle across the room to a catcher in a beanbag.

Giselle reached for Coco's shoulder. As nice as it had been to be welcomed into this underworld for a minute, it might be time for their exit. "I, uh . . . We really need to go."

As the swearing continued, she cupped Coco's ears and began steering her toward the front door, but a smooth, firm voice came rolling across the room: *"Boys!"*

The room stilled.

"That's enough."

The voice came from another tanned, bare-chested figure leaning in the doorjamb, watching everyone, with a black rubbery tube stretched from one hand to the other. He looked older than the others, although Giselle couldn't be sure. He definitely had a more solid body, with actual muscles that looked like they would keep him grounded if a big gust of wind came through. His blond-tipped hair was pushed up as if it had just dried that way. He had on swim trunks, his wide chest boasting the dull sheen that salt water leaves, a dusting of wheat over copper.

He frowned at the boys who were swearing, then motioned with his head toward Coco.

"Sorry, Fin," one of the boys said. He gave one last quiet shove, though, like a puppy frolicking.

Giselle meant to turn her attention back to Coco, but found herself unable to take her eyes off this newest appearance, captivated by his perfect chest, his square jaw, the rock-shaped shoulders. His body was a gorgeous color—a golden brown, with tinges of smoky red at the tops of his shoulders. Giselle thought it would be perfect to paint. Her second thought was that it would be perfect to photograph. And her third was that it would be wondrous to touch.

As her mind lingered on the last thought, imagining her finger running along that ridge that defined his shoulder from his biceps, he met her gaze.

She averted her eyes. *Sweet criminy.* She pulled her cardigan closer and smoothed her hair. She was a stay-at-home mom from Indiana. Comptroller for the PTA. A *scrapbooker.* And he was just a kid. What was wrong with her?

She clasped one of Coco's shoulders and leaned toward Rabbit. "We need to get going."

She'd had enough of the surfer underworld for one day. And this California sunshine was frying her brain—staring at a twentysomething surfer. Was she losing her mind?

Rabbit unfurled his legs. "Join us. We're cooking out."

"Can we, Mommy?" Coco begged.

Giselle ran Coco's braid through her hand. "I'll think about it." But she'd already dismissed it. Drinking beer and eating hot dogs with a bunch of sandy boys that looked barely out of high school was probably not what she and her five-year-old daughter should be doing. And she didn't need that Fin kid distracting her with his golden shoulders and strange blue eyes. Maybe she'd find a nice, clean Olive Garden nearby.

She gathered Coco's shoes, grabbed the empty cookie plate, and hustled out of the room, trying not to look back toward Fin. The other boys called out good-byes—she thought one called her "Betty"—but mostly she focused on getting Coco to the patio without any more gawking.

As she passed the doorway to the bedrooms, however, her curiosity ran rampant against her better sense. Suddenly, wildly, uncontrollably—her gaze swept back.

But he wasn't there.

She couldn't tell whether the air whooshing out of her lungs was from disappointment that she didn't get another glance at his sculpted chest or relief that she wouldn't embarrass herself any further. Either way, she gave up a prayer of gratitude that her decency had remained intact for the next sixty seconds.

After Rabbit and another boy laid the surfboard in the center of Lia's living room, Giselle closed the door and leaned her head back.

She took twelve cleansing breaths.

Starting a new life might have to come in smaller steps.

Giselle and Coco enjoyed a quiet dinner at the Olive Garden that felt, momentarily, normal. They played tic-tac-toe with straws and sugar packets. Giselle thought about how Roy would get annoyed that they were making such a mess, especially when one of the sugar packets might open. She wondered, ridiculously, whether that might be why he left. But then she caught herself. That was exactly the kind of thinking that was keeping her stagnant.

After dinner, she steered the rental car into a curbside parking space after circling the beach city blocks at least four times to find one. She pulled up on the brake, wiped away a tear that sometimes appeared when she was in silence and darkness, and glanced into the rearview mirror: Coco's blond bangs had fallen across her forehead as her head lulled to one side, resting on Ninja Kitty.

Giselle sighed. When Coco used to fall asleep in the car as a toddler, Roy would carry her. Now that her little girl wasn't so little anymore, putting her on her hip was like carrying an octopus. But she hoisted Coco, tucked Ninja Kitty between them, and trudged back the two blocks to the apartment, tucking her daughter's gangly legs around her waist.

As she got nearer the apartment, the smoke of a charcoal grill coiled through the salty air. She managed the last few pebbled-concrete steps and dragged herself to the crest of the railing.

"Hey," shouted one of the boys, "it's Donna." He snapped his bangs to the side and pushed up from the wall to help her unhinge the gate.

She didn't bother to correct him. He probably didn't remember her name because he didn't care. She did welcome his help with the gate, however—it felt like Coco weighed two hundred pounds all of a sudden.

"Big day for the little dudette." He thrust his chin toward Coco.

Giselle smiled tiredly and shifted Coco's legs.

As a riotous cheer erupted over her shoulder, several hyper-charged bodies spilled out Rabbit's front door—all shoving onto the patio. Another of the boys, who looked Hawaiian, stood guard over the smoking grill. *"Easy."* He pressed them back with his elbows.

As Giselle turned from the scent of grilled sausage to fumble for her front-door key, Rabbit appeared.

"Shhhhhh," he told the louder boys, pressing his palms toward the ground. He strode across the patio and took the key from Giselle to unlock her door. While she shuffled into the dark living room, Rabbit leaned in the doorway. Coco's braids flopped across her neck as Giselle laid her on the couch with Ninja Kitty.

"Join us," Rabbit said, tilting his curls toward the patio.

"I can't," Giselle whispered.

"She'll be fine. You can sit in front of the door—we'll leave it open."

"No."

"Just one beer."

She took the key from him and smiled apologetically. "Thanks anyway."

I'm too old, was what she was thinking. *And someone's mother. And I need to make the rest of the cookies.*

He nodded and looked at her soulfully. For a young guy, Rabbit looked like he had a lot of years in him.

"Where does your name come from?" She took off her

jacket. She could make a little conversation. She sort of welcomed the company tonight.

"It's a nickname I had since I was a kid." His syllables fell into a long drawl. "When I was first learning to surf, I used to do my pop-ups really fast, and I guess I looked like a rabbit."

Giselle tried to picture a tinier mop-topped version of him and smiled. "What's your real name?"

"Henry." He laughed abruptly, as if he hadn't heard it spoken aloud in a long time.

"Does a person 'pop up' fast when he's scared?" she teased.

Rabbit's head jerked back. "*Scared?* No. I was just small and skinny." He slumped into the doorway and then seemed to realize she was razzing him. He grinned and inspected the beer bottle in his hand. "I like your sister," he announced.

"It's hard not to like Lia."

"She told me to watch out for you, but you seem to be doing okay for yourself."

She adjusted her jacket on the barstool and sighed. The idea of Lia asking someone to "watch out for her" embarrassed her. They all worried about her now—her mom, her sisters—they all acted as if she were going to fly apart any minute. Sometimes, actually, she did—there were moments after Roy's sudden disappearance when she thought she was looking down at herself from above, watching a complete stranger. But it bothered her that they all knew. As the oldest child, she'd always been the levelheaded one, the responsible one, the one who had it all together. But now they knew she'd lost her footing. It made her feel revealed and vulnerable, like a rabbit herself— exposed out of its den.

Giselle cleared her throat. "Yes, I'm sure I am." She began organizing her belongings along the countertop.

"Lia said she set you up with Dan the Man."

Dan. That was his name. . . . "Yeah, I guess so. Thursday night." She was dreading it, but one date wouldn't kill her. Lia said she had to start somewhere. "What's he like?"

"He's okay. He's a real estate guy here. Lotsa money."

Giselle nodded. Sounded like Lia's type, actually. But he obviously didn't impress Rabbit here much.

"Fin was asking about you, though," Rabbit said.

Giselle's heart skipped, right there, as she stalled with her key ring halfway into her purse.

She went back to fussing with the place mats on the breakfast bar. There must be some mistake. Surfer boys with rock-shaped shoulders did not ask about PTA moms from Indiana.

"I didn't know how much you might want to be bothered during your weeks here, though," Rabbit continued, shifting in the doorway, "so I didn't know what to tell him."

She brushed a few breakfast crumbs off the countertop so she wouldn't have to meet Rabbit's eyes. She didn't want to know whether he thought it was weird for a friend of his to be asking about an older, divorced mom from suburbia. Fin must have been asking about her regarding *work*, or the photographs. Maybe he had wanted a cookie.

"What did he want to know?" she asked.

"If you were married."

Giselle knocked over a saltshaker. Surely, this must be a mistake. Rabbit must have misunderstood. Perhaps Fin needed someone to sew a button on his swimsuit or something.

"Rabbit, how old are you guys?" She rearranged the salt and pepper shakers. She needed to restore a little balance to her universe. "Some of those boys looked like they were barely out of high school—are they old enough to drink?"

"I'm twenty-three—old enough to drink." He winked. "Most of us are twenty-two or twenty-three."

Giselle took her time before asking the next question. "And Fin?"

"Ah, Fin's an old man. He's not one of us."

Giselle wasn't sure which of those two statements interested her more. She cleared her throat while she assembled her next question, but Coco stirred on the couch and wriggled into a sitting position.

"Mommy." Coco shoved her bangs back with her palm. "Can I have water?"

"Sure, baby." Giselle hustled into the kitchen, relieved to be back in her own world.

As she rounded the kitchen corner, her cell phone rang, pulling her even further back into normalcy—it was a tinkling piano sound, Beethoven's Fifth, which her ex-husband had programmed nearly a year and a half ago.

"I'll go." Rabbit ducked his head and waved. "Anything you need, Giselle, just ask."

The door clicked behind him as Giselle rummaged through her purse for the jangling phone. She wished Rabbit hadn't left. Despite how young he seemed, he felt kind, and comfortable, and Giselle had the urge to sit on the floor with him and ask a million questions, as if he held the key to a new world she might want to hear about right now—something foreign and fascinating that could dangle a little magic before her eyes. She knew she couldn't stay in that world, but hearing about it would do her well, like a child who wants a bedtime story about princesses to ward off any monsters that might show up instead.

Beethoven's Fifth pealed again, and she looked at her phone with resignation. "Hello?"

"Giselle," came the voice on the other line. His flat intonation registered right away, even though she hadn't heard much of it in months. Four, to be exact. Four months, two weeks, and two days. She was amazed he could still make her hand shake.

"Yes?" She tried to keep her voice steady, uninterested. She wanted him to think she didn't know who this was. She wanted him to think she had men calling her cell phone all the time, at eight or nine o'clock, and she couldn't differentiate between all their voices.

"He's dead," he said.

Giselle breathed in, let another breath out.

"The funeral is Tuesday. I'm flying out tonight. I know you left a message saying you and Coco would be in Sandy Cove all week, so I'd like you to be there. It's only about thirty miles from where you're staying. It would mean a lot to Mom. And Ray-Lynn."

Giselle's world kept closing in, the voices and names from the past, trying to edge into the new world she was trying to create. She had the foreboding sense that the voices and names wanted to fill her new space, push her out. She imagined herself falling over a cliff.

"Roy, why aren't you returning my calls? I've been calling—"

"This isn't the time, Giselle. My father just died. Are you going to be there?"

She gripped the counter to steady herself. She didn't know

what to respond to first: his typical reprimand, the fact that he was forming real sentences to her on the phone for the first time in four months, the fact that Joe had finally passed from cancer, or the uneasy awareness she was going to have to come face-to-face with Roy again, right here in California, just as she was just starting to get her life back together.

"I'll be there," she said.

He gave her the details; then she put the phone down and went to get Coco her glass of water. She sat on the couch and stroked her little girl's hair until she fell asleep. Giselle's tears these days had a few different wellsprings, but the main one, right now, was the fact that Roy hadn't even asked about Coco.

The squawk of seagulls woke her.

Giselle lay in bed and watched Coco's profile, listening to the gulls' cries and thinking about how different morning sounds were in different parts of the country.

She didn't know how she was going to face Roy. She hadn't seen him once since that humble day when she'd found the note underneath the cantaloupe next to the bowl of breakfast bars: *"I've met someone else, G. I'm so very sorry."*

Since then—since the floor had fallen out from underneath her—she had never managed to put all the pieces back together. He had run away. Their accounts had closed. He hadn't explained. He never returned her calls, only texted her from time to time so they could set up a visit with Coco, which they handled by switching pickups after school. She was served divorce papers in front of the grocery store about four weeks later.

Giselle turned her head on the pillow and studied Coco. She was so bold, so carefree. Giselle wanted, more than anything, for Coco to regain her life. She had been such a trouper with all the Roy hoopla: Her little life was turning upside down, and she rarely cried or complained. She asked for her dad from time to time, but when Giselle said he wouldn't be returning for a while, Coco simply shrugged. She'd been without him enough evenings in her five years to not have it make much difference. In the meantime, Giselle tried to do normal things as often as possible—serve fish sticks on Fridays, get ice cream after kindergarten on the last day of every month, and play at the park on Saturday mornings.

And this getaway, by token of being a getaway, was Giselle's chance to welcome new traditions. It was time to start their new life together, just them.

But now—with this funeral invite—Roy was going to send her two steps back again.

Coco's eyes fluttered open, and her lips curled into a sleepy smile. "Hi, Mommy."

"Hi, baby."

"Why are you looking at me?"

"I'm looking at how wonderful you are."

"You can see that?"

"Mommies can always see that."

Coco unfurled her body into a long cat's stretch. She kicked off the covers and stretched as far as she could, then snapped back into a coil on her side and faced Giselle over her pillow.

"What's a fish with no eyes?"

Giselle frowned. "Is this a joke, or do you mean seriously?"

"It's a joke."

"Hmmm . . . a fish with no eyes . . . I give up."

"A fsh." Coco laughed and threw her legs over the side of the bed. "Can we go down to the water this morning?"

Giselle smiled. "Let's eat breakfast first."

They ate plain Eggo waffles from Lia's freezer while Giselle made a list of groceries they'd need, with a little help from Coco, who quietly suggested hot dogs and fruit roll-ups. Giselle crinkled her nose. But then, at Coco's hopeful eyes, she stopped. A new life. New traditions. She wrote "fruit roll-ups" next to the apples and grapes, and Coco touched her lips and giggled.

They wandered through the corner beach market in sun hats and flip-flops, dropping obnoxiously colored prepackaged items in the basket along with Giselle's fresh fruit. As Giselle stood in front of a display of apples, she thought about how similar and different the experience was at the same time: This was Lia's market, next to the ocean, so different from hers, and yet the Lean Cuisines were still next to the Smart Ones; the Jif still next to the Skippy. Same. But different. It brought her an odd comfort.

"You girls visiting?" asked the elderly lady at the checkout line. She smiled at Coco, whose white-blond waves were barely contained in the narrow braids that bobbed just below her shoulders. Giselle had plaited them while Coco sat in the middle of the surfboard this morning.

Giselle nodded as a rack across the aisle caught her eye.

Hair color. Every color imaginable. She darted across the line and grabbed the first that called to her. Although she'd always been a blonde, the color she held was an intriguing reddish tone. Strawberry, it said.

"And this."

The woman added it to the bag. "You girls have a wonderful time," she said, throwing the color into a bag. "Do you need help to your car?"

"No, thanks," said Giselle.

They were, she decided, fine on their own.

The surf grew louder as Giselle and Coco trekked the few blocks to the ocean. She'd left half the groceries on the kitchen counter—she wanted to mimic Coco's spontaneity, rushing back through the door with only a clear mind and a beach towel—but now she couldn't stop making a mental list of what had been left on the countertop. She didn't leave the frozen strawberries out, did she?

"Mommy, look!" Coco pointed to a caged iguana on a tortilla-colored patio. The home had a Spanish-tile red roof. Hot-pink bougainvillea exploded along one side.

Giselle stepped closer to the waist-high wrought-iron gate and peered over it with Coco, smiling at the funny pet. They decided his name should be Iggy.

Giselle had walked these same sidewalks in Sandy Cove about six years ago, visiting when Lia had first moved in. They had strolled next to these same stucco homes—each a paler shade of sand than the last, with low-walled patios lined with potted succulents. Iron lounge chairs, padded with striped-green cushions fading from the sun and salt, still lay in wait for their owners. Giselle had been about eight months pregnant with Coco then. Rabbit and the boys were probably still living with their parents. Roy was still kind. And the world seemed like it was a flower waiting to unfurl.

She took a deep breath and fought back the heavy pang in her chest. Her sisters had been right about Roy. It was terrible that she'd let him isolate her. Roy had never "approved" of them, and she'd let herself become more and more pulled away, wanting to please this man she'd so admired. He rolled his eyes when Giselle mentioned Lia—saying her independent ways were never going to win her a husband—and spoke with disdain whenever Noelle's name came up—a "girl with her head in the clouds." Then he'd grab Giselle and tell her that he would never be able to stand the idea of "those girls" rubbing off on her. Soon, Giselle began to see the pattern of conversations about her sisters being followed by Roy being particularly paranoid, then demanding, in bed—ordering her clothes off, with a resentful, irritated bark, and throwing a certain aggression into sex that made Giselle's teeth grind. Over the years, she found it simply easier not to talk about them. And certainly not to visit them. It was just one more thing she'd grown to resent.

Coco sank her bare toes in the sand, and they weaved their way past a quilt of colorful beach towels to find a spot near the water. Giselle tilted her head back to the late-day sun, letting it warm her until it reached all the way down to a calming spot in her chest. She sprayed sunblock all over Coco, plus on the few patches of skin she herself revealed—her wrists and ankles—then let Coco make elaborate sand castles near the water.

"You know who lives here?" Coco asked Giselle, pointing at her largest castle. She had just trudged back up from the water's edge for the millionth time with another pail full of sandy, murky water. The sun was sitting low on the horizon.

"Who?" said Giselle.

"Me." She readied her pail with both hands to pour into the moat she'd created around the sand mansion. "And you. And Iggy. And a prince."

"A prince?"

She nodded solemnly. "For you."

Coco poured the water into the moat and sat back on her haunches, the sand granules sticking to her legs in circular patterns, while the water swirled briefly, then disappeared into the sand.

"Oh." The wind swept the tendrils of yellow hair around her

ears while she put together what just happened. "I guess we need soldiers." She scrambled to her feet and ran back to the foamy surf to look for pebbles and shells, which she collected the rest of the afternoon. She spent the good part of the next few hours making sure they all had a specific place to stand guard.

A knock sounded on the front door as Giselle lined the fish sticks along the cookie sheet. The sun cast a golden glow through the curtains.

She padded across the floor in her bare feet, pulling her cover-up tighter, and flung open the door.

"Heeeeey," Rabbit drawled.

Giselle smiled. She liked Rabbit.

Coco ran up from behind and peeked her head around the door.

"I came to ask you two about a party tonight," he said.

"Oh, no, thanks, Rabbit."

"It'll be fun."

"No, thanks."

"You have something against having fun?"

"Of course not. It's just . . . not my thing. . . ."

He smirked. "Fun is not your thing?"

"Parties are not my thing."

A flash of honesty went through her mind, though, of the multitude of charity balls and hospital events she'd attended over the years for Roy, and she felt a pang of guilt for lying. She'd been attending parties for Roy's medical colleagues for years, signing up for committees, standing around in floor-length gowns, doing him proud. "*Beach* parties are not my thing," she amended.

"You have a lot of beach parties in Indiana?" Rabbit said, smiling.

"I just don't—" She began to explain, but then stopped. She was tired of defending herself. She motioned toward the kitchen. "I'm putting fish sticks on."

"Weeeell . . ." Rabbit followed her into the kitchen and glanced over her shoulder at her baking tray. "I'm pretty sure there'll be something better than fish sticks there."

"I have Coco."

"There'll be lots of kids." He took a frozen fish stick off the tray and tried to bite into it.

She glanced at Coco. Rabbit had already found her weak spot.

Lia, too, had mentioned in her phone message earlier that Giselle should go out and have fun. Giselle had been so happy to hear from her—when she'd called back and gotten voice mail, she'd almost asked about Fin—*Have you seen this guy? Do you know who he is?*—but then she chickened out, embarrassed to ask such a thing of her younger sister, who was trying to set her up with a stable real estate investor. Instead, she left a message about Rabbit and how nice he'd been.

Rabbit waved a fish stick. "This is terrible. C'mon."

Giselle felt something inside her give up. Maybe this was the reason Roy left her—maybe she was too cautious, too closed off. Maybe she was going to end up being some old lady, with just Coco and Iggy and some cats. Until Coco left her, too. And then it would just be Giselle. And the iguana. The crazy lady on the hill.

She turned off the oven and put the fish sticks back in the freezer like some sort of wild woman.

"Let's go."

CHAPTER

Three

Leaning forward to peer out the windshield of her rental car, Giselle followed Rabbit's beat-up Volkswagen through the weathered streets of Sandy Cove.

The isolated town bore little resemblance to the flashier beach towns farther north, which she'd visited often when she stayed with her mom. Her mom and younger sisters had eventually made their home in Los Angeles shortly after her parents' divorce, but Giselle had started college that year and fled back to Indiana, happy to be near her father. She hadn't liked L.A. much: It was too pretentious, too much of a show-off. But Sandy Cove, farther south, was different. Weatherworn, with cliffs and hillsides setting it apart and an "Old California" vibe that was ceaselessly forgiving, the little town seemed made for people who wanted to hide.

Coco pointed to a bulletlike train that glinted in the sun, passing through. Giselle crossed the tracks and parked behind a community of narrow, aluminum-sided homes, laid along the sand like piano keys. The bases of the homes were permanent— some with Polynesian-style lava rocks, some with stacked stone. The entire community had a 1950s ambiance—the rental office was flanked by retro tiki torches and miniature palm trees, and many of the homes still had green-turf balconies and Plexiglas-panel windbreaks standing at attention against the ocean. It looked like a community that time forgot.

The party house boasted the same retro feel, but with an updated, million-dollar face-lift. A slate walkway led to a bright white door, and a vintage Sputnik-styled lantern hung in the doorway.

Giselle, Rabbit, and Coco stepped into a small, open living area. Dark wooden floors and wainscoting showed off sleek, masculine furniture. Eight-foot walls of glass showcased a long stretch of ocean and horizon, all the way north and south. The house perched right above the sand, only about twenty feet from the water, but elevated by a wall of rocks. A set of nautical-roped stairs zigzagged to the sand, where several children played. A second patio held a cluster of adults, who sipped colorful stemmed drinks and complimented one another's bright tropical dresses and shirts over the steel-drum tunes that came from a live four-piece band.

Coco spotted a girl about her age sitting in the sand, playing with a bright pink sand bucket off the main-level patio. The girl looked up and asked Coco whether she would like to play.

Giselle wished it were that easy for her. She smoothed her spring sweater and cotton skirt and studied the clusters of absurdly beautiful people.

Rabbit had, as Giselle had feared, slipped away. She took a glass of champagne from a passing tray and wandered toward the patio rail, where she could keep an eye on Coco and her new little friend. The foamy waves of the Pacific rolled up behind the girls, the water glistening like gemstones. Giselle had told Rabbit she'd stay only an hour, but as soon as she saw the view, she decided she might wait until the sun went down. Watching it from here would be magical.

She leaned into the rail, letting the rhythmic roar of the sea envelop her, allowing her shoulders to relax for what felt like the first time in days. She let the seaside serenade lull her.

"You came," said a man's voice over her shoulder.

She whirled, then tripped backward to see Fin.

He had clothes on today—a loose-fitting button-down shirt that draped off his shoulders, narrowing at his hips and falling over a pair of dressy shorts. He didn't have the air of a surfer about him today. He looked like a yachter, perhaps. Or some wealthy woman's boy toy, with his blond tips and expensive clothes. He was remarkably handsome up close—his face lean at the sides, with lines around his mouth—and he offered her the kind of grin that must stop many a surfer girl's heart. But the thing that stopped Giselle's was his eyes. She'd noticed them before, in Rabbit's apartment, but up this close they were stunning: bright blue, with an outline of navy.

Giselle glanced over his shoulder, almost expecting the wealthy woman he must belong to to materialize behind him.

"Rabbit invited me," she blurted out.

Fin seemed to find that amusing. He nodded and looked into the tumbler he held with an amber drink. "I'm glad."

"He said there'd be lots of kids," she babbled, "and that I could invite my daughter, even though we weren't going to come. I wasn't really sure. . . ." She lamely indicated Coco playing in the sand. "I don't even know whose party this is."

She was embarrassed she was talking so fast. She couldn't remember the last time a man had left her so flustered. And this one was so . . . *young*. Wasn't he? It was hard to tell. She stole a quick glance at his mouth, at his square jawline. He could've been twenty-two or thirty-two, really—he had one of those faces that made it hard to tell. But either way, he was clearly younger than she was. She took a deep breath and decided it was safer to simply not look at him.

Taking a sip of champagne, she kept her eyes on Coco. The flute stem provided a thankful distraction for her hands, and she grasped it tighter, as if she could harness some of the recklessness of her pounding heart—perhaps wrap it neatly around the stem.

The music lulled into a Caribbean-sounding number, and several guests began rolling their hips.

Fin leaned closer. "Can we go somewhere?" he said over the music. He reached toward her lower back, not touching her, but indicating he'd like her to move with him.

Her heart thumped again—flipped, really, right there in her chest—at his ocean eyes and coconut scent. She almost snapped her champagne flute.

"My daughter," she choked out, indicating Coco. "I need to keep my eye on her."

"Of course."

The music grew louder and a young couple in matching red bathing suits did a rumba toward them. Fin smiled to the woman and stepped aside, then directed Giselle's attention to a spot in the sand just behind Coco.

"How about there?" he said toward her ear.

A cluster of bright white beach chairs occupied the spot he indicated, just out of reach of the lapping foam.

Giselle nodded, her gaze skimming over his forearms—much too thick, too roped, to belong to a boy.

As she surreptitiously extended her inspection to his hands, he reached back to steer her across the patio to the steel-drum beat, turning sideways through several clusters of people. He nodded to several of them.

When they got to the chairs, she positioned herself to make sure she could see Coco, smoothing her skirt with one hand and balancing her champagne in the other. He studied her carefully. The sun was setting behind him, shining through the blond strands of his hair.

"I noticed you at Rabbit's apartment yesterday," he said.

The waves cracked, and Fin's voice drifted on a current of wind. She pulled the comment back, letting it flutter about her, forcing it into her consciousness while she tried to filter it, process it, put it somewhere inside her normal view of herself. She couldn't, exactly. She nodded, deciding to avoid mentioning that she'd noticed him, too, particularly his bare chest. She was pretty sure gorgeous surfer dudes didn't care about being noticed by scrapbook moms.

She took another sip of champagne.

"I have this event to go to," he went on. "It would be a favor." He took a nervous sip. "I need someone to go with, and when I saw you, I thought you'd be perfect."

It sounded like a compliment, but the fact that he wasn't meeting her eyes indicated otherwise.

"*I'm* perfect?"

He nodded.

"If you tell me it's a mother-son ball, I'm going to kick sand at you," she said.

He squinted at her for several long seconds and then smiled. She had the strange thought that there was a lucky girl somewhere who got to see him smile like this all the time.

"Those boys at Rabbit's must be doing a number on you," he said. "Are they still calling you 'Donna'?"

Her breath caught in surprise. "How did you know?"

"Donna Reed."

The name hung in the air while Giselle assembled it in her mind. Slowly, inside, she began to crumble. She pulled her sweater tighter and looked away.

Fin did a double take through his bangs. "They mean it as a compliment."

She nodded halfheartedly. Of course they did. A pearl-clad 1950s television housewife was exactly who everyone wanted to be compared to.

"You . . . just have an air about you." He shrugged.

"An air?"

"Very maternal."

Giselle sucked in as much air as she could, as every organ inside her seemed to deflate. She could almost feel her breasts flattening against her chest. She looked over the top of his blond head at the ocean, briefly, just to gather her senses, then forced herself to face the fact that whatever reason she'd hoped he'd invited her out here—that wasn't it. Whatever reason he'd noticed her at Rabbit's apartment—that wasn't it, either. She looked away from his tousled hair.

"Do I need to bring cookies?" she said sarcastically.

He laughed. He had a nice, mature-sounding laugh. "I heard they were good, but no. It's a wine tasting and art auction. I have to impress some people. I was thinking about asking your sister, but when I came by to see if she was there, Rabbit said she was gone for a couple of weeks."

Lia? It hadn't occurred to Giselle that Fin might date Lia. She tried to picture her extroverted, hair-flipping little sister on the arm of this magazine-cover surfer boy and felt, first, a stab of jealousy. But then she dismissed it. Lia wouldn't date someone like Fin. Lia had liked serious boys when she was young, then moved on to serious men. First it was boys who wrote dark poetry and rode motorcycles to high school; then it was men who wore black suits and took over companies. Fin wouldn't fit into her worldview at all.

"Do you . . . *date* Lia?" she asked anyway, unable to keep the incredulity out of her voice.

"No, no." Fin shook his head as if the idea were preposterous. "She's not—*I'm* not . . . her type at all."

At least they agreed on that much.

"We're friends. She's helped me out of a few jams. But this one—even she wasn't right for this. But you . . ." He looked her up and down. "You're perfect."

Giselle let the words settle over her for an instant, enjoying their flash of warmth. She didn't hear compliments very often, particularly from her ex, who had looked at her as if she were simply part of the furniture for the last several years. But then she noted another of Fin's skittish glances and reminded herself he was probably up to something.

"You must know a million other women."

"Not old enough."

Her extraordinary reserve allowed her to keep perfectly still. One didn't get through excruciating high-school beauty pageants by letting hurt feelings show. Her eyes, however, must have given her away.

"I don't mean—" Fin lifted his hand. "I just mean I need someone my own age."

Clearly, he'd missed the mark on this one. "How old *are* you?" she asked.

"Twenty-nine . . . soon."

Giselle looked at him skeptically. "When's soon?"

"Next weekend."

She raised her eyebrow. Twenty-eight? She had about seven years on him. Although at least he was older than she'd thought. He'd looked boyish from a distance, but up close he had all the strength that brings a man over the threshold from boyish to sexy. He was definitely already there.

But, even so, this wasn't possible.

"Well." She stood, brushing the sand off her legs. "I'm a little older than that. And besides, it certainly must serve you well to have a beautiful twentysomething on your arm?"

"Not at this event."

He seemed resigned to the fact that she was leaving. He

took a sip of his drink and looked, for the moment, terribly sad and lonely.

"You must know several sophisticated thirtysomethings." She could see at least seven or eight from here—glowing tans, beautiful bodies, windswept hair in shades of gold.

"Too married," he said without looking.

She watched him for a minute as the waves crashed behind them. She almost asked how he knew she wasn't married, but then remembered he'd asked Rabbit. So *that* was it: She was the only thirtysomething who was still single in the state of California. Her fingers instinctively went to her wedding ring. It was a strange habit, keeping the ring on, and she couldn't exactly explain why she did it. She knew it had something to do with Coco—she didn't want people to look at her and Coco, alone, and think she was depriving her daughter of a two-parent home. It was strange and pathetic, but there it was.

"Yeah, that threw me." He nodded toward her finger. "I double-checked with Rabbit."

A quiet tingle ran through her at the thought of being discussed, privately, between two men. But then she told herself to ignore it. She was being discussed as Donna Reed, after all, not Pamela Anderson.

"Rabbit talks too much," she said, with more irritation in her voice than she wanted.

Fin chuckled into his drink. A light breeze came up and blew sand across their shoes.

"Why do you still wear it?" he asked.

She felt her face flush. She didn't want to discuss her personal choices with this surfer. What would he know about the difficulty of having your husband run away from you? Of not being able to face any of your friends or family because you didn't even know what went wrong? Of feeling like you'd failed in a catastrophic way?

"It's difficult to explain."

"Try me." He looked straight at her—as if he actually expected an answer—but Giselle shook her head.

He bobbed his as if to acquiesce that she didn't want to say. The sunlight caught his face as he stared at the ocean. And, as soon as she was about to turn, his eyelashes lowered. He looked knowing, somehow. But also achingly, painfully lonely.

"When is this event?" Her words, now spoken, hung in the breeze between them, seeming like they belonged to someone else.

"Wednesday." His expression shifted from doubt to hope. "Look, uh—Giselle, isn't it?"

"Well, it's not Donna."

He grinned. "Look, Giselle, I didn't mean to insult you. I'm sorry if I did. I just mean that this event is important to me, and I need to bring someone who is beautiful and sophisticated, and when I saw you at Rabbit's place, I thought you were perfect. Even better than Lia."

She kept very still. She was afraid if she moved, her face might reveal her skepticism. He didn't say it as if "sophisticated" were something he necessarily admired, but her heart hung a little over the "beautiful" part. She hadn't heard that compliment from a man in quite some time.

And, really, who was she kidding? Spending an evening in this gorgeous man's company, sipping wine and looking at art, didn't seem like the worst idea in the universe. She could call Lia and make sure he was okay. And she and Coco had their own event to go to this week, after all, and Roy's mom might want Coco to—

An idea hit her.

"Uh—Fin, isn't it?"

"Definitely not Donna."

"All right, Fin. I have an event myself this week. And *you*—" She let her eyes wander up and down, the same way his had, but she didn't quite have the audaciousness to do it right. "You're perfect."

He regarded her with suspicion. "Perfect how?"

"Young enough. Hunky enough. Pro surfer enough."

He laughed a little and stared at his glass. Clearly, he hadn't seen this coming. "How do you know I'm a pro surfer?"

"Rabbit told me."

"Did we already say Rabbit talks too much?"

"I think we agreed on that."

He stared at the ocean for a second. "I'm not on the tour anymore."

"It doesn't matter."

He shifted his attention and studied her suspiciously. "When is your event?"

"Tomorrow."

"What is it?"

"A funeral."

His eyebrows shot up. "Seriously?"

She nodded.

"Why do you need a pro surfer on your arm to attend a funeral?"

"Because I'm swimming with sharks."

Several expressions crossed his face in rapid succession—doubt, humor, maybe even a hint of admiration. He settled on a hesitant smile. "I'm listening."

"It's at one o'clock. I just need you to come along, stand there, and look pretty."

He chuckled at that. "All right. I guess I can do that. What should I wear, my nicest black wet suit?"

"Funeral clothes."

His expression turned somber. He swirled his drink in his glass a few times. "Whose funeral is it?"

"My ex-father-in-law."

He nodded slowly. "I suppose, then, there's an ex-husband on the scene?"

Giselle paused. It hadn't occurred to her that he might not approve of all the details. She nodded hesitantly.

He looked at her for a long time. "All right. As long as this isn't one of those scenarios where you need a stand-in so he can beat the crap out of me."

She laughed at the absurdity of it—her skinny, bespectacled husband taking a swing at anything besides a golf ball.

"I don't think that'll be an issue," she said.

Roy had run away. He obviously wouldn't be jealous. She simply wanted Fin to accompany her because she didn't want to look pathetic. She wanted to look pulled together, like she'd moved on. And not just *moved on*, but moved on with *this guy*. She wanted to show his whole family that she had a new image now: one of strength. One of the ability to move forward, without them, without Roy. . . .

"Any requests for me, for your event?" she asked.

He took a sip of his drink. "Don't look too sexy."

Giselle suppressed a laugh and tightened her cardigan around her middle. As if that would be a problem. "This is a crowd that wouldn't like that?"

"Something like that," he said, avoiding her eyes.

They walked another four or five steps toward the house, until Fin became engulfed by a cluster of partygoers. He looked over his shoulder at Giselle and mouthed to talk to him before she left.

Giselle nodded, then searched for Rabbit. When she found him, she asked just exactly how famous Fin was.

"Pro All-American, World Cup, Brazilian Open, Azores Islands Pro, U.S. Open twice," Rabbit said. "I could go on. He's a god. I'd show you all his trophies, but he's got them locked up in a closet." He shoved his thumb over his shoulder.

Realization was slow in coming, but Giselle's gaze followed Rabbit's thumb. "This is *his* house?"

Rabbit frowned. "That's why I invited you, Giselle. He asked me to." His face took on an air of concern. "It's okay, right? If you want him to just leave you alone, I'll just—"

"No," she interrupted. "It's okay."

She took a deep breath. All right. A gorgeous pro surfer, who had all these people here to see him—including at least forty stunningly beautiful women in very small bikinis—had just asked her on a date. Or, well, not really a date. An *event*. And she'd asked him to a *funeral*.

Giselle looked around and set her champagne glass on a table behind her. She took another breath and tried to speak rationally, like this all made sense and she fit in here. "He said he's not on the tour anymore," she said casually.

Rabbit rolled his eyes. "Unfortunately."

"What does that mean?"

"It means he's not on the Men's World Tour anymore. He's trying to get back on it."

"Why is he not on it now?"

He shook his head. "I'll let him tell you." Then he looked at her with that concern again. "It's okay that I brought you here?"

She nodded.

"Because I promised Lia I'd watch out for you, so if you—"

"*Rabbit.*" Giselle held up her hand. "Stop."

He looked uncertain.

"Lia is my *younger* sister. She does not need to be watching out for me. And you, certainly, don't need to. I'm fine. No more of that, okay?"

He nodded, but looked less than convinced.

They wandered throughout the party, did a couple of turns to the steel-drum band, played with Coco in the sand, then ran into Kino. The whole place was body-to-body people, but she didn't see Fin anymore. After she gathered Coco into her lap to watch the sun set, Rabbit smiled at her over the top of Coco's hair. They watched the setting sun with several other quiet people in the sand.

When she was ready to leave, she finally found Fin in the kitchen with his arm around the waist of the young woman in the bright yellow bikini. Giselle tried not to notice how comfortably his thumb rested near the shockingly low bikini strings.

"One o'clock?" he said, stepping away.

She glanced at Yellow Bikini and pulled her sweater tighter around her. "Yes."

She wondered how difficult it would be for Fin to spend two whole afternoons with her, Ms. Donna Reed, when he was used to these bathing beauties with the long legs and belly-button rings. She fingered her top button and tried to keep her eyes off Yellow Bikini's cleavage. Even she found it stunning.

"One," she agreed.

He nodded and studied her over the rim of his drink.

Giselle abruptly turned to find Coco, and put her hands on her shoulders to hustle her out the door. Fin was probably counting the seconds until he could get his hands repositioned across Yellow Bikini's abs.

This wasn't a date.

She needed to keep remembering that. She was simply filling a role.

She scurried down the pathway with Rabbit, her hand clutching Coco's, and bit her lip while trying not to cry.

She knew she shouldn't feel sad. There were plenty worse things than being Donna Reed.

At least, she supposed there were.

Fin sipped his drink and watched Giselle walk down the pathway with her little girl and Rabbit in tow, then congratulated himself.

Finding an unmarried thirtysomething at this late date had proven nearly impossible, and he had almost given up yesterday morning. But there, in a little floral sweater, walked away his ticket to success.

He turned and moved his smile to the nearly naked Veronica, who looked hot over there in that yellow string bikini, and wished, vaguely, he could bring her. But that would be impossible. Veronica wouldn't be able to get his sponsorship back. And neither would several other women at this party. The contract VP kept telling him his reputation was bad enough with the Jennifer thing and the string of surfing losses since her death but, on top of that, his reckless behavior—and the constant parade of rotating bikini models—was not helping an iota.

Until now, Fin hadn't cared. He liked his dates rotating. But now he'd lost the last of a long list of sponsors, mostly because of his losses since Jennifer. And he only had Mahina left, who was hanging by a thread. That contract was supposed to expire next weekend, on his birthday, and the renewal wasn't looking good. If it happened at all. From what Fin could glean, it looked as if his life of pay-for-play might be over.

Downing the rest of the scotch, he looked at the space Giselle had just vacated, there on the pathway, and wondered how well he'd be able to pull this off.

He couldn't lose surfing.

He'd already lost everything else.

Of course, he hadn't told Giselle all the details. And he certainly hadn't anticipated the fact she'd unnerve him once he began talking to her.

She had kind of a Grace Kelly thing going—something that smacked of sophistication and secrets, but with an innocence that made you wonder what you could show her. And the cookies were a final touch—he didn't even know there were really women like that, who baked cookies and brought them next door on a plate. But what really stayed in his memory were her lips. Clearly, she had no idea of the power they had. Fin eventually had to keep his eyes trained on the ocean while they talked, taking only quick glimpses of her to keep the conversation going. Lia had pretty lips like that, too—it must run in the family—but Lia's mouth didn't make him think of sex like Giselle's did. Something about those voluptuous lips, combined with her prim manner, was an irrational turn-on. And the fact that she didn't seem to know it made it all the sexier.

He ran his fingers through his hair and found a spot on the living room chaise behind Veronica. He was going to have to watch himself. He needed Giselle for this event, but that was it. She was much too entrenched in the people he knew, like Rabbit and Lia, for him to be thinking of her lips. Or wondering about her ex. Or trying to determine how "ex" he was.

He vaulted across the hardwood floor to pour another drink. He poured two, actually, and walked one back to Veronica, reveling in the exotic face she turned toward him. She gave him that secretive smile she always slipped him, while she continued her story with a handful of his acquaintances, who laughed simultaneously at something she said. One or two looked at him with that sad, pitying face he sometimes got—still too often since last August.

He tried to focus on the strings that tied Veronica's bikini together, taking another sip of his drink and motioning for her to do the same. But he was stunned at his lack of reaction. He swirled the drink in his glass, horrified to have his mind drift back to Giselle.

That Donna Reed number she wore was damned cute. He wondered what she wore to bed. He pictured something sort of prim, that she'd undo with her fingertips and . . .

Damn.

He stood again and walked to the window, where he could watch the surf. *Business*. That was it. She was going to get him this sponsor back. And, once she did, he was going to take her home, say good night, and thank her. With words. Then he'd head out to South Africa for the Ballito competition and continue on with his life.

He was *not* going to think about her lips or what she might do with them, or how her legs might feel, or what she might wear in his bed. Despite how pretty she was, any fool could see she was too vulnerable for that kind of thing. And, although his most roguish sense told him that a vulnerable woman was the easiest kind of woman to get, his slightly more decent sense reminded him that Lia would kill him. And Rabbit, with all his gangly loyalty, was acting as if Giselle were his responsibility for some reason.

So no more. There were plenty of other women he could sleep with, to take that edge off. It wasn't like California was having a shortage of women. And Giselle was the type who men fell in love with, not the kind that empty-hearted bastards like him took to bed for as long as a good Ziggy Marley CD lasted.

"What do you think, bro?" Kino materialized beside him. "Dawn Patrol?"

"Tomorrow?" Fin asked.

Kino nodded.

He normally liked to do his morning session without an entourage, but maybe agreeing to go with Kino and the boys would be good for him.

"Trestles?"

"Nah, Rabbit needs to stay here—he's starting his groms tomorrow."

Fin's synapses fired from *grommets* to *Coco* to *Giselle.* . . .

"Is that so?" he said.

"That's so, bro."

Fin nodded. The idea of seeing Giselle again before the funeral—even though there was a good possibility she'd be covered head-to-toe again—felt oddly compelling.

"I might join you," he found himself saying.

He drained his glass again and realized he might already be on a slippery slope. He needed to behave.

CHAPTER

Four

Lia's bathroom mirror felt cool against Giselle's forehead. The grommet surfing camp didn't start until nine, but Rabbit said he was going to surf first with some of the instructors, and Giselle wanted to take pictures of them in the early-morning dawn.

She coiled her hair into another chignon and tugged on another sweater. By the time Rabbit knocked, Coco was up, pulling at the straps of her Pretty Princess bathing suit. She tossed her ruffled towel on the couch and opened the door.

Rabbit leaned in the doorway sleepily, in a hooded sweatshirt and flip-flops, his curls matted to his head. Morning mist settled behind him.

"You'll need a sweatshirt, little grommet," he told Coco solemnly. "I need coffee," he whispered to Giselle.

"I can make you some." She whirled toward the kitchen.

"No, we'll get some on the corner. C'mon."

Giselle tore herself away from her instinct to take care of the gravel in his voice, to make sure another person in her orbit was satisfied and taken care of. Instead, she snatched her camera bag and yelled for Coco. It was uncomfortable but strangely freeing, to not care. Her arms felt light.

The morning fog drifted between the palm-tree trunks as they made their way down the narrow, tiled sidewalks, bright green ice plant pushing out of the sand around the sidewalk's edge. Rabbit shuffled tiredly, Coco bounced behind him on the sidewalk, and Giselle fielded questions from Coco about how early seagulls awoke, and whether or not it was possible to "open" and "close" a beach. Rabbit gave a weak smirk once or twice.

A doughnut shop materialized out of the mist, with seven young guys waiting in molded plastic chairs, Styrofoam coffee cups cradled in their palms. Seven surfboards were stacked against the wall behind them. Giselle smoothed her Ann Taylor slacks and slowed.

The light was stunning. All she saw were the bright blues, reds, and oranges of the boys' caps and clothes, the amber cast of the early-morning sun, the yellows in the surfboards—gorgeous contrast.

As she focused her camera, she wondered whether the boy in the bright blue knit cap belonged to that sunset-orange board right over his shoulder, but decided it didn't matter. He twisted his neck to laugh at one of the kids next to him and blew the steam off the top of his cup.

She zoomed tightly—the line of the board, the line of his jaw, the circle of white Styrofoam, the sun rising against his face. Click. Perfect.

"Jensen, Corky, you remember Lia's sister Giselle?" Rabbit motioned toward her.

Giselle wondered whether they had been in the apartment yesterday, because she didn't remember any of them, although their heads bobbed.

"She's going to take some pictures for the brochure." He grabbed one of Corky's doughnut remains and popped it in his mouth. "Be sure to look pretty for her."

They all inspected Giselle with renewed interest.

"Mmm." Rabbit bent toward Coco. "Do you want a doughnut?"

"Can I, Mommy?"

Giselle sent Coco into the shop with a hesitant nod. She hated the idea of her daughter eating a doughnut without any fruit or nutrition yet today, but . . . well, they were *relaxing*, and starting new traditions, and starting a new life. . . .

She wiped the morning dew off a plastic chair and reintroduced herself to the boys, shaking their hands primly. She found out who belonged to which board.

The other boys were much more animated than Rabbit had been, fueled already by a first cup of caffeine. Jensen tugged his sweatshirt over his hands and told her about the photographers who combed the beach area for the local surf magazines. Giselle adjusted her posture and tried to look nonplussed. These guys were almost pro already—used to cameras clicking on them, photographers following them out into the water, being interviewed for surfing magazines and sports television shows. And Giselle, with her little scrapbooking camera, was out of her element, once again.

"Let's hit it," said Rabbit as he emerged from the doughnut shop, bag in hand. The rest of the guys gathered their boards and followed.

The sidewalk broke off into tan, grainy sand, and they all took their shoes off to wade through the cold granules. There was only one towel on the beach—about a hundred feet away—and no people. Once near the water, the boys plopped their boards upright and shielded their eyes against the sun that was just starting to break through the fog.

"Bro, did you see that left?" said Jensen, pointing.

"Killer," said Corky.

Without taking their eyes off the waves, they wriggled into wet suits. Rabbit smiled to Giselle. Coffee did him well. He was back to his regular self, and she raised her camera to capture him. Warm eyes. Orange sun. Click. Perfect.

"You comin' in?" he said over the top of her lens.

She laughed. *Never in a million years.* "I think I'll shoot from here."

He stepped into his wet suit—a sleek, black short-sleeved number that ended just above his knees. He tugged the zipper up his back with a long neoprene loop.

Giselle tossed her sandals into the sand, trying to find a warm spot to sit. Straightening, she gazed at the dozens of seal-like surfers out in the water atop their boards, necks turned toward the horizon. She couldn't believe so many normal human beings would be up at six in the morning in the freezing Pacific on a Monday.

"Why are so many people out there?" she asked.

"Dawn Patrol," Rabbit said. "You've got CEOs to accountants out there. They come to get their session in before they get behind their desks and spreadsheets for the day. Gets their head in the right place. This place used to be the best-kept secret in Southern California, because a cove doesn't sound like a great place to surf, but actually there are two reefs out there that make for some killer waves."

For the rest of the morning, as the sun slowly revealed itself, Giselle pointed her camera, keeping Rabbit and the others in the viewfinder. A few times, Giselle put the camera down in awe, to watch as they took their waves with grace and speed. Rabbit and Corky and Jensen and Kino were like different people out there—no longer lanky-limbed boys, but acts of strength, with beauty and speed, bending and moving and lowering themselves in a rhythm only they understood.

"Mommy, why do penguins eat fish for breakfast?" Coco yelled from down the dune, where she was doing cartwheels in the sand and inspecting the prints her hands and feet made.

"Is this a joke or a serious question?"

"A joke."

Giselle tried to remember whether she'd heard this one as she adjusted a towel around her shoulders.

"Um . . ." She steadied her camera for the next shot, searching for Rabbit. *Why do penguins eat fish for breakfast,* she mused, trying to think of the answer but mostly trying to get Rabbit's mop-top in her viewfinder.

"Because doughnuts get soggy," said a man's voice behind her.

Giselle whirled to see Fin blocking the morning sun, boasting the same-style short-sleeved wet suit that Rabbit had worn, although Fin's arms and legs filled it out more considerably. A bright blue surfboard was beneath his arm, and the morning light caught him beautifully on the side of his face. He smiled at Coco. "That sounds like one of Rabbit's jokes."

"That's *right*," said Coco. "You're the *winner*. You win a *prize*." She galloped around him in a circle.

"A prize?"

"Um . . ." she said. "A shell. Just a minute." She shuffled her feet through the sand to search.

Fin turned toward Giselle and raised his eyebrows.

His hair was wet, standing on end, as if he'd just pushed it up with his hands. The damp edges at his neckline curled around the high neck of the wet suit. She had the strangest urge to reach out and touch it.

Instead, she forced her attention to her camera, hoping the air would cool the heat in her cheeks. She raised the lens. Zoom. Frame . . .

"Whoa," he said, putting his hand up. "Hold on. What's that for?"

She lowered the camera. *Because you look like a god,* she thought. "The light is great on you," she said instead.

"I don't like having my picture taken."

Giselle tried to wrap her mind around that. How could you look as good as this guy, with those made-for-a-camera teeth, and not like to have your picture taken? Plus, as a pro surfer, he must certainly be used to being in the limelight.

"Rabbit and the boys out there?" he said, peering out at the surf.

"Yes," she said, still mulling over the last point.

He nodded toward her camera. "Is this for Rabbit's brochure?"

"Yes, but why don't you like having your picture—"

"Are you a professional photographer?"

She couldn't tell whether he was annoyed by that or impressed. "It's just a hobby. Lia mentioned Rabbit might need help."

"Well, if Lia recommended you, I'm sure you're good."

Giselle bit her lip. *Lia recommended me because I'm her sister and she feels sorry for me.* She turned, instead, toward the water. "So were you out there? I didn't see you."

"I usually do a morning session down there, by my house. The swells are good here, though." He gazed at the water longingly.

"Have at it," she said, motioning toward the waves.

She was curious to watch him. After watching Rabbit and the boys this morning, she was eager to see, now, what Fin could do out there—how he could defy nature with the strength in his legs, push up off the board with the power in his arms. She wondered what he would look like, taming what seemed untamable.

"Too many people." A strange flicker went across his face. "So about our agreement—we didn't get a chance to talk much after the party. You're still okay with it?"

"Yes." She glanced up to see whether perhaps he was changing his mind.

Coco came bounding up from the side, her palm outstretched. "It's broken, but it's the prettiest I could find."

Fin bent forward and gingerly picked up the small piece of shell she had in her hand. "An abalone."

"Bologna?"

Fin laughed.

Giselle couldn't help but smile. It was nice to see the life come back into his face.

"Abalone. It's a mollusk. This type of shell is used for lots of jewelry—see how shiny it is?" He pointed to the swirls of blue and lavender inside the broken piece and Coco nodded. "Nice choice."

Coco beamed. "It's your prize."

"Are you sure you don't want it?"

"No, it's your *prize*. But you have to take good care of it."

"I will. Thank you." His fist swallowed the shell. "I'd better go," he said to Giselle. "So one o'clock? I'll pick you up at Lia's?"

Giselle nodded.

"Thanks, little grommet." He lifted his fist with the shell inside.

Fin began trudging back up the coastline, his body rippling under the sleek black suit, his backside curving into thick, muscular thighs.

Giselle caught herself gawking, and immediately pretended she was getting something out of her camera case. As soon as Coco resumed her cartwheels, though, Giselle allowed herself a nice, long stare.

Fin pulled his bare feet through the dry sand and began his mile-long trudge back to his place.

He'd trekked all the way down here to see if he could get a glimpse of her—cursing himself the whole way, because it was a goofy, juvenile reaction to a woman he shouldn't even be paying attention to.

He'd thought maybe his reaction last night was due to too much scotch—he really needed to stop drinking like that—but today, like last night, the sight of her was enough to rattle him.

He'd come down to tell her the details of the wine and art event—what he was going to need her to do, in case she wanted to back out. He needed to be honest. But watching her eyes this morning—that curious stare that dove through him—was enough to clam him up again.

He wondered whether it was because he was attracted to her, but dismissed that. He never worried about what women thought of him—even gorgeous ones who looked like Grace Kelly.

No, this discomfort seemed to come from some kind of assessment she was making. And, for some reason, he wanted it to go his way.

With *Giselle.*

Lia's sister.

Whom he didn't even know.

And couldn't sleep with.

What the hell?

He trudged the last half mile trying to clear his mind, then propped his surfboard along the wall of his patio. He swore at himself again for not coming clean—now he'd have to hope for the best, even if his scheme repelled her.

He'd just tell her today at one.

A funeral seemed like an appropriate place anyway.

CHAPTER

Five

Giselle opened and closed the refrigerator seven or eight times while she waited for Fin to arrive.

"Do you want an apple?" she asked Coco.

"I already had a banana after surf camp," Coco said, spreading her Polly Pocket dolls across the dining table.

Giselle closed the fridge again. She hadn't been able to eat a thing this afternoon, but she knew she needed something in her stomach. Coco had had fun at surf camp—already perfecting her "pop-up" under the proud grin of Rabbit—and Giselle had gotten some good photos. But now her stomach was in knots: She was jittery about seeing Roy again, about facing his family, about Coco's reaction to going anywhere with a strange man in a strange car. Plus she was flat-out nervous about seeing Fin again. Spending an afternoon with a man who made your heart pound could be thrilling under normal circumstances, but when it was set up as a favor, not an actual date, it seemed like it had disaster written all over it. She already regretted coming up with this cockamamie idea.

When the knock finally sounded, she took a deep breath and smoothed her dress.

"Hello!" she breathed out as she swung the door open.

Fin filled the doorway, wearing some kind of Armani suit—a rich, double-breasted fabric that lay in a flat, black sheen along the contours of his body. The crisp white at his collar—secured with a simple black tie—contrasted with his golden tan and made his eyes especially blue. He had one hand in the trouser pocket like some kind of cologne model.

She'd expected . . . Well, she didn't know what she expected. But she didn't expect *this*. She expected him to maybe be a little shocking, like a good renegade surfer date should be—maybe messy hair, or a mismatched suit, or a childish tie. Instead he just looked gorgeous.

"You look . . ." She searched for words.

He stood quietly, waiting for her verdict.

". . . like a Wall Street broker," she said.

His mouth quirked up at one side. "How tragic."

"I don't mean—"

"Do you hate Wall Street brokers?"

"No."

"Is your ex a Wall Street broker?"

"No, it's just—"

"All right, then." He shifted his attention to Coco, who was dipping her head beneath Giselle's arm to see around the side.

"Hi!" She bounded out the door in her little navy dress with the butterflies on it and reached for Fin's hand. "I surfed today!"

"How was it?"

"It was *stellar*."

He laughed—a real, from-the-gut kind of laugh she hadn't heard yet from him. "Spoken like a true surfer."

"Mommy was scared."

He glanced up at Giselle, but she let her gaze slip away before that line of questioning could get started.

"Do you still have the abalone?" Coco pressed.

"I do."

"Then we can go." She thrust her hand out again.

He stared at her little fingers, as if not sure what to do with them, then finally tucked her hand into the crook of his arm. "M'lady, your chariot awaits."

Coco giggled. "Just like the prince." She started her rapid-fire steps across the patio, dragging Fin behind her.

"The prince?"

"The one for Mommy, who lives in the castle."

Fin raised an eyebrow back at Giselle, but she ducked her head to lock the door.

"Your abalone will help," Coco told Fin in a very loud whisper.

"My abalone will help with what?"

"It'll make you a prince," she said, as if the answer were obvious. "It's used for jewelry, so it makes you a prince. But you have to carry it with you, so it will work."

Giselle watched Fin nod, seemingly trying to follow the turns the conversation was taking. She wondered whether she should try to rescue him.

"Are you carrying it with you?" Coco asked sternly.

"I put it on my window ledge," he said.

"In your kitchen?"

"In my bathroom."

Giselle followed them down the stairs and wondered again whether she should intervene. Obviously, Fin thought he could spin a tall tale with her little girl, but maybe she should put a stop to this. He probably wasn't used to getting the third degree from a five-year-old, but it was brutal, and they were truth detectors.

"But if you want to be a prince, you have to carry it with you," Coco said.

From the back, she saw him nod again. "I'll remember that." His voice sounded more amused than annoyed.

Fin beeped open his car. As she got closer, Giselle came to an abrupt halt on the sidewalk. He drove a BMW—much like the car Roy drove.

"What's the matter now?" he said.

"I just thought . . ." She shrugged. "I thought you'd drive something else."

"Like what?"

"I don't know."

He smiled. "Like a surf van?"

Her cheeks heated. Maybe. It wasn't that she thought he was Jeff Spicoli from *Fast Times at Ridgemont High* or anything, but she wanted to make a splash. If he dressed like a doctor and drove a doctor's car, what kind of new image was she showing off?

"Sorry to disappoint you," he said, yanking open the passenger door.

"I'm . . . sorry. This is nice." She was lucky he was deigning to come at all, really. She needed to pull herself together and stop projecting her anxiety. She'd lost him at "hello."

He lifted the leather seat to let Coco climb in the back, then leaned in to tug at the seat belts. Giselle caught a great view of his behind, supported by some amazing hamstrings, as he held himself steady in the frame with one hand. The seat belts were still wedged between the cushions.

"Is this a new car?"

"No—three years."

"You've never used the seat belts?"

"Not back here." He tugged the plastic off one of the buckles.

Giselle raised an eyebrow. Must be a bachelor thing.

"Sorry again about what I said," she said, trying not to stare at his behind. "This is a beautiful car. I just wanted to . . . make a *point*, I guess."

His body slid fluidly out of the backseat. "You want me to play a *part*," he said, not as a question.

"Yes, but—"

"As the surfer dude."

"Yes, but that's not necessarily how I see you, it's just—"

"It's okay," he said. He held the door wider.

Giselle bit her lip. This was a stupid idea. She had been so upset that he saw her in a singular role—Donna Reed—but here she was, doing the same thing. She thought he'd appear to be some kind of renegade coming to hang out with Roy's family—the laid-back, good-looking young athlete who gave her hot nights and great sex and had chosen *her* among the dozens of women at his beck and call. And she wanted to look like the renegade ex-wife who loved it. She just didn't want the pity anymore. The pity was burying her alive.

"If you don't want to do this, I'll understand," she said.

"It's fine." He moved the door, as if hoping she'd just get in.

She paused, guilt curdling in her stomach. Maybe she should backpedal this whole plan—this was ridiculous, wasn't it?

"Do you want me to start saying 'dude' and 'hella'?" His mouth drew back into a crooked grin. "I could throw in some 'bro's, too."

Relief flooded through her.

The tiny sports car smelled like leather and aftershave. Fin slid in and glanced at her sideways, offering an ornery smile, complete with laugh lines where she imagined blond stubble would poke if you woke with him early in the morning. "I could call you a 'Betty.'"

Her eyes widened. That was what one of Rabbit's friends had called her. "What is that?" she asked cautiously.

"It means a pretty girl." He leaned forward and started the car. "You said we're heading to Arroyo Viejo, right?"

She swallowed hard and nodded at the map in her lap, trying to ignore the tingling in her stomach. "Well," she added primly, as he pulled out and gunned for the road, "it sure beats Donna."

Fin studied the road as they drove past beachside florist shops and ice cream stands.

"You know that's a compliment, right?" he said, shifting gears.

"Donna Reed is a compliment?"

"Pretty wife, someone you don't mind coming home to every night . . ."

"You would want to be married to *Donna Reed*?"

"Well, I don't want to be married at all, so I'm the wrong one to ask. But those boys mean it as a compliment."

Giselle thought maybe they had visions of milk and cookies floating through their heads. They certainly weren't imagining long nights of silence in a huge, cold house. She stared at her hands and summoned the courage to ask the next part.

"Why don't you want to be married?" Her voice had a thin, stretched quality to it she didn't recognize.

"Just . . . not in my game plan, I guess."

She'd have guessed as much. Why settle down with one woman when you must have so many swimming up to your door every day?

"Well"—she cleared her throat and went on with her point—"would you call that woman with the yellow bikini—the one at your party—would you call her 'Donna'?"

"Veronica?" Fin chuckled. "Not if I wanted to live through the night."

"Would you call her 'Betty'?"

"It's '*a* Betty.' Like a noun."

"But would you call her that?"

"Absolutely not."

"Why not?"

"Because I'm not stupid. And not eighteen."

She ignored the heat in her cheeks and rearranged her hands in her lap. She was probably irritating him already, so instead she watched a couple of primary-colored beach cruiser bikes glide by.

"Are you trying to make some kind of point?" he finally asked.

She couldn't quite read his face—whether he was irritated or amused—but she took a deep breath and went on with her argument. "I'm just saying, 'Donna' is not the compliment you think it is—to me. And 'Betty' is probably not either, to someone like Veronica."

Fin seemed to think that over as he merged into traffic. "All right, I suppose if I were eight years younger, and hanging with Rabbit and the boys, I might still use that line on her. Because it's not meant to be mean. Guys mean it as a compliment."

She ignored the tiny ping of jealousy that ricocheted in her chest and leaned back in her seat. "Fine, then. You've made my point. Let's nix the 'Donna' thing."

Fin glanced at her one more time, but then kept his eyes on the road.

She thought she saw him smirking.

The drive was long.

And Fin was amused.

Although his amusement was pricked with pangs of confusion, like a balloon letting out air, as he kept glancing at Giselle and trying to figure out what was going through her head.

She was beautiful. His heart had flipped, right there, on the patio, as soon as he saw her in that dress. It was black, of course. Funeral, after all. But there was leg. Lots of leg. And there were curves all over her body—waist, hips, curves everywhere, sloping in a very touchable-looking fabric that he longed to test.

But this was no time to be losing sight of the plan.

She was putting him through the paces, though. For whatever reason, she wanted her ex to think she was seeing a van-driving hippie surfer dude. He filed that one away. She also smelled like wildflowers. He filed that away, too. And she was fiercely protective of her daughter. And had the softest voice. And didn't like being associated with Donna Reed. . . .

He kept a mental tally of each detail. The curves and the voice and the wildflower thing might be for his own edification, but the rest seemed like details he might need to know to play this well. He wanted to do a good job for her today.

"So is there anything you want to tell me about this family?" He glanced toward the backseat to make sure Coco wasn't listening.

She leaned toward him, bringing the scent of wildflowers with her. "I was very close with his parents. I have trouble with the rest of the family, but Lovey and Joseph always treated me well. Lovey's going to be devastated with the loss of Joe, but she's strong. You'll see it today. Joe was . . ." Her eyes began glistening.

Fin rubbed his chin and focused on the car in front of him. Damn. Even though he knew he was playing a ruse here, stuff like that brought home the fact that this was a part of her real life. He waited for her to go on.

". . . Joe was a good man," she added. "He was a doctor. Quiet, but always kind."

"And your ex?"

She shot him a strange glance.

"I mean, was your ex a doctor, too?"

"Roy," she said.

"What?"

"His name is Roy."

"I prefer 'ex,' thanks." He cleared his throat. "So is he a doctor?"

"Yes, a heart surgeon."

He let out a low whistle. "Nice."

He wondered again what happened here—what would cause a man like that to give up a woman like this, or if it might be the other way around—but it wasn't in his nature to get involved. He liked his life to be lived on the outer edges, worrying about his own behavior instead of the behavior of others. His own was bad enough.

"How did you know?" she asked.

"Know what?"

"How did you know they were both doctors?"

"Seems like the kind of thing that runs in families. Father's expectations, all that." He gripped the steering wheel harder. He knew that one well.

"Yes, they were both doctors. Roy came out here a few times a year, in fact, to work with his dad on research and some charity events they did out here. He was here a lot."

"Did you ever come to Sandy Cove before?" The odds seemed high that he might have run into her before, around Lia.

"Only once, when I was pregnant with Coco. Roy usually came out here alone."

"Did you stay with Lia?"

"Yes, one night."

"I used to live next door to her. In the apartment Rabbit is in. That's how I met her."

"Really?"

"Yeah, that would have been about . . . six years ago?"

"That's about when I was there."

He nodded. It would have been great to have met her back then. Those days had been fun and carefree, when he hung out with Lia and they were all younger and more idealistic. When surfing was for love and made him feel whole. Giselle might have liked him back then.

"So why don't you compete anymore?" she asked.

The change of subject threw him. "I, uh, do, but—" He checked his side mirror and changed lanes before answering. He didn't want Giselle to know all this. "Let's get back to you. I need to make some crib notes."

The tires popped and crackled over the gravel in the church parking lot as Fin found a spot in the very back, against a chain-link fence woven with oleanders. He pulled on the emergency brake.

"Ready?" he said.

Giselle nodded, although she wasn't sure.

She glanced into the backseat. Coco had fallen asleep.

She was grateful Fin was taking care not to say too much in

front of her little girl. She didn't want Coco to see her playing these games. And good thing Giselle wasn't going to know Fin forever—she would be embarrassed to even run into him in the supermarket four months from now, after this display. But she also couldn't help herself. She just felt so frustrated by Roy. She wanted a little dignity back after spending so many nights in tears, alone.

"So how long were you married?" Fin asked into the quiet of the car.

Giselle blinked. She still wasn't used to hearing her marriage discussed in the past tense. It made her feel lost all over again. As if everything she'd built—the marriage, the relationship, herself as the perfect wife, the perfect hostess, the perfect mother—was gone.

"Ten years." Her voice sounded far away.

Fin nodded slowly. Maybe, to a guy like this, in his twenties, that sounded like a lifetime.

"Does that sound awful?" she asked.

"Not at all."

"But not in your game plan?"

The corner of his mouth quirked up.

"Too many bikini-clad women on the tour?"

He laughed at that, but didn't answer.

She wanted to know more, but felt wildly out of her element again. Here she was, about as far away from her cul-de-sac and peanut butter sandwiches as possible—sitting in a seductive leather-trimmed BMW with a sexy, tousled-hair athlete who surfed for a living—and she didn't really know how to proceed from here. Did twentysomethings feel comfortable talking about their dating lives? Did pro surfers like to talk about the girls they met? Did they even call it dating anymore? Maybe they just "hooked up"—a phrase that always gave Giselle a bad visual.

Unable to form a sane question, she reached for the handle.

"Hold on," he said.

She shifted back in the seat so she could face him.

"Why didn't you visit Lia more often in ten years?" he asked.

Why did he keep coming back to this? And how was he managing to zero right in on one of the major issues between her and Roy? As if he knew how guilty she felt, how many nights she'd cried. She tried to think of an explanation she could say out loud. *Talking about my sisters elicited rough sex from my ex-husband* seemed distinctively out of the question.

"Roy wasn't fond of my sisters."

"How could anyone not like Lia?"

Her sentiments exactly. "I don't know. It was complicated."

"Tell me later." The edge of protectiveness in his voice sent a shimmer of warmth through Giselle.

She stepped out of the car and smoothed the pleats of her dress, already feeling vulnerable in the bright sun. She dipped her head and studied the others arriving. So far she didn't recognize anyone.

"Giselle," Fin called. His heels made a crunching sound as he approached from the other side of the car. He shoved his hands in his pockets and nodded toward her hand. "You might want to take that off."

She followed his gaze. Her ring. Of course. She twisted it off with more force than was necessary and threw it into her purse as if it burned her fingers. "Thanks."

She trudged through the lot, unable to meet Fin's eyes. He kept pace beside her while Coco galloped nearby.

"It makes me look pathetic, doesn't it?" she whispered, fighting tears.

He didn't respond, only matched her strides with his own. Eventually, they got to the picket fence that led to the church sidewalk, and he opened the gate to guide her through.

"I asked for purely selfish reasons." He bent toward her ear. "I don't want people to think I sleep with married women."

Giselle stumbled across the wooden gate frame. She was unable to look Fin's way the rest of the walk.

The church vestibule bulged with funeral guests. Giselle and Fin pressed their way into the warm center, the heavy scent of perfume catching in Giselle's throat. She hoped no one from Roy's family would take notice of her yet. Showing up with a hot young man at her elbow and a fake new life was one thing, but having to spin the lie inside a church was another. She gripped Coco's hand and inched toward the main double doors.

"Gis-*elle*," said a woman's voice from beside her. Giselle recognized it immediately, and took a deep breath as she turned to greet Roy's sister, Ray-Lynn, who was sidling toward them. Ray-Lynn's voice was laden with sadness—dripping all over that second syllable. It was unclear whether the sadness was for Joe's death or Giselle's divorce.

"Ray-*Lynn*," Giselle replied in a matching tone.

They exchanged hugs, and Ray-Lynn bent to give Coco a squeeze, commenting on how big she'd gotten and how much she looked like Roy, which Giselle didn't really see.

Giselle watched Ray-Lynn's eyes dart toward Fin. For a moment, Giselle simply relished: in Ray-Lynn's speculation, in her confusion, in her probable thoughts that maybe she didn't need to be as sorry for Giselle as she had been these last several months.

But Ray-Lynn took the mystery into her own hands, and extended her ring-laden fingertips. "I'm Ray-Lynn, Giselle's ex-sister-in-law."

"Fin Hensen." He shook her hand gently and threw her a grin that sent her other hand fluttering to her collarbone.

Ray-Lynn didn't let go, seemingly waiting for him to clarify. He leaned forward and whispered, "I'm sorry for your loss." He brought the wattage of his smile down with his voice.

Ray-Lynn opened her mouth, but closed it again as Giselle took Coco's hand and snuck her toward the doorway.

Fin's fingers touched the small of Giselle's back as he led her down the aisle.

This was definitely her best plan yet.

As the minister spoke, Fin glanced around, absorbed in the smell of shoe polish and bad aftershave. He wondered which was the ex. Must be the dude sitting up front, with the doctor glasses on—the one who kept twisting his neck toward Giselle.

At his fourth or fifth glance, Fin was certain. He reached for Giselle's hand in her lap.

Giselle about leaped out of the pew.

He let go quickly and reassigned his hands to peeling off his jacket. Damn, it was hot in here.

He didn't know what she wanted. And he didn't know whether he should touch her. Touching her, in fact, just might be off the table because now, after touching her hand in her lap and accidentally brushing her thigh, his mind had gone into complete sexual overdrive. He let it continue for about twenty seconds, but then reminded himself where he was, and who she was, and how inappropriate this was on so many levels. He inched away and pretended he needed to get something out of his jacket pocket.

A wrapped mint crinkled against his fingertips—it must have been from Javier's Cantina down on the beach— probably his last date with Catalina Caesar. He held it across Giselle's body to Coco, who sat on the other side. She took it and swung her little shoes back and forth under the pew.

He leaned back and pretended he was listening to the minister. This might have been a terrible idea. He needed to talk to Giselle. Maybe they needed some ground rules.

"As we all come here together," the minister continued, "to grieve for Joseph, we allow ourselves to think back to all the joy he's brought us. . . ."

Fin surveyed the crowd. A lot of people here. Jennifer's funeral had brought about this number of mourners, too—all those surfers from around the world. He'd been a pallbearer at the request of her parents, who had regarded him kindly but probably wished he'd never met their daughter: *If only he hadn't convinced her of her talent. If only he'd been watching her more carefully on that last session . . .* They probably had a million regrets about him.

Fin accidentally met Giselle's eyes, which seemed to carry some kind of apology. God. That look was so sweet it killed him. Sort of like Lia, only Giselle had a wisdom about her that Lia didn't quite have yet. He knew there was another sister too, but he didn't know much about her. Giselle was enough of a surprise—her kindness, her humor, her patience with Coco, her curves, her softness. But he knew he'd be doing her a service by getting the hell out of her way as soon as possible. He wasn't a good person for her to have brought here. She should have brought someone with honor—someone who would impress these people, who were all losing a man who brought a crowd like this to his funeral. She shouldn't have brought a guy like Fin, who let his life go from bad to worse and didn't seem to know how to stop the train wreck.

Fin glanced again at ex-husband-the-doctor and wondered

what kind of man he was. Obviously a fool for letting Giselle go, but he must have had some kind of redeeming qualities to have won her over in the first place. And he sure helped create a cute kid. That, in itself, was something to be proud of.

While he watched, the ex cast another glance over his shoulder. And then Fin saw it.

Or *her*, actually: the young blonde at ex's side, who leaned toward the good doctor's shoulder, whispering something to get him to focus on the sermon.

Damn.

Now he got it.

He shifted in his seat and blew out a breath.

Giselle was a scorned wife.

And left for a younger woman.

She was bringing him here to get even. She'd said so in the sand—*young enough, hunky enough, pro surfer enough*—but he hadn't fully understood. But now he did.

Damn.

What was the matter with that guy? He must be some kind of jerk to take off for that young thing there, who probably didn't have half the grace of Grace Kelly here. And to leave a *daughter*? Who was only five?

But this was none of his business. He needed to stay removed. She hadn't invited him here to get involved—she had invited him here to look a certain way and play a certain role.

The ex turned around again, as Fin figured he would. Although the asshole waited, at least, for an appropriate moment, when the congregation was turning to one another to give peace. Fin leaned forward, just as the good doctor turned, and put his lips against Giselle's ear.

"How sexy do you want me to be?" he asked.

Giselle froze against the wood of the pew.

Fin's breath against her neck was so unexpected, so unprecedented, she couldn't meet his eyes.

Goose bumps prickled down her arms. She wasn't supposed to have goose bumps. She was supposed to have fake feelings, with fake shivers. This was her fake date. She needed to separate her attraction to a man of twenty-eight from *real* feelings that were *supposed* to elicit goose bumps—things she could look forward to, perhaps, in the future. Maybe from a nice accountant who would speak nicely to her and wouldn't mind taking on a new daughter.

Of course, she had had real feelings for Roy and couldn't quite remember the goose-bump stage. Maybe it had just been short.

"Joseph was survived," continued the minister, "by his wife of forty-seven years, Lovey; his son, Roy; his daughter, Ray-Lynn; and a granddaughter, Coco. . . ."

Coco twisted in her seat with wide eyes.

"It just means you were Grandpa Joe's granddaughter," Giselle whispered.

Coco nodded, still uncertain, and wriggled back into her

seat. She clutched Giselle's arm and nestled her head near her shoulder, putting her thumb in her mouth.

Giselle bit her lip. Coco hadn't done that since she was two. She reached over with her other hand and stroked her little girl's hair.

The minister's words danced through the air like a lullaby and, for a second, Giselle's shoulders began to relax. She even thought it might be safe to glance at Fin.

He'd spotted Roy. He'd taken her hand, leaned in, and had even asked her that exquisite question at a moment when Roy had turned to gape at them. So Fin knew. She was glad she wouldn't have to spell it out, say the words: *He abandoned me for a younger woman.* . . . She was glad she wouldn't have to risk crying. She was glad she wouldn't have to seem even more pathetic.

". . . and as Joseph goes to his new place in Heaven," the minister went on, "so, too, will we prepare for ours, and for the day when we will meet him, once again. . . ."

The minister's words sent a sudden wave of shame through her.

"As we live our lives in preparation of that wondrous meeting . . ."

She closed her eyes. *Live our lives in preparation.* . . . Her breath shook as she tried to fill her lungs. She shouldn't have brought Fin here. This was a *church.* She was supposed to feel *forgiveness.* So what if Roy had this laughably young nurse at his side? So what if everyone blinked at Giselle with pity? She was used to it in Indiana, with the neighbors giving her sidelong glances in the grocery store; she could get used to it here. And the funeral was only one day. Was her pride so great she couldn't deal with a day of pitying glances?

"As we prepare ourselves for that meeting . . ." the minister said.

And what about Fin? He didn't deserve to be here as some kind of fraud, being forced to lie. He probably wanted to be anywhere but here—anywhere but with a woman almost a decade older than he was, who was covered in black funeral clothes and trying to seem like she didn't deserve to be left for a beautiful younger woman. Maybe the decent thing to do would be to let him go. Just because she was playing some kind of sick game of one-upmanship didn't mean she was free to drag along innocent bystanders. What was she *becoming*?

"Fin," she whispered. The minister was saying something about preparing their souls to meet God.

"What do you need?" He covered her hand, right there in her lap, then let go quickly and dipped his head to try to meet her downcast eyes. He smelled so good—like intrigue and dubious morality. It sent a delicious shiver down her arms.

"Giselle?"

She couldn't look at him. She shook her head, tried to focus on the minister: ". . . the glory of the kingdom of Heaven shall await . . ."

She'd talk to Fin outside.

When she could breathe again.

The June sunshine assaulted her as she tugged Coco to the car, hoping to avoid Roy's family. The three of them scurried through the gravel until Fin grabbed her arm and swung her around.

"What's wrong?" he said.

"I shouldn't have . . ." Tears burned the backs of her eyes. She was a terrible person. How could she bring this guy, whom she didn't even know, and ask him into a *house of God*, to *lie*, straight out, along with her, to all these people who loved her—or once did—in front of her *daughter*? At a *funeral*?

"Giselle . . ." He started to reach toward her, but then dropped his hand and studied the other mourners, the cars—anything but the tear that just escaped down her cheek.

"Hey, Coco," he called, stepping toward the fence where Coco was searching for big rocks among the gravel. "Can you pick some of those flowers over there?" He pointed to a group of daisies that ran along the fence below the oleanders.

Coco squinted. "How many?"

"A bunch."

"Like a bouquet?" she asked delightedly.

"Yes, big," he said, showing her with his hands.

"We can bring them to Grandpa Joe!"

"Great idea."

She nodded and ran off.

Fin spun toward Giselle and grasped her elbows in both hands to move her a few steps away. "I pushed it too far, didn't I?" His hands felt warm and solid. "We might need some rules. I don't fully understand this situation or what you want me to do. You didn't mention the hot number in the high heels."

Giselle shot Fin a frown. That was all she needed. The stand-in fake boyfriend leaving her for the young nurse, too.

Her shame pulled at her until she felt like sinking into the gravel, letting the pebbles cover her, bury her. But instead she brought her hand to her eyelids and pressed. She couldn't cry like this. She needed to be strong.

"I shouldn't have made you come," she said. "This is awful. I'm terribly sorry. Do you want to drop me off? I can find a ride back."

He frowned. "We're at a *funeral,* Giselle. I'm not dropping you off." He stepped back for a second and took a deep breath. "I just need to know what you want me to do. I thought you wanted me to . . . you know, be the bastard who stole the doctor's wife."

Giselle sucked in some air and ran the phrase "stole the doctor's wife" through her head a couple more times, memorizing the sexy way he'd dropped his voice, and then had a hard time remembering what she'd planned to say.

"I need to know if the touching is too much," he said quietly.

Oh yeah, she thought. *The touching is definitely too much. You're sending shivers down my spine, and you shouldn't even be here, and you shouldn't have to know that a PTA mom is feeling hot for you, and you shouldn't have to be part of this at all.*

Coco's patent-leather shoes began crunching through the gravel behind them. She would have a big bouquet by now— an overachiever just like her mom.

He glanced over her shoulder at Coco and stepped closer to prompt an answer. "What do you want?"

The footsteps came louder. Crunch, crunch, crunch, crunch . . .

"Quickly," he said.

"Gis-*elle,*" she heard from a different direction—Ray-Lynn. Criminy, Ray-Lynn was coming.

"Kiss me," Giselle whispered.

Fin's eyes widened. "What?"

"*Kiss* me. Now."

He glanced over her shoulder. Ray-Lynn was yoo-hooing again through the parking lot, and Giselle could see the exact moment Fin put all the pieces together. He took Giselle's jaw in both hands and leaned toward her—but stalled before touching his lips to hers. All sound fell away—the crunching, the calling, Ray-Lynn, the crowds, the cars' tires pulling out for the procession. The world simply, softly, came to a halt. Fin's lips moved gently across hers, then pressed more seriously. His fingers entwined in her hair, and he covered her mouth with his. He kissed with a sense of discovery that Giselle met, pulse for pulse, while her bones melted into something warm and slow, sliding down her body. She brought a shaky hand toward his jaw, but before she could touch him, he stepped away. Averting his eyes, he dropped his hands and retreated, looking as if he didn't know what had just happened.

"My, my," said Ray-Lynn, who was now at Fin's shoulder, grinning from one to the other.

Giselle's face grew hot. She'd thought maybe Ray-Lynn would give them some privacy if she saw an intimate kiss. But apparently Ray-Lynn didn't do subtle hinting. Or not-so-subtle. Whatever. Either way, she was right there. And now Giselle's newest plan had backfired in more ways than one: The expression on Fin's face bordered on something between shock and horror.

Coco tugged at Giselle's skirt. "I told you he was a prince." She shoved the daisy-and-oleander bouquet toward Giselle.

"We have to go, Ray-Lynn," Giselle said, trying to disguise the tremor in her voice.

Fin grabbed Giselle's arm, steering her toward the car. With his other hand, he took Coco's bouquet and guided her, too, past the dispersing cars in the parking lot.

"Hope I'll see you at the house," Ray-Lynn singsonged toward Giselle's back.

Giselle didn't know who, exactly, Ray-Lynn was talking to. But she guessed it wasn't her.

Okay, Fin thought, as he marched Giselle and Coco to the car. *Okay, okay.* He pressed Giselle's elbow to speed her along, causing dust to fly over the tops of their shoes. *That meant nothing.*

But he refused to meet Giselle's eyes.

He got Coco buckled into the backseat, the flowers settled in her lap; then he straightened and finally faced Giselle.

If this were any other woman, he'd step out of the line of sight of her kid and would grab her, right here, and see if that kiss could generate more of the heat he'd felt back there. He'd have her bent back across the trunk of his car—kid or no kid—and would be seeing whether those lips of hers—which, hot damn, were everything he'd imagined them to be—were as yielding as the rest of her body. And—if this were any other woman—she'd comply. Because he dated those kinds of women.

But this was Giselle.

And *damn*. But *damn*. That was hot.

He motioned with his hand for her to get into the car.

This was Giselle.

He walked to the other side and ran through all the reasons to ignore that kiss: He was supposed to be doing her a favor. And she was too sweet to comply with his usual debauchery. And her kid was too sweet. And Lia was one of his only true friends. And he was in a *church parking lot*, for Christ's sake. . . .

By the time he got to the driver's side, and his jacket off, he was pretty sure he'd convinced himself it was a temporary madness.

"Hot today," Giselle said quietly, after they'd driven a mile or so.

He murmured an agreement, loosening his tie.

"Is it always like this?"

"Not usually this early."

"Thought so."

That was all she said until they got to the grave site. Fin didn't know what the hell they were talking about, but he had the strong feeling they were both talking about a lot more than the weather.

———— C H A P T E R ————
Seven

The grave site gathering was as awkward as anything Giselle had ever experienced, with ex-aunts, ex-uncles, ex-cousins, and even an ex-grand-aunt who cast glances her way as they got out of cars and wandered over the low green hills.

Giselle's stomach knotted. She worried about seeing Roy up close. Worried about what he'd say. Worried about Coco. Worried that she'd just kissed her fake funeral date—and about melted into the gravel—and he'd responded with a look of horror. . . .

A few of the relatives pointed toward Coco, probably wondering whether they remembered her from Indiana family picnics or trying to recognize her from Christmas photos Giselle had sent to Roy's seventy-seven friends and relatives for ten long years. Giselle glanced down the paved road that bisected the rolling green of the cemetery, searching for Roy's car. Certainly, he would say hello. But Giselle wished it were sooner rather than later. Coco was glancing from side to side.

Meanwhile, Giselle continued her list of things that needed to be banned from her thoughts: Coco's probable abandonment by this family, and now Fin's kiss.

She bit her lip and tried not to think of how soft his lips

had felt. She hadn't experienced a kiss like that since . . . well . . . she supposed since she met Roy. But Roy didn't kiss like *that*.

A bead of sweat slipped behind her ear as she tried to keep up with Fin's footsteps. He'd been frowning pretty much the entire drive. He frowned as they got out of the car. He fell silent as they balanced across the mounds of emerald grass. He refused to look at her as they found a place at the back of the grave site gathering. While she was obsessing over his lips, his arms, the way he'd gripped her elbows, he was frowning as if he'd just made the worst, most regrettable mistake of his life.

She touched Coco's braids and managed to square her shoulders. She reminded herself of her goal: All she had to do was appear as if she'd moved on. She just had to get through one day at a time. After this week, she'd probably never see Fin or Ray-Lynn or Grand-Aunt Esther or Uncle Frank or that young nurse ever again.

"Where's Daddy?" Coco whispered.

Except Roy. He was someone she'd unfortunately have to deal with forever.

"He'll come."

"Darling." Lovey reached for Giselle's hand. She dipped her champagne-colored coiffure toward Coco and kissed both her cheeks with an exaggerated smack. Coco giggled and threw her arms around her grandmother.

"I'm so glad you came," Lovey said. "Come join us." She tugged at Giselle's hands, but did a double take when she realized Fin was part of the entourage.

Shame and pride warred in Giselle's chest, but Lovey simply held out her hand. "I'm Lovey, Giselle's former mother-in-law."

"Fin Hensen."

"The surfer?"

Fin's hesitation was noticeable only to Giselle. "Yes."

Giselle took another long look at him. She thought his name might be recognizable to one or two of the younger people here, but she didn't expect him to be recognized by her sixty-nine-year-old mother-in-law.

"Please." Lovey motioned toward the row of seats that sat like little soldiers around the raised casket.

"I'd feel more comfortable back here," Giselle whispered.

Lovey started to say something, but then acquiesced. She shot a glance toward her son, who had just arrived and was taking a seat in the front row, staring toward the casket, his young nurse at his side. The nurse studied the crowd through wide-rimmed sunglasses and a patterned head scarf that gave her a mysterious Jayne Mansfield look.

"It's awful," Lovey whispered. "I'm sorry he brought her here. Are you sure you won't join us?"

Giselle nodded. She was having a hard time taking her eyes off Roy and his nurse. Roy seemed . . . *smaller*, somehow. Even from just four months ago.

"Can I take Coco?" Lovey asked tentatively.

Giselle had been gripping Coco's shoulder with a certain protectiveness, but releasing her to Lovey was the right thing to do. Of course Lovey would want to spend time with her only grandchild. She'd always adored her, sending her cards and games in the mail, calling her on the phone on the first Wednesday of every month to share knock-knock jokes, and coming to visit Indiana when she could so she could take Coco to the lake.

"Can we take her to the house?" Lovey's eyes begged.

Giselle nodded again. But she shuddered at the deep loneliness already creeping up her spine.

She bent to remind Coco to mind her manners, and Coco held out her palm. "Kissing hand?" the little girl whispered.

Giselle planted a kiss right in the center before Coco bounced away with Lovey.

"What's a kissing hand?" Fin said from behind her.

Giselle wiped an errant tear from the corner of her eye. "It's from a book. The mother raccoon kisses her baby's hand and leaves the kiss in his palm. That way he can press it against his cheek whenever he needs it."

Fin nodded solemnly and shoved his hands in his pockets. He took a few steps closer. "Are you okay?"

She was swept with gratitude that he was here. If he hadn't been, she'd quite possibly be standing here, on the outskirts of this grave site, on the outskirts of this family, feeling more alone than she'd ever felt in her life.

"I will be," she said.

And, for the first time, she had a tiny ray of hope that it might be true.

* * *

When the grave site ceremony ended, Fin turned, like a body-guard, to scout for the good doctor. And spotted him, imme-diately. Heading their way. Alarm for Giselle ignited through him. He scanned the crowd to see whether the hot girlfriend was in tow.

"He's coming to talk to you. Want me to stay?" he asked.

Her gaze slid over his shoulder, her nod barely perceptible.

"Giselle!" the doctor called.

"Roy." Giselle gave him a tight, sort of keep-away-from-me hug; the doctor returned it with a little less keeping away, as far as Fin was concerned. But at least the girlfriend wasn't around.

A silence fell. It occurred to Fin that the doctor was wait-ing for an introduction.

"Fin Hensen." He thrust his hand forward. That was all he was going to say. Let the bastard wonder.

"You're the surfer," he said as the name registered. His handshake was fishy and wet.

"Yes."

"Roy Underwood."

Fin nodded curtly.

Roy stared at his ex-wife with curiosity.

That's right, you idiot, Fin thought. *You're not the only one who can sleep around.*

Although, of course, Giselle *wasn't* sleeping around. Which was too bad for Fin. But the point was, she *could* if she wanted to. Fin went back to slandering Roy in his head.

"Are you coming to the house?" Roy asked, pointing his question to Giselle.

Fin shoved his hands in his pockets and sized Roy up. He'd expected Giselle's ex to be tall for some reason, but he was just average, unremarkable, with a froglike shape. His suit was nice, though—he'd give him that.

"Coco looks great," Roy said into the next silence.

Fin glanced at Giselle to see her reaction to that. It seemed like a weird thing to say about your kid. As if she were a pot of daisies, or the new siding on the house.

"She's doing well," she responded politely.

Fin spread his legs and dug his heels into the grass. He and Giselle had come up with two signs just moments before Roy had arrived—a touch to his forearm meant: *Do not leave under any circumstances*. And a mission—*Fin, could you go check on Coco*—meant she needed time alone. They weren't clever signs, of course—pretty damned straightforward—but he wanted to be sure they had this all under control.

But now she did neither.

"My dad would've appreciated your coming," Roy went on, polite as all get-out, as if he were speaking to the cleaning lady.

Fin allowed himself another glance toward Giselle. He expected her to seem a little strained. But, instead, she was the epitome of reserve. He wondered whether Roy thought of how beautiful she was when he ran into her—did he think he'd let her slip away? Or was he already so wrapped up in his own life that he didn't see it anymore? Fin remembered the hot number in the high heels. She was gorgeous, too, in a very come-fuck-me way, but Giselle's beauty was different. It began at her spine, or maybe at her soul, and radiated from there. He'd read once that a pretty woman was only pretty while she was young, but a beautiful woman was beautiful her whole life. The line finally made sense to him.

"Can I talk to you privately?" the good doctor whispered toward Giselle's shoulder.

Ah, here we go.

Fin waited for his cue.

"Actually, anything you need to say, you can say in front of Fin." Her fingers curled at Fin's biceps—a detail the ex didn't seem to miss.

"I'd rather not," the doctor said.

"I'd *rather*." Giselle raised her chin. Fin couldn't help but feel a flash of pride in her.

Roy crossed his arms and dropped his gaze to his shoes. The gesture was so one of a surgeon, coming to tell the family that the patient had died—that Fin had the irresistible urge to put his arm around Giselle, before she heard the bad news. But he refrained. Aside from the "don't go away" sign, they'd decided on only necessary touching, which was Giselle's request, but he hadn't argued. He figured having rules about touching was good. Although her fingers wrapped around his biceps right now weren't escaping his notice. But *he* was the one who needed the rules. After that kiss, he wasn't sure he could trust himself.

"I just wanted you to know . . ." Roy angled his shoulder to block Fin out. ". . . Kimber is pregnant."

Fin glanced at Giselle. *Kimber?* Was that the hot blonde? Roy's delivery seemed so overdramatic, with that lowered voice and exotic name, that Fin half expected Giselle to rail in some over-the-top soap-opera way. But instead she held her neck up as if Roy hadn't spoken at all. As if she were still waiting for the interesting part.

Roy blinked a few times and glanced at Fin, as if they were just two men now, both confused by a woman's behavior.

"I haven't told Coco," Roy went on. "I'd rather not say anything until later."

Giselle stood completely still, the epitome of poise.

"We'll see you, Roy," was all she said, and she started stepping toward the car.

As they walked away, Fin couldn't help it. He reached up and put his arm around her. He figured this time, of all times, was one of the necessary touches.

"Of all the cockamamie, for-crying-out-loud things," Giselle said out the car window, as Fin pulled through the cemetery.

He let her curse in her beauty-queen way while he maneuvered from what looked like a luxury-car sales lot.

"He never even wanted *Coco*," she said, exasperated, flinging her hand toward the window.

That got his attention.

Damn. The more he was learning about this bastard, the more he wanted to beat the crap out of him.

"What do you mean, he didn't want Coco?"

Giselle blinked at him, as if she suddenly realized she'd been saying all these things out loud. Her attention drifted to the hills rolling by.

"When I told him, he said he wanted me to get an abortion." Her voice cracked over the last word. "He was barely out of medical school, and still doing his residency, and he thought it would be too hard for us. He even came to me with a business card of one of his associates—someone he trusted. I doubt he's handing *her* that card."

The sadness that hung over Giselle was so palpable, Fin felt like pulling over and doing whatever was necessary to stop it. But he had no idea what that would be. He felt helpless—a feeling he hated more than anything in the world. Instead he just sat there, at a stop sign, ready to pull out of the cemetery site. He kept his hands on top of the steering wheel.

"Can you roll the window down?" she said, touching her throat.

He quickly hit the button.

She leaned her head back and took in big gulps of air.

"Look, Giselle, how about if I take you somewhere? Get something to eat, get your thoughts together? You can pay your respects in your own way, later."

He didn't really know how to handle a situation like this, but he did know that she'd rip herself apart by showing up at that house. She'd have to watch that Kimber babe from across the room and know that Coco was going to have a new little sister or brother someday soon.

"No," she said, with surprising conviction. "I need to go."

"Of course you do, but you don't need to go for four *hours*. How about if we go somewhere for an hour or so, let you take a few deep breaths, and then we'll arrive at the house in the middle of the reception, make an appearance, gather Coco, and leave? Will she be okay for an hour?"

Giselle thought about that for a minute. "She's fine with Lovey."

Fin switched his blinker to the opposite direction and squealed into the street before she could change her mind.

"Have you ever had a fish taco?" he asked as the wind whipped through their hair.

She shook her head. She was still looking out the window as if her world had just caved in. Which, he supposed, it had.

"Well, welcome to Southern California, home of the best fish tacos in the States."

A polite, beauty-queen smile forced its way across her face. "And *outside* the States?"

"That would be Mexico. That's where we learned it. But let me take you to my favorite place. It's not far from here."

Fin threw the car into fourth and took Giselle away from everything.

Even if only for an hour.

CHAPTER

Eight

The smell of grills and salsa mingled through the small room as Giselle followed Fin all the way to the back, toward a turquoise Formica table under a makeshift thatched palapa. Surf pictures and boards hung from the ceiling and walls; tiki lights draped from corner to corner; and surfing and skateboarding stickers covered every conceivable surface: booths, chairs, tables, walls, floor, doors, and even the windows. It struck Giselle as a decidedly mixed atmosphere of rope hammock, crashing wave, and daring athleticism.

She scooted in her chair as Fin slid out of his jacket and nodded hello to one of the workers.

"Do I even want to know what 'sex wax' is?" she said, squinting at the bright red letters of one of the stickers slapped to the table.

Fin took his seat and rubbed the side of his nose, as if he weren't sure he wanted to answer. "Not as interesting as it sounds."

"What is it?"

"It's a wax you rub on your board. Keeps your feet from sliding."

"Why is it called 'sex wax'?"

Fin glanced at her from under his bangs, then looked away. "'Wax your stick,' that kind of thing." He suddenly seemed to find his receipt very interesting.

She felt her face go hot and tried to think of something else to say.

She tried to imagine how she must appear to him—in her low-heeled proper shoes, someone you couldn't say "sex wax" to without lowering your eyes—and wondered what this whole marital drama must look like to a young, single guy. Especially the part with the ex-husband strutting around with a D-cup mistress, then dropping the news at a funeral that he'd gotten the girl pregnant. She wondered whether Roy seemed ridiculous to Fin—as if it weren't occurring to him that if he kept turning his mistresses into mothers, they'd lose their appeal. Didn't a doctor know better? And she wondered whether she seemed pathetic for sticking around while it happened.

Especially a second time.

Jillian had happened two years ago, when Coco was only three. Giselle had been devastated that there would be another child in this world who would be related to Roy and Coco, whom they'd all be bringing into their lives. Who would involve weekend visits and birthday gifts. Who would represent Roy's disrespect. It was almost more than she could bear, but she took Roy back anyway. She didn't want to deprive Coco of a two-parent home, and her love for Roy had turned into a sort of desperation. Plus she had nowhere to go—she hadn't planned a career, had no real life of her own. She figured she could suck up a little disrespect so that Coco could have as close to a normal life as possible. But then Jillian lost the baby. And Roy said he was coming back to Giselle and Coco "for real." No more infidelities. He'd learned his lesson, he'd said. He'd given Giselle his pager and cell phone, asked her to check it every night. He'd made his life an open book—all in an effort to prove to Giselle that he was devoted to them, that he'd never make such a foolish mistake again.

But then D-cups had come a-calling again. A different set. And Giselle and Coco were left in the wake again.

That was when Giselle found the note underneath the cantaloupe: *"I've met someone else, G. I'm so very sorry."*

Giselle had sat for four days in a darkened house, telling

Coco that she had a tummy ache. She'd made brief sojourns to Coco's preschool in her slippers and pajamas and then gone home and cried for hours.

Roy didn't call. He didn't return her messages. She had no idea what had happened.

But then, about a week later, she'd snapped herself back together.

She'd gotten up, gotten a haircut at the most expensive salon she could find, charged it to Roy, gone shopping for the most expensive clothes she could find, charged those to Roy, and then packed up and found a place at a swanky hotel in Indianapolis, where she could still take Coco to school every day but where they could dine in style, on Roy's dime, and she could think.

She'd called a lawyer. Collected the divorce papers. And then she'd called Lia to ask if they could stay in Sandy Cove for a little while, just to clear her head. Her hands had shaken through every one of these activities, but she did them.

Calling her sisters and her mom had been the hardest part. She knew there'd be an element of "I told you so." And she didn't even have a good explanation for why he'd left. She'd always been the responsible oldest sister, the one to do the right thing, the smart thing, to take care of everyone. And admitting that she'd made the most enormous mistake of all—but wasn't sure what it was—was almost more than she could bear. She had no bank account, no job, no work experience, no skills, not even her own friends. Her Audi wasn't even in her own name.

But she'd swallowed her pride, made the calls, listened to Noelle's sighs of pity, listened to Lia's list of things she would have done to be more financially independent, listened to her mom's litany of all the reasons she never liked Roy in the first place, and then started packing for Sandy Cove.

Roy stayed oddly away. He tried to contact her only a few times, to see Coco, and always through texts. They arranged for him to pick Coco up after school on a couple of Fridays; then Giselle would pick her up after school on Mondays, so they still didn't talk. When she caught him answering his phone in real time once, she jumped at the chance to ask him what she most wanted to know: "Why?"

"I can't explain it," was all he said. His voice was robotic.

He listened to her sobbing and then said they'd talk later, and hung up.

Giselle eventually talked herself into starting over. She didn't have any answers about what went wrong in her marriage, but she couldn't stay stagnant forever. Her own mother had divorced twice, and Giselle had always promised herself her life would be different. Her daughter would *never* suffer through a broken home—separate Christmases, competitive birthday gifts, shuffling of weekends. She'd *never* fail her daughter.

But then she did.

And now she had to live with the fact that she'd failed in the only thing she ever wanted to be: a good mother, with a strong family.

"That wasn't what he wanted to tell you," Fin said, leaning across the aqua Formica and running the receipt through his fingers.

"What?" Giselle cleared her throat and forced herself out of her reverie.

"I know it was devastating enough, but it wasn't what he wanted to tell you. He wanted to tell you something else, but he didn't want me there to hear it."

His eyes darted toward the counter, waiting for their food. As if on cue, the T-shirt-clad server appeared with two porcelain plates piled high with white rice, black beans, and fish tacos, all covered in bright red salsa.

"Can you autograph this?" she asked shyly, handing him her cap. "To Tilly?"

"I thought I autographed everything in this place already," Fin said, smiling up at her.

"I'm new." She handed him a pen.

He scrawled his name across the brim.

"Thank you," she said breathlessly, flinging her ponytail over her shoulder and sliding away.

Giselle gaped at him as he loosened his tie and began moving the salsa bowls closer to each of their plates. "Do you always get asked for autographs like that?"

"Oh." He waved his hand back. "Not here. They've known me for years. The new girl threw me."

Giselle nodded. She thought *her* life was held up to scrutiny and judgment, but this put things into perspective. The snowboards and surfboards that hung at odd angles around the room did, indeed, have autographs all over them. She let her gaze roam over them until she gasped to see a huge graphic on a wall with Fin's image, along with two other men, in colorful, Andy Warhol–style negative.

He followed her eyes. "I was trying to position you so you didn't see that. Crazy, huh? Those others are Kelly Slater and Taj Burrow. Kelly Slater is a modern legend. Taj Burrow beats me every year. And that's Laird Hamilton." He nodded with his head in another direction. "He's a big-wave surfer."

"Kelly, Taj, Laird, and Fin? Do all surfers have to have ultracool names to compete?"

"Yeah, Coco will fit right in. You need to get her on the Women's Tour ASAP."

She smiled and tried to ignore the fact that she was sitting with a guy whose picture was a designer graphic on a restaurant wall and had girls named Tilly following him for an autograph. And that she happened to know he was the most amazing kisser.

She watched him divest himself of his tie and fling it on the back of his chair, unbuttoning his shirt at the collar. His thick, tan knuckles undid the buttons deftly as she wondered what else his hands could do, what his fingers could trigger, who else's zipper or dress he could unravel. . . . Embarrassed, she redirected her attention toward her meal.

"This looks delicious," she said.

"It is—the three brothers who started this place have a Chinese-Brazilian heritage, so you have the white rice and black beans, but they learned the fish taco thing from their surf days in Mexico. I come here all the time." Fin spooned extra salsa across his rice and held the bowl out to her.

That was about as many words as he'd strung together the whole day. She felt a slight sense of accomplishment.

"So how do you know?" she asked.

"Know what?"

"About Roy and that he wanted to say something else."

He attended his plate for a few seconds. "He just had that look about him."

Back to the short, choppy sentences.

Giselle nodded. She'd noticed much the same thing—it did seem like Roy had begun with one agenda and switched to another. She was just surprised that Fin could read it.

"So what did you think of him?" she asked.

He gave her a wary look and didn't answer.

She watched him dig into his meal, then studied her own plate for a moment. The sex wax sticker poked out from under her plate and now said "ex ax."

"I'd like your opinion," she prompted.

"It's none of my business, Giselle."

"I'd like it anyway."

He raised his eyebrow as if he didn't quite believe her, then shrugged. "He has a kind of shiftiness, if you don't mind my saying."

"I said I wouldn't mind."

"I don't want to insult you."

"Why would I be insulted?"

"You married him."

Giselle's spine stiffened as she pretended to move her rice around.

Fin bit into his taco and watched her for a minute. "See? This is none of my business. I'm sorry. Go ahead and eat— you look like you're going to fall over."

"Are you wondering *why* I married him?"

He glanced at her between bites of his taco. "Doctor, good living, secure, probably smart. I can figure that out."

Giselle tried not to react. She did *not* marry Roy because he was a doctor. Or because he had money. That had been the furthest thing from her mind. In fact, when they were first married, he was a med student. They barely made ends meet. "Are you saying I married for materialistic reasons?"

His mouth quirked up at the corner. "Giselle—I didn't say that. You're beautiful. And smart. And sophisticated as hell. So I figure he must have some redeeming qualities. But right now, he just seems like an asshole. That's all I'm saying." He took another bite.

Giselle started to respond, but then closed her mouth. Fin was right. Roy did seem like a jerk. But he *did* have some redeeming qualities when she met him. And what did a twenty-eight-year-old who played in the ocean for a living know about what you searched for in a good marriage, anyway? She wanted a good father, of course. Someone who was solid . . . secure . . . certain of his future . . . Of course, Roy had turned out not to be *any* of those things. . . .

And did Fin just say she was beautiful?

She dragged her napkin back across her lap.

"So tell me why he didn't like Lia," Fin said.

Giselle shook her head.

Fin finished one of his tacos and took another long sip of his drink. He pushed his plate back. "I want to know," he said.

Giselle paused, but then shook her head again. "It'll only make him seem like more of a jerk."

"Try me," he said tightly.

"It's not wise."

He busied himself with the salsa on his plate. "So was I right about why you married him?"

"For money?"

He smirked. "I didn't say that, Giselle. I said he was probably smart. Secure."

Giselle sat straighter in her chair. She didn't know, now, whether she'd made the right decisions. Maybe she had married Roy for the wrong reasons. Maybe she should have waited for those goose bumps, not pinned her sights on what seemed like security. Or fatherly material.

"Maybe these questions are too personal, after all," she said.

"Well, I figure—being the new lover and all—I should know some of these things."

Giselle's face flushed. She rearranged her napkin again. She didn't want Fin to make fun of her. She didn't want his pity, or anyone else's.

"Giselle," he said, putting his taco down. "I'm sorry. I'm trying to lighten the mood here, but—"

"I married him because I thought he'd be a good father," she blurted.

His expression registered surprise—clearly, he'd thought that line of questioning was over. But now he searched her face. "And *is* he?"

Giselle managed to maintain eye contact for five full seconds before the tears stung her eyes. She shook her head. She'd been wrong on so many levels. She'd never been able to admit it to her mother, or her sisters, or her friends, or even herself: *She'd made a terrible decision.* Roy was a terrible husband. And a terrible father. And rather than facing that truth, or even admitting it, she'd kept living in denial. As the ugly honesty of the situation hit her, she tried to avert her eyes as a couple of tears escaped.

"Wait," Fin said. "No, don't cry. . . . I'm sorry." His hand moved across the table, but before he touched her, he seemed to think better of it. "Please." He found a napkin to hand her. "I brought you here so you could get your thoughts together and . . . Damn, don't cry."

She dabbed at her eyes with the paper napkin. He was right. This was no time to fall apart. She lifted her eyelashes to one of the surfboards hanging from the ceiling to let the tears well back down. Criminy, what was the matter with her? She didn't even know this guy. And here she was, crying all over her tacos.

"Let's talk about something else." His voice was laced with desperation.

She nodded again.

"You steer—what do you feel comfortable talking about right now?"

She kept her focus on the board—Fin's autograph was on that one, too, along with Laird Hamilton's. She took a deep breath. "Surfing."

An expression of surprise crossed his face.

She poked at her taco with her fork and pushed some lettuce around. "Tell me how you learned," she added, her voice still wobbly. "Where, when, why."

She figured this conversation would give her enough time to let the pressure in her head die down.

Fin surveyed the room for a few moments, then took a deep breath and wiped his mouth with his napkin. She couldn't help but stare at his lips when he did so—that full bottom lip, and the strong upper one, and what soul-stirring feeling they'd ignited when he'd stepped into that kiss. . . .

"Well, the 'where' would be San Onofre," he said.

Giselle cleared her throat and tried to focus on what he was saying.

Fin paused, as if that were all he planned to say, then looked at her nervously as if he were worried another tear might escape if he stopped talking. "That's about fifteen miles south of here," he added quickly. "The 'when' would be age four. And the 'why' would be because my parents were both surfers at the time. I suppose I had salt water in my blood."

"Really? Your parents were surfers? What was that like? Wow, Fin, these tacos are amazing."

"Aren't they? Here, have some more salsa."

"So is that why you're named 'Fin'? Is it your real name?"

"Finnegan. But I've been 'Fin' for as long as I can remember."

"So tell me about growing up with surfer parents."

He studied the room for a minute, as if trying to decide where to start. Or whether he wanted to. "It was a nomad existence. We were traveling all the time, which wasn't so bad—I got to see a lot of beautiful coastline from Indonesia to Hawaii— but we weren't exactly staying in luxury hotels. It was a lot of camping in vans, sleeping in the sand, eating what fish we could catch, that kind of thing. My parents weren't pro surfers like nowadays—with sponsors and magazine ads. They were amateurs who were the real deal. They surfed for love."

The long swig he took of his drink hinted at some finality to this story. But Giselle imagined there was a lot more to it.

"That must have been hard, not knowing where your real home was," she prompted.

He shrugged.

She waited for him to go on, but he focused on his food. Fin didn't exactly seem like the type to tell his whole life story in the first hour or so. In fact, he didn't seem like the type to tell his life story at all. So she decided she'd have to either pry or stick to the basics. Her sense of upbringing, though, held her to basics.

"Where did you go to school?"

"Didn't."

"You didn't go to school?"

"School of life: Tahiti, Bali, Costa Rica. We traveled with a group of my parents' friends, all surfers."

"You never got a formal education?"

He shrugged. "I'm sure my parents thought they were teaching me more important things than algebra and cursive, so not until about the sixth grade."

"That must have been hard."

"Not really."

She waited for him to go on.

He ate another chip and finally gave her a crooked smile. "I was a weird kid. I had been traveling with all these Zen surfers who were reading Jack Kerouac and Robert Aitken and who could talk all kinds of circles around Rick Griffin's transcendental art. They taught me meditation and self-realization techniques at nine."

"You sound like you were an interesting kid."

He shook his head and laughed. "Definitely weird."

"So where did you finally go to school? Here?"

"A little farther north: Central California, where the surf is good. We moved there in the eighties. But, you know—I never had the right sneakers, never had sack lunches with fruit cups in them. I had long hair, and 'nomad' written all over me. I saw what the other kids had—normal lives, new clothes for school, new folders with *Knight Rider* on them, or whatever, and they'd play together after school, or play in Little League. I just wanted that. I thought that would be the ideal life."

"So was it?"

He took a deep breath. His tanned fingers touched the rim of his plate.

"My parents were still competing. My mom—she's an amazing surfer. So they made another tour, but I had a friend named Ronny Romano—he lived inland a little—but he had a nice, normal family. And I wanted to live there. So my parents let me."

"They *left* you there?" Giselle gasped.

His jaw muscle began to dance. "They're good people, Giselle. I was fine."

"Where are your parents now?"

"Bali."

"Brothers, sisters?"

"Just me."

Giselle couldn't imagine not having any family, not having her sisters. Even though they didn't all stay close all the time, she knew they were there. Fin, however, seemed terribly alone. She thought back over his house, his car, his suits. He'd accomplished a lot for a twenty-eight-year-old, all by himself. There was much more to this man than she realized.

He shifted in his seat. "So where did you grow up? I can't remember what Lia told me."

"Mostly Indiana."

"What was it like there?"

She wanted to turn the conversation back on him—wanted to know more about his family, when he moved to Sandy Cove, when he last saw his parents—but she had the sense he'd hit his limit.

"Typical," she answered. "We had a very normal lifestyle. We were those kids with the Knight Rider folders and new shoes."

"Nah, those kids I'm talking about were jerks. You were probably very sweet. You and your sister. Or sisters. Isn't there another one?"

"Yes, Noelle. She's the youngest."

"Is she as pretty as you and Lia?"

Giselle felt herself flush. Fin was awfully free with the compliments—she wasn't used to it, having had pretty much a dry spell for the last ten years.

"Thank you," she said, remembering that was what you were supposed to say. "I always thought Noelle was the prettiest, actually. She has this long, auburn hair I always admired. Lia and I got stuck as the blondes."

"You seem to hold your own." He smiled. "Tell me you weren't the homecoming queen, or Miss Indiana."

Giselle sucked in her breath. "Did Lia tell you that?" she whispered.

He raised his eyebrows, then chuckled. "Uh—Lia told me *nothing*. But I just impressed the hell out of myself. You've got 'beauty queen' written all over you."

"I was Miss Strawberry," she said with mock indignation.

"I have to hear this."

Giselle laughed. She hadn't thought about this in a long time. "Dane County has a strawberry festival every year in June, and they crown one of the girls from the local high schools as Miss Strawberry. There's a parade, and you ride in this red convertible and wave your hand. But you get a scholarship, so that was nice."

"Did you wear a crown?"

She nodded.

"Sash?"

She nodded again.

The corners of his mouth quirked up. "Did you have to cut a huge slice of strawberry shortcake?"

Giselle's eyes widened. "How did you know?"

"We have something like that here. I can picture you sitting on the back of some red convertible." Fin chuckled down at his plate, cleaning up the last few remnants of fish and rice.

A smile escaped Giselle's lips.

After the table was cleared, Fin leaned toward Giselle, his muscular arms on the table so he could be heard at low volume.

"One more thing, before we go back . . ." The merriment was gone from his eyes. The navy rim was thicker now, making his eyes darker. He took her in for a while before shifting his gaze to tell her the one more thing.

"That kiss—" he finally said.

Oh, no. Giselle closed her eyes. She didn't want to talk about this. She knew he was going to say it was off-limits, that she had no right to ask that of him. She'd been way out of line. But goodness, that kiss was amazing. She wondered whether he'd felt the heat rising in her when he kissed her like that. He could probably feel her ready to ignite, for criminy's sake. And he was probably putting a stop to that right now. Twenty-eight-year-old surfer dudes did not need to make out with thirty-five-year-old soccer moms.

"I know," she started to say, shaking her head.

"—I'm sorry," he said.

She glanced up at him. *Sorry?*

"I . . ." he began. "Well, it got out of hand. I didn't mean to . . ." He seemed to be searching the room for the answer. "I didn't mean to let it get out of hand."

Giselle cleared her throat and looked at her fingertips, which were now up on the table playing with her paper napkin. She could hardly meet his eyes. Out of hand? Well, she had certainly thought so. But she knew what he was saying— he simply wanted to play this part, to reciprocate this deal they had going, but he didn't need her to get swept away.

"I understand," was all she could manage. She shredded the edge of her napkin and hoped he'd change the subject. "No more," she reiterated.

He watched her eyes for a long time, then nodded.

"Got it," he said. "Are you ready to go back?"

They went over their signals: a signal for when she needed him to stay by her side and another for when she needed some privacy. She suggested they stay a half hour, just to pay their respects to Lovey, then collect Coco and leave.

Fin put his tie back on and collected his jacket off the chair. "And be prepared for that second bombshell your ex is going to drop. Maybe you should just paddle out—you know, take the wave full-force. Don't put it off. Be ready for it. I'll be there for you."

Giselle watched as he patted his pockets, making sure he had his cell phone, his wallet. A warm feeling began in her stomach, and she forced herself to walk back through those last few words to make sure she'd heard him correctly: *I'll be there for you.* Those words meant more to her than he could possibly know.

He glanced up. "Okay?"

"Okay."

And, for a moment, she felt she'd be ready for anything.

The house was stellar.

Fin wandered past the living room bar and mused about what it would have felt like growing up here, with a doctor for a father, a boat dock in the backyard, and fancy living room furniture, instead of wondering where his next meal was coming from. The house backed up to a man-made lake, rimmed around its two-mile perimeter with enormous homes, white-stucco condos, and hillsides of tile-roofed townhomes standing shoulder to shoulder. Pristine sailboats and motorboats left a sparkling wake on the water.

"Here you go." He handed Giselle a mimosa and leaned against the cement balustrade, staring at the boats and homes below. It was a beautiful place, but the man-made nature of the lake bothered him. He loved the grit of the ocean, throwing its sand and seaweed and debris around—debris that had been collected for years, even centuries, stolen from shores all over the world. This man-made lake was nice and all, but it wasn't anything like natural beauty, which always had stories behind it.

"Cheers to us for handling this crowd so far," Giselle said, lifting her glass.

Fin toasted. What he really wanted to do was hand her a scotch. She'd had a hell of an afternoon, with her ex giving her speculative glances as soon as she stepped through Lovey's threshold, and that strange sister-in-law Ray-Lynn dripping with all those platitudes about how much Giselle was missed.

In fact, Fin could use a good scotch, too. But he figured it would be obnoxious to ask Lovey where she kept the Glenlivet.

He downed his mimosa and stared over the balcony railing at the sun, which was still hanging high in the sky. He wondered what the surf was like at home. But he stole a quick glance at Giselle and decided she was a beautiful distraction anyway.

He hadn't known what had made him open up like that at the restaurant. That was strange. But it was nice to talk—he hadn't told anyone about Ronny Romano in years. And hearing her stories was nice. *Miss Strawberry.* Good Lord. He'd had her number from the start. All those Rose queens and homecoming queens he'd seen on television had that same aura. Somewhere, God was still churning out that caliber of woman from his famous queen-making machine: They knew how to use the right forks; they cursed with words like "darned" instead of "fucking"; and they had elongated, pretty necks.

Like Giselle's.

Which looked pretty fucking kissable from here.

He sighed and leaned into the rail. He wasn't going to let his mind go there anymore. No more thinking about kissing Giselle. She was in another league.

He put his empty glass on a table behind them and moved farther down the rail.

"All right, thirty minutes and counting," he told her, consulting his watch.

"You don't want to stay another excruciating second?"

"Look, I could stand here forever—good champagne, pretty view, pretty Betty . . ."

She gave a mimosa-induced giggle. "I like . . ." She shifted her gaze before she could finish the sentence.

"You like what?" He couldn't help but smile. And he knew he shouldn't ask. He knew she was going to say something that was going to make him reverse all his well-laid plans and remind him of what a jerk he was. But he watched her anyway and waited for her answer.

"I like when you call me 'Betty,'" she whispered, her voice dropping to a girlish level of inebriation and vulnerability he recognized as dangerous.

"It's 'a' Betty," he said.

"Like a noun."

"Like a noun."

Fin closed his eyes. *He was a mess.* He wanted her. She was so unlike any woman he'd ever allowed himself. So elegant. So smart. So pulled together . . .

"So should we stay?" she said, moving closer.

He stepped away. "No."

Her smile faded.

As she pivoted away, he caught her arm. "Giselle, I mean, we can stay as long as you like. But I don't think it's good to be here if you don't want to."

And my good intentions are slipping away by the minute.

The wind came up off the lake and tossed tendrils of hair about her face. Rather than fuss like most high-maintenance beauty queens he imagined, she simply turned toward the wind and pulled the hair away from her lips. He loved her ease with her body, her minimization of movement. It was much like surfing—keeping movements to where you needed them, moving with nature, not against it. He'd never seen anything quite like it on a woman like her.

She twisted toward him. "You're right. Let's go with twenty-seven and counting." She downed the last of her glass and glided through the sliding door.

Fin followed her around for the next twenty-seven minutes like a bodyguard, hoping she wouldn't drink any more champagne. Twenty-three of those minutes went off without a hitch.

They moved through the house, Giselle nodding toward numerous people who took her hand or leaned toward her with a polite hug. Coco held Lovey's hand and glowed like an honored guest. Coco was apparently planning to stay behind this evening. Lovey and Giselle spent a good ten minutes in the kitchen, writing detailed instructions regarding Coco's peanut allergies and her eating schedule. They worried aloud about something called Ninja Kitty—a stuffed animal or something—and even discussed Coco's clothing size in case Lovey needed to get her a swimsuit.

Fin stood at Giselle's elbow and stared at the saltshakers. A strange sensation swept over him—something of a recognition of a life he may have wanted. Something of a settled life—saltshakers, daughters' schedules, a grandmother writing down notes for a sleepover. He had never thought of any of these things before and knew he hadn't ever longed for them as an adult, so he didn't know what the feeling was. He shook it off and moved toward the kitchen window to admire Lovey's view of the lake.

The rest of the minutes were spent circulating. About fifteen people knew Fin's name as soon as they heard it, and he signed six autographs, all under the stunned stares of Giselle. She clearly didn't know who he was. Which was pretty refreshing. He felt like he could be anyone. Or, rather, he could be himself.

The last four minutes were the troublesome ones.

"Giselle," Roy called, as the two of them were almost at the door. The good doctor sauntered toward them in the vestibule.

Giselle stiffened. Fin had suggested, twice, that she head Roy off—accepting bad news was always easier when you were prepared and aggressive about it—but she had shaken her head. She wanted to escape without talking to Roy at all. *He's refused to talk to me for four months. Now maybe I feel like being silent,* she'd said. So Fin had acquiesced, figuring it wasn't his business. But now her shoulders squared.

"Roy," she said, "thank you for making sure we were able to say good-bye to Joe. We'll keep him in our prayers."

Fin turned so he could make eye contact with her. *Do you want me to stay?* he tried to convey. Giselle smiled in a way that was unreadable. Roy moved so he was exactly between them, then dropped his mouth toward Giselle's ear.

Giselle paused for a long time to listen. Then she glanced over Roy's shoulder.

"Fin, if you'll go wait in the car . . ."

Fin hesitated. This was their agreed signal, of course, but it was always unnerving to leave a woman with a man she didn't like.

"We're this way," he said, giving her one more chance.

She nodded. He paused a second longer before finally loping down the brick driveway. At the bottom, he turned once more, but Roy had closed the door.

* * *

"We need to talk." Roy pressed the huge mahogany door with his palm. A tight *whoosh* sucked the air from the entryway.

Sounds of the reception—forks scraping plates, hushed tones, glasses set on polished end tables—swirled from the level above while Roy inspected her through his glasses as if she were some kind of cell he couldn't figure out.

"Only for a minute," Giselle said.

She knew she'd had a little too much to drink, and didn't want to start a heavy conversation in this state, but her curiosity took over. She'd waited so long to hear what Roy had to say. Was he going to give her a clue about what happened?

"Do you want to sit down?" he asked.

"I don't want to stay long."

"Sit."

She was tired of him bossing her around, having the upper hand in this separation, while she waited for answers, waited by the phone, cried because she didn't know what was going to happen next. How could she plan the next step of her life when she didn't even know if he was going to sell the house, ask her to leave, or even finish filing the divorce papers? And how could she move on when she didn't even understand what went wrong? And why was he the one who got to dictate when they talked and when they didn't?

"Please," he added belatedly. "Sit. You're very pale."

She was feeling unsteady. She reluctantly followed him through a doorway off the vestibule, into a small parlor that Lovey adored, where a rose-colored fainting chaise sat right inside the doorway. Giselle propped herself on the velvet piece. Roy shut the door.

"How do you know Fin Hensen?" he asked.

Giselle lifted her head heavily. *That* was what he wanted to talk about? Roy hadn't talked to her in months, and he wanted to start *there*?

"Roy, I agree that we need to have a conversation, but this isn't where I want to start. Why don't we meet for dinner and we can discuss all we need to discuss? Not now."

"Why not now?"

She didn't answer. She wished she hadn't had that last glass of champagne. This wasn't how she'd imagined her first conversation with him would go. She tried to thrust herself up from the chaise but her legs felt wobbly. She grabbed the upholstered arm.

"You drank too much. Do you think that's the proper thing to do when you have your daughter with you?"

Disbelief swept through her, followed by a quiet rage that began in her ears. She opened her mouth to respond, but Roy stepped forward and guided her back toward the chaise. "I just want to know how you met him."

She gripped her purse and felt a twinge of dizziness. But she refused to let him grill her. *How dare he question her on who she was dating?* Or . . . well, *fake* dating. Whatever. The point was he had left *her* for another woman. He had no right to start questioning.

"Move aside, Roy."

She pushed herself up again and tried to move around him. She was done here.

"Did he approach you, or—"

"It's none of your business."

He was blocking her path, and she tried to step around him, but he kept sliding into her line of trajectory.

Startled, she paused. He wouldn't physically stop her, would he? With all those guests upstairs? Roy had never been violent, except those few times in bed where his grip on her wrists could surprise her. But, despite his small stature, he unnerved her. He often vibrated like a tightrope ready to snap.

"Roy, this is crazy." She tried to keep her voice steady. "Step aside."

"I don't want you seeing him."

"That isn't any of your business."

"He's not good for you, Giselle." He slid in front of the door handle and dropped his forehead to catch her gaze, as if he were being caring, comforting. His voice went soft: "He's known around here as someone who's wild and reckless. He's in the paper all the time. He's dropped out of surfing—probably from being on drugs—but he's still dragging whorish-looking girls to every event. You're a *mother.* You need to make better decisions. I need you to take better care of Coco."

Better care of Coco? Disbelief and rage warred through her head.

"This is hugely hypocritical of you," she said, in her best voice of reserve. She took a chance and pressed his arm to get to the door handle, but he shoved her hand away.

"Listen," he hissed, moving his face closer. Her heel wedged against the leg of the chaise. "Fin Hensen is *trouble*, Giselle. I don't want him around Coco. If you continue this lapse of judgment, I'm going to have your custody reconsidered."

Giselle took a deep breath and tried to get her breathing back under control. She couldn't even make sense of anything he was telling her. *Her custody reconsidered?* Was Roy insane? Coco was *everything* to her—he knew that. She would lay her life down for her little girl.

"Let's talk about this later," she whispered. Maybe the champagne was making something difficult to understand here. She needed to get out of this room.

"He's dangerous, Giselle."

She took a small step back, a little off balance. Could that possibly be true? She'd wanted her family to think she'd moved on with a hot professional surfer, not a drug addict. Lia wouldn't associate with him if he were, right?

But a sickening drop of doubt fell through her stomach as she reached again for the handle. She'd had Coco around him. . . .

"Listen to me," Roy hissed.

She could barely focus on what he was saying. She couldn't even believe this was Roy. He'd donned Roy's glasses and wore Roy's suits, but this was not him. Her Roy loved her, and loved their life. Her Roy loved his daughter. Her Roy would not ignore her for months and then talk to her like this. Her Roy would not hiss at her and say, *"Listen,"* and grind his jaw. Her Roy would never accuse her of being a bad mother. . . .

The thought forming in her head slipped out as a whisper: "I just don't understand what happened."

An expression she hadn't seen in years—well before the cantaloupe—softened his face. Years of lines suddenly seemed to disappear. He studied the marble tile.

"You're right." He moved aside, revealing the door handle like a beacon of hope. "We need to talk. Dinner is a good idea. I can . . . I can take you now."

"Not now." She opened her purse for a Kleenex but, poking around, all she could find was a tiny sequined skirt that belonged to one of Coco's Polly Pocket dolls. The sequins felt sticky at the tops of her cheekbones. "Let's do it later, when I pick up Coco."

"How about Friday night, then?" He reached for her shoulder. "Let me take you home."

"No. Fin's waiting. I need to—"

"I thought I just said I didn't want you to see him?" His hand dropped back to his side. Dark, angry eyes met hers from behind his rounded lenses.

"I need to go, Roy."

"Did you hear what I said?"

"Of course. You're sneering from about two inches away." She sidled around him. "He's a friend of Lia's, and Lia is a good judge of character."

"Yeah, Lia is a model citizen," Roy scoffed.

"Roy, *move*."

"I'm worried about Coco."

"She's with *you*, Roy. Worry about yourself." The fear that had been gripping her turned sharp inside. "Take care of her. Be a dad. She's missed you. She waits for you to call her every night, and when you don't, she just looks heartbroken." A sob caught in her throat as her feelings continued to churn, not knowing whether to settle on fear, confusion, anger, or sadness. She needed to get out of here. She was having a hard time breathing. These feelings like panic attacks were increasing, whenever she thought about Roy, or Coco sitting by the phone at night, or what her life was going to become. "Let me out of here."

"*Giselle?*" She heard a muffled voice from the other side of the door. It was Fin.

Roy leaned on the handle and threw the door outward. Giselle heard a sickening *thud* on the other side, then, "*WHAT THE F—??*"

When she peered around the opening, Fin was doubled over, his hands cupping his nose.

"*What the—??*" He spit out a few more epithets, then looked at Roy with disbelief and rage. A trickle of blood slid through his fingers.

"Oh my God." Giselle rushed forward. A small shriek

came from the other side of the vestibule, and Lovey and Ray-Lynn charged toward them, staring at the drops of blood on the marble flooring. They each tried to peer into Fin's face. Lovey clutched Fin's elbow and tried to move his hand away.

"I'm fine; I'm fine," Fin said, trying to push them all back, but he glared up at Roy, who said nothing.

"Goodness, let me get some ice," Lovey said, turning on her heel and scuttling back into the main part of the house.

"I'll get a towel," Ray-Lynn said, fleeing toward the downstairs powder room.

"Fin, let me see. . . ." Giselle tried to move his left hand—was his nose broken?—but he stayed doubled over and held her off with his right.

"I'm fine," he said irritably as she tried to dab at the blood with the Polly Pocket skirt. He frowned at the sequined fabric. "Let's just—" He motioned toward the door. "Do you want to go? I heard you trying to leave." He threw another glare Roy's way.

"Yes, I . . ." She turned toward Roy, who stood there saying nothing. "What's *wrong* with you?"

"I didn't do it on purpose," Roy spat. "Here, man, let me take a look."

Roy stepped forward, but Fin gave him a suspicious scowl. "I'm fine." He turned the other way. "Giselle, if you want to go, let's go."

"Let me see," Ray-Lynn said as she swept back in with a lace hand towel, reaching toward Fin's face and cooing toward his chin.

"I'm fine, seriously." Fin tried to get her to back off. "Really. Thank you, but I'm fine. Giselle, let's go."

Giselle threw the sequined fabric back into her purse and tried to put her arm around Fin's shoulder as she followed him toward the door, but he shrugged her off and opened the door for her instead.

"We're all doctors, Fin; let us help," Ray-Lynn called. "At least take this!" She ran back and grabbed the bag of frozen peas Lovey had hustled through the house, and delivered it relay-style to Giselle.

"I'm so sorry," Ray-Lynn whispered.

Giselle nodded and threw one more glance back at Roy,

who was the one who should be apologizing, but he stood in the doorway, expressionless.

Fin leaned his head back on the couch with which he was very familiar, and moved the bag of frozen peas to the right.

"That's turning to mush. Let me get you something else," Giselle said, leaping off the couch.

"I'm *fine*." He grabbed her wrist to make her stop getting up—he wished to hell she'd stop—but his peripheral vision was off, and he missed. She flitted away.

"I have a Boo Boo Buddy," she said. "Let me get it."

"A what?"

"A Boo Boo Buddy. It's Coco's. Just a sec."

She was gone into the kitchen, and he leaned his head back again, exasperated, the pea bag still over the bridge of his nose. Condensation dripped down the side of his face.

He didn't want to be here. He just wanted to get home, take a long dose of scotch, and call it a night. Everyone's fussing had made him uncomfortable, and Giselle's was embarrassing him to no end. But he thought coming in for five minutes would alleviate some of the guilt he didn't want her to feel.

He was done now, though.

"Giselle, I'm heading out." He stood, still holding the peas against his face, but she came flying back into the room.

"Fin Hensen, sit down *right now*."

He bit back a smile at her command, amused that it might be her sternest voice. Damn, she was cute. He watched her hustle into the kitchen through the eye that hadn't swollen yet. She opened the freezer and fussed with something in the dark. He settled back down.

"This isn't a big deal," he mumbled. "I've had boards fly back and hit me a hundred times."

"Just . . . hush."

He sat quietly and surveyed the living room. He was intimately familiar with this room. He'd been here on several occasions with Lia and their friends, especially in the early days when he'd lived across the patio. He'd sat on this couch a multitude of times—in fact, he thought he'd even made out with Lia once on this couch, although they'd both been young and drunk and stupid at the time. After that—a clear lapse of judgment on both of their parts—she'd started dating an investment banker, and they'd committed to just being friends.

But the room seemed different now with Giselle's presence. He moved a bowl of fresh flowers on the coffee table to see the stack of oversized books underneath—*Stellaluna* was the first one, with *The Kissing Hand* underneath. He tilted his head to read the other spines: *Chica-Chica-Boom-Boom*, *The Velveteen Rabbit*, and *Disney Princesses*. He smiled. Must be where Coco got all her prince talk. A small bowl of grapes sat next to Coco's big stack of books. He took one.

"Sit back for me." Giselle came back to the couch with some kind of terry-cloth thing in her hand.

"What's that?"

"Just sit back."

For some reason, he did as he was told. He leaned back into the couch and let Giselle sit near his hip. She brushed his hair off his forehead and rested her terry-cloth thing on the bridge of his nose. He had to admit, it felt good. He closed both eyes and let his head sink farther into the cushions.

"What is this?" he murmured when a wave of euphoria washed over him. Relaxation prickled around his hairline.

"The Boo Boo Buddy was out of use, so this is our backup," she said. "See? It's a bear."

He lifted his head and peered through one eye at a terry-cloth ring with a blue bear-head shape on the end.

"You bring backup ice holders everywhere you travel?"

"Of course."

Fin leaned his head back again, hoping she'd put it in the exact same spot. He waited for the calm to return through his chest, feeling Giselle's fingers brush against his eyebrows. She stroked there about twenty times, then pressed tenderly at the top of his cheekbone. His nose felt like it was cut across the top, stinging like a bitch and three times its size, but he focused on Giselle's touch. He'd never felt so relaxed. This was better than scotch.

"I'm sorry for dragging you into my mess of a life," she whispered. "Roy, and Ray-Lynn, and now . . ." He flinched when she touched the side of his nose. "Oh, Fin, you're going to have a shiner in the morning."

"It's okay."

"It's not." She stroked his eyebrow. "What are your coworkers going to say at your event tomorrow?"

He had thought of that during the drive home. Fox was going to kill him. He had made it clear that Fin was supposed to arrive tomorrow night looking as "stable" as possible, preferably with someone who could pass as a fiancée. The press was going to be there, Fox had said, and this date needed to be someone Fin could be photographed with. Fin was sure his boss didn't mean to arrive with a black eye from the fake fiancée's ex.

"It'll be fine," he lied.

"I'm sure you didn't intend to sign on for all of this when you made that deal with me," she said quietly.

"You did say your ex wouldn't beat the crap out of me." With his eyes still closed, he tried to smile.

"I did promise that, didn't I?"

He could hear the smile in her voice.

"Don't move," she added, holding the terry cloth steady.

They sat together in the silence of the living room, a small clock ticking from the corner and Giselle's fingertips lulling him back into euphoria.

He could feel the softness of her hand against his jaw.

He could feel her body shifting slightly in the cushions.

He could feel the heat from her leg against his thigh. . . .

He shifted uncomfortably. "What was he telling you?"

"Be still."

He let a few more ticks of the clock go by. Her issues with her ex were none of his business. Especially now that her event was over. He didn't know why he even cared.

But he listened to the clock tick another few seconds, letting his mind recall her voice from behind the door: *Let me out of here.* . . . Anger swept through him, which confused him. Maybe he was just feeling a residual protectiveness because she was Lia's sister.

"What was he saying when he had you in that room?" he said, trying not to move his face too much.

Giselle paused for a long time, shifting her weight on the cushions. She lifted the terry cloth and peered underneath it, touching the bridge of his nose gently. He kept his eyes closed.

"He doesn't want me to see you anymore," she said in almost a whisper.

He raised his head at that.

"Be still," she whispered.

"He was bullying you behind a closed door because of *me*?" he asked.

"Are you a drug dealer?"

Fin whipped his head up higher. "Is that what he said?"

"Don't move." She rested his head back and readjusted her terry-cloth bear. She brushed the hair off his forehead again. "Something along those lines, yes. Maybe he said addict. I don't remember."

Fin ground his teeth. "I'm not a drug dealer or an addict, Giselle. My parents dragged me all through that hippie life-style growing up. Trust me, it leaves an impression."

"He said you've been losing competitions because you've been involved in drugs."

His jaw tightened. "I've had some issues with competing, but it has nothing to do with drugs. Look, I think it might be a good idea if we call the rest of this off. I don't want to cause more trouble for you and Coco."

"What? No! Fin, I want to go to your event—I agreed."

"You don't have to. We didn't know all this going in."

"I don't want Roy to have control over what I do."

He paused. He could understand that. But he had to know first: "Are you in any danger?"

She hesitated.

He removed the bear, the ice, and set them on the coffee table. He sat forward so he could stare straight at her. "Giselle?"

"He would never hurt me."

"Has he in the past?"

"No."

"Has he ever hurt Coco?"

"No."

Fin had a hard time seeing through his right eye, but he peered at her face to see whether she was telling the truth. Not that he would know. He wasn't used to grilling strangers, or even knowing this much about them, and he didn't neces-sarily know what truth looked like. But she gazed back at him earnestly. And damn it all, but all he could think of was kissing her. . . .

"You're going to have a terrible black eye." Her eyes moved across his face; then she brushed his eyebrow again. The effect was strangely erotic. It caused a warmth deep in his belly—like a belt of whiskey—and he wanted to just sit there forever, and let this beautiful woman touch his battered face, making him feel healed, and whole again. . . .

Abruptly, he pushed up from the couch. He didn't deserve this. "I've got to go."

She nodded and stood, wringing her hands. She picked up a blanket of Coco's that had pink and lavender cartoon characters all over it, then bent over and slipped the ice cubes out of the terry-cloth bear.

"Take this home." She tucked the bear into the pocket of his jacket. "You can use it tonight. It'll help get that swelling down, and it might not look so bad tomorrow."

"I don't want to take Coco's thing, Giselle. I'll—"

"Bring it back tomorrow if you like."

He shrugged and took it. He didn't want her fussing anymore, or picking up after him, or touching his forehead like that.

He was an asshole, lusting after her all day. He didn't deserve to have her caring for him.

He grabbed his jacket, headed for the door, and turned toward her once more before heading to the patio stairs.

"Tomorrow at five," he said curtly.

And she nodded.

He'd need a new game plan.

CHAPTER

Nine

The next morning, Giselle woke to the sound of the gulls and ran her hand across the pillow next to her, finally remembering that Coco was with Lovey.

She sighed.

The morning sunshine cast golden streaks across the ceiling, which she watched move slowly while she ran last night's events through her head. She skipped some of the more painful ones with Fin, like the way he'd dashed off at the end. She hadn't known what she'd said, or what she'd done, but he'd bolted as if she'd just admitted out loud how much her heart was pounding as she'd touched his face. Or how much her body began tingling when her fingertips hovered over his lips. She'd almost leaned in to kiss him right there, in fact—even just a brief kiss to his bruised eyebrow—but she'd refrained.

She groaned. She was pathetic. He probably fled because this divorced mom was getting all swept away again. It was probably like having one of his groupies turn up at his doorstep. Only this time, instead of a hot, young, long-haired girl, he was being gawked at by a woman nearly ten years his senior, who sat him in the middle of a Dora the Explorer blanket and began cooing at him over the top of a Boo Boo Buddy. . . .

She flung her arm over her face and let another wave of embarrassment wash over her.

But then she allowed herself to run through some of the less painful memories: like the sound of his moan when she'd tended to his wound; or the feel of his strong hands cupping hers during the church service; or the velvet brush of his lips in the parking lot. . . .

She ran through the conversation they'd had at the fish place, too. She couldn't believe his parents had left him while they pursued their dreams. Giselle rolled over and wondered how they could have done such a thing. And she wondered whether Fin really wasn't hurt about that, of if that was all a cover he ran.

But she told herself not to care. She couldn't get too attached to him. She was going to go to his event tonight and that would be that. The poor guy probably realized he was already in way too deep—Lia's crazy sister, indeed. And with an insane ex, to boot. She'd do the part she'd promised—undergo her traditional role—and they'd release each other from these roles neither probably wanted to play.

She launched out of bed and dialed Lia's number. As usual, the phone went to voice mail. "Call me" was all she told her sister. Discussing whether Fin was a drug thug or not, and admitting she'd roped him into attending Roy's father's funeral, and mentioning she couldn't stop obsessing about his lips now, would all have to wait for a live voice. Shame heated her cheeks when she thought of what Lia was going to say about all of this.

As the gulls cawed through the window, and the steel drums of Bob Marley traveled through the air from Rabbit's place, her heart fell into a softer rhythm. By the time Giselle pulled her hair into a simple ponytail instead of her usual chignon, she found she was anticipating the day. She'd see whether she could catch Rabbit and the gang. Without Coco, she felt listless, but these new friends and the photography gave her something to look forward to.

Plus, the more she thought about it, the more she was excited to see Fin tonight. Despite her potential for embarrassing herself, she deserved a little giddiness, didn't she? She'd handle it as a treat, like the fruit roll-ups—something you usually denied yourself, but you could have a little of on vacation.

The gulls continued squawking through the '50s-style frosted window in the bathroom as she brushed her teeth. She heated up a quick mug of tea, threw on a sweatshirt, and took her mug, along with her camera, to the beach.

It was time to focus.

Giselle took about twenty pictures of Rabbit and the boys surfing.

The light wasn't very good—the morning sky fell gray and overcast, which edited out the gold tones of the sun—but she knew, from experience, it was hard to predict when a magical shot would show up. Overcast days often gave the best blues and greens.

Rabbit emerged from the water, panting, his board tucked under the armpit of his spring suit. He'd told her that was what the short wet suits were called, and she'd filed it away with "bottom turn" and "cutback" for possible use in her brochure.

He threw the board into the sand and sat on top. "Where's the grommet?"

"She's with her grandmother for a couple of days."

He ran his hand over his forehead, still breathing heavily, and pushed sheets of excess water back into his curls. "How'd it go yesterday with Fin?"

"It was fine." Her voice sounded clipped. She was already trying to rearrange the ending in her mind. She wished he hadn't left so abruptly. She wished she hadn't caused him to.

"He was fine? He treated you nice?"

"Of course."

He nodded and studied the ocean.

Giselle watched, too, for a couple of seconds, but then she couldn't help but ask the lingering question: "Did you think he wouldn't?"

Rabbit shrugged. "I don't know much about what Fin does and doesn't do when he's alone with the femmes."

That sounded ominous. But she let him catch his breath.

They quietly wriggled their feet in the sand and watched the crashing waves, seagulls squawking overhead.

"They're rippin' it out there." Rabbit smiled.

He leaned back on one elbow and pointed out the "soul arch"—where Kino stood on the very tip of the board and leaned way back, pelvis thrust forward, one arm back over his head for balance. It was a lovely shape for the human body. Jensen did a few moves, too, like a "cheater five," which Rabbit explained was five toes over the nose of the board, versus both feet in the "hang ten."

Giselle nodded, working up the nerve to venture another question: "So is Fin a little notorious around here?"

The bright noon sun glistened over the water droplets across Rabbit's face as he shot her a sideways glance. "Listen, Giselle, I don't want to get in the middle of any of this. If you want my help with something, that's cool. But otherwise just leave me out."

"But is he safe?"

"*Safe?*"

"My ex said something about drugs."

"Drugs? Nah. That's not even close to true."

"My ex said he started competing badly because of drugs."

"Fin's had a gnarly time; I'll give you that. But it's not because of drugs."

"What's it because of?"

He watched the surf, or maybe Corky, for a while, and didn't answer right away. Then he pushed up and brushed the sand off his palms. "I think you should ask Fin all this, to be honest. He'll tell you. If you're interested in him, you should hear it from him."

"I'm not . . . *interested* in him, Rabbit," she sputtered.

"Whatever you say." He smirked and turned his attention to the waves again. It felt like he was giving her permission. Permission to act like an idiot.

"Does it seem like I am?"

"I'm just saying most femmes are."

"So by 'most femmes are,' you're saying he dates a lot? My ex said he's always bringing different girls around, and has a bad reputation."

"Your ex seems to have a lot to say about Fin."

"Yeah . . . I guess so."

Rabbit shook his head, but then, reluctantly, shrugged. "Well, I wouldn't call him a player. For the most part he's a loner. He goes out with different Betties, but he doesn't let anyone get to know him. He's going to turn out to be that mysterious old man who lives on a hill, you know? The one who'll have birds and iguanas, and he'll scare little kids away."

She laughed. She could relate. Maybe she could introduce her cats to his iguanas.

"Well, he can't be that much of a loner—he had that big party the other night."

"That was a *sponsor* party." Rabbit spit out the phrase, as if he were disgusted with sponsor parties, whatever they were. "Those are totally gnarmin'. Those people think they're his friends, but I doubt he'd call 'em friends. Most use him. He's got a lot of cash. Nice digs. Nice surf out his front door. They come for the handouts. And the sponsors come because he makes them tons of dough."

Giselle winced. The idea of people just using Fin's house and things seemed so overwhelmingly sad—like when he said his parents were in Bali, or that they left him with that other family when he was a child.

"Lia's nice to him, though," Rabbit said. "Fin likes her. And I think he trusts me. I mean, he *could* if he wanted to. He's a brosef to me—I feel loyal to him. But I think he sees me as too young. Kinda like you do." He winked at Giselle. "But me and Kino and the crew—we don't weigh him down with a bunch of wants and needs."

Giselle ran her hands through the sand. That sounded about right.

"And he definitely likes you." He smiled at her sideways.

Giselle ignored the fact that her heart leaped like a junior high schooler. "Please. I'm too old for him, Rabbit."

His eyebrow arched. "That's bogus. How old are you?"

"Guess."

Criminy, she was going junior high all the way. But she was playing with fire here. He could say forty, and then how would she feel?

"You've got one of those faces that's hard to tell." He let his eyes rivet down her body playfully. "You've got young-looking feet, though. Let me see your hands."

She brushed the sand off, then held them out, flipped them back and forth.

"What's with the wedding ring?"

"Oh, I—" She felt herself blushing. "I just wear it sometimes. When I'm out with Coco, usually."

"All right. Well . . ." He shifted his attention back to her hands, stroking his soul patch, having fun with this now. "Twenty-nine? Thirty?"

"Older," she admitted. "But I'll take thirty."

"Well, you're not too old for Fin. He's an old soul, anyway."

Giselle nodded. Something about that rang true.

"What about that woman at the party?" Giselle blurted. Despite her schoolgirl attraction, she almost wanted Rabbit to tell her Fin had a girlfriend, or an ex, or *something*. She didn't want him to be alone in the world. It just seemed unbearably sad. She held her breath for Rabbit's answer, though. She wasn't sure which way she wanted it to go.

"Which woman?"

"The one in the yellow bikini—I think he said her name was Veronica."

"Oh, Veronica. Well, I'm sure he sleeps with her, but they're not an item or anything."

Giselle's breath caught. She didn't expect that comment to knock her in the gut the way it did, but there it was. And there was her answer, too: He may find his connections through casual sex and empty relationships. She had to remind herself that Fin wasn't of the world she was from—a world of suburban dads who committed themselves to families and drove their five-year-olds in SUVs to soccer camp. Who wore slacks to backyard parties, and stood around with expensive wines, and talked about getting new decks built and the stock market. Although, of course, that world was not perfect, as Giselle had once dreamed it would be. It was filled with insidiousness, like doctor dads who screwed around with their nurses and pharma reps. The idyllic life she'd always wanted for her daughter was coming with plenty of holes in it—plenty of ugliness and falseness. But it was the only life she'd ever trained herself to want.

And Fin's was a world she simply couldn't comprehend. One in which she didn't know the rules. His world seemed filled with young, available, stunningly beautiful women, there for the taking, standing around on ocean-view patios with champagne glasses, but it seemed to have no boundaries or emotions. He probably slept around, which was a lifestyle she would never understand or be able to participate in. She would never be able to separate sex from romantic feelings like some people could do—people, probably, like Veronica. Giselle had only ever slept with two men: her husband, and one man before him she'd thought she was in love with. She couldn't imagine having sex with a man and not getting tangled in emotion. She'd always be the worst kind of clingy.

"Hey, want breakfast?" Rabbit slapped her knee with his knuckles.

"Oh—no, I don't think so. I was going to . . . um, just take care of some things in the apartment." What she really meant was "Google Fin" and "call Lia," but she didn't want to sound like a bigger goofball than she already did. "And maybe get some sun."

"In that?" Rabbit smirked at her long-sleeved shirt and pants.

"I have a bathing suit."

"Thought you were going to stay covered up the whole time here." Rabbit bit back a smile. "Don't forget sunblock." He unraveled his legs and scanned the horizon for his friends.

She followed him to a standing position and gathered her towel and camera.

"Hey, Giselle?" Rabbit called. He threw his beach towel over his shoulder and used one edge to wipe the salt water out of his hairline. "He's a good guy. And he's safe to hang out with. He just . . . Well, don't expect to get too close."

She started to protest that she wasn't interested in getting "close," but somehow she lost the momentum, and wasn't entirely sure what she wanted anyway.

She simply nodded. "Thanks, Rabbit."

Once home, Giselle scrambled for her laptop with an energy she pretended was for the new brochure, but—without opening a single brochure photo file—she managed to find herself a half hour into perusing a Fin Hensen wiki.

Next to a photo of him in the surf was a caption that he'd been pro since he was seventeen, sponsored by two major surf-wear companies right after high school. It said his father was a famous surfer, once world champ, and had also ridden for Mahina. There was a separate link to him.

Giselle opened it, hoping for a photo of Fin's father, but there was only a grainy thing from the '70s, shot from far away.

Fin's own wiki listed all the years he'd been on the World Tour—first qualifying when he was nineteen, then surfing it every year since, usually ranking in the top 5 percent. His "home base" was listed as Sandy Cove, but it said he was there for only about nineteen weeks a year. His earnings from contests and sponsorships were listed at $1.2 million. But then, according to the write-up, on a break during last year's tour, he'd been surfing with close friend Jennifer Andre when she was involved in a surfing accident and died. A link to Jennifer Andre's page showed a beautiful young Hawaiian woman in a bikini, leaning against a hibiscus-strewn surfboard.

In the three Men's World Tour events following her death—one in Portugal, one on the southwest coast of France, and one in Hawaii—Fin only placed twentieth or twenty-first out of twenty-five, causing the surfing community to "assume he'd given up," the wiki speculated. It also said Mahina would probably not renew his next contract, despite their history together with him and his father, but no source was given. The article also linked to several photos of Fin supposedly on "guilt benders" and to tabloid-type articles with photos of him at parties with various women.

Giselle clicked through each of the tabloid stories, and zoomed in on each of the photos, but she was beginning to understand why Fin didn't like his picture taken—all the captions seemed as if they were trying to show him in as terrible a light as possible: "Fin Hensen Now Seeing Catalina Caesar?" (a photo of him sitting next to a pretty young woman on a couch); "Fin Hensen Stoned in Teahupoo?" (a photo of him mid-blink); "Why Didn't Fin Hensen Show Up on Time at the Hurley Pro?" (a photo of him leaving what appeared to be his own hotel room).

Giselle clicked through articles for about twenty minutes, but what caught her eye for the rest of the morning were the professional photos of him in the surf. Although the tabloid reports now took up his whole first page on Google, the second page was filled with the material he probably wanted next to his name: dozens of articles and photos dating from the last nine years, of Fin on his board, glistening in the water, stooped low to keep his balance, coming through waves. . . . There was an article about a foundation he was part of to save the oceans, and another of an environmental study he was helping with. . . . There was a cover story in *Surfer* magazine from two Julys ago, with a photo spread of him in artful and athletic positions. . . . The photos took her breath away. He was strong and sleek and powerful, staring off camera with that grin she was coming to love. Only the photos since August had that sad, lost expression.

Giselle picked up her cell and dialed again.

"Lia," she said, exasperated, into her sister's voice mail. "*Please* call me." She stared at a photo of Fin surfing through a riot of whitewater. "It's about Fin," she added at the last second, then hung up. There. That ought to get Lia to call back. She quickly closed the Web pages down before she began drooling all over the keyboard, then logged on to her e-mail. Much to her surprise, there was an e-mail from Lia from earlier that morning.

"Hope everything's good with the apartment. I meant to tell you that you can park in space 119 in the underground garage. And that the 'hot' and 'cold' faucets are backward in the tub. You probably figured that out. And, if you're reading this on your laptop, you probably found the router in the corner of my bedroom. Lost my phone in Bryant Park. I'll probably come home early, July 5. E-mail if you need anything. Kisses to Coco. XOXO"

Giselle hit reply and stared at her blinking cursor, wondering how much to say, how much to ask, how much to admit about Fin. But she really wanted to have those conversations with Lia in person. And it looked like now she would, on July 5.

"Things are great," she finally wrote back. *"We can't wait to see you."*

She hit send, then rummaged through the dresser for her bathing suit, bumping her fingertips against Lia's red bikini.

She almost laughed before shoving it aside to find her conservative one-piece.

She slipped on a cover-up, then tossed a towel, sunblock, and bottled water into her tote bag and headed to the beach.

She'd be fine. Even without Lia's input. This was her own new life now, and she could forge ahead.

And she might have some ideas about tonight with Fin. She may not ever fit in with his world—with his sexy Veronicas and one-night stands—but she could certainly play for a bit. It was like being afraid of the ocean, but knowing how to dip your toe in—to enjoy the cold shock of the sea, know how vast it was, know it could swallow you whole—but enjoy your shivers from shore.

CHAPTER

Ten

Giselle perched on the edge of a dining chair before Fin arrived so she wouldn't wrinkle her new dress, astounded that she didn't have anything to do. Without Coco, without Roy, without her home in Indiana, without her chores or her basil on the windowsill, she didn't have anything to rush around for. She smoothed her skirt and took twenty cleansing breaths.

A knock sounded at the door, and she lunged to yank it open.

Fin lounged against the doorframe, meeting her gaze with an embarrassed grin.

Yesterday he'd been all sharp angles in his business suit, but this afternoon he exuded a masculine elegance: double-breasted tuxedo, bow tie nestled beneath his Adam's apple, hair slicked back. The six-o'clock light cast him in shades of gold. He had a small white-strip bandage across the bridge of his nose and a dark purple line that curved away from his eye. But Giselle still thought he looked gorgeous.

As she took in her full appearance, though, he pushed up from the doorway. His smile faded.

"Too much?" She touched her new "strawberry blond" hair. But he wasn't paying attention to her hair. His gaze was

caught at her breasts, which showcased her other new purchase today: a halter-style red dress. The salesgirl on Sandy
Cove's Main Street—a friend of Lia's named Vivi who worked
in a vintage clothing shop—had helped her with some "tape"
to keep the strips of chiffon in place, but they were creating a
sharp *V* down her front that showcased her pillowy new cleavage, courtesy of her new Bali push-up bra.

"Giselle," he breathed out.

"It's too much, isn't it?" She let go of the door handle and
began to twist, but his hand shot out and grabbed her wrist.

She was afraid to meet his eyes. She knew she'd gone too
far. After Rabbit's discussion this morning, she thought maybe
she'd try to be the sultry kind of woman Fin longed for, the
kind like Veronica, with the remarkable breasts and beautiful
bare shoulders. And then, seeing him in all the Internet photos, she came up with some sort of crazy bravado, probably
fueled by groupie-ism.

But now—seeing him in real life, looking like a cover model
under this deep, golden sun—all of her insecurities were back.
She'd gone too far with this dress and this hair color. They
weren't her. She probably looked like a hooker.

She pulled away, and he used the momentum to step
inside. The door clicked behind him.

"You look beautiful," he said huskily. But he sounded like
he was trying to convince someone.

Pressing back tears of bad judgment, she pretended to fuss
for something inside her purse. She heard him take a deep
breath. He was probably trying to think of how he was going to
break it to her—*Honey, you absolutely can't go to my wine-
tasting event looking like that. I'll get arrested for pimping.*

Finally, she got up the nerve to face him.

He ran his hand over his face. "I did say not to dress too
sexy."

"I'm thinking I look more ridiculous than sexy."

"You look *sexy*," he said quietly.

"And you don't want sexy?"

He let out a sound that seemed meant to be a laugh. "Well,
that would make me a fool." His eyes slipped again. "But these
people . . ."

"They don't like that," she filled in for him.

"Something like that."

"Who are these people?"

"Idiots."

She laughed. "But you want to impress them?"

"I *need* to impress them." He paused, still seeming to struggle with where to rest his gaze. Eventually, he frowned at her head. "New hair?"

Her hand flew to the red curls that flew around her shoulders—not exactly Ronald McDonald, but definitely more than she'd bargained for. Another wave of shame swept over her. This was the stupidest idea she'd ever had.

"I just wanted . . ."

He waited, frowning, for her to finish the sentence, but she didn't know how. What had she wanted? To impress him? To look younger? To be someone else for an evening?

"You wanted what?" he prompted.

"To be someone different." She spun away this time, because admitting that definitely made her want to cry. She'd worked so hard, for so many years, to cultivate the image she thought was expected of her: good daughter, good wife, good mother. Proper. Reserved. Quiet. Put your own needs aside and serve others.

But now she was wanting her own things—passion, excitement, adventure, *this man*—and she didn't know how to get them by being herself. She began shuffling through her purse again, but her mind was on Lia's closet, wondering what she could change into.

"Why do you want to be someone different, Giselle?"

The gentleness she heard in his voice shook her, but she couldn't answer or she'd really start crying.

Criminy. He'd been here all of two minutes and was already being subjected to more of the drama he'd put up with all day yesterday. He was probably *so* over her.

She shook her head and begged her emotions to quiet.

"Well, mission accomplished. You don't look much like the Giselle I met the other day."

When she mustered the bravado to turn and face him, she saw his mouth quirk up on one side. He rubbed the back of his neck. "But *that* Giselle—the one from the other day—she's the one I need to bring to this party."

"And this one?"

"This one . . ." Fin let his eyes roam openly this time. "This one, I'd have some other ideas for."

Giselle's breath caught, and her hand flew to cover her new snowy friends. "I can wear something of Lia's." She bolted for the bedroom, practically taking her shoulder out on the corner.

Mother-of-pearl, what was she thinking? She didn't know what to do with a guy like this. He was used to Veronicas. Women with no stretch marks. Women with no ex-husbands. Women who knew how to be sexy and fling their hair around. Her life was about sippy cups and playdates—not sex and real dates. What would she do if Fin came on to her? She wouldn't know the first thing about making an energetic twenty-eight-year-old happy.

Fin's voice drifted from the living room: "Lia wore this black dress once to an event I dragged her to. It was sort of plain, straight. Do you see it? It went all the way to her neck."

Giselle was flinging hangers back in Lia's closet, trying to get her breathing back under control. Black, plain, straight? She found a black shift, a boatneck, cut just below the knee—vaguely Jackie O. It might be the one he was talking about.

"I think I see it," she yelled back.

She checked the size. It was a size small for her, but the stress of the divorce and not eating much was making some of her clothes hang in a gangly way. This might actually fit.

She slipped out of the siren-red concoction and flung it across the bed, chastising herself again for trying to be something she clearly was not and for wanting something she couldn't even define. She wriggled the plain black dress up over her hips with a desperate sort of hope, poking her arms through the sleeveless armholes and tugging at the zipper in back. She noted, with relief, that it zipped all the way.

She went to the mirror.

Huh. Not bad.

And it made the red hair appear slightly more natural. Regardless, she decided to pin her hair up. This wild look wasn't her either. She scooped it into a chignon—not her best, but it would do—and slipped on a pair of sensible black heels. She felt a lot better.

Fin was standing by a bookcase, checking out Lia's CDs,

when she reemerged. He turned to say something, but halted. She couldn't read his expression.

"Better?" she asked.

He cleared his throat and put a Ray Charles disk back. Shoving his hands in his pockets, he walked over and held out his arm, much as he had for Coco the other day.

"My chariot awaits?" Her voice shook. She noted that he skipped the compliment.

He nodded curtly, and she took his arm, smiling politely but wanting, inside, to die.

She was back in the role of Jackie O. Or Donna Reed. Or whoever he expected her to be. Which was not what she wanted, but what he needed.

Fin had played his part for her yesterday, doing exactly what she needed when she needed it, so the least she could do was respond in kind.

"Let's go," she said, trying for cheerful, but hitting a note that she hoped he didn't recognize.

Because if he heard it right, it would have sounded like her terrible, shattering disappointment.

Fin put the car into gear, pulled out into the quiet sandy streets, and tried not to look at Giselle any longer than he had to.

He was already sweating from the heat, and he wasn't going to appear any more presentable at this wine-tasting event if he were dripping with perspiration from the way she looked in that dress.

The disturbing thing, of course, was that the dress itself was nothing to make note of—not like the first number she'd had on. He'd hardly recognized her when she opened the door in that red thing—her oyster-white skin, the incredible cleavage she had going—and he'd pretty much lost his ability to speak. "Wanting to be someone else" in a dress like that might mean tapping into a new, post-divorce sexuality—but damn, that couldn't be on his watch. He was supposed to become a better person, not seduce his closest friend's sister.

But now, even though she'd changed into this new number, with no plunging neckline, no racy color, it made him sweat all the same. Her breasts still rose deliciously with every breath; the clingy fabric still coiled around her waist and emphasized the sway of her hips. And she'd pulled her hair up, so now he could see her neck again, which he had an absurd obsession about kissing. Just once. He had the sense that she'd make a very sexy, breathless sound if he kissed her, right there, on that little curve of her neck. And he had to focus on his rearview mirror so he didn't think about that anymore.

"Do you have enough air?" He adjusted the dials on the dash.

"I'm fine."

He needed to stay focused on his goal—which was to impress Mahina's board of directors. They needed to think of him as stable. Mahina had had a string of bad luck with their riders lately—Jennifer, their favorite, had died; an East Coast surfer named Caleb had gotten arrested and spent most of last year in jail; and Fin had begun losing all his heats and dropping in the rankings. He just couldn't pull it together after Jennifer's death. Every time he went out there, into the rolling surf of Portugal or the barrels of Hawaii, he couldn't get his head in the game—relying on the luck of the waves, doing the tricks the judges wanted to see, hoping his competitors wouldn't get the same waves—it all just seemed so fucked-up after Jennifer died. There didn't seem to be a point to any of it.

So he resorted to drinking through most of the competitions, isolating himself. And when he did show up at parties he didn't want to be at, all he seemed to do was get incriminating photos plastered all over the press. He was embarrassing Mahina.

"Nice night," she said.

"Mmmm," was all he could give. He made the mistake of glancing toward her and caught sight of her body again. He moved the A/C vent so it was blowing right onto his face. "It's only about twenty minutes from here," he said, more to himself than to her.

"Okay," she said quietly.

He could tell her face was turned toward him, maybe trying to read him, maybe hoping he'd be a damned better date. Lia and Rabbit would be horrified if they knew where his thoughts were going right now—*soft dress, rustling off, soft skin, lace panties, his fingers exploring . . .*

He rubbed his forehead.

Eyes on the road. Hands to himself. That was tonight's new mantra.

"Your eye doesn't look too bad," she said.

He grimaced. It did. Fox was going to kill him. "Thanks for trying to fix it up last night," he said anyway.

"Did you use the Boo Boo Buddy?"

"I did. I couldn't make it feel as good as you did, though." *Damn*. Did he just say that? "I forgot it. I'll have to give it back to you another time."

"That's fine. So what do I need to know about your event?"

He cleared his throat. Yes, sticking to business would be better here. He was on the verge of admitting he'd dreamed about their damned kiss, which was something he couldn't remember doing—dreaming about a *kiss*—since he was about fourteen.

"There'll be a couple of key players," he said. "I'll point them out to you when we get there. It'll be the company vice president, named Fox, who's my boss and very cool; and the owner, Mr. Makua, who's powerful and holds my career in his hands. The company is Mahina. My contract with them needs to be renewed."

"Oh, I read that. . . ."

He took his eyes off the road to glance at her. "Where did you read that?"

"Online."

As her words sunk in, he glanced between her and the road. "You *Googled* me, Giselle?"

"A little."

The blush that stole across her cheeks was incredibly cute, but Fin's back stiffened thinking about what she probably found.

It had been refreshing yesterday being with someone who had never heard of him—it felt like a fresh slate, where he could make his own impression and not be at the mercy of rumors or wikis. And he thought he'd done pretty well, considering. But now . . . Now the media would have its influence on this woman, too. This woman, who seemed all things good and innocent, and would now see him at his bottom-dwelling worst. It made him feel hopeless.

"If there's anything you want to know, Giselle, you can ask me directly. You know that, right?"

She nodded.

He wondered what she'd thought of all the photos of him—the photos of all the booze, the groupies who hung around the hotels, the general downward spiral since Jennifer died. He *had* been drinking way too much, especially as they'd tried to finish the tour in Portugal. The tour had moved on to the Quiksilver Pro in the southwest coast of France, but Fin and a few others flew back to California with Jennifer's body, where they'd done a small tribute. About a hundred surfers did a traditional "paddle out" in Sandy Cove—they'd formed a ring with their boards in the deep water, out behind the wave breaks, and had thrown leis into the center, as was custom. But it wasn't enough for him. It wasn't enough for Jennifer. The guilt of not saving her was eating him alive.

When he flew back to France, he began having nightmares that she was in his grasp, but he couldn't lift her, which wasn't the way it had happened, but it kept him awake most nights anyway. In Portugal, for the Rip Curl Pro, he dreamed she fell out of an airplane and he was supposed to catch her. By the time they'd hit the Billabong Pipe in Hawaii, he began dreaming that her body fell apart in his hands. He was a mess. He began spending much of his time alone in his hotel room with a couple of bottles of scotch, dreading and willing sleep at the same time.

"I'd rather you ask me than read crap online," he said quietly.

"Mahina's the company you've had your contract with for years?"

"Is that all you're wondering?"

"Just trying to understand this."

He tipped his head. "That's right. I've been with Mahina for years."

"What's the contract for?"

"I ride for them—which means I wear their gear when I'm competing—wet suits, board shorts—and use their leashes and boards. And I pose for photos, show up at events, sign autographs, that kind of thing."

"Do you like it?"

Colorful summer plants whisked by his window as they picked up speed. He wasn't used to anyone asking him whether he liked his job. Most people thought it was a dream job—surfing for a living—but in reality it could feel stifling when you did it for money. Wearing the sunglasses and hoodies and crap and posing for photos could make you feel like a sellout faster than you could blink. But he always felt like an asshole for complaining. He knew he had a lot of people's dream job.

"Can't complain," he said.

"But you're worried they won't renew the contract?"

"Right."

"Why wouldn't they?"

He took a deep breath. "Well, some of the stuff you saw when you Googled me is part of the reason."

He braced himself for her judgment. It had been nice being the protective arm for a smart, beautiful woman who thought he was "hunky enough, pro surfer enough" to help her somehow with her own problems, but all that was over now.

"So why do you need *me*?" she asked.

He glanced with disbelief between her and the road, then dropped his car visor to ward off the bright sun that came through the windshield, slicing through the dry summer canyon. She was just going to let everything go—whatever she did or didn't see online—and let it zoom past, just like the golden canyon hills out their windows. The thought buoyed him, but made him feel guilty at the same time. He didn't feel he deserved her trust. He hadn't been on the receiving end of trust in a long time.

"I'm on the older end of this sport," he finally answered. "Companies like Mahina want seventeen- and nineteen-year-olds to sell their gear. I don't have the jutting hip bones anymore to hang board shorts on." He tried to smile, but her eyes went wide before they darted away.

He cleared his throat. Damn. He had to keep reminding himself not to talk about body parts, sex, or even sex wax to her. Topics like that made Grace Kelly here look like she was going to combust.

"As nervous as they are about me," he went on, "they're even more nervous about the groms coming up. I'm hoping they'll see me as their better, more mature candidate."

"You're mature?"

He snapped his head in her direction.

"I mean . . ." she stammered. "I just mean 'mature' in the sense of 'old.' You seem so . . . *young*."

He didn't answer. Women like Giselle were probably always going to see him as an immature beach bum.

"So I'm the old lady to make you look more mature?" she asked.

That brought a smile to his face, but he kept his eyes averted. "You're my sophisticated date, to show that I make good decisions. And that I'm popular among the people they care about."

"And those people would be . . . ?"

"People with money."

From the corner of his eye, he could see that her face changed then—that probably hadn't been the best way to phrase things. But keeping this to facts was the best thing for both of them. He had played a role with her, and she was playing a role for him, and it was best they just stick to their scripts. It was better than trying to impress her, or worrying about what she thought of him, or blurting out his whole life to her. And definitely better than obsessing about seeing her naked.

"So what do you need me to do?" she asked.

A stab of guilt went through his chest at the hurt sound in her voice.

"Just be . . . *you*," he managed to say, shrugging. He couldn't think of how else to explain it. She was perfect, just the way she was. She was smart, well educated—exactly the kind of woman the board at Mahina loved. The kind of woman Fox wanted him to bring tonight. The kind he could be photographed with.

He leaned forward to find the main canyon road, which would lead to the cliff-top entrance to the gallery. His tires popped over the gravel of the turn, which took them up a winding road through a grove of silvery eucalyptus trees. There was a magical quiet to the eucalyptus canyon, which Giselle seemed to sense. She sat forward, lips parted, gazing toward the top of the hill, where the gallery was lit like a modernist cube, glass walls showcasing the elegance inside.

"Beautiful," she whispered.

He stole a glance at her. The evening sun dropped in

through the windshield and cast her in a ringlet of gold. "Agreed."

The dirt parking lot was full, and they had to park toward the back with a few other arrivals right behind them. When Fin cut the engine, the quietness of the canyon seeped into the car. He turned toward her, the leather creaking beneath him.

He cleared his throat. He didn't expect to be nervous about this. "Giselle, could you . . ." He nodded toward her wedding ring. "Could you take that off again?"

She paused for a second, seemingly confused, then followed his line of vision to her hand. "Oh! Of course . . ." She began wrestling with the thing, then tugged it off and threw it in her purse.

But he continued to stare. Now, instead of her ring, she had a nice white tan line—a classic "cheater's band."

He ran his hand over the back of his neck. "Well, that's not going to do a thing for my reputation."

She followed his gaze and then rubbed her finger, as if shocked the ring of white were there. "I'm sorry, Fin. I must not have put sunscreen on my hands today. The breeze made it seem too cool to tan."

"It's all right. Rookie mistake." He opened his ashtray and started rummaging around. This would make things a lot easier. "Do you have any other ring you can wear?"

She shook her head, still staring at the ghost of her marriage.

He leaned toward his ashtray and found what he was looking for. It was a small woman's band, with a single turquoise stone, that he'd gotten in Mexico during one of his surfing trips years ago. He had purchased a cheap nickel band for himself that had long since tarnished, buying it off the sidewalk from a woman who was selling jewelry off a Navajo blanket with her four children, who all sat there disheveled and hungry. Fin had given her the five dollars she'd asked, then threw in his last hundred when he saw her limp forward on her badly burned legs. She'd thrown her arm around his waist and put this skinnier nickel ring in the bag as well.

He found it now, pulling it out among the quarters, and held it in front of Giselle.

He had intended to keep this light, keep it playful. He had

intended to give it to her and say, "Hey, will you marry me?" and they'd both laugh about it as they climbed out of the car and she put it on for this part of the charade.

But a wave of embarrassment now swept over him. He stared at it between his fingers and tried to think of what to say.

"Are we supposed to be married?" she finally asked, saving him the humiliation.

"Engaged. I won't see most of these people again—they're almost all from corporate. My boss, Fox, just thought it might help my case with Mahina and thought it would be . . ." He tried to think of what he meant to say, but words were eluding him.

He waited for her to respond as the car grew warmer, holding his breath while she turned the ring over and over.

"I know it's not much," he said.

He almost bit off his tongue. Damn, he was an idiot.

The ring was large for her finger, and the turquoise weighed it down so it slipped toward her palm, but it would do. And it covered enough of that damned white band of skin.

"It's beautiful," she said.

Fin began breathing again.

"But I need to know what you're doing with a woman's ring in your ashtray. I'm not wearing someone else's ring, am I?"

"God, no."

Her expression remained dubious. "Fin?"

"*No.* I got it in Mexico a long time ago." He told her the whole story, about the woman with the burned legs, and even dug out the man's ring from the ashtray to show her the original purchase. But he left out the part about the hundred bucks, not wanting to seem like a complete sap, just saying he paid a little extra.

Giselle nodded, seemingly satisfied, then grabbed the door handle.

"Uh . . . there's one more thing," he said.

"There's more?"

"One more detail. It's a bit crazy."

"Crazier than the fact that we're supposed to be engaged?"

"You're a baker."

"What?"

"A famous one."

"A famous baker?"

"You write cookbooks and you sell cookies all over the world. You're like Mrs. Fields, only newer and hipper."

Her eyebrows knit. "Because . . ."

"Fox—for some godforsaken reason—blurted out at the last contract negotiation that I was 'settling down' with the next Mrs. Fields. When you came in with those cookies at Rabbit's, I just thought . . ."

Her face fell. She turned back toward the handle as if she couldn't get out of the car fast enough.

"Wait, Giselle." Did he say something wrong? Was it just too much? "If you don't want to go through with this, I understand."

She settled back down and stared into her lap. The sadness in her face, the slump of her shoulders, made his chest clench. . . . He was an asshole. She was trying to be someone else, and he was forcing her back into a role she probably didn't want to play anymore. He stared out the window and tried to figure out how to fix this.

"Is Fox the cool vice president?" she asked.

He paused. *Was she considering this?* "Yes."

"I'm not doing some kind of cooking demo, am I?" She avoided his eyes, but didn't look quite as horrified.

"No, nothing like that. But someone might ask what you do."

"All right, then," she said, opening the door. "Let's go. While we're walking, you can tell me the rest of our story."

He was so relieved that the slump to her shoulders was gone, so grateful she was agreeing, and so amazed that a woman like this would help him, he simply blew out a breath and followed her through the parking lot.

Eleven

"So how long have we been dating?" Giselle said, slipping her fingertips into the crook of Fin's arm.

Her disappointment continued to fall around her at each crunch of gravel beneath her heels, but she smoothed her sensible dress and glanced at him for an answer.

"A couple of months?" he said.

She nodded and slipped her hand farther into the fabric. This was the fourth or fifth time she'd held his arm already, despite having known him less than thirty-six hours. Yet it felt strangely comfortable. And it kept sending a shiver through her as she felt the ball of his biceps beneath the suit fabric.

His body was rigid as they made their way through the parking lot. It probably took a lot out of him to give her that ring—to have any kind of hint at having a fiancée. He kept averting his eyes. Normally, she would have been irritated that he hadn't told her all of it from the beginning, but she figured she'd put him through some hoops, too. They were both just doing their best, grasping at something in each of their lives that was slipping away, each with what reserve they had left.

"Do I own a local business or national?"

"Local, but you're thinking about expanding; you just moved here."

"From where?"

"Wherever you want." He glanced down at her. "Want to say Indiana? Make things easier?"

"Perfect."

She watched her footsteps to make sure she didn't slip, and he slowed so she could maneuver the steps in her high heels. The evening's honey-colored light made the pebbles around the shrubbery sparkle like metal.

"How did we meet?"

"Through Rabbit?"

She nodded.

"You were here in California, scouting a new location, and he invited you to a party I was having." He pulled a cell phone out of his pocket and glanced at it. The bandage on his nose and the start of the black eye, along with the tuxedo, made him seem like a tough, young James Bond.

"What about Coco?" she whispered.

"Yes, I'm marrying into a family."

Another shiver shot straight to her fingertips at the ease with which he said that, right before he slipped his cell phone back into his pocket. *Silly,* she reprimanded herself. *Get ahold of yourself.* He was spinning this story as he thought of it, not having romantic visions. He only picked her because of her cookies.

She tightened her grip as they crested the top. The sounds of an orchestra billowed across the courtyard. Strands of tiny white lights swung against the surrounding trees, sparkling against the light blue sky and lending the terrace a theatrical feel. Clusters of people milled on the concrete, all in tuxedos or long gowns of silky fabric. An ocean breeze swept along her ankles.

Giselle smoothed her dress against her thigh. Thank goodness she'd changed out of the fiery red number. Fin was right—it wouldn't have fit in at all.

"Fast engagement. When are we supposed to be getting married?" she whispered.

"Let's keep that part vague."

"Spoken like a man."

Fin chuckled. His shoulders relaxed, and her own hand softened, too.

"Finnegan Hensen," came a booming voice from their right.

"Mr. Randolph." Fin held out his hand to a balloon-shaped man with clusters of white hair around his ears.

"What the hell happened to your face, son? Don't tell me you got clocked by a board?" Mr. Randolph turned to a colleague beside him and pointed at Fin. "This is our wet-suit model. We have to protect this investment." He laughed and gave Fin a fatherly hug. "We're going to have to move you to Mahina flip-flops if you don't watch that face of yours."

"Mr. Randolph, I'd like you to meet Giselle . . . McCabe." Fin's hesitation over her name was barely noticeable, but Giselle almost laughed. He didn't even know her last name. He'd simply attached the name he knew as Lia's. She bit back her amusement, but it was starting to mingle with worry.

"Lovely meeting you," she said.

Mr. Randolph pumped her hand with an enthusiasm that didn't seem warranted, then refused to let go as he turned to wave down a companion. "Let me introduce you to . . ." He waved again. A slender, silver-haired woman in an eggplant-colored suit caught his greeting and approached. "Donna! I want you to meet someone."

Giselle's eyes met Fin's. *Donna?* The corner of Fin's mouth quirked up as he focused on his shoes.

"Donna, this is Fin's friend, Giselle McCabe. Giselle, meet my wife, Donna."

Another silvery couple came up behind them, the man clapping Fin on the back and asking about his face. The evening breezes ruffled through the trees, and sent the lights dancing to the orchestra. A distant scent of night jasmine drifted up around them. Giselle kept shaking hands with new couples from the board of directors—all with white or silvery hair—until one of the women in a wildly patterned scarf noticed her ring.

"Oh!" she exclaimed, taking Giselle's hand and holding it up. "Tom, look." She gazed into Giselle's eyes with interest. "Is this what I think it is?"

Giselle swallowed. She glanced at Fin while words and lies eluded her.

Fin met Giselle's gaze and smiled grimly, as if this were all a runaway train he couldn't stop. His face grew ruddy.

"When did you get *engaged*?" the woman asked Fin.

He cleared his throat. "A little while ago."

"Oh! How romantic!" Another older woman grasped Giselle's hand and turned toward Fin. "I'm so happy for you. It seems like we just met—" She moved her hand as if to call a name out of her memory, but then flushed in embarrassment. "Well, anyway, it doesn't matter. We're so happy for you, Fin. We've been hoping you would settle down soon. You two make a dashing couple."

"Thanks." Fin avoided Giselle's eyes while the orchestra grew louder. A metallic sound clanged behind them, and they all turned to see the huge steel doors of the gallery swinging open.

"Let's go inside," he said in a rush, resting his fingertips at the small of her back.

Fin pressed her forward, slipping his fingers just low enough to send goose bumps down her back. She couldn't remember ever having a man touch her there, not even her ex, who didn't like public displays of affection. Fin glanced down at her right then, his eyes dark.

"Thank you," he said into her ear.

The low whisper of his voice sent a chill across her neckline. She wanted to meet his eyes, decipher that darkness, but a balding man in a dapper tuxedo whirled toward them as they crowded through the doors and shouted to Giselle to ask whether she liked art.

"I do," she admitted, tearing her eyes away from Fin. "I always like learning more about it." She enunciated everything clearly, since the man's decibel level hinted that he was hard of hearing.

"What kind of art do you like?" the balding gentleman continued.

Giselle tried to concentrate, ignoring Fin's fingertips at the top of her panty line. She wondered what he was thinking. She wondered whether his eyes went navy because he was uncomfortable, or because he was grateful, or for some other reason she had yet to learn. She had the vague notion he might look that way in bed, and a runaway fantasy flitted through her head and made her drop her gaze before anyone could see her blush.

"I don't think I've ever met an Impressionist painting I didn't like," she said.

The man nodded with enthusiasm. "Are you familiar with California Impressionists?"

Another gentleman pulled Fin away as soon as they shuffled into the glass-walled lobby, wrapping an arm over his shoulders in a fatherly gesture, and Fin broke away, leaving a coolness at the curve of her spine.

"I'm from Indiana," she enunciated to the balding man, "so if there are California Impressionist paintings here, that would be a real treat."

"*Oh*, you're in for a delight," he shouted. "There are amazing California Impressionists on the second floor. Let me take you."

As Giselle followed him toward a circular marble staircase, she glanced back at Fin, who had kept her in his radar as soon as they separated. He raised his eyebrows and smiled.

Another well-dressed gentleman—this one a bit younger than the other board members—approached Fin from behind like a shark and clapped him on the back.

"Hey, Fox," she heard Fin say as he turned away.

Giselle left Fin surrounded by several other tuxedoed men, who began laughing boisterously. She followed the balding man, who reminded her a bit of a condor and whose name turned out to be Turner, to see the California Impressionists.

She'd make her own impression.

For Fin.

Fin watched Giselle glide up the staircase with Mr. Turner and felt a strange rush of relief and gratitude, combined with a terrible discomfort, all at once. An emotional cocktail. He turned back to Mahina's VP and did his best to smile.

"Fuck!" Fox frowned. "What the hell happened to your face?"

"Would you believe I got hit by a door?"

"Would *you*?"

Fin smirked. He liked Fox. He was the contract VP, so Fin worked with him most. They'd been working together since

Fin was about twenty-one—the year Fox started at Mahina. Fox himself was probably only twenty-nine at the time, and Fin was his first contract. They'd hit it off from the start, and—even though they had to maintain a professional relationship in contract negotiations—in their off-hours, Fox would invite himself surfing with Fin, or they'd knock back a couple of Coronas at the beach bars on the weekend. Fox had always seen something in Fin that went well beyond what he could do in the water. And Fin had been eternally grateful.

Now, however, he stared at Fin in disbelief. "What the hell is *wrong* with you?"

"Honestly. It was a door."

Fox shook his head. "I'll tell people you got hit by a board."

"That's what Randolph concocted anyway."

"You're a fucker. Are you *trying* to make my job hard?"

The main-level exhibit was modern art, and the two of them wandered through the sculptures, their dress shoes shuffling along the travertine. The sky was turning a brighter orange behind the glass walls, providing a quiet illumination for the shining materials in the artwork.

"Good job on the date, though. She's beautiful," Fox said.

Fin nodded once, not wanting to say any more. He didn't want to perpetuate this lie. But Fox said he knew what he was doing. He wanted Fin to get the contract with Mahina—more than he wanted Caleb to get it, or any of the other new "piss-ers," as Fox called them. But Mr. Makua, the company owner, had issues with Fin's behavior over the past few months. Mr. M had worried that Fin was too depressed to compete, and that he'd never rally back. But Fox had been willing to bet otherwise. And Fin was grateful for that.

They stopped in front of a red-copper twisted structure, raised on a pedestal in the middle of the floor, illuminated from its base.

"I don't understand this stuff," said Fox, shrugging.

"I don't think it's part of our job description."

"Thank God." Fox waved down the waiter with the wine tray and snagged two off the edge.

They moved toward another piece made out of painted license plates.

"Make sure to have your picture taken with her, okay?"

Fin nodded.

"And make sure they get your left side."

Fin nodded again. But this felt wrong. He felt like a sell-out. He felt like a liar for maneuvering photos, faking his acceptance. And he felt bad, all of a sudden, for using Giselle.

"You're still heading out to South Africa for the Ballito competition?" Fox asked.

Fin managed to get another sip of chardonnay around the sudden tumbleweed in his throat. "Yep."

"Do you think you'll do well?" Fox asked.

Fin studied another piece of sculpture that resembled a female form. He *should*. He'd won it before. But, given his strange year of losses after Jennifer, he really wasn't sure.

"I should do all right."

"Mr. Makua might delay your contract until you compete there. And win."

Fin stared at him.

"I know. It sucks. You'll have to get back on the tour to get the contract, I'm thinking. You'll have to win Ballito, and probably the U.S. Open, too. Sorry, Fin. It's the best I could do."

Fuck. Fin shook his head. He didn't know whether he could win both of those.

"And, you know, you'll have to be on good behavior," Fox said, low. "How's the drinking?"

"It's . . . under control."

The phrase "your contract" was still hanging there like a carrot—at least he thought he'd heard it. But he switched his thinking to follow Fox's train of thought.

"We just need to know you're stable, Fin. We don't need to be employing another Caleb Anderson. His year in jail killed us."

"I understand."

"No more benders, wild parties in Bali . . ."

"No."

"No arrests, no fights . . ."

"No."

"No more fucking *black eyes* . . ."

"Got it."

They shuffled into the next gallery, where a small crowd had gathered. They stood behind the others, eyeing the splotchy paintings on the walls.

Fox regarded him with sympathy. "Look," he said, his voice dropping. "I know you're not the asshole the press is making you out to be, but they're ripping you up, man."

Fin nodded.

"You being a loner all these years—it's not doing you a bit of good. Get out there if you can, but doing . . . you know . . . *good* things. Show off your Surfrider Foundation work, or talk about your Make-A-Wish stuff. Talk about how you're financing that kid's surf school. . . . Or be seen with people like her." He nodded back in the direction of the staircase again.

"Her name's Giselle." A wave of irritation rode through Fin.

Fox shot him a sideways glance.

Fin didn't do the environmental work or the Make-A-Wish work to show it off; he did it because he wanted to. And having to posture for the public—when all he wanted to be judged on was *how he surfed*—was making his skin crawl.

"Listen, man." Fox turned toward him. "I know this is fucked-up. But this is part of the game. I hate it, too, but I've been playing for years. It's all about image now, Hensen. Sorry, but true." They circled an orange sculpture made of rods. "Introduce your lovely lady to Mr. Makua."

"Giselle."

A strange smile crept across Fox's face. "Of course. Introduce her. And do well in Ballito. And the Open. I need you back on board, man." He clapped Fin on the shoulder as the board of directors' treasurer, Pete Wilkins, approached from the side. Before Fin could press for more details on the contract, Fox sauntered away, deep in discussion with Pete.

Left alone amid the marble, Fin drained the rest of his glass and turned to find Giselle.

From the second-floor landing, Giselle watched Fin take the stairs with his hand in his trouser pocket, all elegance and fine lines, with the little bit of roughness in his battered face. But this time there was a strange, distant shot of anxiety. She smiled at Mr. Turner's description of the painting they admired.

It was a smile she was used to presenting, and a role she was familiar with playing—she'd done it often enough with

Roy's colleagues at the hospital. This event, in fact, was almost identical to those she'd attended with Roy: same wine, same conversations, same appreciation for the arts, same philanthropic goals, same pasted smiles. She'd done it for years. She'd thought she was doing it for him. But for what? To have Roy leave her for someone else?

Of course, there were a few key differences with tonight's scenario: Here, she was with a man who sent goose bumps down the backs of her legs when he touched her or glanced down at her with those navy eyes. And whose low voice could make the tendrils of hair stand up on the back of her neck. But the end result, she kept reminding herself, was the same as when she played the roles for Roy: He would be done with her once the evening was over.

"Hello." Fin's soft baritone rolled over her shoulder. And again, she ran her hands over her arms.

"What are we looking at?" The painting drew his attention.

Mr. Turner launched into a repeat of the story he'd just told Giselle. "This is one of William Wendt's springtime pictures. . . ."

Pretending she was listening, Giselle stood as close to Fin as she could and imagined what his arms would feel like wrapped around her. She knew she shouldn't be indulging in foolish fantasies, but it was just for one night—and he didn't seem to notice. She hadn't allowed herself feelings of yearning in so long—yearning for *anything*. She deserved one night of flirtation, didn't she? One night to be without worry, without responsibility, to simply enjoy the rapid heartbeat that this exquisitely molded man inspired every time he slid his eyes toward her. She took a sip of wine and stared at his tanned wrists, coming out from sharp white cuffs, and let herself imagine his fingers tracing a line down her stomach . . .

"Yes, she is," he said, glancing down at her.

Giselle's neck snapped up. She tried to find her place in the conversation.

"And pretty, too," said Mr. Turner.

She glanced back and forth and wished she'd been listening to the first comment Fin had agreed with, but they both swiveled to view a Guy Rose painting. Fin reached for her elbow.

"Excuse us, Mr. Turner—we're going to find Mr. Makua. I haven't said hello yet."

"Of course." He directed a nod toward Giselle. "I hope you'll come back. You can tell me more about that exhibit you saw in Indiana."

"Pipes," she said.

"Pipes!" Turner said, letting out a sharp laugh. "Can't wait to hear it."

Fin steered them down a glass-sided catwalk to the other side of the mezzanine and gave her a warm glance. "You know art?"

"A little."

"You keep impressing me."

She let her heartbeat escalate over that comment—her new permission—but that was as far as things were going to go this evening. Fun flirtation. And that was it. Fin was out of her league.

"So what *is* your last name?" he whispered.

"Some fiancé you turned out to be."

"I know. I can't even get the basics right. Did you go back to McCabe?"

"No, I kept Underwood."

Fin nodded; then irritation crawled across his features. He moved his hand away from her back as they approached the next crowd, and she felt a brief sadness.

"I need to introduce you to a few more people," he said curtly, shoving his hands into his trouser pockets. "Most importantly to Mr. Makua, the company owner. You up for this?"

"Of course. That's why I came."

He nodded again.

Giselle was glad she reminded herself.

Mr. Makua stood at one end of the gallery, surrounded by too many people, as far as Fin was concerned. He was a small man, leaning against a twisted wooden cane, flanked by two enormous Samoans ready to take his elbow at the slightest indication of wavering.

Makua still made Fin's palms sweat—if ever a man held his career in his hands, it was him. He'd met Mr. Makua about three times—had been "presented" to him, really—and his contract had been renewed two days later in each case. Fin didn't know what Mr. Makua wanted in a company spokesman, but he figured, until recently, he'd been it. Or maybe Mr. Makua just kept him around because he'd known his father—the two had been competitors in the '80s, although back then the industry was not the cutthroat, multibillion-dollar one it was now.

Fin followed Fox's advice and pressed Giselle forward. A photographer from the newspaper, wearing a badly fitting tux, swung into view. Fin thought he'd remembered him. J.J. or something. He aimed his camera. "Hey, Hensen!"

Fin pulled Giselle to his side and averted his black eye. The flash went off.

He kept moving Giselle toward Makua, but a sudden, strange wave of guilt swept over him as she half stepped in front of him. An image in a book he'd seen as a child flashed through his mind—a volcano, with a God of Thunder seated in a chair, and a virgin being sacrificed.

A waiter swung by with a tray of merlots, and—as soon as J.J. left—Fin grabbed two. He handed one to Giselle and took a deep gulp of his. The guilt didn't dissolve in his throat in the slightest.

"Thank you," she mouthed, over her shoulder. He watched her lips pucker into that sexy "ooo" from "you."

He settled into the crowd and tried to pull himself together, stopped thinking about the virgin sacrifice, forced himself up to speed on what the conversation was about. A restaurant, apparently . . . the restaurant up the hill in the art-festival grounds.

"Mr. Hensen," Mr. Makua called in a thin, creaking voice. Everyone turned.

"Nice to see you, son. How's your father?" His heavy Hawaiian accent was raspy.

"He's fine, sir. Still in Bali. Still surfing every day."

Mr. Makua grinned. "Good to hear. I see you've had a run-in with a board."

Fin didn't correct him.

"We're talking about Canyon Terrace," Mr. Makua said. "Have you been?"

"No, sir, I haven't."

"I was just telling the others how good the food is." He leaned on his cane, and one of the Samoans guided him by the elbow toward a chair at the side of the exhibit. Mr. Makua had been in a terrible surf accident in the late '80s—similar to Jennifer's, actually, where he'd been thrown against some rocks. He'd survived his. But his legs had broken in so many places they'd never been the same.

He sunk into the chair placed for him while the crowd pressed closer. A sheen of sweat trickled along the back of Fin's neck. He was a sellout and a liar for doing what he was about to do, but he guided Giselle into Makua's line of vision.

"Mr. Makua, I'd like you to meet my date this evening, Giselle . . . McCabe." He somehow couldn't get her married name out of his mouth.

Makua nodded gently. He turned to set his cane to the side.

"Nice to meet you, Miss McCabe. I noticed you and Mr. Turner enjoying the Impressionists earlier."

"I studied the French Impressionist period a little back in college."

Fin twisted his neck toward her. *She had?* She hadn't mentioned that part.

"I love how the paintings showcase the passing of time through light," she continued in her soft voice. "Mr. Turner mentioned that the Southern California painters used a lot more light than the Northern California artists did."

Makua nodded. "You'll have to come see *my* collection some time, in Oahu."

The comment was laden with a question about the years folding ahead—Fin couldn't tell whether Makua was referencing Fin's future with Mahina, or Giselle's future with Fin.

"We'd like that," Giselle said.

"Have you and Mr. Hensen been to the art festival this year?"

"No, we haven't."

"It's breathtaking. I should invite you."

Fin took a long swig of wine. He was an ass. She seemed like her normal self when she was talking about art, but being forced into lies seemed to deflate her about an inch. *A baker? What was he thinking? Saddled to him?* Nightmare. He'd given her a wrong name, a false life, different clothes, and a different career. . . . Doing what her ex had done—making her into what he wanted her to be. He remembered the way her ex had kept her stifled behind that door. . . .

Stepping backward into the crowd, he tugged her elbow. He had to get her the hell out of here. And out of his fucked-up life. "It was nice to see you again, Mr. Makua," he mumbled.

His chest felt like it was going to explode. He saw a tray going by, and slid his half-empty glass onto it and reached for Giselle's waist.

She looked at him with surprise, bumping against him. "Fin?" she whispered. Her voice was filled with so much concern for him—so much of the Boo Boo Buddy, let's-fix-Fin-up voice—he wanted to let out some kind of war yell.

He pressed her forward, steering her through the crowd, toward a dark corner he could see at the end of the mezzanine. He deposited her into the stillness and gripped the rail behind her to take a deep breath.

"Fin?" she whispered again. "What's wrong? Should I not have said we'd like to see the art in his home? I didn't mean we would necessarily see it in the—"

"Giselle."

The harshness of his voice caused her eyelashes to lift toward him.

"You didn't do anything wrong." He met her eyes, trying to eliminate the worry.

She looked doubtful, her hands lifted toward her collarbone as he crushed her toward the back corner. Another stab of guilt went through him, and he backed off, stepping away to let her unfold.

"I just—" He shook his head. "I shouldn't have brought you."

"It's fine."

"It's not."

He needed to get out of here. He needed to get *her* out of here, and keep her from his deranged behavior. He was an asshole. And he needed to handle this on his own. He needed to present his honest self to Mr. Makua, present his right side to the camera, and let Mahina and the public take him for what he was. And if they didn't? Well, then he'd have to deal with that in the next phase. He was tired of selling out, tired of apologizing for who he was. And he certainly wasn't going to make this crumbling, vulnerable woman do the same.

"I need to get you home."

Her beauty-queen brows furrowed in the center, giving her a delicate look of confusion. "If you . . . if you must, of course. Whatever you need . . ."

He took her elbow and began hustling her down the mezzanine.

Giselle worked hard to keep up with Fin as he swept her down an open-sided spiral staircase back into the main gallery.

"Let's get your things," he said, angling her toward the concierge. His voice sounded strangled and contrite.

As she skipped over her steps across the bright orange light in the glass-walled lobby, she was sad the evening would be over, but she understood. He needed to get far away from here, now that the main goal was done. He probably just wanted this business deal, and this night with her, over.

As the concierge desk came within view, a female voice called out from behind them like a lasso.

"Fin!"

He squeezed his eyes shut and slowed.

A slender, dark-haired woman with an edgy bob approached from behind. She had long, storklike legs and wore a pantsuit of brown and gold, with shimmering silk that gave the suit a feminine elegance. She seemed to be about Giselle's age, yet held her chin just a little higher in a certain badge of worldliness.

"Giselle, right?" she asked, extending her hand. "Tamara Fox."

Her hand was long and cool to the touch. "I'm so pleased to finally meet the woman to steal Fin's heart," she said.

Fin smiled wanly. "We were just leaving, Tamara."

"You're not staying for dinner?"

"I, uh—I'm going to take Giselle to dinner on the way home."

"Please don't go." Tamara grabbed the fabric at Fin's wrist. "You're the youngest people here. Or, well, Caleb's here, I think, but he's an idiot."

"We need to get going. I've got to get Giselle home."

"I can imagine," Tamara said with a ribald grin. "A more

delicious offer waiting?" She winked at Giselle, who felt her face flush.

Fin's shoulders relaxed and he laughed. He didn't seem to find Tamara embarrassing at all. "Tell Fox I said good night, and I need to talk to him. I'll call him tomorrow."

"You can tell him yourself." She threw her chin toward a point behind him.

Fin turned to catch Fox's masculine slap on the shoulder. "Hey, I need you to meet someone," Fox said, dragging him away.

Giselle straightened and prepared to make small talk with Tamara.

"I've heard all about you tonight." Tamara flashed a beautiful smile. She wore a sophisticated shade of copper-colored lipstick.

Giselle wasn't sure what to say to that, so she simply glanced back toward Fin, catching sight of him through a set of glass panes, shaking hands with a small cluster of suits.

"You are *so cute* together," Tamara whispered. She grabbed Giselle's arm and strolled with her toward another set of sculptures. "Fin has been bringing a parade of women to these events for years, but they usually can't string four sentences together, and I don't think I've ever seen the same one twice. And I've never seen him look at anyone the way he looks at you."

Giselle tried to conceal her smirk. Where, oh where might she put her Oscar?

"Do you like art?" Tamara went on, turning toward a three-dimensional stone piece that sat as the centerpiece in the small room they'd entered. It was a riot of blues and greens made of copper and iron. "Mr. Makua is really into art. That's why he loves to come to Laguna."

"He and I talked about the Impressionists upstairs."

"Oh, he must've loved that. You should see his place in Hawaii. Whenever he comes here, he wants to see all of our exhibits. And you're a pastry chef, I heard?"

"I make cookies." Giselle tried to swallow.

"Terrific—you'll have to tell me about starting a business sometime. So how did you and Fin meet?"

Giselle tried to remember the story she and Fin had concocted. She told it the way it really happened, with Rabbit introducing them, but shorting at the fact that Fin asked her on the first "date" to play Donna Reed. Instead, she said he'd asked her to an art exhibit. She mentioned that they brought Coco, then waved her hand as if that were a whole other story. "Enough of us—tell me about you and Mr. Fox. How did you two meet?"

Tamara paused, as if hanging on to something from Giselle's story and finding a problem with it, but then she dismissed it, seemingly happy to talk about her husband. "Oh, everyone just calls him 'Fox'—first and last, one and the same. We met at a farmers' market. We were both there to buy sunflowers." She took Giselle's arm again and resumed their stroll toward one of the long windows that looked out over Laguna. The evening lights stretched out for miles until they suddenly stopped, falling off into the black abyss of the ocean.

As Tamara glanced through the paned balcony doors where her husband and Fin gathered with a growing group, the adoration in her eyes was unmistakable. But it slowly melted into a strange sadness.

"He works too much now, though," she said. "The surf industry has turned into a crazy business."

Giselle encouraged Tamara to tell her more, but Tamara changed the subject and asked about Coco. Tamara and Fox had a little girl in kindergarten also, named Toni, so they discussed art programs in schools, and then talked about the new modified schedules that were starting in California.

"Giselle." Fin's voice came over her shoulder.

His hand went straight to her lower back. She wasn't sure whether it was the touch, or his voice, or the wine, or his breath on her ear, but she knew her hyperawareness must have been transparent because she met Tamara's amused eyes, staring at her over the rim of her wineglass.

"There's a slight detail," Fin murmured. His eyes begged her for something, then mingled with apology. "It seems Mr. Makua wants us to attend a dinner with him tomorrow night." She couldn't tell whether he was imperceptibly shaking his head, or begging her to say yes.

"That's . . . fine."

"It's mandatory." Fox slapped Fin's back jovially. "You must be Giselle." Fox held out his hand. He looked slightly older than Tamara—maybe forty—and had a head of short-trimmed, prematurely silver hair. He was impossibly hand-some, with a lean face and chiseled chin. He reminded Giselle of a presidential candidate. "It's great to meet you. Fin's told me a lot about you."

Fin frowned at him, and Giselle felt a flush up through her cheeks. Clearly that was a lie.

"This dinner tomorrow is just for fun—no business," Fox said. "But it's good for business." He looked pointedly at Fin. "Mr. Makua wants you to try Canyon Terrace and wants you two to see the art. Tamara and I will see you there. Let's meet at the wine garden at six. Tamara, we need to say hi to Munton." He nodded at Giselle and steered Tamara away, but not before she could wave to Giselle and call, "See you," over her shoulder.

Fin turned to face Giselle across the empty space Fox and Tamara's personalities had vacated. He muttered a curse word under his breath, followed by a quick apology.

"It's okay," Giselle said. "I don't want to ruin anything for your deal, but I'm not sure I can go tomorrow night. I have a . . . Well, Lia is setting me up. On a blind date."

Fin frowned. "Lia set you up with someone?"

Giselle nodded.

"Who?"

"Um . . . I keep forgetting his name. . . . Dan? Mansome-thing?"

"Dan Manfield?"

"I think that's what she said."

"Dan the Man?"

"I guess so. . . . That's who Rabbit thought it was. . . ."

But Fin was already staring out past the guests, a look of incredulousness on his face.

A tuxedoed man stepped out to the entrance to a set of double doors where dinner was being held, ringing a bell in the orange lobby light, while guests began funneling into the room in a swirl of haloed gowns and tuxedoed legs.

Fin watched them vacantly. "Dan the Man?" He frowned at her again.

"Do you know him?"

"Yeah," he said, but then shook his head. He took her elbow and steered her toward the stairs. "I should get you home."

He directed her through the set of doors on the opposite side of the lobby, cradling her elbow as if he were directing an elderly aunt.

A lump rose in Giselle's throat at how quickly he seemed to want to get rid of her now. She was probably too matronly for words. Maybe he was used to young and exuberant bikini models, thrilled to be near a famous surfer. Maybe they did things like sneak him out here among these patios, finding hidden railings and pressing him against them to kiss him, pushing their hands through his tousled hair. Maybe they touched his crotch while he was driving, leaning in and smiling suggestively. Maybe they took their underwear off and stuffed it in his jacket pocket.

Giselle glanced at the outdoor rail as they shuffled past. It seemed pretty cold and metallic.

She inspected the front of her dress, trying to remember what underwear she was wearing, wondering whether she could manage to get it off. But she remembered it was a very plain, dull white—cotton, nonetheless—it wouldn't look very sexy sticking out of his pocket. Plus she'd never in a million years get it off gracefully like his bikini models probably could.

The temperature had dropped about ten degrees when they stepped out, and Giselle completed the image of the elderly aunt by tugging her sweater over her shoulders. She didn't care anymore. Fin pressed her toward the parking lot, and she did her best to keep up, her lungs filling with salt air and despair.

When they got near the car, he beeped it open, but then stopped, his hand on her door handle. He stared at it as if he weren't sure what he wanted to do next. Their breaths were coming short and harsh. A few crickets were making an early-evening trill.

"Giselle—" He studied his shoes then, as if deciding whether he wanted to say what was on his mind.

Then he ran his hand down his face.

"Never mind," he said. "Let's get out of here."

Twelve

Fin punched through six or seven songs in the car, then leaned back to something loud and cutting. He knew Giselle wouldn't like this song, but he needed to get rid of her now. She was just reminding him of what a jerk he was. And obviously Lia thought so, too.

Dan the Man?

What was Lia thinking?

Clearly she wasn't thinking of *him*.

But he knew that, right? Why would Lia set her perfect, beautiful sister up with a loser like him when she could instead set her up with . . . *Dan the Man*?

Dan Manfield was the local real-estate-agent-turned-investor mogul. Everyone in Sandy Cove knew him—he had his mug plastered all over the place. He was about two hundred years old, but rich . . . steady . . . smart . . . *stable*. . . .

Damn. Fin pulled his driver's-side visor down as low as it could go against the assaulting setting sun. Those were the things Giselle said she'd wanted in a husband, weren't they? And why was he upset about this?

He jabbed his way to a Van Halen song and sat back into the seat.

"Are you mad at me?" she whispered.

He frowned. "Of course not." *I want to take you home and fuck you.* But he bit his Neanderthal tongue and looked away.

He needed to get out of this mess now. She had served her purpose—just as he'd served a purpose for her—and now they needed to get out of each other's way. He wanted her—suddenly desperately—but he knew he shouldn't. Lia wanted her with someone like Dan. And how could Fin ever be any more than a lay anyway? And he was leaving for South Africa in three days, and she was going back to Indiana. Certainly Giselle deserved more than that, especially right after being jilted.

"I can go with you tomorrow night if it'll help," she said quietly.

"No." He took a deep breath and loosened his bow tie. He needed to stop acting like an ass. But he *really* had to get rid of her. Every second in her company was giving him another chance to be the jerk he didn't want to be.

He also needed to stop thinking about her going out with Dan. The jealousy that was engulfing his ears right now was a strange and loathsome new feeling for him.

But first he needed to feed her. He hadn't thought this part through. What kind of asshole invites a woman to do him a favor, plies her with booze, then takes her home with no dinner? Trouble was, he didn't know where to bring her. Sitting across from Giselle at a table for two—-where he could stare at her cupid-bow lips and the way her breasts rose when she sighed—might be the end of his good manners tonight. He tried to think of a place nearby where they could fill up and not sit too close together. . . .

"What did you want to say back there—in the parking lot?" she asked.

He glanced at her. The *parking lot*? Oh. He shook his head. He hadn't known, really. He'd been about to apologize, he supposed. Or maybe tell her how much he appreciated her being so great with Mr. M. Or maybe lean her against the car and kiss her again until neither of them could think. He wasn't sure which way it was going to go.

"It seems you have trouble expressing yourself," she said. "Sometimes it's best to just blurt out what's on your mind. That's what I always tell Coco."

He slid her a sidelong glance. "You don't want me to blurt out what's on my mind, Giselle."

He needed to shut this conversation down. An apology took on a vague form in his mind, like a vapor trying to materialize. He'd had fun with her these two days, and she'd helped him. She was sweet, and good-hearted—she certainly didn't deserve to be shuffled out of an event like that. He loosened his tie to tug it out of his collar and tried to formulate how he was going to say this.

"It's because I'm too old, right?" she said softly.

He set the tie in his cup holder and frowned. *"What?"*

"You don't want to bring me tomorrow night because I'm too old and matronly."

"What are you talking about?"

"Well, I mean, I'm a decade older than you, and—"

"You are *not*."

"I am."

"You are not. How old are you?"

"Some fiancé you turned out to be."

He smiled, despite himself. "Yeah, I suppose I should ask some of these things beforehand, like your last name and general decade of birth. But really, how old are you? You're not forty."

"You're not thirty."

"I'm twenty-nine . . . *almost*."

"I'm thirty-five . . . *already*."

He shook his head. "Well, math was never my thing, but I'm pretty sure that doesn't add up to a decade."

"It's close enough."

"It's not close at all."

She turned away, toward her window, allowing the now-setting sun to illuminate the side of her face in goldenrod as they sped down the freeway.

"It's six years," he said gently. "How is this making sense to you?"

"It just matters."

Thirty-five? Didn't bother him in the least. And obviously other parts of his body didn't care, either. But this discussion, as amusing as it was, was getting him nowhere. He was not going to seduce her. And bringing her tomorrow night would just test his limits.

But the expression of "failure" on her face was starting to kill him. It reminded him of her devastated eyes when they were sitting at the church and she was glancing at the hot number next to her ex.

"I should take you somewhere to eat," he offered.

She blinked back surprise, maybe at the turn the conversation just took. "That's not necessary. I have fish sticks at home in the freezer."

"I'm not dropping you off to have frozen fish sticks, Giselle."

"This isn't a real date, Fin. It's fine."

A wave of anger, or guilt, or some such thing rose from his collar. The tiny tuxedo button was stubborn, but he managed it loose. He hit his blinker and merged furiously. Logic forced him to acknowledge that he wasn't angry at Giselle—he knew that—but he couldn't quite corral all the other things he was angry at. He was angry at himself, for making Giselle feel even the remotest sense of the insecurity that her ex had made her feel. He was angry at Fox, for wanting him to play to the public just to prove he wasn't an asshole. He was angry at Lia, for not wanting to set him up with Giselle. And even angrier at himself that Lia was right—he wasn't capable of dating Giselle. Dating was what normal people did—people who didn't have careers that took them around the world for forty weeks of the year. It was what you did when you wanted to get to know someone better, in hopes that you might carve out a possible future with this person where you both resided on the same continent. His version of "dating" had deteriorated into flat-out sex. Ten years of one-night stands with groupies in other countries and women like Catalina and Veronica, who waited for him for the few weeks he'd be in the U.S. for the year, but never pretended to have feelings for him.

He sped off the freeway, cutting off a bright red Mercedes, whose driver promptly leaned on the horn, and headed toward Sandy Cove Pier, where he could hopefully get her some food, get this night over with, and walk her home. He didn't quite know how to deal with all the anger, resentment, sadness, sexual frustration, jealousy, loneliness, and embarrassment. It felt like every emotion he'd been tamping down over the last year—or, who was he kidding, over the last ten years—was simmering under the surface of his skin.

All tracing back to Giselle.

Who he wanted to be with, and get rid of, at the same time . . .

Damn.

Thirteen

Giselle maneuvered down the sandy sidewalks onto the wooden slats of Sandy Cove Pier. Alone. The sun was beginning to set, and the light blue wooden rails of the pier stood out against the pink-orange sky.

She put her name in at the place Fin told her, The Captain's Hull, the only restaurant on the pier. It sat teetering above the waves on wooden pylons that held it over the lapping foam of the ocean. Fin had offered several excuses for why he should drop her off to put their names in, but it was becoming clearer and clearer that he wanted to spend as little time with her as possible.

Giselle wandered down the uneven wooden pier to begin the wait, then drifted toward the right-side rail where she could lean over and see nine wet-suit-clad bodies bobbing in the ocean, waiting with hopeful expressions for evening waves. The wind picked up the farther down the pier she walked, whipping tendrils out of her chignon.

She leaned against the rail and twisted Fin's turquoise ring around her finger as she tried to ignore the tightening in her chest. It was the same tightening she always felt when she knew she was letting someone down.

She'd had a wonderful time with Fin these two days—despite the bizarre circumstances. She'd loved every touch of his fingers against the small of her back, every glance he gave her from beneath his bangs, every flex of his muscles when she held his arm, and especially the way his eyes had lingered over her tonight. It had been such a thrill to have a man gaze at her that way for the first time in so long. And especially *this* man—this hunky, golden, chiseled man, who had youth and energy breathing through his fingertips. It was sad to have it end this way. She wasn't sure whether she'd let him down, said something wrong, or if he was just cutting the attentive act he'd been pretending for forty-eight hours. Either way, it was clear he wanted to be rid of her now.

Which reminded her of Roy.

Why did she have this effect on men?

She took the ring off and pressed it into her palm as she gazed at the surf. Seagulls called overhead, and she could smell bonfires starting up in the sand. Her mouth felt like it was filled with cotton.

When Fin approached from behind, about fifteen minutes later, he stood well apart from her.

"You should take this back." She held out the ring.

A few beats went by where Fin stared at it, almost as if he didn't recognize it, but then a light dawned. "No, you keep it."

"I can't keep it, Fin. It's yours."

"No. Just . . . keep it." Guilt or maybe some kind of sadness etched his features. "How long is our wait?"

"They said thirty minutes." She reluctantly put the ring in her purse.

The surfers were lined up where the waves broke, and she tried to focus on the beauty of the rugged palm-tree-dotted coastline of Sandy Cove. The horizon was a distant line, separating the orange sky from the blue ocean, and the fiery sun was dropping steadily. Thin rows of clouds were colored like rainbow sherbet.

Ignoring the sunset, Fin watched the surfers, who continued to bob on their boards, waiting for waves that were barely rolling in.

"They're not going to get much," he mumbled, pushing up his sleeves. He still wasn't looking at her. Instead, he took a deep breath and leaned into the rail, tugging at the black-corded bracelet that had been under his shirtsleeve.

"Listen, Giselle . . ." He licked his lips and studied the ocean. "I'm sorry for rushing you out of there tonight."

He started to say more, but then closed his mouth and ran his hand over his jaw. Giselle stayed quiet with hope he'd continue. She hoped she hadn't let him down. The wind rushed up again from beneath the pier, and she smoothed tendrils of hair away from her lips.

"I felt bad I was"—he shook his head—"making you pretend to be something you're not. I don't know what I was thinking. I shouldn't be pretending *I'm* something I'm not, and I shouldn't be dragging you to do the same." He stared at the ocean, seemingly drained already from so many words.

Relief swept through her. Maybe Fin hadn't been *angry*—maybe he'd simply felt guilty, the same way she had at her event.

"That's how I felt when we were at the church," she said. "I felt terrible for bringing you to the funeral, and making you lie."

"I didn't mind that, though."

"I didn't mind this. I felt bad for asking you to lie, and to be someone you weren't."

"The dude who drove the surf van?"

She laughed. "Right."

"I didn't mind that, though. But this—I was asking you to play a role you were uncomfortable with."

"Honestly, Fin, it's fine. I had fun. And I'd really like to go tomorrow, if you want me to. It might help with your contract, meeting your boss and—"

But he was already shaking his head and turning back toward the ocean. He rested his arms along the rail. "I can't bring you, Giselle."

She straightened. She tried not to think about why he didn't want to bring her, and—more important—not to *care*. But she couldn't. All of her insecurities rose like the ocean wind, and she felt frozen, her chest tightening, standing there watching the orange sun sink into the sea. Fin was saying the same thing Roy had: *You didn't let me down, but I can't be near you anymore.* She didn't understand what was wrong with her. She wanted to slip through the pier slats.

The sherbet light threw shadows across his face as he

glanced at her across his shoulder and then did a double take. *"Giselle."* He squinted at her. "Whatever you're thinking right now—that's not the reason."

"How do you know what I'm thinking?"

"Based on your expression, I've got a pretty good guess."

She tried to rearrange her face, but ended up just turning away because it was too exhausting.

"You've got that beaten-down look you have when your ex is around," he mumbled.

Giselle's spine stiffened. *Beaten down?* "Is that how I come across?" She could hear a note of anger rise in her voice.

"Only around him."

Giselle was stunned into silence. No one had ever told her that before. She wondered whether this was what Lia saw, too. And Noelle. And their mother. She wondered, with horror, whether Coco saw it, too. . . .

"Look, Giselle, that's the last thing I want you to be feeling at the end of our night—whatever it is your ex makes you feel. I think he's an asshole for making you so insecure about yourself that you want to be someone else. So, to make sure I'm not doing the same thing, I'm going to admit a lot of stuff to you right now that I have no business saying out loud. I'm just going to blurt it out, like you said."

He glanced at the ocean as if summoning some kind of strength. "I'm not sure what all to admit to, here." He ran his hand down his face. "I guess, for starters, I'll admit I've been picturing you out of that dress for the last four hours."

Giselle's breath hitched. She glanced up to make sure she'd heard him correctly.

"And I'll admit that the first time we talked, at the party, I couldn't stop staring at your lips. You've got an incredibly sexy mouth."

Giselle's hands began shaking.

"And I asked you not to dress too sexy for my event, not because I thought the board members might not like it, but because I was afraid I'd be staring at your body all night. And that kiss in the parking lot?" He turned and caught her gaze, holding it hostage. "As embarrassed as I am to admit it, I think I even dreamed about it last night." His attention drifted to her lips. As the seagulls cawed overhead, though, he looked away.

"So if you're thinking I don't want to bring you tomorrow night because you're too 'old' or that I'm not attracted to you, or any such foolishness, just . . . stop. Nothing could be further from the truth. I don't want to bring you because I'm doing way too much thinking about how to get you into bed. And I shouldn't."

"Why *not*?" The words flew out of her mouth before she could stop them. Belated, she brushed her fingertips over her lips.

Fin laughed and gave her an embarrassed glance from under his bangs. "I'm flattered, Ms. Underwood."

An automated voice floated toward them—with words Giselle couldn't quite understand through the pounding of her heart—and Fin turned toward the restaurant.

"That's us. Think we can make it through this dinner?" He gave her a sympathetic smile. "I'm going to have to stop picturing you out of that dress, and you're going to have to try not to blush to death."

Giselle gave a weak nod and followed Fin inside.

The sun fell into the water just as they were being seated, throwing its last burst of orange through the tiny dining room. The room was designed like a ship's hull, with small dark-wood tables and brass handrails. Outside the tinted windows, a wrap-around balcony hosted white tables and chairs underneath bright blue umbrellas that almost touched one another. As the sky shifted from orange to lavender, waiters in shorts and sweat-shirts hustled to take down the umbrellas, and heat lamps began their low burn.

The waiter sat Giselle and Fin at an impossibly small table right next to the window. Giselle was able to face the sunset and see the silhouettes of couples who'd taken places along the pier rail, huddling close in romantic poses. She watched one couple kiss, then dropped her gaze and pulled in her chair.

Fin studied the menu in silence. She forced herself to focus on her own, and tried to tamp down her nervousness. *Had Fin just said he was picturing her naked?* She couldn't quite con-nect the pounding of her heart with how much air she needed, or connect the words she'd just heard with her own reality. She tried to keep her menu from shaking.

". . . drink?" she heard.

She snapped her head up.

"Um . . . iced tea," she stammered to the waitress.

"Water for me," Fin said.

When the sweatshirt-clad waitress left, Giselle wanted to go back to taking surreptitious glances at Fin, but he'd set his menu down. She couldn't stop her hands from shaking as she tried to comprehend the menu selections.

"I don't know what to get . . ." she said.

"Take your time."

How can I read with you staring at me like that? And after you just told me you're picturing me out of my dress? She squirmed a bit in her chair, and had to rest her menu on the edge of the table to keep it from vibrating.

"What are *you* getting?" she finally asked.

"Fish tacos."

"I'll get that." She set the menu down and searched desperately for her iced tea. . . . Or water . . . Water would do. . . .

"So have I made this unbearably uncomfortable for you?" Fin asked.

A waiter came by and thrust his arm between them to light the tiny candle on the table. They waited an excruciatingly long time until the young man moved out of the way; then Fin leaned closer, the flickering candle illuminating his jaw. "You said to blurt out what I was thinking, but I'm not sure you were really ready for that."

"It's okay. I thought . . . something different. So I'm glad you . . ." Her cheeks were on fire. "I'm glad you said those . . . nice things."

"Did they sound nice?" He raised an eyebrow. "I must not have expressed myself correctly."

"I just mean—"

"I know, Giselle."

The candle illuminated the sharp planes of his cheekbones, the darkening edges of the bandage on his nose, and then a strange sadness in his eyes. . . .

The waitress brought their drinks on small cocktail napkins, and Giselle went about the business of sweetening her iced tea with exactly two tiny shakes of Splenda. She wasn't used to Fin's direct compliments, wasn't used to the sultry stares he was shooting her way, and certainly wasn't used to being within touching distance of a man who had just admitted he was picturing her naked. Especially a man who could make her heart pound like this. She folded her yellow packet into neat rows and tucked it under her bread plate.

"I'm not clear on why you haven't mentioned any of these things, if they're true," she said.

"*If* they're true? You still don't believe me?" He shifted in his seat and seemed to be thinking over how to phrase the next thing he wanted to say. He gave up when the waitress came to take their order.

After she left, he leaned forward again. "The reason I keep my thoughts in check around you is because of Lia."

Lia? Giselle had to throw her train of thought into a U-turn. She couldn't imagine how Lia had entered this scenario—this stunning scenario that had Giselle fast-forwarding to how she could get herself wrapped, naked, into those arms of his.

When her voice came back, she shook her head. "What does Lia have . . . ?" But then a thought hit her. "Oh Fin, you said you and Lia weren't—"

"*No.*" He held up his hand. "No, no, no. We are *not* seeing each other and never have. I'm just saying she wouldn't approve of . . . of *me*, probably. And my thoughts. And what I want to do with you."

Giselle took a long gulp of water. It took her a minute and a long, deep breath to ask the next question. "And what would that be?" she squeaked.

Fin shook his head. "Let's keep those thoughts in check, okay?"

Giselle's heart began pounding again in her chest. "Maybe Lia doesn't know what I want," she said in a voice that came out as a whisper.

Fin cocked an eyebrow.

She was on the verge of doing something she'd never done before: stating what she wanted and going after it. *She wanted Fin on her summer vacation.* That was what she wanted.

Despite what Lia wanted for her, or what her Indiana mom friends might think of her, or what her mother or Noelle might expect of her, or what Roy thought she should do—she wanted to go out, for the short time she was here, with this sexy twenty-eight-year-old. She wanted him to kiss her like he did in that parking lot, and have his gaze hang up at her breasts like it did earlier this evening, and wanted him to take her in with his dilated navy eyes, the way he was doing right now. Even if it was only for two weeks. Or maybe just a few days, since that was when Coco would be back.

And she wanted to have sex with him.

That last thought almost caused her to knock the sugar holder over. She'd never admitted anything like that to herself—having been the perfect girlfriend, then the perfect wife and perfect mother for so long, she'd never allowed herself to think about sex with anyone but Roy. But *yes*—she wanted to have sex with an almost-stranger.

She glanced at his tanned hands, which lay languidly on the dark-wood table, and thought about how they would feel running down her naked hip. . . . She took a gulp of air and hoped Fin couldn't tell that her heart was nearly pounding out of her chest.

"This sounds dangerous, Giselle," he said, low.

She moved her silverware around while she garnered the nerve to tell him what she wanted. Now that she knew, the next step was saying it.

"Lia *thinks* she knows what I want. She—and everyone, really; my mom and Noelle and my friends—they all seem to know what I 'need' these days. They tell me I *need* to rekindle a career; I *need* to move back out here to California; I *need* to meet a nice new man; I *need* a more involved father for Coco. . . ." Her mouth went dry, and she took a long sip of iced tea. "But I'm so tired of everyone else telling me what I need, or what I should do. They don't know what I need." She let out a long breath. It felt good to say that part out loud. She hadn't been able to share that with anyone. It felt like a yoke had been lifted off her shoulders.

Fin was nodding, turning his water glass between his palms. "Are they wrong?"

It wasn't a challenge. It wasn't a criticism. It was pure, unadulterated interest. It had been so long since anyone had asked her such a question, asked what she really needed, or what she wanted—maybe even dating back to high school, or college, when she was first mapping out her adult life—that she didn't even know how to answer. She met the ocean blue of his eyes, filled with actual *concern*, and felt a flutter deep in her stomach.

"There are differences between needs and wants," she said.

Fin gave her a sad smile. "And I'll bet you go after the needs, but ignore the wants."

She shrugged. She supposed that was true. But that was the responsible way to live, right?

He moved the candle to the side. "I think I'm interested in hearing your wants right now," he said in a voice that went suddenly husky.

Giselle took a deep breath and thought about this for a second. She wanted Fin. Right now. But she also wanted, maybe, someday, to get married again. And those two things weren't on the same brass ring.

"Long-term or short-term?" she asked.

He gave her a long, slow smile. "Long-term. But I might be interested in your short-term answer, too."

"You might be involved in the short-term answer." As soon as the words left her lips, she marveled at them. She couldn't remember ever saying anything so direct, so flirtatious, and here she was, saying them to this man who made her hands shake. And her hand didn't even flutter to cover her mouth. And the world didn't fall apart. In fact, the world seemed to open up. He moved back a fraction of an inch and eyed her with what looked like playfulness. She felt a huge surge of . . . *relief*, strangely. Relief that this blunt directness felt so good. Emboldened, she sat up in her chair.

But the playfulness she'd seen flash in Fin's eyes turned to sadness. He twisted his water glass. "Unfortunately, I might need the long-term answer first," he said.

The waitress arrived with their dinners, and he leaned back to let her place their plates in front of them. They each had two enormous fish tacos, wrapped in paper cones, with cabbage and tomatoes spilling out onto the plate. Red, white, and blue tortilla chips covered the other side, presumably as part of the upcoming Independence Day celebration.

"Are you Fin Hensen?" the waitress asked, as she let go of his plate.

He gave a brief nod.

"Oh, wow. Could you sign something for me?" She searched her waist apron.

"No problem, but I'm on . . ." He glanced at Giselle. "I'm on a date right now. How about if we do this after?"

"Oh, yeah, absolutely." She looked at Giselle. "Absolutely. When I bring the check." She flashed a huge set of teeth at Fin.

Once she left, Giselle smiled. "So we're on a *date* now?"

Fin was already scanning his plate for the best place to dig in to his meal. "It sometimes keeps another ten people from funneling past our table."

"Ah."

Although she knew he threw the word in there as a ploy, she still felt a vague comfort in the fact that he wasn't embarrassed to call her a date. Especially to a pretty young waitress he could've snagged instead. Her confidence went up another notch, and she tucked her hair behind her ear.

"Do you date much?" she asked.

"Probably not your definition of 'date.' "

"What do you mean?"

"I mean I don't date one person with the idea they'll be in my future. Sharing my life with someone isn't in the cards for me. I ask women out to have sex."

Giselle blinked against the assault of honesty and reached for her tea.

"Sorry," he said, low. "Sad but true."

"Why do you assume sharing your life with someone isn't in the cards for you?"

"I travel forty weeks out of the year, Giselle. I can't even own a turtle, let alone have a girlfriend. It's easier to just live a week at a time, with no responsibilities. That's sad but true also." He threw her a smile to try to make the comment ironic, but somehow too much sadness remained in his eyes.

"Do you like surfing, then, because it's so independent? You like living life alone, on your own terms?"

He thought that over. "No. I love surfing because it's . . . *surfing*." The word held a sort of breathless wonder the way he said it.

She couldn't imagine loving something that much, except Coco. She followed his gaze toward the ocean and wondered what it felt like, what could be the pull for so many people like Fin and Rabbit and Kino and the others. "What's it like?"

He shifted and picked up his water glass. "Maybe you can try it while you're here."

"No."

"Rabbit's a pretty good teacher, and so am I. We've got several boards between us—he can even let you try on one of the kids' foam boards."

"No!"

He stared at her over the rim of his glass. "That was emphatic."

"Yes, I'm very emphatic about that. But tell me: What's it like? Is it like sex?"

She didn't know what made her blurt that out—it was either his openness earlier, or his sexy eyes half-lidded over this flickering candle, or something, but she let it escape her lips before she could recapture it.

His face registered surprise before dissolving into an I-was-just-discovered kind of grin. "There *is* an element of that, yes."

"Ah, so did I just stumble upon the massive surfer secret? The thing that makes legions of twenty-year-olds go out and chase the surf?"

He laughed. "You might have. There *are* some comparisons."

"So tell me."

He sighed and looked around the room, but then shook his head. "It's hard to explain."

"Try me."

He took another bite of his taco while he thought that over—maybe deciding how much he wanted to say.

"There *is* a kind of high to it. A 'stoke.' If all the conditions are exactly right—the wind is right, the wave is right, you're the right one in the lineup to catch it, you chose the right board that day—if all that is ideal, sometimes you're rewarded with an incredible ride. You have to be subservient to Mother Nature, though, which is unlike other sports. But when Mother Nature delivers you that perfect rise, you know it. You see the rise, and you know it's got some face, and you get in there, and you hear that *whoosh* of wind right up the wall of the wave, and your board catches, and you find that hollow and start to fly. And the rest of the world falls away. It's just you, and the ride, and the massive ocean, and nothing else."

Giselle's face went hot. It did sound a little like sex. Although not the kind of sex she'd had in a long time.

She cleared her throat. "So that's what surfers chase? The perfect wave?"

"Well, the perfect moments. There's not just one. You can have lots of them. Surfers will give up careers, relationships, homes, jobs, just to spend their days chasing those moments. One good stoke can last you a long time. You can mind-surf it for days."

"Mind-surf it?"

"Relive it in your mind."

"But then you'll chase the next one," she said.

"Yeah." He nodded, almost sad. "Yeah, there's always a next one."

They both ate in silence for a moment.

"I don't know how the hell you get me to talk so much, Giselle." He laughed and dipped his chips in the salsa. "But now we're going to talk about you—spill it. Long-term wants and short-term. Long-term first."

"Why do you want long-term first?"

His eyes lifted up toward her without moving his head. "Depending on your answer there, I might not be able to hear the short-term."

"What do you mean?"

"As enjoyable as I think your short-term wants might be— and as much as I'd like to help you out there—I'm guessing your long-term answer involves some of those things your sister wants for you—a nice, stable guy; maybe marriage again; maybe a father for Coco; at the very least, maybe a guy who can take you out for dinner without wanting to get you into bed before dessert. And I can't give you any of those things. Which is why Lia would be pissed that you were spending time with me instead of going on your date with Dan Manfield."

Giselle caught her breath at his brutal directness and took another sip of tea to cool herself. "Maybe Lia's not paying attention to what I want short-term."

"I'm sure it's because she cares about you, and doesn't want you to get hurt."

Giselle eyed her plate. Despite the fact that Fin was turning her down for things she wasn't even admitting to him, maybe he was right. Maybe Lia wasn't trying to be pitying, or overbearing. Maybe her mom and Noelle weren't trying to direct her life or save her from "ruin." Maybe they all just cared about her, and their advice was meant to help, not to take over because they thought she was incompetent.

She picked up a red chip and nibbled on it. "I don't think you would hurt me."

Fin froze. Without taking his eyes off hers, his throat worked a few times. It felt like an eternity before he spoke. "I'm trying not to," he said, his voice a rasp.

"Everything okay here?" the waitress interrupted in a much-too-chirpy tone.

Fin cleared his throat and nodded without looking up at her.

Giselle nodded her own agreement until the waitress went away, and then moved some food around on her plate. She wanted to spend more time with him—and would love to go to his event the next night instead of going out with Dan Manfield—but he was clearly not going to go there. The fact that he was citing Lia as the main obstacle seemed a little silly but, at the same time, his love and respect for Lia filled her with warmth. It was such a contrast to what she'd been dealing with for the last ten years with Roy, who couldn't stand her sisters. And she couldn't begrudge Fin the attempt to act with what he thought of as honor.

In fact, it made her want him all the more. . . .

"So you don't want to know my short-term wants, then?" she asked.

"Was I wrong about the long-term ones?"

"I don't think so."

"Then no."

Giselle sighed. Darn. Maybe if she lowered her expectations, wanted less . . .

"Maybe my short-term wants are simpler than you think. Maybe they just involve gaining a little confidence."

He eyed her suspiciously and then went back to his plate. "Define 'gaining confidence.' "

"Learning to surf."

He choked on his taco and had to swallow several sips of water. "I was under the impression you were afraid of the water."

"Where did you get that impression?"

"Your emphatic reply about two minutes ago. And Rabbit."

"I think you and Rabbit are doing too much discussing of me when I'm not around."

He gave her another grin. "That's probably too damned true. So am I wrong about your fear of the water?"

She wanted to say yes, but . . . "No," she admitted. "Lia says I should learn to be unafraid of the ocean, so I don't inhibit Coco."

"I would agree with that."

"So I think you could help me out there."

Skepticism carved a line between his brows. "Okay . . ."

"Lia also tells me I need to learn to be more confident meeting new people. I'd love to go to your event tomorrow. I think that would help. If I could help you out, that would bolster my confidence."

"Uh-huh."

"And . . ."

Fin wiped his hands on his napkin and waited.

Giselle shrugged and moved her taco around, trying to garner her courage.

"And what?" Fin prompted.

She stared at a blue chip and forced the words out: "Maybe I want a little summer fling."

There. She said it. Having gotten the words out, she felt another surge of bravado—even enough to glance up to see his reaction.

Which was . . . impassive at best.

He cocked his head to one side and squinted at her. "And what exactly is involved in your idea of a 'fling'?"

"Maybe . . ." She shifted in her chair and leaned forward to whisper. "Maybe *casual sex*?" The words sounded foreign coming from her lips.

Fin sat back and stared without much emotion. "Is this the part I'm involved in?" He didn't seem too happy about it.

"Well . . . if you'd *like*."

Fin shook his head. "Giselle, you're not getting what I'm saying. What I'd *like* is not on the table here. What I'd *like* is to bring you back to my place and strip that dress off you and do amazing things to you in my bed. But, despite what you say you want, Lia would see this as taking advantage of you, or using you—*hurting* you—and she'd never speak to me again."

Giselle couldn't believe she was having an open conversation with a beautiful almost-twenty-nine-year-old about having casual sex. And it was a little humiliating that he was turning her down. And because of her sister.

"So you want me to go out with Dan?"

His Adam's apple worked a few times, and he stared down at his plate. "What I want is not part of this discussion."

She took a deep breath and poked at her tortilla chips. Maybe Lia and Fin were right. Maybe this transformation wasn't right for her after all. Maybe she needed to stick with her reserved, unassuming demeanor. She wanted passion in her life—a sudden thought, just awoken from deep in her belly, by this incredibly beautiful man who said things like "bed" and "clothes off" and "rise" and "hollow" in a deep, husky way—but she would have to tiptoe into this new want of hers. Maybe women like her were not meant to have men like him.

"Can we at least be friends, then?" She could barely get the words out of her throat.

Relief crossed Fin's face. He moved his napkin around on his lap and studied the table. "I think that'd be best."

"Can you still teach me to surf tomorrow?"

He moved his water glass to another point on the table. "Rabbit's a pretty good teacher."

"He says you're better."

He lifted an eyebrow. "Sounds like you and Rabbit are discussing me when I'm not around, too."

"That's probably too damned true."

Fin chuckled. "I hope swearing like a sailor isn't one of your short-term wants."

"Did that sound awkward?"

"A little."

She smiled and took a deep breath. "I want *you*, Fin," she said. This freedom for direct talk was kind of fun. And darned liberating. She grinned at his expression, which was nothing short of panic. "I want you to *teach* me, that is."

His shoulders relaxed. He sat back in his chair.

"You just offered a minute ago," she pressed. "How about

tomorrow? I'll be at the grommet camp taking some pictures for the brochure. When's your morning session?"

His shoulders still carried a stiffness as he adjusted in his seat. "I see you're adjusting to your new surf lingo. Morning session is around seven. Although tomorrow's tide will be best at eight, so I'll go out late."

"Come meet me after camp."

He eyed her with something that looked like curiosity, but if she didn't know better, she might have seen a little respect in there, too. "Maybe."

She sighed. "What's it contingent on?"

"If I dream about that kiss again tonight."

"Which way rules in my favor?"

"If I don't."

They finished their meal, Fin paid the bill and signed about seven autographs, and they walked back to Giselle's apartment in the dark, the smoky scents of fire pits drifting around them, and the crash of the black waves in the background.

Fin kept his hands in his tuxedo pockets for the whole stroll, and Giselle tried not to say anything too flirtatious, or even direct, so as not to scare him off for the next day. In fact, she finally relaxed, not feeling any pressure to be like his bikini babes—she now saw it as a liability.

Instead, her laughter bubbled up naturally. They climbed the sidewalk leading away from the beach, and she was able to ask him more personal childhood questions—and even shove him off the curb once when he challenged her sense of direction.

In response, Fin relaxed, too. He laughed openly and without restraint. They stopped to pet a border collie in the park, Fin's corded bracelet bouncing along his forearm, and he asked whether she and Coco had had any pets. He shared a tale about surfing in the Hainan Dao Sea in East China when he was eleven, described how to spear fish, and chuckled through a story about a haircut he received from a blind woman in Southern France.

When they got back to her place, she hugged her purse and sweater to her chest and turned toward him. "I'd give you a kiss on the cheek, but I don't want you to go dreaming about any kisses tonight, so . . ."

He smiled. "Courteous of you."

"So tomorrow at noon?"

"We'll see." He turned on his heel and walked away, glancing once back at her when he reached the stairs.

Giselle stepped inside and felt more relaxed than she had in years.

Even without her twenty cleansing breaths.

CHAPTER

Fourteen

The seagulls woke Giselle before her alarm did. She rolled over and sighed that Coco wasn't there, then thought of Fin. And sighed again.

She reached for her cell phone on the nightstand and dialed Lovey. Coco gave her a full report of making pancakes with Grandma, going to the park, then going with Daddy to see some "fifteens cars."

"Fifties' cars?" she asked Coco.

"Maybe." Giselle could even picture Coco's little shrug.

After hanging up with only one small escaped tear, Giselle dragged herself out from under the sheets.

The shock of her hair color in the mirror made her gasp right into the silence—Gosh, what had she been thinking? She did want to be someone different, but why she thought hair color would do it was beyond her. She finger-combed it into a ponytail and washed her face. She'd even fallen asleep last night with her makeup on. A giggle escaped. It seemed so rebellious.

With the tantalizing thought of Fin seeing her today—which, honestly, sounded as nerve-racking as tantalizing—she pulled her two favorite suits from the now-messy dresser. She held them both up, deciding on the one with the most coverage—a light green.

She tugged it on, then inspected herself in the mirror. Criminy, she looked like a forest fairy with this green suit and red hair. She'd have to make an appointment soon.

The suit looked good on her, though. She ran her hands over the fabric and wondered whether Fin would show up to teach her to surf. She turned to inspect her bottom. . . . And wondered whether his hands would land anywhere on this suit today. A small shiver ran through her, and she couldn't quite figure out who was gazing back at her from the mirror.

Toting her bag and chair, she made her way down the Spanish-tiled sidewalks that lined the park, past the palm trees and greenbelts, along the same path she and Fin had walked last night. She was glad she had something to do, something to keep her mind off the fact that she missed her little girl so. And off the fact that she could barely breathe every time she thought of Fin saying he'd been picturing her naked.

This early in the morning, Sandy Cove's beach and park were quiet—only a few people out, jogging along the sidewalks like apparitions through the morning mist. Eventually, she made out the instructors' gear and boards in a pile near two large wagons: an island of familiarity surrounded by emptiness.

"Mornin'," Rabbit said, smiling from his perch atop his board. His curls—still dry—blew around his face. "What're you shooting today?"

"Some of the class, then the pier." She plopped next to him.

"Stellar. Hey, are any of the pics of me coming out?" He leaned over her shoulder to inspect her viewer. "Can I use one for my Facebook page?"

"I know just the one." She pulled her sweatshirt over the heel of her chilly hands, then rewound through several shots to find the one she was thinking of. She'd caught a beautiful profile of him the other day, his head turned toward the sunrise, his light brown eyes reflecting a million specks of gold.

"You look good," Rabbit said. He leaned back and took a closer inspection. "Relaxed." He nodded toward her head. "Should I start calling you Red, though?"

Her hand flew to her hair. "I don't know what I was thinking yesterday. I'll make an appointment to tone it down."

"It's cute." His eyes, crinkled into a smile, suddenly shifted to a point past Giselle's shoulder. "Oh man." He concentrated on the sand as if he wanted to sink into the granules.

A willowy young woman—in her early twenties or so—made her way down the dunes, holding the hand of a bouncy brown-haired boy who seemed to be about five. She had long, tanned legs, extending from a pair of extremely short shorts, and straight dark hair to the middle of her back.

"Who's that?" Giselle asked.

Rabbit had his face buried. "Just talk to me like normal," he whispered.

"Okay, well . . . I have . . . um, just the picture you can use," Giselle went on in her regular voice. "And I have some action ones, too, if—"

"Hey, Rabbit," came the woman's voice behind them.

Rabbit peered up at her without lifting his head. "Oh, hey, Ms. Sandoval." He got to his feet casually. "I see Jordan's ready to go." He held his palm out to the small boy, who gave him a low five. "You ready, buddy?"

The mystery woman laughed and released Jordan. "Call me *Callie*, Rabbit."

"Hey, I'm a professional here."

"So you say." She pushed her hair over her shoulder. "Should I come back at noon?"

"Unless you want to stay." Rabbit gave her a shrug that even Giselle could see was filled with hope.

But Callie didn't seem to see it. She bent to come eye to eye with Jordan. "Be *good*," she said firmly. Then she flashed Rabbit a breezy smile. "I'll be back at twelve."

As Rabbit watched every leggy step she took back to the sidewalk, Giselle couldn't wipe the grin off her face.

"What?" Rabbit laughed.

"You're like a junior-high-school boy."

"I know," he mumbled, his voice filled with misery. "She makes me stupid."

"What's the story here?"

He glanced at Jordan, who galloped over to the blue foam boards lined up in the sand and tried to find his favorite. "I've known her since high school," he said, low. "I was surprised to see her here the other day, signing up as a single mom with a five-year-old kid. She still has the same effect on me she did back then." Another few parents coming down the dune caught his eye, and he waved. "I'll tell you more later."

Giselle moved to the side so Rabbit could greet his groms, and Jezzy and Corky came out of the water to help.

The joy on the kids' faces was infectious as they picked out their boards and practiced their pop-ups; then Rabbit drew them into a circle for stretching exercises. Giselle's camera kept clicking.

At noon, which came faster than she expected, Giselle glanced up the coast to see whether Fin might be coming, but he wasn't. Her shoulders slumped as she began packing up her camera gear. Jezzy, Corky, and Rabbit hauled the boards, snacks, wet suits, and leashes into the wagons as they released each child to his or her parents.

Giselle supposed she should feel flattered to curl up at night with the knowledge that perhaps Fin had dreamed of kissing her again. But she didn't want to curl up with knowledge. She wanted to curl up with him.

"What's wrong?" Rabbit asked, tossing towels into the wagon.

"Fin was going to teach me to surf today, but I don't think he's showing up." She looked wistfully down the coast. "He said you were a good teacher, if you have time. But you're probably wiped."

Rabbit glanced down the beach in the direction of Fin's house, then back at her. "He said that?"

"Why do you sound so surprised?"

"Well, I don't want to move in on Fin's woman."

"Rabbit!" She squirted a stream of sunscreen at him. "Maybe it would take too much time from moving in on Ms. Sandoval."

He laughed. "Whatever you say, miss. Let's go."

Giselle self-consciously peeled off her Ann Taylor slacks, then followed Rabbit down to the water. When she tested her first toe in the white foam of the Pacific, she sucked in her breath.

"That *is* cold!" she squeaked.

Rabbit had already waded to his waist and sent a spray of water back in her direction.

She giggled and backed up onshore.

Rabbit motioned up the dune to get Jezzy and Corky's attention. "Head back!" he yelled to them. "I'm waiting for Fin! Leave a foam board!"

Giselle shot him a look of skepticism.

"He'll show," Rabbit said. "But I have a feeling it's going to take us another hour to get you out here, so Fin should be right on time."

She arranged to have the boys bring her camera equipment back up, too. Then, inch by inch, Rabbit coaxed her out, tossing seaweed out of their way and pointing out the millions of holes the sand crabs made each time the water hissed back. The sun rested on her shoulders, and several children played in the wet sand near her. They made it out to about her knees when she started to get nervous. The rush of the water as it rode back—hard and pulling against the backs of her legs—began to terrify her. There was so much power out here.

"Once your stomach's wet, you're almost there," Rabbit said.

"I'm not almost there."

"No, you're not." He smiled and gazed at the sparkling horizon.

"I'll take it from here," said a voice behind them.

She and Rabbit both whirled to see Fin sloshing through the shore break with a bright red surfboard under his arm. A pair of light blue board shorts hung low on his hips, the classic string tie crossed in *X*s down his groin. His abs and chest were all muscle, tan skin glistening from the water as he made his way toward them. Salt water slicked his hair back, and his low abdominal muscles formed a wide *V* from the edge of his waist into his low-hanging shorts. Giselle took a deep gulp of air. She didn't know men were actually built this way in real life.

"I've got her," Fin told Rabbit.

As her heart began to hammer out of her chest, she wondered whether this might not have been such a great idea after all.

After a bumbling apology from Rabbit that didn't make much sense, and a quick switch of surfboards, Fin was left alone with Giselle in the thigh-high surf, trying to keep his eyes off her bathing suit. If he'd been shocked at the reveal of her shoulders yesterday, he was struck dumb at her legs today—so shapely, but with a whiteness that showcased a ridiculous vulnerability. The suit amplified every curve she had—especially the beauty of her backside and the fullness of her breasts, which he now wanted to reach out and weigh in his palms more than anything. He did his best to cut his eyes away, but her cleavage kept drawing his attention back like a magnet.

He rubbed the side of his nose and kept his eyes trained downward. "Is this as far as you've gotten since noon?"

"I'm a little cold."

I see that. He threw Rabbit's foam board in the water to give himself something else to focus on and attached it at his wrist with the leash.

"So no dreams last night?" she asked.

He smiled. He knew she'd ask right away. "I did," he admitted. "But there was no kiss."

In fact there'd been more—much more. But she didn't need to know that. And he'd taken the loophole of no *actual* kiss, because . . . Well, damn, he'd just wanted to see her again today.

He'd admitted that to himself sometime in the middle of his morning session, right after paddling out at T Street and catching two glassy barrels. The surf was beautiful; the morning was perfect; he'd slept through three nights without any nightmares about Jennifer; and Giselle Underwood was constantly floating on his mind. . . . He hadn't been this happy in a long time. He finally decided to stop fighting it. Though he didn't exactly know what he was "fighting"—an obsession? A crush? A tantalizing tease of something he couldn't have? He had no idea what was going on here, but he did know that right after those barrels—which normally would have kept him stoked all day—he'd found himself counting the hours until he could make it down here to see Giselle.

When Fox had texted at ten to verify that Fin and Giselle would show tonight—apparently Mr. Makua had scored tickets for all of them to see Laguna's Pageant of the Masters art show—he'd written back that yeah, they planned to be there. He hoped her offer still stood. But he knew it was just another excuse to see her again, even if it was going to be platonic.

"Are you still up for going with me tonight to the art show?"

Her eyes widened as she glanced up at him. "Of course." The waves were lapping against their knees, and she held her hands out in a cute way to keep her balance when the tide went hissing back into the ocean, the way a four-year-old might.

"Fox texted this morning. He seems pretty insistent that I bring you. Mr. Makua got us tickets for a show."

"A show?" The rush of water swallowed her words.

"It's a 'living art' show. It's kind of famous around here. Mr. Makua wanted you to see it, being my fake fiancée and all." He smirked. "Hard to get tickets, so it would be rude if I showed up without you."

"Of course!"

"So you can move around that date with Dan?"

"Absolutely."

He nodded. He was much too gratified about that. Maybe he was further from being a better man than he thought.

"Conditions are great for learning today," he said, rubbing his neck and keeping her breasts out of his peripheral vision. "You can wander all the way out there and still be at your waist. C'mon." He tried to motion for her to move into the water, but he didn't want to touch her, so he made a herding gesture.

"I'm still nervous."

That was apparent, given the terror in her face and the way her hands were splayed like she was on a tightrope.

"Does your fear come from something specific? Like an accident, or . . . ?"

"I fell once in the ocean when I was a kid. I was with my mom, and my sister. And . . ." She squealed as another wave hit her thighs, and he lunged toward her, but she seemed more cold than scared. ". . . I just remember the next wave coming down on me, and being underwater for a long time."

He nodded. That could be terrifying. He had to hand it to her for at least trying.

His hands hung on his hips as he watched her for another few minutes, letting her know it was okay, just being near in case she needed anyone. He was going to have to take this slowly. "Let's work on just getting you in to your waist today."

The relief that crossed her face was palpable. That was what Giselle needed—she just needed a damned break.

Her full breasts—even more tantalizingly visible now through the wet bathing suit—came into his peripheral vision again, and he sucked in his breath. He turned his body toward the ocean in case it decided to broadcast a little too obviously what she did to him. The cold would help—he needed to get in to his waist.

"Let's walk a bit." He cocked his head south. The water rushed back against their legs and she held her arms out in her cute way again. When the tide relaxed, she gave him the sweetest smile—filled with a kind of trust he knew he didn't deserve—and reached toward him.

He stared at her extended fingers for a beat too long. Fuck it. He'd be strong. He reached out and pulled her hand into his.

Still trying to avert his eyes, Fin led her. And not astray. He'd be good.

Giselle followed Fin through the shore break, gripping his hand as if her life depended on it. Although, thankfully, she was temporarily distracted from a potential watery grave right now because of Fin's body. She glanced at his muscled chest and tried to concentrate on pulling her legs through the rushing water.

He told her to wait a second, then jogged up to toss the board onshore next to her tote bag. When he came hustling down again, he frowned at her outstretched hand.

Hurt, she began to drop it. Maybe he truly didn't want to touch her anymore. Maybe he was being uberstrict about this "just friends" thing.

Before her hand hit her thigh, though, Fin snatched it up again. His hand was large and warm—more callused than she'd guessed, maybe from the boards? The sand? The wax? But its roughness was sexy—so different from Roy's surgeon hands. It engulfed hers in a way that made her feel safe. She knew he wouldn't let her go under, or let her get swept away.

They headed down the coast, toward the pier, but also angled deeper into the water, splashing through the glittery ocean. The waves splashed to her thighs, but maybe this wasn't quite so scary after all. When you were holding Fin Hensen's hand, anyway. She liked moving her feet and not feeling so stuck in the sand.

And did he just ask her to his event tonight?

She tried to shift her thoughts from the terror of the water toward the brief conversation they'd just had. He did ask her, didn't he? She, of course, was thrilled to go. She'd hoped he would change his mind. But she also knew he wanted to keep things light—there'd be no intimate touching, certainly no more of that kissing. He'd made himself clear last night. She might get as far as gripping his hand like this, and she'd even settle for wrapping her fingertips around that biceps ball, which she was itching to do right now. But she'd behave. He'd said this was Fox's idea, not his. And his reticent behavior said enough.

As their suits got more drenched, though, she couldn't help but notice she was at least scoring furtive glances from him. A feeling like warm carbonation filled her chest at the idea of him looking at her like that. At the idea of *any man* looking at her like that, actually, but especially *this guy*. . . . Holy Toledo.

She couldn't remember Roy offering that kind of attention in a long, long time—perhaps ever. And she was shocked at the tingling it left throughout her extremities. She didn't know where all this new, awakening sexuality was coming from, but there it was, and it was freeing her in a way that all of Lia's blind dates, hair appointments, and red bikinis never could.

"Are you okay?" He glanced over his shoulder at her.

With her breath still gone at the cold, not to mention her new wayward thoughts, she simply bobbed her head.

He stopped and took her other hand as if this was where he meant to bring her. She couldn't believe she was holding on to this guy. She couldn't believe she was *all the way in*, or . . . well, *almost* . . . to her waist, anyway. She followed him another four or five steps into the ocean, and a low wave hit him from behind. He blocked some of it from her, but the white sea foam wrapped all the way around her, reaching around her bottom. She sucked in some air through her teeth.

"You're here," he said, grinning.

The water rushed back to sea, pummeling the backs of her legs with sand and power. She let it push her—Fin was right there, after all. He grabbed her waist, as if he were catching her, but as the water pushed, she let the ocean press her all the way against him. She folded against the length of him, her bathing suit against his flat abdomen, her breasts pressed against his hard chest, her fingertips on his biceps. He was warm and sinewy, a rock-solid wall in this chaotic ocean, his muscles taut, body warm. Her legs entangled with his as the water rushed. He squinted over the top of her head as the water finished receding, his hands on her waist, waiting it out. Then he pressed his mouth into her part. "Giselle," he groaned against her hair. It was an admonishment.

When the tide relaxed, he set her back from him. "Stay there," he said hoarsely. With three large strides, he was in the ocean, diving under a very shallow wave that was coming their way.

He was at her side before the same wave was even ripping back into the sea, slicking the water back out of his hair, standing near enough that she could grab him if she needed to, but letting her balance herself.

"You're like a regular wahine here now." He smiled ruefully.

"Wahine?"

"It means 'woman' in Hawaiian, but we use it here for a female surfer. Usually gorgeous. Let's head back."

She followed the direction he'd nodded, relishing in the fact he'd just called her gorgeous, that he'd just maybe been turned on by her, that he'd just helped her get into the ocean *all the way to her waist.*

But they took it slow, keeping a distance all the way back—close enough in case she stumbled, but far enough that she felt empowered.

As they stood in front of her tote, dripping into the dry sand, Fin's gaze swept her body appreciatively. He still cut his eyes away, but this time he let her see the heat there. She grabbed for her towel.

"Don't you have a towel?" she asked, snapping hers around her body.

"Nah."

"Do you want one of mine? I have an extra." She rummaged through her tote for the other towel she always brought for Coco. "It's Polly Pocket, but . . ."

"I'm fine, Giselle."

"I know I have it here. . . ."

"Giselle."

She glanced up at the harshness of his tone. When she met his eyes, he was frowning.

"I'm *fine.*"

A warmth rose around her ears. She needed to stop behaving so maternally around him. That heat in his eyes wasn't going to last long if she started throwing the words "you need a towel" and "you need a jacket" around. What was the matter with her? Next thing she knew she'd be cutting his food. She wondered whether Dan Manfield had children. Maybe that was where Lia's logic was going. . . .

"So we're okay for tonight?" he asked.

"Of course. I was wondering if you might—or if we might—I'm glad we're—" She cut herself off. *Quit while you're ahead, girl.* . . . "How can I help?"

Droplets danced along his hairline, dripped off his eyelashes. He hung his hands low on his hips, and Giselle watched the rivulets of water that curved down his chest and raced toward the waistband of his shorts, which seemed to be sitting even lower now, if that were possible, revealing those lowest, sexiest abdominal muscles that shouldn't legally be shown in public. Children's voices laughed behind her in the far distance.

"Just . . ." He shook his head. "Be you. You don't have to be anyone different. And . . . let's not complicate things, okay?"

She didn't know where to rest her gaze. "I, uh—of course." She swiped at her face with her towel. She must seem like a crazed—possibly horny—drowned rat.

"And, Giselle?"

She tended to her towel, tugging it tighter around her.

"Sorry about that, back there." He nodded his head toward the pier.

She realized he was referencing his hard, warm body, pressed against hers. Or her body pressed against his. Whatever.

She closed her eyes. Guilt swept through her. *She* was going to have to behave. *He* was trying to be noble.

She opened her mouth, but he spoke first.

"No complications," he reiterated gently.

She bobbed her head in an embarrassed gesture but swiped the Polly Pocket towel out of her bag and shoved it into his waist. "Then use this."

Snatching her tote, she trudged up the dune, sidestepping the patchwork of beach towels that now stretched as far as the eye could see.

Fin followed behind her, chuckling lightly. By the time they got back to the sidewalk, he had the Polly Pocket towel spread over his shoulders, billowing in the breeze down his stomach.

CHAPTER
Fifteen

The art festival was tucked away, nestled in the chaparral canyons of Laguna Beach. The earthy scent of California sage hung in the air, mixed with the aroma of wine. Fin had been here once before—also with Fox and Mr. Makua, for a company-sponsored work event on the grounds—but he'd never been here on a triple date, being treated almost like one of the board members. He adjusted his dress shirtsleeve at the wrist and swept his hand for Giselle to enter first, beneath the entry arches designed to resemble a Roman ruin.

Apparently she'd spent the afternoon at some beauty salon and had her hair done back to the way it was, pretty much—more of the blond Grace Kelly thing. He didn't care either way what color her hair was—he was more obsessed with the tendrils that moved along the back of her neck, directing his attention to exactly where he wanted to kiss her.

But he wasn't going to kiss her tonight. Not her neck, not her lips. Nothing. He was going to show her a nice time while she was in Sandy Cove, because she was the sister of one of his closest friends. And he was going to attend this event tonight with his sponsor company because they were good to him and he wanted to continue.

And that was the extent of tonight.

They followed a paved, winding path past angled booths displaying oils, photography, mosaics, sculptures, and jewelry.

They were early, so he didn't search for Tamara or Fox yet. He wanted to give Giselle a chance to really take in the art here, which was all local. He knew she'd love it.

The sky was turning a deep gold, and mini-lights sparked to life in the sycamore branches. He glanced around for Fox and Tamara and Mr. Makua around six. Live jazz struck up from the center of the grounds, offered by two guitarists who stood on a grassy hill amid wrought-iron café tables.

He wished, now, that they weren't meeting anyone. Watching her face light up with passion at each booth was strangely edifying to him. It reminded him of how he felt when a perfect wave was rolling his way—that joy that comes from your gut. But Giselle's joy seemed as if it were awakening from a long-dormant sleep. He felt honored being the one to watch it stir.

"There they are." Giselle nodded toward one of the tables, where Fox and Tamara were pulling up a few chairs. If he'd heard it right, her voice held a whisper of disappointment, too.

Next to Fox and Tamara were Mr. Makua and another woman Fin didn't know. Behind them were Mr. Makua's Samoan bodyguards, trying to blend in at a nearby table, although they were each about 280 pounds and shoved into wrought-iron chairs.

At their approach, Tamara pushed out a chair with her foot. "Hi, you two! We just got here."

Fin self-consciously touched Giselle's back and gave her the chair. They should have gone over some ground rules again—how much touching, how much they were going to extend this farce. He'd asked her to wear the turquoise ring again when they'd left the apartment, but mostly to cover up her white band. Beyond that, he didn't want to continue lying. He wasn't sure what Tamara knew, or whether Fox had come clean with Mr. Makua.

"Mr. Hensen, this is my friend Charlene."

Charlene was a beautiful Hawaiian woman, about Mr. Makua's age, who wore expensive-looking clothes that teetered on the edge between business and pleasure.

Fin leaned over. "Nice to meet you. This is my . . . *friend* Giselle."

"Oh, I think she's more than a friend," Tamara guffawed. She'd taken only a few sips of wine, but her voice was already up an octave.

Fin had spent many an event with Tamara, most of which involved Tamara getting tipsy and moaning about how Fox always abandoned her for work colleagues. But, despite all her drama, he got a kick out of her.

"Once a woman is sleeping with a man, she's more than a *friend*," Tamara admonished with a finger pointed at his chest. "He becomes a *boyfriend*. And note the 'a.' "

Fin glanced at Fox, who raised his eyebrows in a you're-on-your-own-buddy note.

"What would you two like to drink?" Mr. Makua interrupted.

Thankful for the reprieve, Fin turned to Giselle. He didn't know what she drank, which seemed to sum everything up in one quick realization.

"I'll take a Moscato," she said.

Ah, Fox would like that.

As predicted, Fox lit up. He drew Giselle into a conversation about local vintners and how many of them produced Moscato, and how it was all the rage lately. Fin bit back a grin and congratulated himself again on picking Giselle.

The beer and wine garden was about ten tables away, so Fin started ambling. On his way, Fox caught up with him.

"Your lady has good taste."

"You didn't tell Tamara?" Fin mumbled as they took their place in line.

"Tell Tamara what?"

"About me and Giselle."

"What did you want me to tell her?"

"That we're not really dating."

Fox frowned. "What are you talking about? You asked Giselle to come?"

"Well, yeah, but—"

"You're not paying her?"

"Of course not."

"That, my friend, is a date."

Fin started to respond, but then thought better of it. He absentmindedly flipped through his wallet to make sure he'd brought his card. "She's the sister of a friend."

"Still a date."

"Well, we're not engaged," he said. "And I feel like I was leading some folks to believe that. I don't want to lie."

"Then don't." Fox shrugged. "You brought a beautiful young woman here who makes you nervous, who probably gives you a hard-on every time you look at her, and who you're clearly starting to fall in love with. . . . No lie."

Fin laughed. "Starting to fall in *love* with?" That was the only part he could argue with.

Fox smiled but didn't answer.

"So we're not talking about business tonight?" Fin changed the subject.

"He might pry a bit—you know how he is. He'll ask about your dad. He might ask about Jennifer. He'll probably get you to share some of your glory days—he loves that kind of stuff. But no, he's not going to grill you about the contract or ask you why you haven't won a fucking competition since last July."

A wave of guilt swept through Fin.

"It's all right, man." Fox clapped him on the shoulder. "I'm just fucking with you. You've had a rough year. But you've got to stop the self-destructive shit, okay?"

Fox wanted to buy Giselle her Moscato, so Fin let him while he studied the handwritten blackboard menu himself. He didn't want to drink tonight—something told him he needed to be alert—so he ordered a pinot noir he didn't like and planned to leave it untouched.

"Actually, I might have something else in mind for you," Fox said.

Fin frowned and put a tip in the tip cup. "What are you talking about?"

"It's something I've been thinking over." Fox swept his two plastic wine cups off the table and nodded for Fin to grab Giselle's.

"What is it?"

"How about if we get together after this? I think the show

ends at ten—we can grab some beers at Javier's Cantina or someplace and I can run this idea by you." As they approached their table, Fox's voice dropped to a mumble. "Mr. Makua doesn't know about it yet."

Fin nodded. "Sure."

The guitarists on the grassy stage struck up a Simon & Garfunkel tune, and Fin mulled over what Fox might be talking about as he handed Giselle her drink. "From Fox," he admitted.

She bent her neck in an elegant gesture toward Fox, and Fin felt a ridiculous jolt of jealousy.

Through a sort of fog, he heard someone say their reservations were ready, and he helped Giselle out of her chair. He took a deep breath before walking toward Mr. Makua's questions. He didn't want Giselle to hear about his father, or about his parents abandoning him for Bali, or about his impoverished past, or about Jennifer dying right before his eyes. Although he didn't know why. It didn't matter. He'd never see her again after this week unless she came to visit Lia. But, even so, he didn't want her to see what a mess he was.

He headed toward their reservations as if walking toward the gallows.

Maybe this wasn't such a good idea after all.

For dinner, they were seated on an outdoor patio among the bougainvillea. Mini-lights hung above them, strung through the eucalyptus trees, and stained-glass windows hung from sycamore branches, illuminating jewel-toned fish, flowers, trees, and surf. Giselle stared at one that had a wave on it and smiled at Mr. Makua, who nodded his head in appreciation.

Tamara wriggled out of her sweater, sending her colorful art-glass necklace clinking against the china place settings. "This place is *so* romantic. They have lots of weddings here, you know." She threw a smile at Giselle. "Have you guys talked about a wedding?"

"Tamara," Fox warned. He leaned across the table toward Giselle and Fin, and dipped his head apologetically. "She loves weddings. And how-you-met stories, despite how private they may—or may not—be. Don't encourage her."

Tamara lifted her menu. "Oh, Fin doesn't mind. Do you, Fin? I was going to ask how you two met. I feel like I've heard a couple of different stories."

Fin twisted his full wineglass at the stem. "We're not—"

"Better yet, your first *kiss*," Tamara said, leaning across the table, her glass beads forming a pool on the tablecloth. Her jaw dropped in an actress's openmouthed surprise, a smile tugging at the corners.

"*Tamara,*" Fox warned again. "I'm having the pork chops. Fin?"

Fin rubbed his eyebrows. "I'll, uh—have the fish."

Tamara looped her finger through her necklace and smiled coyly. "You all don't have to get so uncomfortable on me— it's *fun.* I played it at a party once. Fox loves to tell these stories." She hit him on the arm.

"With *you.* In *private.*" He shot her a chiding glance, but it was clear he adored her. He turned toward Charlene and Mr. Makua. "Seriously, ignore her. If you encourage her, she'll get worse."

"I'll play," Charlene said in a rolling Hawaiian accent.

Everyone at the table turned to stare at her. "Kai first kissed me . . ." She turned and grinned at Mr. Makua, who was blushing but smiling. "Hmmm, on a boat dock. It was on our third date. Third! I thought he would never move faster."

Giselle laughed with the others, but a rivulet of perspiration ran between her breasts. She glanced at Fin. He seemed more amused by Tamara than afraid of her question, and was sitting back, running his fingertips along his wine stem, smiling at Charlene while she told the rest of her story.

Giselle couldn't hear the story due to her pounding heart. It was hard to tell lies.

"Giselle?" Tamara prompted when it was her turn.

Fin leaned forward. "I first kissed Giselle in a parking lot."

Giselle let out a breath of relief at the interception and brought her water shakily to her lips.

"A parking lot?" Tamara scowled. "Oh, Fin, you could've done better than that."

"Yes," he said, stealing a glance at Giselle. "I think I could have."

"I bet you regret that."

"I regret the location, but I don't regret the kiss. I mind-surfed it for days." Fin smiled, his eyes still on his wine stem.

Giselle fluttered her menu to her face, which she could feel turning bright red.

"I hope you made up for it," Tamara said.

"I'm working on it."

Giselle took a tentative peek at him from behind her menu. He chose the same moment to draw a heavy-lidded gaze at her that could have held a promise or a question. She darted back toward the salad selections.

"For us, I was the one who kissed Fox first." Tamara grinned, leaning into the conversation.

"I'm sure everyone's shocked," Fox said dryly.

"We were on a boat, too, Charlene," she continued. "I thought he was attracted to me, but I wasn't sure, and I just got . . . *impatient*."

"Can I take your order?" the waiter interrupted.

Throughout the rest of the dinner, they talked about boating, and art, and traveling to Belize, where Charlene had been twice, and where Fox and Tamara had just returned from an anniversary trip.

Fin relaxed as the dinner went on, leaning back in his chair, laughing openly, especially when the conversation shifted to Tamara and Fox. Giselle stole a few glances at him during dinner, and caught him staring at her. Instead of lowering his eyes again, though, he smiled.

When the talk turned to his father, however, he stiffened.

"Yep, he's doing great," he answered toward Mr. Makua as he shifted forward.

"You said he's still surfing every day?"

"He is."

"Did he ever get that company off the ground? You mentioned he might start—"

"No." Fin shook his head. "He's happy with where he is. Have you ever surfed Padang Padang or Uluwatu there?"

Giselle glanced up. Fin was trying to steer the conversation away. She wondered again about the tightening in his jaw when anyone brought his parents up.

"Yes, Uluwatu!" Mr. Makua said, pleased. "Those reef breaks . . . Like a dream."

"Is that where your parents live now, Fin? In Bali?" asked Tamara. "I didn't know that."

"They live in a small fishing village, on the eastern side. But Uluwatu." Fin gave a groan of approval. "Those reef breaks—perfect barrels."

Mr. Makua nodded, seeming to drift back on a memory. He turned toward Charlene. "You should see Fin doing the long barrels. He still has better form than any newcomers. They all want to do airs now—flying into air over the top of a wave. But Fin still does amazing long rides through tubes. He goes into the hollow, and the wave is crashing all over the top of him, and it goes on and on for miles; you can't see him anywhere. You think he went down with the whitewater, but then—there he is! Riding out to the left!" His grin took up his whole face.

Fin's cheeks grew ruddy. "But the airs are where it's at now, Mr. Makua. The new judges—that's what they're scoring highest."

"Jennifer, too," Mr. Makua added, ignoring the comment about the judges. "She does beautiful barrels."

Fin nodded. "She did."

A pause hung over the table as everyone stared at the tablecloth, lost in their own thoughts about the lost Jennifer.

"So you're heading to South Africa?" Mr. Makua said, breaking the silence.

Giselle glanced around the table. To her surprise, Fin nodded.

"Two days," he said.

She tried to keep the shock out of her face. He was leaving in two days? He hadn't mentioned that. . . . Although, on the other hand, why would he? But the thought made her strangely sad. She had hoped she could finagle more time with him. She liked the way his voice softened when he spoke of the sites in Bali; she wanted to hear more about South Africa; she wanted to know more about his father and what was going on there; she wanted to see more of the laugh lines around his mouth when he talked about reef breaks. She also wanted more of the shivers he gave her when he fixed her with that heavy-lidded smile.

Fox chimed in about South Africa, and how one of the tour surfers from Australia was making his home there now.

As Giselle tipped her wine and tried to hide her new disappointment, the conversation turned toward food, and then—somehow—art again.

The dinner came to an end over a raspberry-swirl cheesecake and a molten chocolate cake, which they shared six ways.

"The show starts in ten minutes," said Mr. Makua.

"Now, what is this show?" Giselle said.

"You'll like it," Mr. Makua said, helping Charlene scoot back her chair. "It's an original tableau: Actors pose in the paintings. They do the lights and makeup to make them appear flat, as if they're in the painting. They've been doing it for seventy-five years. I always come in July to make sure I see it."

The show was on the festival grounds, so it took only about five minutes to walk to the entrance. A set of majestic double doors, which were really just archways to the outdoors, opened to red theater seats that rose sharply, stadium-style, as if molded into the canyon. The sky provided the ceiling; the falling dusk and emerging stars counted down to showtime.

Mr. Makua handed out the tickets while Fin rented binoculars at a nearby booth. Fox stood in line for blankets, and came back with three—one for each couple.

Fin took Giselle's elbow and steered her toward their seats. A slight chill hung in the air with a growing mist that was settling in the canyon, cooling the evening sky as the sun went down. Giselle spread the blanket across her and Fin's laps.

"You're going to South Africa in two days?" she murmured.

"Yeah. Ballito—the Mr. Price Pro. Nice purse—quarter million."

She straightened the blanket on her side. Her hands shook.

"Was that something I should have told you?" he whispered.

"Well, I figure—being the new lover and all—I should know some of these things."

Fin chuckled at her repetition of his line, but his laughter died as he watched her obsessive smoothing.

"Seriously," he whispered. "Is this upsetting you?"

"I just—" She leaned forward to tuck the blanket around her ankle and took a deep breath. She didn't know what to say. *I'm going to miss you? Why didn't you tell me?* It sounded so silly. She didn't even know this guy. This relationship was fake. "I just didn't want to mess up your scenario for your boss," she finally fudged.

He stared at her for several beats after that, as if about to say something, but didn't.

Fox's voice rang across the row: "Everything okay?"

Fin turned to respond as Giselle continued to smooth the blanket. The scent of coconut swirled off Fin's hair when he moved.

"We're good," he told Fox.

"Good evening, ladies and gentlemen," the narrator's voice boomed.

The show launched into the first act. It was as terrific as Fin and Mr. Makua promised. The theme was "The Muse," and Giselle brought her binoculars to her eyes for every painting and sculpture, watching in amazement to see whether they were truly real people. The makeup and lighting nullified depth perception, making the actors look flat and helping them blend right into the painting. Sometimes life-sized statues were unveiled in the bushes at the sides of the stage, each posed by a real actor sprayed completely in bronze or gold. The works were accompanied by narration that explained the muse in each painting and how she shaped the work. A live orchestra played between each set.

Giselle was transported to this world of art she had once loved and lost between *Parenting* magazine and playdates. Between each piece, she applauded with the rest of the audience, then snuggled beneath the blanket and gazed at the outlines of the canyon, the ocean fog sitting just outside the rim of the bowl, as if it, too, wanted to swirl to the orchestra. The night air smelled clean.

One of her favorite parts was the work of Frida Kahlo. The narrator told stories of Diego Rivera and Kahlo's tempestuous marriage, riddled with infidelities. Giselle gaped at the devastating landscape of Frida's *On the Borderline Between Mexico and the United States*, and could see that the painting could just as easily represent the feeling of being between marriage and divorce, carcasses and sadness strewn throughout the foreground.

She lowered the binoculars.

"*Land of Make Believe*," Fin whispered in her ear.

"What?"

"That's the one that reminds me of you."

A shiver ran through her at his breath against her ear, racing against the sadness she felt for Frida. Her emotions were a cacophony: despair for Frida, sadness about Fin leaving, joy when his thigh brushed against hers under the blanket, hopelessness at the idea of shattered marriages, and sexual jolts when Fin's breath tickled her neck and told her that works of art reminded him of her.

Giselle shakily lifted her binoculars to study *La Valse*, a bronze sculpture by Camille Claudel, and her sadness evaporated—replaced with a warmth that curled her toes. The sculpture portrayed two lovers in a sexy, yet chaste, embrace. The actor was bronzed with paint, shirtless, longish hair, holding the woman in what appeared to be ocean water. The woman leaned in, back bare, snuggling his neck. They weren't kissing, just holding each other in an embrace of love, safety, adoration. . . . He had his arm wrapped firmly around her waist, as if to keep her cherished.

Giselle's breath caught at the beauty of the piece, as it transported her to a memory of Fin this morning—the way he'd held her in the surf, the way she'd felt so safe snuggled against his chest, the way his lips had whispered that warning against her hair.

Giselle brought the binoculars down. She glanced at Fin's profile. He was watching this one with interest.

The last piece was *The Last Supper*, but Giselle didn't lift the binoculars. Mostly she needed to stop her heart from thundering. The idea of being in Fin's arms for real, or just having him kiss her once more, the way he had at the funeral, was crowding into her thoughts. She didn't know what she was allowed to want. Long-term, she wanted a family again. Suburbia. Some sense of normalcy for her daughter. And what Fin had said at the restaurant on the pier made sense: If she wanted all that long-term—the happy family, the suburban life for Coco—then she shouldn't take advantage of something cheap and easy, like him, short-term. Dismissing the easy thrill was the moral way to behave, the responsible thing a mother of a five-year-old girl should do. When Coco was older, she could tell her that she shouldn't lust after a man she didn't have a future with.

Yet, after years of putting her life on hold for Coco and Roy, her own wants were being unleashed in a chaotic way, powerful as the ocean against her body, ready to knock her down.

A sudden shuffling was going on at the other end of their row, and Giselle leaned forward to see Fox discussing something in low whispers with Tamara.

Fox leaned toward the rest of them, his cell phone in his hand. "I have to go," he whispered. "They stopped the presses at the magazine. I have to see what's wrong. Fin, can you take Tamara to Javier's Cantina? I can meet you there after the show." Without waiting for Fin's answer, Fox headed out the aisle.

Giselle glanced at Fin, and then at Tamara, who sat stonily, refusing to meet anyone's eyes.

Tucking the binoculars into her lap, Giselle joined the audience in another round of applause.

Sixteen

Fin could barely concentrate on the rest of the performance, focused now on how he was going to keep Tamara happy until Fox returned. And how Giselle's thigh felt under this blanket.

For a night that had started pretty well, it was sure starting to suck.

He'd enjoyed the rest of it, though. Although Mr. Makua had been veering into dangerous territory with too much talk about his dad.

Fin was embarrassed that his parents lived such an impoverished life. It was what they wanted, though. Fin kept trying to send money, but his dad would send it back. Usually with angry notes. His dad came close, several times, to accusing him of selling out, of losing sight of what surfing was all about. His dad said he didn't need much in Bali—just good surf, his good woman, and a bowl of rice three times a day. Fin himself had always felt hungry as a child, and often unsafe, and couldn't understand how his parents could have chosen that as their level of "enough." They'd slept under trees on hard beach sands in Mexico or South Africa, Fin shivering against the siren howls of the wolves or jackals. Sometimes they'd sleep in the van, the gas fumes clogging their throats as one of the Zen surfers sat guard, freezing, in the driver's seat. They learned to hide their food in hanging nets, against animals and vagrant thieves. Because Fin had lived a childhood that always felt uncertain, he now relished having money. He kept most of it in the bank—he didn't have many needs—but having it made him feel safe. He knew he would never have to wonder where his next meal was coming from.

Despite that brief side trip during tonight's dinner, he had enjoyed the rest of the night. He got a kick out of Fox and Tamara; he loved talking surf with Mr. Makua; and he loved watching Giselle. Watching her laugh. Watching her close her eyes against the deliciousness of cheesecake. Watching the passion spark in her eyes when she talked about art. Seeing that smoldering sexuality bubbling closer and closer to the surface. . . . He was lucky he was heading out to South Africa in two days, because whatever this obsession with her was, it was starting to feel dangerous.

At the Roman-ruins exit, the five of them shook hands, and the women exchanged hugs. As they waited for Mr. Makua's driver, Mr. Makua tugged on Fin's elbow and held him back from the others.

"Your father is proud," he said, low.

"What?" Fin couldn't imagine what Mr. M was talking about. He hadn't talked to Fin's dad in years.

"His heart swells with pride."

Fin smirked. Maybe right between sending his money back and ignoring his phone calls. "How do you know that, Mr. Makua?"

"Because *my* heart swells with pride."

A strange lump formed in the center of Fin's throat. He tried to swallow around it.

"You are a man of respect," Mr. M said quietly. "I knew you respected the ocean, and I knew you respected your father and mother, but tonight I saw you respect life, and Jennifer's life, and your lady. This will take you a long way, Mr. Hensen."

"But Giselle—she's not—"

"You have respect for her." Mr. M waved off Fin's response. "That is what matters. I don't care about what the tabloids say, Mr. Hensen. I care about what I see. Respect for others, respect for Mother Nature, respect for self." He ticked each one off with a finger. "This is all your father ever wanted for you."

The car pulled up, and Mr. M leaned forward on his cane as the bodyguards came close, helping him and Charlene into the car.

Fin wanted to continue the conversation, but all he could do was lift his palm in an inadequate good-bye.

As soon as the car pulled away, Tamara's smile left her face. She hooked Giselle's arm in hers and headed down Laguna Canyon Road toward Javier's, several steps in front of Fin.

He cleared his throat and pressed his fingertips against the bridge of his nose, against a strange pressure of tears that dammed there, and glanced at Tamara's deliberate tugging of Giselle.

This was going to be a hell of a night.

Javier's was crowded, as usual.

Fin ushered Giselle and Tamara off the beach sidewalk, through the shoulder-to-shoulder crowd within the white-washed adobe walls. They made their way to a bar table and ordered a round of margaritas under the open beams of the night-lit patio. But Fin, at the last minute, called the waitress back and changed his order to a club soda.

The wooden casement windows on the far end of the bar opened toward the night ocean, with only the Pacific Coast Highway and some sand between. The misty air, mingled with the evening fog, smelled like salt and left a familiar film on Fin's arms. He rolled his dress sleeves past his elbows and continued to think about what Mr. M had said. Respect? Was that what Mr. M had been looking for all this time in his Mahina spokesman? Was that really all Fin's father had wanted? And was that what was so different about Giselle—was he stumbling over himself with respect for her? Was that why she felt so special?

"The melon margaritas here are wonderful," Tamara told Giselle, pushing hers across the table for Giselle to try.

Tamara was talking again, trying to maintain a cheerful note, but obviously still seething. He wondered how often Fox pulled this kind of thing. Of course, he didn't ask: He didn't want to get her any more riled up than she already was.

The music grew louder as the night grew longer. The Eagles' "Tequila Sunrise" came over the speakers. Soon Tamara was slipping into alcohol-induced revelations, leaning heavily toward Fin's shoulder.

"So I didn't embarrass you earlier, did I, with the first-kiss story?"

He took a sip of his club soda and looked at her sideways. "No," he lied.

"I just love a good love story." The tequila was causing her *L*s to become labored. "And you two are *clearly* in love," Tamara went on, leaning now toward Giselle.

Fin glanced across the table at Giselle, who was avoiding his eyes.

"I wonder if Fox is on his way." Fin dug his phone from his pants pocket to check his messages. Damn—he'd forgotten that he'd turned it off during the performance. Had he already missed Fox's call? "If he doesn't come soon, maybe we can take a walk along the beach," he tried, as he came upon three messages in a row from a number he didn't recognize.

Shit, it *was* Fox. Fin could barely hear Fox's message above "The Piña Colada Song" on his end. But he could make out the whirling of the presses on Fox's side. *"I'm waiting for Chartreuse to bring its new ad by, and as soon as this asshole gets here with it, I'll head back over there. Should be no more than two hours."*

Crap. He couldn't keep Tamara sober here for that long.

The table trembled as Tamara leaped off her barstool, her own phone pressed to her ear. She must have gotten the same message.

"Tamara!" Fin lunged across the table to try to stop her, but she was quick. She spun past a burly man in a bright red Hawaiian shirt at the bar table behind them and headed for the front door. He swore under his breath and turned toward Giselle. "Wait here."

He elbowed his way through palm- and hibiscus-decorated sundresses and dress shirts and tried to catch Tamara at the door, but she moved too fast. He got caught up behind a party for six and lost her.

"Tamara!" He spun out to the sidewalk. The bars were still teeming with people. Live music and suntanned bodies spilled out onto the sidewalks, carrying the heavy scent of suntan lotion and perfume. Fin turned sideways through the next crowd.

"Tamara!" He spotted her and lunged forward, catching her wrist. "What are you *doing*?"

As she whirled to face him, he was stunned to come face-to-face with the most pitiful expression he'd ever seen— mascara streaming down her cheeks, mouth long and sad, and wisps of dark hair sticking to her neck. He felt so damned sorry for her.

"He keeps *doing* this," she wailed. "He keeps *leaving* me."

"Tamara, it's a work emergency. What's he supposed to do?"

"I think he's seeing someone."

Fin stepped back, startled by the preposterousness.

"I could hear presses in the background," he said. Her accusation seemed so absurd he didn't think he needed to say more than that, but she shook her head.

People jostled them, and the scent of coconut oil swam heavily in the air. She swayed to the right.

"Let's go back to the restaurant," he said. "Giselle is still there."

He thought that would appeal to Tamara's protectiveness, but Tamara looked farther down in the direction of the beach. He tried again: "We'll pay for our drinks. I'll take you wherever you want. I'll take you home, or . . ." He left that open-ended. He wasn't really sure what their other options were.

"I liked your idea about the walk on the beach."

"Okay." He began nudging her back toward Javier's. "But let's get Giselle first."

"Or your house?" she asked, in full vulnerability mode now. She leaned into him and swiped at the mascara under her eyes. "Can we go to your house? You and me and Giselle? I like her, Fin."

"Sure. We'll go wherever you want. And I like her, too." God, he hated to see women cry. He never knew what to say, or what to do.

He directed Tamara through the sidewalk crowds, past beer bottles clinking inside the restaurant patios, past bursts of laughter punctuating the swells of live bands. When they made it back to Javier's, Giselle was standing in front, holding her purse primly.

"I paid the bill," she said.

Fin winced. "Let me pay you back."

"No, it's okay—" She caught sight of Tamara's tear-streaked face and gasped. "What *happened*?"

"Fox is cheating on me." Tamara threw her arms around Giselle.

Giselle looked wide-eyed at Fin over Tamara's shoulder, but he shook his head.

"Tamara wants to go somewhere," he announced. "I think we all need some fresh air and fewer crowds."

A few guys suddenly recognized Fin on the sidewalk and came over for autographs. He scrawled his name and handed hats and other items back, desperately trying to keep track of Tamara, who was stumbling down the sidewalk toward the car, leaning into Giselle. He was pretty sure there'd be an article in the paper tomorrow about what a jerk he was, not signing enough autographs, not signing that guy's skimboard, not even focusing on his fans. He took a deep breath and tried to keep Tamara in his line of vision.

Once he escaped, and made sure Giselle and Tamara were both in the car, he leaned against the hood and left messages at the pressroom to let Fox know where they were.

Damn, things weren't going the way he'd hoped.

Tamara was undone by the time they got to Fin's place. Her dress was crumpled around her hips, and mascara formed jags down her face.

"I was a *debutante*," she whined from the backseat. "My father was the CEO of *Pique*. How could Fox *do* this to me?"

"I'm sure it's all a misunderstanding," said Giselle, double-checking her assumption against Fin's profile. He nodded.

When they arrived at Fin's house, he ushered them down his front walk, past the sounds of the dark ocean that roared up between the narrow homes, and into his living room, where he left the two of them in the center while he flipped on the lights.

Giselle laid her purse on the low, midcentury-modern couch and wondered whether she should keep up the ruse for Tamara that she and Fin were engaged. Should she walk into the kitchen and pretend she knew where the water glasses were?

One glance at Tamara, though, swaying from her standing position, and she had her answer. There would be no need. She led Tamara toward the couch. "Have a seat, sweetie," she said, easing her into the thin, rectangular cushions.

Fin watched both of them warily.

"Let's get her some water," Giselle said over her shoulder, and Fin nodded, escaping into the kitchen.

Giselle settled Tamara against the back of the couch and then joined Fin. He helped her get down a coffee mug and turned on the tap water for her. The mug had a lewd picture on the side.

"You don't have any glasses?" she said.

He smiled. "Afraid my china for twelve is in storage, Miss Strawberry Queen."

Giselle walked the mug to Tamara, but Tamara had gotten up and found some scotch Fin had on top of a wet bar by the window. She held up a shot glass that had the name of some Vegas showroom scrawled across the side.

"Tamara," Giselle said in her den-mother voice. "I don't think that's a good idea."

"Oh, Giselle, *please*. If Fin were cheating on you, you'd be doing the same thing."

Giselle glanced at Fin, who simply raised his eyebrow at that.

"I want to sit on the beach," Tamara announced.

She pushed past Giselle to the center sliding door. Fin had three sets of sliders, spanning the front of the house. Tamara stumbled over an expensive-looking telescope in the center of the room, chose the slider on the farthest side, and tugged at the lock.

"Tamara, why don't you relax." Fin moved her hand away. "The tide's all the way in. Sit down. Let me get some lights on out there."

Tamara backed off, and Fin herded her toward the couch. He threw Giselle a pointed stare that seemed to beg for help.

Giselle took Tamara's hands and guided her toward the couch, sitting with her, this time, on the edge.

"I just love him," Tamara whispered to Giselle, her mouth forming a grimace as the tears began to flow.

"I know you do."

"I just want him to stay with me." Tamara buried her forehead into Giselle's shoulder.

Giselle patted her head. "He will, Tamara. He loves you. He's just working." She fluffed two couch pillows, which were leather and not very fluffy, and helped Tamara lean back.

Outside, Fin flipped on two enormous rooftop floodlights that slowly hummed to attention. As they warmed up, the lights threw their illumination about thirty feet across the water in front of his house. With the tide all the way in, the water completely submerged the sandy area below where Coco had played the other evening. The thought sent a violent shiver through Giselle. The ocean roared toward the house, violently meeting the rocky break below and sending rooster tails of spray into the black air. The ocean hissed each time it made its way back out.

"Do the waves ever come up to the windows?" Giselle asked, stroking Tamara's hair.

"During storms," Fin said, stepping back in. "This is high tide—that's as high as it'll get. But during a storm, yeah, the waves hit the glass. It's kind of awe-inspiring."

"It doesn't scare you?"

He shook his head. "I respect it."

"It scares me."

He gave her a gentle nod, then searched for some long matches, which he carried back out onto the balcony to light four tiki torches that stood taller than he did. As the flames sputtered to life, Giselle watched him from behind. He stood with his hands low on his hips, watching the water. The torches cast golden flickers across his profile, lending ritualistic tones. His jaw set like some sort of Polynesian god, thinking back through the way the evening had played out, perhaps.

Giselle didn't want to, but she turned away, to attend to Tamara, who—surprisingly—was crashed against Fin's uncomfortable leather pillow.

"You know you can't leave tonight." Fin handed Giselle a Beatles' *Abbey Road* mug, then set down his own, one with Darth Vader on the side, and climbed to join her on the brick-lined concrete ledge, where their legs dangled over the waves below.

He had changed clothes. He was now barefoot, wearing a simple pair of cargo shorts, with a navy T-shirt that had the logo of one of his sponsors splashed across the back. They watched the surf for a second. The rooster tails created an awesome show, the floodlights giving the white foam and black water a movie-reel intensity. Every third wave threw off just enough sea spray to send a sticky sheen across her legs, just below the hem of her yellow skirt. She clutched her sweater closer and sipped her coffee.

"You're not letting me leave?" she asked playfully.

Fin glanced back at Tamara asleep on the couch. "There's no way in hell I'm going to be caught alone with my boss's wife passed out in my living room. So, no."

"You need a chaperone?"

"Well." He took a sip from his mug and thought about that. "Not with her." He avoided Giselle's eyes.

A breeze blew up off the navy water, and she pulled her sweater tighter.

"I'm not sure how Fox is going to react to all this," he said. "I have the sense he's either going to beat the crap out of me or fire me."

"It isn't your fault."

He gave a humorless laugh. "I'm sure when he asked me to take her to Javier's, he didn't mean for me to get her plastered and running through downtown Laguna."

"She's a grown woman, Fin. It's not your fault," she repeated.

He took a sip of his drink and eyed the water as if he weren't entirely certain.

"Is Fox really cheating on her?"

Fin gave a snort of disgust. "There's no way that's true. She just had too much to drink. I never met a man more crazy about a woman."

A hum slipped from Giselle's lips, but she realized it sounded wistful. She cut it short and quickly took a sip of coffee.

Fin glanced at her. "Maybe all marriages start out that way." His voice sounded conversational, but the comment was laden with a question.

"I only have experience with one," Giselle said.

"So did yours?"

She winced. Fin may not speak all that much, but when he did, he zeroed right in on what he wanted to know. She took another sip so she could compose herself before answering.

"I don't recall that stage, actually." She kept her voice prim and emotionless.

"Tell me about it," Fin prompted.

"You don't want to know about my marriage." Giselle couldn't decide whether Fin was flirting in some odd way or teasing her. All she knew was that talking about her marriage made her feel like a terrible failure.

"Maybe I do." His eyes met hers. But, instead of pressing, he turned back toward the ocean. They watched the navy water wash in below. "You fascinate me," he finally said.

Giselle gave a little laugh. "I'm so far from fascinating, you can't even imagine."

"Try me."

She shook her head. What did he want to know? Anything she told him would only make the distance between them elongate—dull stories of her laundry days and carpool runs to contrast nicely with his life of international travel. But, on the other hand, maybe it would be good. It would force her into reality, reminding her that all those glances from him, all those lingering stares and brushes against her thigh, were only temporary. Deliciously temporary, of course, but only temporary. She would be out of his thoughts as soon as Veronica showed up with her belly-button ring.

"I have a pot of basil on my windowsill that I've thought about more this week than would be considered normal by most human beings." She drew a resigned breath. "I spend hours in the grocery store every week, comparing the sugar content of yogurt for Coco. I have a cupboard full of sippy cups but I don't own a single shot glass with the name of a Vegas showroom on it. And I've never been to South Africa. Or Brazil. Or China."

Fin nodded slowly and stared at the ocean. She was sure she'd lost him now. He probably couldn't even think of a response to such a boring life.

"How do you spend Thanksgiving?" he asked.

She blinked back her surprise at the random question and shrugged. "The normal way, I guess. We have people over—friends, or family if they're in town."

He nodded. "How many people?"

"Six? Eight sometimes?"

"Do you ever spend it with Lia or your mom?"

"I have, though not in many years."

Fin nodded again. "She's invited me a couple of times—to your mom's. I always wanted to go. I picture a big table, with a lot of people. Turkey in the center. Napkins, candles." He smiled, embarrassed. "I never did that. Even at Ronny's. It's always been around the O'Neill Classic, or the Reef Hawaiian Pro, so ever since I was a kid, I've been on a plane on Thanksgiving—lately playing Scrabble on my phone."

Giselle noted the sadness in Fin's face and wondered again whether that was what she'd been glimpsing this whole time—a longing for family? For normalcy?

"So when did you know you were in love with your ex?" he asked.

Telling him all this seemed embarrassing. She had loved the furtive peeks Fin was taking at her body; she loved the way he looked at her with half-lidded eyes. Revealing how unsexy and unromantic her marriage was would certainly make all that go away.

"I can't imagine why you want to know any of this," she said.

He nodded and wrapped his arms around his widespread knees. "I shouldn't."

A few black waves rolled in, misting them with residual spray. He waited until the sound retreated and then went on as if the conversation had never broken:

"I'm just asking because when I kissed you, that one time, you let out this little sound that made me think you're the kind of woman who likes some passion in her men. And I've been trying not to think about that sound, or what I can do to hear it again, but I was just wondering."

Giselle tried to swallow. *Passion?* In *men*? She didn't have "men." She had "a man." And passion seemed like something that belonged in Humphrey Bogart movies.

"That's"—she sputtered for an answer—"really . . . *none* of your business."

He smiled into the ocean and gave her an acquiescing nod. "You're right."

They watched the water in silence for a moment, and Giselle tugged her sweater around her shoulders. "So you've been putting me on the spot for the last ten minutes. I think it's my turn."

He regarded her warily.

"You said you'd never been married, but have you ever had a serious relationship? Been in love?"

The water demanded his attention again. "No."

"You've *never* been in love?"

"I don't believe so."

"Tell me the closest you came."

He shook his head.

"C'mon, Fin."

He laughed. He was clearly uncomfortable, but he didn't look like he wanted to shut down. He simply looked like he wasn't used to talking this way.

"There was a surf instructor, once, I met in Hawaii," he finally said. "She was Oregonian. Amazing surfers come from Oregon. Anyway, I liked her a lot."

Giselle waited for more, but he took another sip from his mug and redirected his attention back to the surf.

"That's *it*?"

He glanced at her and shrugged.

"That's your big 'love story'? That's not even going to get you a Hallmark card. What made you think you were in love with her?"

He thought about that for a while, as if the question had never occurred to him. "She was . . . smart. Confident. Older than me." He winked. "Made me want to be around her a lot. She was teaching some students, and I was at a meet. She cheered me on. That was strange, and different. Nice."

"So what happened? Did you stay together?"

He smirked. "I didn't say we were 'together,' Giselle. It was just a surf meet. It ended on a Sunday, and she went her way and I went mine."

"You never stayed in touch?"

"Nah."

A wave of sadness swept through Giselle, imagining Fin on the plane on Thanksgiving, imagining him coming home to an empty house every time he traveled. It seemed as if he went out of his way to stay cut off from everyone—even this Oregonian woman he felt came the closest to representing love.

"Were you ever in love with Jennifer?" she asked.

"No."

At her look of skepticism, he shook his head. "She was

always seeing someone off and on. She wouldn't tell me who he was. She was embarrassed because he was married—some high-powered hotshot—and he'd told her he was leaving his wife, but of course he wasn't, and she didn't want her brother or her parents to know. I was always just a friend. Kind of a mentor. I taught her how to surf."

"What happened to her?" Giselle asked hesitantly.

Fin didn't answer right away but brushed some stray sand off his bare ankle and then went back to watching the ocean. "We were filming for some sponsors," he finally said. "It was a foreign company—Kimiko, which makes wet suits—and Jennifer and I rode for them once or twice, along with a couple guys from the Men's Tour. They wanted us to do a little surfing for a commercial in Tahiti, and we—the guys—were in Teahupoo for the Billabong Pro, so Jennifer flew in to meet us there. I told her it would be a good idea."

He watched another wave turn to foam as it rolled under them, slapping against the rocks.

"She was acting strange—almost as if she were off balance on certain sets. I mean, she's Pro–All American, Grand Am Hawaii; she won the Australian Open twice—she's not an off-balance surfer. I taught her. And I've traveled with her for years. And that's the thing that pisses me off: I *saw* her looking off. And I didn't think it through, or say anything.

"So a big set came in, and I looked back, kind of challenging her. I wanted her to take it. So she paddled out, and I saw it again. It was this odd hesitation she had, and this leaning to the left. And then . . . that's the last I saw of her."

Giselle's heart began pounding. . . . To lose someone, right in front of you . . .

Fin shrugged. "I was so wrapped up, you know—I was scrambling for the next set, and I wasn't watching out for her, and I was just 100 percent focused on getting the next wave. By the time I took another few waves, and watched the other two guys—no one noticed she was gone. We assumed she'd called it a day.

"But when I came back onshore, an Aussie kid named Booker was running down the sand and said he'd found her board, broken apart, against the rocks. We found her about twenty minutes later. In a pile of boulders."

"Oh, Fin."

He shifted his position and stared at the Pacific's unending blackness. It resembled the edge of a cliff, dropping to an abyss.

"I haven't told anyone this in a long time," he said.

She touched his shoulder. He leaned away casually.

Giselle's stomach clenched to see Fin's pain. For someone who had so few people in his life, losing someone—especially someone he felt protective of, and responsible for, and losing her in such a senseless, violent way—must have been devastating. She rubbed his shoulder, but he reached for his mug so he could get out from under her touch.

"I'm not trying to get your sympathy, Giselle."

"I know."

He stared at the rooster tails shooting out from the rocks. "It was called as a coroner's case. They found drugs in her system. Xanax."

How awful for Jennifer Andre. Giselle pulled her sweater tighter.

"But it was complicated, being in a foreign country, to open an investigation. Her parents just wanted her flown home. Everyone was left with a lot of questions."

"What do you think happened?"

"I'm not sure. Some people take it recreationally, but she didn't do drugs that I knew of. Although I wouldn't necessarily know. She'd been with her married asshole boyfriend a long time, and she and I didn't see each other much anymore. But why she would take anything right before that set?" He stared out at the ocean, as if the answer might be there, always elusive.

"The fact that she wanted to talk is what bothers me—if I'd just talked to her, or just listened . . ."

"Fin, you can't blame yourself for that."

He pressed his fingers against his eyelids. "I should have been watching her. I should have trusted my instincts."

"It's not fair to put all that responsibility on yourself."

He shook his head.

"Who was the man she was seeing?"

"He never stepped forward. Bastard. I never knew who it was. She knew I didn't approve, so we didn't talk about it much."

A wave hit the rocks right then and they leaned back. The mist settled around them, and Fin wiped his forearms. He watched her hands run down her legs and then cleared his throat and averted his gaze. "Giselle, how the hell do you get me to talk so much?"

She met his vague smile with a gentle one of her own. "Doesn't it feel good? To just let it out sometimes?"

He stared at her for a beat too long—one that moved from comfort, to trust, into a point of intimacy. He seemed to be searching for something in her eyes—some kind of answer, or maybe asking some kind of question. "Yeah," he finally said.

She looked away first, and a comfortable silence swelled. Giselle enjoyed the sound of the water, roaring up and hissing back. A strip of light shimmered against the ripples.

"Moon is full," she said.

He murmured an agreement. "Strawberry Moon."

Her eyes widened. "How did you know that?"

"I study moon and tide charts every day, Giselle. They're the homepage of my laptop."

"But how did you know it was the Strawberry Moon?"

He frowned. "That, I'm not sure. I learned that at some point—probably one of the Zen surfers."

"My dad taught me."

"Why does your dad study moons?"

"He teaches Native American literature. He always said the full moon is the best time for change."

He stared at her for a long time; then they listened to four or five good waves. Suddenly, she felt his fingers touch hers on the concrete.

She jumped, and gasped.

"That's the sound I was talking about. The one I'm not supposed to think about anymore." His body unfolded. "Come with me."

He moved through the glass doors, his heels thudding against the hardwood floor, but turned abruptly when he realized she wasn't following. After hesitating a few seconds, he walked back and held out his hand.

"I'm not going to jump you, Ms. Underwood. As tempting as that sounds. I just want to show you something."

She took his hand uncertainly. He lifted her from the concrete ledge, and she followed him down the hall, past the passed-out Tamara, and into his bedroom.

Seventeen

Giselle hesitated in the bedroom doorway.

The room had the same feel as the front of the house—sort of a retro Polynesian look, with dark woods set off by white walls and linens. A bamboo fan hung over the bed, moving ocean air through the room. A desk and dark cabinetry ran the entire length of one wall, and a row of photos ran along the connecting wall—all framed in dark bamboo against the stucco. The photos were black-and-white, of surfers from other eras with their boards, sometimes with vintage cars.

"Who decorated your house?"

He found whatever he'd been searching for in a walk-in closet, and emerged with six or seven loose eight-by-tens in his hand. "You can tell I didn't?"

"It just seems awfully detailed for a man to do."

"Well, you're right about that. I had a designer do it."

She raised an eyebrow.

"That's when the money was rolling in, and my agent suggested it. What do you think?" He surveyed the room himself. "Would it impress someone like you?"

"What do you mean 'someone like me'?"

Fin just smiled. "Here are some photos I wanted to show

you. Remember I was talking about the perfect moments? These are some."

Giselle remained near the door while they studied the photos. He was the sole surfer in each one and looked spectacular. He pointed out the "corner" of the wave, or where the "wall" was. A few of the photos were close-up, his face fierce and focused. In some, he was crouched so low it was hard to imagine him balanced, coming through a tube of water, right at the camera.

"That was on the cover of *Surfer* magazine." He handed her the next photo, in which he was hanging in the air over a wave, sideways, the board seeming glued to his feet, his tan arm flexed as he gripped the side. The sun glinted off the ocean in diamonds all around him.

In another, he was doing one of the "soul arches" she'd seen Kino do. His board shorts hung low on his hips, and his body arched back in a work of art.

"That was in Levanto, Italy, for *Longboarder* magazine. This one was in Sri Lanka." He handed her the last one of him doing the soul arch, the water crystalline and blue behind him, the sky a saffron yellow.

"These are gorgeous," she said. "I thought you didn't like to have your photo taken?"

"I don't mind having my photo taken doing something *real*."

The whirling of the ceiling fan and the gentle ticking of a clock were the only sounds in the room as she took her time gazing at each of the photos, taking in his handsome face, the sexy flex of his forearms, the muscles in his thighs, the ridges of muscle across his stomach—then marveling that it was all within touching distance right now. Her breath quickened.

Fin leaned against the desk that ran along the one side of the room, his heavy arms crossed, watching her.

Giselle didn't know what to do with his perusal. She shuffled the photos, then glanced around the room. A wall of framed shots caught her eye. "Who are these?"

Fin's gaze dragged away from her. "My parents." He pushed up from the desk. "That's my mom in a competition she won in the seventies, and that's my dad, accepting a trophy for the Honolulu competition. This is both of them, in Tahiti."

The photos were all black-and-white—perhaps orchestrated by the designer—but Fin's parents appeared timeless anyway.

They looked like teenagers, with a tiny Fin between them—a towheaded, wide-eyed boy sitting in the crook of his mother's legs, with her chin on his hair. Giselle couldn't imagine how a mother could ever leave her child in another country, but in this picture she almost looked like a child herself—nineteen at best.

"Do you miss them?"

Fin dropped his gaze. The sound of the clock ticked clearly again into the silence.

"Coco's lucky to have you," he finally said. "You're a good mother."

Tears pricked her eyes at the compliment. It was one she always longed to hear, and coming from the least likely source she could imagine. She searched for something to focus on so he wouldn't see her tearing up again. She shuffled through the photos and selected the two she liked best. One was the soul arch.

"Can you scan these for me?"

Fin frowned. "Why?"

"So I can remember my week here, with you."

He stared at her a long time, not seeming to know how to react to that. He pushed them back toward her. "You can have them."

"But these are your perfect moments."

"There'll be more."

"Because you're always looking for the next one."

He smirked. "I am."

"I'll scan them and send them back," she whispered.

A wild rush of despair swept through her, similar to the art show only more intense, causing her heart to accelerate in an out-of-control way. She hadn't had an anxiety attack in a long time. She brought her hand to her chest. Usually they came on when she was terrified, like the first week she'd been alone with the newly born Coco. Or the week Roy had left.

"What's wrong?" He was trying to duck his head down to see her face.

"Fin, I—I'm having a great time with you." Giselle could hear the apology in her voice.

He laughed with discomfort. "I'm having a great time with you, too, Giselle." He said it in a polite way, the way you speak to a child.

She was anxious about missing him. He made her feel accepted in a way she hadn't felt in years—so unlikely, yet there it was. A twenty-eight-year-old pro surfer in California, making her feel she was good enough, smart enough, beautiful enough, and even a good enough mother—when it was all she'd been looking for from everyone she knew all her adult life. When she glanced up, he was frowning in confusion.

"I mean—I'm having a *really* great time with you, and I don't know why I can't . . . let myself . . ." She shook her head. She knew what she wanted. She whispered the next part: "Why I can't let myself have *casual sex*."

Fin seemed to find that amusing. He took the photos from her and walked them back to the desk. "Giselle . . ." He straightened some papers, then leaned against the desktop. "This is a dangerous conversation."

"I really think—"

"It's not a huge mystery. You can't let yourself have casual sex because you play for keeps. And that's great." He gave a rueful laugh. "It's healthy. Just stay that way."

"But maybe I want . . ." She wrestled for what that might be.

"What?" he asked, frowning.

What *did* she want? What Fin had said earlier—that had touched on something that felt true. "Maybe I want passion, like you said." She whispered it. She was shocked she even let it slip off her tongue, but there it was. Between them. Floating like truth. "Maybe I want to be . . ."

The clock ticked off the seconds while she tried to formulate what it was.

"What?" He stepped closer.

"Desired."

Fin's chest rose and fell rapidly under his navy T-shirt. He dropped his head back. "Giselle," he whispered. "What are you doing to me here?"

"I'm not trying to do anything," she said. "I'm just confused and I . . ."

She turned toward the door. She didn't mean to torment him. But before she could reach it, his hand snapped around her wrist. "Listen," he rasped.

When she turned, he let go and stepped away from her. He took a deep breath. "You *are* desired. Half those boys at Rabbit's stare at you as if you're dessert. And, on the other end of the age spectrum, I think you had Mr. Turner's heart-rate monitor up a few notches. So if you think you've lost that somewhere, don't. And if your ex forgot to tell you, he's an idiot. You're beautiful. And sexy. And those lips . . . You're the type of woman who will *always* be desired. And I—well, I haven't made it a secret that I've been desiring you since the second I laid eyes on you."

He took a hesitant step toward her.

"But I'm standing here thinking you want something more than that. I'm thinking you want to be in love, maybe, long-term. Or married again. Or maybe you're looking for a good father for Coco."

He searched her face, scrutinizing it for his answer.

"So I'll ask you, one more time . . ." His voice was quiet, tinged with something that sounded like desperation. "I'm asking what you want. Because if you say you want a long-term relationship, I'm going to spin you on your heel and march you right back out of this bedroom, because I can't give you that. I'm not equipped for long-term.

"But if you say all you want is to be desired, or to know how much you're desired, I'm going to lock that door and hope to God that Fox doesn't come back for the next couple of hours. Because *that* I can show you."

Giselle stood very still, worried that even the slightest movement would upset the equilibrium of the room. She took in his rock-solid shoulders, his darkening eyes, his sun-kissed hair, and wondered whether she could touch him, have part of him, and then go nonchalantly back to real life. Would one night of passion help her get her life back on track? Was that all she'd been missing?

She could tell he knew the answer already. He turned to collect the photos. He seemed already resigned, already reeling himself in.

The old Giselle, she knew, would continue to wring her hands and say yes, she wanted the long-term relationship. It was what she was supposed to want. It was what everyone told her to want.

But the new Giselle would not.

The new one would lock the door.

* * *

Fin heard the click of the lock, and stood there dumbly for a second, wondering whether he'd heard it right.

Did she just—? He turned his head.

Holy fuck, she did.

He faced her, but then caught her terrified smile, and wondered what he had just unleashed here. Giselle had some kinks in her that she seemed to feel the need to work out, and here he was—lucky bastard—the recipient of her newfound depravity.

But guilt rose like a tide. He hung back to see where she wanted to go with this. "I guess that's my answer," he said.

"I guess it is." Her breasts began rising and falling rapidly.

And damned if his heart wasn't pounding a hundred miles an hour. He couldn't remember the last time he'd felt nervous about touching a woman, but there it was. With Giselle. Damn.

"I can't be anything but a lay right now, Giselle." His voice was husky. He hardly recognized it.

"It's okay," she said on a sweet whisper.

"This is a one-night stand."

"I know."

He closed his eyes against the fragility of it all.

She wasn't ready for this. One-night stands were good for raw sex; good to scratch that itch; good for men like him who didn't want anything more than that. But Giselle would feel hurt by the coldness this always ended with. She was coming off a relationship that sounded like it lived and died in coldness—this was not going to make anything better for her.

And Lia was going to kill him.

But even as he was coming to those very logical conclusions, and knowing he didn't want to be the jerk in this scenario, his brain was short-circuiting at the sight of her trembling fingertips going to the top button of that damned sweater. He swallowed hard. He was caught between his own base desires—amplified, tenfold, for some reason with this woman—and the stable, responsible person, the better man, he wanted to be.

"You won't be hurt by this?" he reiterated, his voice barely coming out. He knew he was rationalizing already—the desperate man's last resort.

But the way she shook made him feel bad. As much as he

wanted to see her naked, touch her, be in her, he didn't want her staring at him with that terrified expression all night.

She stalled at the button she'd been about to undo while her smile began to dissolve at his last question. His baser side batted twelve good curse words through his head for his idiocy.

"Because once we get started," he went on, hoping she'd continue. He wanted that button undone. He wanted that cleavage revealed. He wanted her breasts in his hands, his lips buried there, her clothes coming off. ". . . I don't know if I'll be able to stop."

Well, that was fucking true. What if Fox decided to come banging on the front door about now? How was he going to stop here? Did he even turn off the torches outside? Did he close the slider door? Did he—

His brain stalled as Giselle undid her top button. It was exactly the way he'd imagined it, from that very first night he sat with her on the sand—that primness, juxtaposed with a simmering sexuality that was coming from beneath a very shallow surface, very close to the top. She was so curious, so willing. . . .

His erection pressed hard against his shorts. His glance swept her dress for a zipper or button or some way he could get the whole thing off her in about five seconds. But he stopped. This needed to be her idea.

His breathing went shallow, and a line of sweat broke out along his hairline. Watching Giselle strip for him—wriggling out of that dress, stepping out of her underpants—would be something he didn't want to miss. But given their situation here, this might be their one and only time together. He didn't want to rush a single second.

He clenched his back teeth and focused on keeping his feet planted on the wood.

"Are you sure you still want me?" She seemed uncertain.

"Gi*selle*." He tried to keep his voice in a gentle reprimand— the one he used when she doubted her beauty—but it came out on a rasp, as if he didn't have enough air. "Can you see how hard I am for you right now?"

Her eyes darted around, not landing anywhere near his shorts. He bit back a smile. "I'm not faking that."

Nodding hesitantly, she finished wriggling her sweater

over her elbows, giving him a nice jiggle of her breasts while the sweater slid to the floor.

He caught his breath. He'd been right about that top. It had a sort of Marilyn Monroe appeal to it and made her breasts look very, very ... *full* ... and very, very ... What was the word? ... *Touchable*. Shit, his brain was giving out. He might not make it through this strip show. His palms began to itch.

She reached for the hem of the billowy skirt and pulled it up. He swallowed hard. Beneath, he could see milky-white thigh, a color he didn't see often on the beach. A color he didn't see often at all, in fact. A color that hinted at unexplored secrets.

Most of the women he'd been with were coming on to him at this point—experienced, aggressive, ready to move things to the next level they could all predict. He'd never had a woman staring at him like this from across the room—eyes wide, unsure, trusting, hopeful, eager to please, eager to *be* pleased.

His breathing went shallow. He had to close his eyes for a second.

When he opened them, she was wriggling off her panties from under the skirt, bending forward and giving him a glorious view of her breasts almost falling out of that top. Her skirt fell back over the part of her body he most wanted to see, the one he wanted to touch, the one he wanted to be buried in. . . . She delicately pushed the lace-trimmed scrap of underwear to the side with the pointed toe of her shoe, then leaned against the door.

"There," she whispered.

He laughed to himself. They were nowhere near "there." He glanced at the panties on the floor and swallowed hard, again, imagining the bareness underneath that skirt. It was all he could do not to rush her, run his hands up under the fabric, slip his fingers inside her, take her right against the door. He took another step, although he didn't mean to.

"That's not 'there,' Giselle," his throat scratched out. "I'm not standing here, hanging on by a thread, to see you in a dress." He tried to smile to lighten the desperation in his voice, but a flicker of nervousness came across her face.

"You first," she whispered.

"I'll be happy to strip for you, too, when it's my turn. But please don't deny me this pleasure." His voice had a despair laced around the edges that he found embarrassing. "You hold all the power here, Giselle. Look what you do to me. This is desire."

Her gaze finally fell to the tent in his shorts. She nodded. The realization seemed to give her strength, and her fingers went to the *V* of her dress, running toward the crease of her cleavage, exactly where he wanted to be. He imagined kissing her down through that *V*, his lips moving against soft skin, his hands running up her legs. . . . His mouth went dry. *Hang on, man. . . .*

She reached up to untie the dress at her neck. "You have to turn the lights off," she whispered.

"No," he managed to choke out.

"Fin."

"No."

She bit her lip. "Please."

He shook his head. "Do you always have sex with the lights out?"

She hesitated for what felt like an eternity, then nodded a little.

"That's your mistake number one," he said. "Or . . . well, your ex's mistake. I don't make that kind of mistake. I want to see you. And if you want to feel desired, all you have to do is watch my eyes." He took another forbidden step. "Watch how crazy you're going to make me with every piece of your clothing that hits the floor."

Her eyes became glossy with something he'd never seen before. Maybe it was her own desire. Maybe it was a challenge. Maybe it was something deeper, something like trust. It made him want to reach out and wrap his arms around her, protect her from guys like him. So he held back, his breath animalistic, his hands desperate, his erection pressing. He listened to the clock ticking in the background and waited for Giselle Underwood to show him her white body and invite him in.

She started to undo the gigantic belt that was the same color as the dress. Since it looked like part of the fabric, he hoped it would let the whole thing unravel.

As he stood dumbly, his hands just inches away from ravishing her, a powerful bang exploded in the front room.

Breaking glass shattered the silence.

The roar of the ocean got louder.

Giselle's face went white as she scrambled for the lock, and Fin lunged forward and yanked the door open.

CHAPTER

Eighteen

Fin was in the front room in five strides.

He whirled toward the couch where Tamara had— *Fuck*. She was gone.

He leaped over a floor lamp that had crashed to the floor, its bulb lying in bits and pieces, then rushed through the open slider and thudded down the concrete steps.

His eyes went to the rocks.

The tide pulled back and he was able to scan them, hoping he'd see something. Or hear her. Or something. *And holy fuck, where had she gone?*

His heart pounded as he ran across the wet sand, scanning the rocks and the black ocean, waiting for the next wave to roll back to see whether he could see anything in the sand. *Could she have gone in the water? How could she have moved so fast?*

He scrambled down to the foamy surf, which was wet and cold, feeling like quicksand as the tide hissed out. He ran the length of the house to make sure she hadn't gotten stuck in one of the breaker rocks. As he took in another lungful of misty air, the ocean roared behind him and the freezing night tide slammed against the backs of his legs.

"Fin?" Giselle's soft voice floated on a pocket of mist behind him. She was on the stairs.

"Get back up there," he yelled over his shoulder, still moving along the rocks, pulling through the water as the tide retreated, scanning them first, then scouting the ocean.

Giselle hadn't moved.

"Now!" he yelled at her.

Satisfied there wasn't a body in the rocks, he turned and ran into the ocean, scanning the black horizon. The floodlights illuminated about fifty yards, but beyond that was a complete abyss.

A tiny voice—small, far away—drifted toward him. He whirled to see a figure in the water, bobbing in the darkness, about forty feet out, sputtering for air.

Tamara!

She floated in the darkness like ripped seaweed, getting swept back by powerful waves that were rushing out, fast and furious, in a riptide.

His voice was meant to let her know someone was there for her, but he had the sense it was getting caught on the ocean wind and thrown back at him. He sloshed through the surf, trying to find a spot deep enough to dive. She went under again, but she was still about twenty feet away when the next wave came rising up behind her like a black hand—curling over the top of her, its white foam wrapping like menacing fingers—

Fin opened his mouth to yell, just as it crashed down, roaring.

Tamara disappeared.

"Tamara!" The white foam slammed him the other way, but the water was deep enough now to dive into. He threw himself in, his head exploding from the stabbing cold. He paddled hard, then popped up for a deep breath. When he saw the next wave, black as night, rising like the fists of hell, he dipped under and let it roll over the top of him as he dove toward the sandy bottom. It was so black under there—eerie and silent, like death.

He came up for breath and searched frantically. He'd been swimming in the right direction, but it was hard to tell which way the waves would carry her. She could have been anywhere, tossed around like debris in this raging tide. He twisted to find her, just in time to see the next wall come up in front of him—black glass, rising. He threw himself underneath, but he knew he'd been late seeing it. The ocean punished his negligence by tossing him to the bottom—sand scratching his face and arms—until he got his footing again.

"Tamara!" he finally hollered, taking a lungful of seawater.

He twisted his body in time to see her—about twenty-five feet away—getting swept farther out. His arms and legs felt attacked by nails, the water so cold, but he pushed forward. She didn't appear to be moving. Fin drew a deep breath through frozen lungs and lunged again.

He caught another wall, rising, getting ready to rage, right in front of him, and—*Damn! He just needed one minute*. But he had to go under again, this time paddling hard in the iciness to propel him in her direction.

When he came up on the other side of the wave, she was about fifteen feet away, getting batted. Her movements were labored. He knew from talking with her that she was a strong swimmer, but this tide was powerful. The blackness was disorienting. And alcohol in your system never helped.

He threw himself toward her—closing the gap between them to about ten feet—but the ocean lifted her out of reach. The next swell propelled him closer and he grabbed. He caught her hair, then her arm. He gripped fiercely, but had to bring them both under while the next huge wave crashed over their heads, and he felt the white water hammer over his head. He knew he was going to lose her—the ocean was pulling her the other way—but he held on as best he could and managed to keep his fingers manacled around her upper arm. Sand slashed their skin. He felt her slip. But the water retreated, and he was able to shoot up for air on the other side. He spouted water, his lungs feeling like knives were slashing them, but stunned that he still had a grasp on her. He had about a quarter of a minute before the next wave. He yanked her toward him and got her into a lifeguard's hold, across her chest and under her arms.

She fought. It was a natural reaction. But he held firmly, the way he'd been taught.

"It's okay." His voice rasped on a breath. They were in a riptide, the water below rushing off to sea. He'd have to pull her farther out, just to get out from the wave breaks so they could swim parallel to shore. He began lugging her, and she gurgled, clawing at his forearm.

"It's okay," he breathed into her ear. "We have to move. To the right. Riptide is"—he caught his breath—"right underneath us."

He wanted to go out about another ten feet, "behind" the waves. There wouldn't be any breaks to bat them around.

But the next wave rose. He hollered for her to hold her breath, and she screamed again, a series of "no's" that broke his heart, but she finally gulped for air and held her breath. He pulled her under. He knew that was the last one until they could get behind the waves. All he could do was hope she'd hold her breath and survive. She went limp under his arm.

He sputtered back to the surface, yanking her with him, and searched her face. For a second, he thought he'd drowned her. But she coughed and reached back, trying to grab his hair.

At first, he welcomed the battery, grateful she was moving at all, but then her grasping was pulling him under.

"Tamara," he tried, grabbing her wrist. It was impossible to hold her, fight her, and paddle at the same time. "It's okay," he shouted above the waves. "It's okay now, Tamara; we're okay." He pulled her close. The water calmed as they floated to a place behind the waves. An eerie silence fell. Her body stilled with it.

"It's okay; it's okay; it's okay," he whispered, over and over into her ear. His breath caught through half the litany, but she was calming. The ocean bobbed them up and down. She stopped thrashing and clutched his arm.

"Hang on," he sputtered, taking a small, smacking wave of salt water and choking it out. He wanted her to catch her breath so she could swim on her own, but there was no time. He had to get them out of this thing or they'd both be under.

He swam as hard as he could to the left, dragging her like a corpse. He glanced at the shore, which was painfully far away, and wondered whether they were going to make it.

"Tamara, stop . . . kicking." He took a deep breath. "Go limp."

She did. He breathed a sigh of relief and paddled for about thirty feet. *I cannot let her die out here.* The ocean settled under him. They were out of the riptide. But damn, he was exhausted. They coughed together as lapping water slapped their faces. His arms were lead. His feet had weights attached.

The smaller backwater waves threw another mouthful of seawater down his throat, but he coughed it out and turned his face toward her. His arms could not lift her, but he had another thought—a deep, ugly thought from the recesses of his memory, of Jennifer, limp on the rocks, her black hair in clumps around her face, her mouth blueish ash—and he found some strength to pull Tamara upward. He slipped his arm across her chest and began to pull—kicking, paddling, desperately pulling through the icy water, moving them toward shore.

The last of his energy got them to the wave breaks, where the tide began pushing them in the right direction, but they had to deal with crashes and foam. The next few waves battered them, and Tamara was starting to fight again, but at least he could use the momentum to let the waves drag them to shore. He paddled with all the strength he had left. When he got to the point where his feet could touch the ground, he sputtered and stood, wobbly. His knees wanted to give out, but he got Tamara to her feet and helped her across the sand. Her legs were crumpling beneath her.

Suddenly Fox was there, reaching toward her—*where had he come from?*—and Giselle rushed forward, too—*damn it, hadn't he told her to go back?*—and they both fell toward him, getting their calves and thighs wet, and reached for Tamara, dragging her back toward the beach stairs, limp and sputtering.

Fin bent over with his hands on his knees, trying to get some air back into his lungs, and next thing he knew Giselle was back, her arm slipped around his waist, pulling him the rest of the way onto the beach.

"You shouldn't . . . be . . . out here," he sputtered. He tried to push her away, but she clung voraciously and dragged him out of the water. He had to be heavy on her. When they were out of the shore break, he went down on one knee.

She knelt with him, and he turned, for some reason, and kissed the top of her head.

He felt as if she were the one lost. Panic seized and froze his muscles for a second—as if he almost lost something he really wanted—although he was confused about what it was. He inhaled gulps of air and tried to speak, but it was too painful, so he simply snapped the water off his face and sat in the sand, knees up, dropping his head into his forearms.

Giselle leaned against him and wrapped her fingers around his arm. He thought she might be crying.

He had lost Jennifer. He'd let her down. But there were others in his life that he didn't have to let down. It wasn't a chain reaction. He could break the cycle, come back from the dead.

He leaned over and kissed the top of Giselle's head again, then settled his hand over hers, pressing the turquoise ring between them.

He knew who he might start with.

The smell of chocolate and strong coffee mingled in the kitchen as they sat around the small table, mugs between their palms. Only Fox was still on his feet, pacing. He threw fiery glances around the room, as if he weren't sure where he wanted them to land. Mostly they landed on Tamara, much to Giselle's dismay.

"I still don't understand what went on here," he said.

Fin glanced up tiredly. "That's enough, Fox."

Giselle pressed her mug between her palms. They'd spent the last half hour getting Tamara warmed up and changed. Fin had given her an enormous sweatshirt and pajama bottoms that she clutched at her waist. While Fin warmed up in the shower and changed, Giselle searched for her underpants. She shuddered to think where or when they might turn up. For now, she returned to the kitchen and sat with Tamara, a blanket over her yellow skirt, warming her thighs and calves.

Her heartbeat had slowed, but still had not found its normal rhythm. Watching Fin and Tamara get swept farther and farther away was like witnessing death right before her eyes. She'd never been more terrified in her life.

Fox obviously felt the same way. He leaned against the kitchen pillar, his face ashen.

"What *happened*?" he asked again, exasperated that no one was ready to talk. He marched into the living room for the tenth time, studying the blanket on the couch, inspecting the broken lamp Tamara must have knocked over on her way out.

Fin moved into the kitchen and filled another novelty mug with water. "She thinks you're cheating on her," he finally said.

"*Cheating* on her?" Fox twisted toward Tamara. "Is that true?"

Tamara stared into her coffee—tired, weary, half-drowned, defeated, embarrassed, barely sober. The cuffs of Fin's pajama bottoms swam around her bare feet. With her face scrubbed clean of her makeup and polish, she looked like the vulnerable human Giselle herself always felt like.

"You're always leaving me." Tamara's voice was small and far away.

Fin walked the water back to Tamara with two aspirin. "You're going to need this," he muttered. "Sorry about the profanity on the mug."

"I'm not *leaving* you." Fox moved toward the table.

Fin slid quickly out of the way.

"I just . . . *worry*," Tamara said.

The ocean sounded far away as the four of them huddled in the dining room, Tamara sniffling and Fox delivering apologetic kisses into her bangs. Giselle stole a glance at Fin. She couldn't tell whether he was touched by the scene or relieved it was over. Mostly he looked grim.

"I don't know whether to give you a medal of honor or beat you senseless," Fox said to Fin, without any animosity. He drew Tamara closer to his chest.

"Don't say that," Tamara said, sniffling. She pulled away from Fox and turned toward Fin, her hand clenched at her waist to hold the pajamas up. "Thank you." Her eyes became moist. "This was my fault, and you were . . . *amazing*."

Fin blinked hastily. He started to say something, but before he could, Tamara's chair scraped across the floor, and she threw her arms around his neck.

Abruptly, she removed herself and faced her husband. "This is *not* Fin's fault. I drank too much. I was going down to the water to be mopey, but I got caught up in that tide, and that damned water sucked me right out. And thank God for Fin."

"What the hell were you doing, going into the water?" The veins swelled in Fox's forehead. He turned toward Fin. "And where were *you*?"

"Don't blame Fin," Tamara reiterated. "I went outside because I was sad. I thought you were cheating on me because you keep having these late-night emergencies, and it seems suspicious. There was that one two weeks ago, when we got in that huge fight when you had to leave—"

"That was the Toyota thing," Fox interjected.

"I know. But then there was that Thursday, when you were out until three, and—"

"We had that event with the regional medical offices, and the awards ceremony." His voice was straining for patience. It was obvious this had been discussed ad nauseam between them.

"I know that's what you said. But then there was last Wednesday, too, with Evangeline—"

"Tamara, I have to *court* these people."

"I know, but you see this is a pattern on Wednesdays and Thursdays, and it just made me nervous. I thought tonight would be a good night to plan something with another couple, on a Wednesday, but then you—left—" Her face crumpled.

"Tam." He wrapped his arms around her.

Fin stood stiffly, eyes averted, then cleared his throat.

"Fin, listen, I'm sorry," Fox said. "You were—well, you were something out there. Really. But I saw *this*." His hand swept across the living room and the broken lamp. "I didn't know what to think. I thought of . . . Jennifer."

Fin's face turned to stone.

"But I know . . . I mean, I know you didn't . . ." Fox glanced at Giselle.

"Drug her?" Fin spit out.

"Yes."

Fin moved across the room and straightened the lamp with enough force to snap it in two.

Giselle felt something collapse inside her chest for Fin. Even those who believed him would bring Jennifer up again, unspoken thoughts hanging on tips of tongues, released when stress and pressure became too great. No wonder he wasn't able to forgive himself.

Fox moved closer to Fin and shoved his hands in his pockets. "Listen, Hensen, I know this has been a hard year for you. And I'm sorry. That was a shitty thing to say."

Fin nodded but didn't turn around. He threw an errant blanket back on the couch.

"Fin is a *hero*," Giselle announced. As soon as everyone turned to stare at her, she felt a wave of horror. She sounded like an idiot.

But Fin turned last and set her with a shocked stare.

"He saves these women, and cares about their safety," she went on. She knew she sounded like a simpleton, or—at best—a groupie, but she wanted to make sure everyone saw the obvious. "He is more responsible than most men I know, and he takes on everyone else's problems. But these are *grown women*. He's not responsible for watching them."

"I've been telling him that," Tamara said. "Giselle's right." She turned toward Fox. "Fin isn't responsible for babysitting me. I think you owe him a bigger apology."

A strange understanding seemed to pass between the two men. Fox nodded, mollified, then offered a hand. Fin stared at it for a couple of seconds before shaking it.

Tamara walked over to pick up her purse, the pajama cuffs dragging behind her. "We should go." She stood there looking like a vagrant who managed to have a great Gucci bag. Impulsively, Giselle rushed over and threw her arms around her. Tamara might be a little wild and crazy, but, for some reason, Giselle adored her.

Tamara laughed and leaned toward Giselle's ear. "Hang on to that guy," she whispered. "He's got amazing arms."

She slipped her fingers through the crook of her husband's elbow. "C'mon, baby. Let's get our sitter home, and then you can show me how glad you are that I'm alive."

Nineteen

Giselle watched Fin run his hand through his hair and stare at the place in the entryway just vacated by Fox and Tamara.

"Thank you," he said over his shoulder. "For what you said."

She stared at his back. "It's important that you believe that, Fin."

He nodded but didn't turn around.

"You believe it, don't you, that you're a hero?"

"I think I have a hard time believing that." He went out to the patio, where he quenched the tiki torches with a metal snuffer. The sliding door gave a quiet *hiss* as he came back in, then snapped off the floodlights. The sea went black.

"It's how I feel about you," she said quietly.

He studied the floor for a long time, then snapped off two more lights from the kitchen. "Do you want to stay?" He didn't look at her.

Giselle swallowed. It would be strange to pick up where they left off. But she did want to stay. She wanted to hold him, actually. It was the same compulsion that made her throw her arms around Tamara. An acknowledgment that life was fragile, and that it could end for anyone, anytime. That when you found something worth hanging on to, you should hold on to it.

"Would it be weird?" she asked.

"I don't know if the night got too crazy for you."

"Was it too crazy for you?" she asked.

"Too crazy to have sex." He turned off the coffeemaker and set the carafe in the sink, then turned and caught her expression. "Kidding."

"Oh," she said, as her heart resumed beating. "I didn't . . . I didn't know. I . . ."

His low chuckle fell into the wooden floorboards. "I'm a *guy*, Giselle. Guys can always have sex."

He planted his hands on his hips and surveyed the living room to see whether he'd turned everything off. "But you . . . I don't know how this night felt for you. I don't know if you want to stay. I don't know if we were saved from ourselves, or what." He gave her a strange look, then glanced over at the sliders again. "Damn, I should have closed that. I can't believe I left it open." He glared at it as if it were his new archenemy.

"It wasn't your fault."

He moved toward it, as if to inspect the lock. "It even crossed my mind when we were in the bedroom. Not that— you know—not that my mind was wandering. I was pretty focused on what you were doing with your clothes. Or, you know, focused on where your clothes were going. But I should have come out here. If I weren't so wrapped up . . ."

"Fin." She stepped toward him. "You are *not* responsible for these women. And you're not responsible for me, or what I decide to do. Or if I want to have casual sex or not. *I* am."

His body seemed a shelter to her now, and she had a stab of courage that allowed her to step into it. She laid her hands on his chest, dragging them across his sweatshirt. She wanted to test the strength underneath. Feel its tautness. Feel the beating heart . . .

"Do you really see me as a hero?" he asked quietly.

"I do."

"I don't want to let you down."

"You're not."

"Or Lia." He frowned and shook his head, as if frustrated he couldn't make his point. His hands remained on his hips.

Giselle would have to keep the momentum going for both of them. Her fingertips continued moving across his shirt. "Lia wants what's best for me. And what's best for me right now is you. And I'm a grown woman, and can make my own decision on this."

He looked at her skeptically. "I don't want you to get hurt."

"I'm not hurting."

". . . at how temporary this is, Giselle. I actually care about you. But I can't stick around."

"I understand." Her hand made its way up his chest. It was as muscular as she'd imagined. "Fin, can you take this sweat-shirt off? I've been wondering what—"

She didn't even have time to finish the sentence. He yanked it off with amazing speed, the way he must do it when it was his turn for a set. And wow, he was stunning. A light came in from the hallway, hitting the tops of his shoulders and illu-minating the side of his face and neck. His shoulders were hard and round, his skin a glorious color of sunshine. Giselle allowed herself a thorough sweep of his pectorals, his shoul-ders, his biceps, those abs.

She ran her finger along the ridge that formed between his shoulder muscle and his arm, the one she'd seen the first day she'd spotted him.

"You were wondering what?"

"What you looked like here." Her heart was thundering. "What *this* . . . felt like . . ."

He frowned at the line she was tracing on his arm. "That's it?"

She smiled, embarrassed.

He shrugged. "I guess that's a start."

Pulling her closer, he pushed a strand of hair away from her face. "When were you wondering that?"

"The first time I saw you."

"In Rabbit's apartment?"

She nodded.

"Really? I thought you weren't paying any attention to me."

"I was." A heat rose up through her cheeks.

A chuckle rumbled in Fin's throat. "I didn't think women like you noticed guys like me."

"What's that supposed to mean?"

"A sophisticated, smart, doctor's wife like you—I didn't think you'd notice a beach bum."

As he watched her reaction, his grin went from embar-rassed to a little wolfish.

"I did," she squeaked out, dropping her gaze.

He kissed the corner of her mouth. "So we're good with this, then?"

The deepness of his voice, the smile against her mouth, the tease of his lips, were all conspiring to turn her knees to jelly already. He slid a row of kisses down her neck.

"Yes," she breathed out, giving him further access.

"Because . . ." He drew a long teasing pull to that point below her ear that curled her toes. "You were looking a little terrified earlier, if you don't mind my saying." He leaned back to gauge her reaction to that.

"Terrified?"

He nodded.

"I guess . . . you make me a little nervous. . . . I don't think . . ." She stared at her fingertips across his sculpted chest and wondered how much to admit to. "I don't think I'm very good at this."

Fin's eyebrows shot up. "At sex?"

She nodded.

"What on earth makes you think that?"

"Well . . . my ex's two affairs, mostly."

Fin pressed his lips together and looked at a point over her shoulder. "Giselle. Did we say your ex is a complete idiot? Because if we didn't agree on that yet, we should."

She let her fingertips rove across the carved canyon of his pectorals. Roy did make her feel dowdy: undesired, matronly, set out to pasture already. But here she was, in the arms of a Greek god who was staring down at her with a heat in his eyes. Maybe Roy *was* an idiot.

"He was stupid for letting you go," Fin said quietly, tucking her hair behind her ear.

She let the words float around her, along with the light touch of his fingertips and the tenderness of his voice. They were the words she'd been longing to hear.

She'd thought she'd wanted them from Roy—an admission of sorts—but now she realized how much more satisfying they were coming from a man who was looking at her like this, who was going to have her clothes in a heap on the floor and his gorgeous body wrapped around hers in another five minutes. . . .

But there was another worry pressing on her chest.

"And . . . well, I'm not perfect, Fin."

A crease formed in his forehead. "I don't expect you to be perfect."

"But you're probably used to . . . well, you know. Women like Veronica, bikini models . . ."

The crease deepened. He shook his head. "No, I'm not used to that. And besides, only nature delivers perfect. And only sometimes. The most interesting parts of nature—the imperfect leaf, the imperfect rock—are the best parts. They make you feel real, and whole, like you belong and can fit in. Because we're all imperfect."

She ran her finger down the center of his chest. This chest seemed pretty perfect to her. But she saw his point. It was exhausting trying to live up to an expectation that could never be met. Fin saw that clearly, and he didn't want to try to live up to it, either.

And he certainly wouldn't expect her to.

She smiled. "Are you calling me an imperfect rock?"

"How about an imperfect leaf? The most beautiful of all." He smiled, as if his point had been proven, and turned his attention to the finger running down his chest. "But if that finger goes any lower, this conversation is going to get harder and harder for me to continue."

She slowly dragged it down across his stomach.

His breath caught and he held her gaze in a half challenge, half reprimand. "Giselle."

She smiled and ran it farther to his waistband.

"*That's it*," he choked. He stepped into her and covered her mouth with his.

She stumbled back as he pressed into her and slammed against something sharp, which she thought might be the television wall unit. She felt with her hands to move around it, but rammed instead against the glass of one of the sliders. She could feel the night chill, trying to reach in from the other side. But Fin's mouth was warm—demanding—pulling on her lips. His biceps came up on either side of her and pinned her against the glass. She could smell coconut coming up as a tribal heat from his chest.

"I'm glad you're okay with this because I have to hear you make this sound," he whispered.

She was breathless, incapable of making sense of his words, as she tried to concentrate. "Sound?"

He broke the kiss, but kept his lips near hers, as if he weren't committed to leaving just yet. "Turn around," he muttered.

Giselle faced the slider, bringing her palms up and leaning into the glass. Fin drew them higher with one of his. Fog misted around her fingertips.

Fin tugged at the sweatshirt around her and pulled it over her head from behind. He flung it on the floor, and she shivered again—her back and shoulders exposed now from the halter top. He guided her hands back over her head and against the glass, the turquoise ring caught between them, and used his other hand to trace the valley of her back.

She shivered, dropping her head and resting her forehead against the cool slider. He stepped closer and pushed her hair up off her neck, then leaned down and kissed her, right there, just below his palm at her nape. She gasped.

"There we go," he whispered.

His mouth curved against her skin as his lips moved across her neck, delivering a row of electrical kisses that brought her to her toes. She continued to let out little gasps, rolling her shoulders against the chills he gave her. She pressed her cheek into the glass as he found every exquisite pulse point across the back of her neck and behind her ears. She couldn't stop the sounds escaping from her throat.

"Gis*elle*," he whispered, as if he were thrilled, or surprised; she couldn't tell.

She laughed, embarrassed.

"I knew you would make that sound." He kissed her again, and she gasped, and he chuckled. "But there are some other things I want to get to."

He leaned into her, his full body now pressing her harder into the glass. She could feel the length of him, aroused, and she marveled at the idea that she could elicit that reaction in this gorgeous man. He reached down for the hem of her dress, bunching it in his fist to start working it upward.

"Did you put your panties back on? Because they're coming off right now."

"I couldn't find them."

Fin stilled. "You don't have your underwear on?"

"I couldn't find them."

"You've had your underwear off all night? While we were sitting here with Fox and Tamara?"

She meant to answer again, but he'd already run his hand up her bare thigh to find out for himself, and then up and over her behind. He moaned. "God, Giselle," he breathed out.

The glass was fogged in an outline from the heat of their bodies. He got her skirt pinned against the slider so he could explore her bottom. His hand traced the shape of her behind, pushing away any fabric that dared get in the way; then he opened his palm and slid it over her hips and down her front. She sucked in her breath as he slipped his finger between her legs.

He seemed to like that sound, too.

"*This* is where I want to be," he said into her shoulder.

His mouth moved against the back of her neck, sending chills through her arms. But his fingers, now between her legs, were delivering a new level of ravishment. He parted her, and she drew in a sharp breath. He nudged her foot with his, and she spread her legs, a little, but the last vestige of her primness kept her from moving any more. The sensation was almost more than she could stand—the air swirling up from the ground, cooling where he parted her, making her feel too vulnerable, too open. He nudged wider, saying something into her ear that she couldn't begin to make sense of, and his fingers explored inside her, stroking lightly, sending spasms through every nerve ending. Her legs were going to buckle. She concentrated on breathing, not just gasping, as she leaned hard into the glass and heard the ocean roaring on the other side. His fingers went deeper.

"*God*, Fin." She didn't want him to stop. She let herself live in the emotion for a moment, focusing on the sensations that were rocking her: Cold glass. Coconut scent. Heat from his body. Hands sliding. Slick fingers. And then his thumb, pressing down from the top, drawing circles, pressing harder, finding that delicious nerve. Her legs were going to give, and she felt her own wave rush up to overcome her, like it was enveloping her in blackness. She called out—something, she didn't even know what—and then she crested, and floated,

and came down in the darkness, and pressed into the glass.
Everything else fell away.

The perfect wave.

Fin caught Giselle as she slumped forward, and resisted the
urge to breathe out *holy fuck* as he managed to remove his
fingers from her body and get her turned around and facing
him. He watched her expression—he wanted to see her eyes,
but she wouldn't meet his—so instead he lifted her so her legs
were around his waist. He wanted her in his bedroom.

He pushed her skirt up again so he could reach underneath. He couldn't believe she'd had her underwear off all
night—that was about the hottest thing he'd ever heard, from
this prim woman who could barely say the word "sex" out
loud—but now he just wanted her nakedness against him, and
he bunched the skirt against his chest so he could feel her
against his stomach. *Damn*, she was wet. As he carried her
into the bedroom, he touched her once with his fingertip,
from underneath, and she bucked against him but didn't let
go—just let out another of those breathless gasps.

He needed to get his clothes off *now*.

He shoved his sweats down with one hand, balancing her
with the other, and they were almost near the bed, but she had
her arms clasped around his neck, clinging to him as if she
couldn't let go.

"Giselle?" he said, muffled. "You okay?"

She nodded, so fastened to his body—her arms and legs
both—that he could let go with both hands and she'd still
cling. It gave him a chance to push his pants down, at least to
his thighs, and he kicked them off the rest of the way with
both of his feet and then stood naked. This was an excellent
position for both of them—if he just *sliiiiiiid* her down, just a
little, then he could press her up against that wall right there
and be inside her in—

A tiny sob interrupted his game plan.

"Giselle?"

She shook her head and buried her face in the crook of his
shoulder.

What the hell?

He held her across her back with one hand and tried to lay her on the bed, prying her arms from his neck. He got her perpendicular to the edge, resting her back onto the comforter, until she finally let go. She flung the back of her hand over her eyes before he could see them. She was definitely crying.

"What's *wrong*?"

"Nothing."

"How can you say nothing? You're crying."

"It's okay. It's nothing."

"But why are you crying? Is this—"

"*Fin*," she said sharply.

He simply stared at her.

"It's *nothing*. Seriously. I'm just . . . emotional."

"*Emotional?*"

"You could have died out there tonight. Tamara could have died. And I . . . I'm . . . happy."

He peered at her to see whether she were telling the truth. This was a new one on him. He'd never had a woman cry, like this, underneath him. And then say she was *happy*. And . . . emotional? He nodded. Okay. Maybe emotional could explain it. He was feeling something, too, that felt pretty foreign— something that smacked of . . . *gratitude*, or something. The precariousness of life. The fact that it could be over at any second. He didn't know. All he knew was that he wanted to kiss her in a thank-you kind of way, along her cheek, then down her collarbone, then along her shoulder. To thank her for not getting swept into the ocean. For being there when he came out. For wrapping her arms around him that way, on the sand. For being here, now, before he went to South Africa. . . . He just wanted to kiss every inch of her—her hair, her eyelids, her nose, her lips, her neck, her breasts. . . .

He focused on the last thought. That felt normal. Wanting to see her breasts, then rip her clothes off—*that* he was familiar with. Focusing on raw sex was much easier than focusing on the feelings that were tightening his throat.

He stood at the edge of the bed and tried to figure out the fastest shortcut. He shoved her dress up, pushing it past her waist as she wriggled her naked bottom to help him.

"Spread for me, Giselle." He wanted more of those gasps.

She hesitated. So prim. Her skirt was up by her face and she couldn't see what he was doing. She paused for what seemed like an excruciating eternity. She gave him about an eighth of an inch.

"Farther."

She gave him about another sixteenth.

He smiled and waited.

"Farther, baby."

Maybe another eighth.

She couldn't seem to move more than that. It would have to do. He brought his mouth down, between her thighs, and she about bucked off the bed when his lips made contact. *"Fiiiiiiiiinnnnnn,"* she cried out.

But he just smiled. Debauching Giselle wasn't making him feel guilty at all. He could show her desire. He had it in spades. And it was going to be a long night.

Giselle couldn't remember when one experience ended and another began, but Fin was everywhere—his mouth was everywhere; his fingers were everywhere. He undid her dress in a wild desperation, bent her into several delicious positions— over the side of the bed, across his lap, her hips high on a pillow—and explored every inch of her body with his finger- tips and lips, across her breasts, down her stomach, over her hips, between her thighs, murmuring things like, "That's what I wanted to hear," until she tingled through every raw nerve.

By the time he rolled away to reach into his nightstand for a condom, she thought she was going to combust. She squeezed her eyes shut and held her breath while he tore the packaging open with his teeth. When she opened her eyes, he was frown- ing at her.

"We're okay?" he whispered.

She gave him a smile that she hoped conveyed all the head- iness she felt. "We're more than okay." She pulled him toward her, her hands splayed across his shoulder blades.

He took her mouth again, frantically rolling on the con- dom, then hovered over her, triceps shaking, ready to enter her. His eyes opened suddenly and caught her gaze, as if he didn't mean to.

He stilled. "Giselle," he said in almost a whisper, as if something were surprising him.

It seemed some kind of question—a question he'd been trying to ask all day, but had been unable to formulate. And she didn't know what it was. But somehow she knew the answer—she simply nodded, not letting him look away.

He kissed her tenderly, then thrust, hard, catching her in a rhythm she quickly picked up. She went over the edge quickly this time, and opened her eyes to watch him—reveling in his squeezed eyes, trembling triceps, and spent glance at her, which came with a smile.

They took a catnap and awoke at five—he reached for her, looked her straight in the eyes without a word, and her body arched toward him with a need she never knew existed.

Late in the morning, she lay with her cheek on his chest, tracing the shape of his pectorals with her index finger as the morning sun came in through his bedroom window and cast shadows over the blond stubble on his jaw.

"I'm usually surfing now," he said in a gravelly, drift-away way.

She lifted her head. "Do you want to? You can go."

"No," he said quickly. "No. This is . . . infinitely better."

"I thought you said surfing is like sex."

His deep chuckle rumbled within his chest. "I said there are *comparisons*. Sex is definitely better."

He stared at the ceiling for a while. "Your ex is an idiot." He looked down at her and smiled. "Got it?"

She nodded.

"And I might have to redefine my idea of perfection. That might have been it." He lifted her palm off his chest with his other hand and kissed it once right in the center.

She let his warm lips, and his words, surge straight into her heart and settle there, comfortably, where she knew she'd pull them out and unwrap them again in the future. She'd turn them over in her mind—not examining them, just listening to them—whenever she was feeling bad about herself, or feeling too much like someone's mother, or feeling too much like the "good girl." She'd press them against her cheek, like the kissing hand, and make use of the memory when she needed it most. Perfection. Fin Hensen. With her. She'd think of it every time she saw his picture on a surfing magazine, every time she saw him online—every time she saw that intense expression, balancing on his board.

"You make a lot of sexy sounds," he said.

"I do not."

"You do. Do you seriously not know that?"

"I do not."

He ignored that. "I knew you'd be vocal in bed. You're so reserved in your beauty-queen way, I just knew that once you got worked up, you'd be one of those gaspers."

She laughed this time. It pleased her that he thought so— both that he spent time predicting it and found it to be ultimately true.

"Does it bother you?" she asked.

"Well, if 'bother' is a euphemism for 'make you go hard,' then yes. But I could get used to it."

The comment sent a strange rush through her, just for a second. But the hope turned to sadness, and she let it wash over her. *This was temporary.*

She traced another figure eight across his golden pectorals. "I have to pick up Coco today."

"Oh."

It was just a single sound, but he spoke volumes with it: disappointment, guilt.

"So, I guess . . . you know . . . I'll have to go," she said.

He stroked her hair for almost a minute and thought that over. "What time do you pick up Coco?"

"At noon."

He glanced down at her. "All right, then. Are you hungry? Because I can feed you, but we're in no way leaving this bedroom." He got up on his elbow and tilted his alarm clock. "I have two hours to see how many times I can make you feel desired."

"I'm not hungry," she said, a little breathlessly.

He gently pushed her shoulder toward the bed. "Then turn over." He adjusted her naked body, facedown on the sheets, and pulled the blankets away so he could see her more fully in the daylight. Then he pushed her hair up off the back of her neck and started the slow process all over again.

CHAPTER
Twenty

At eleven thirty, Giselle leaned against the marble bathroom countertop and ran Fin's brush through her hair. She scanned his bathroom counter, peeked into his medicine cabinet. Everything about him suddenly fascinated her— what deodorant he wore, what type of brush he used, what his soap smelled like. She stopped short at inspecting the hamper, but only after she'd begun to open it. Her hand drifted to her side as she tried to get ahold of herself. This might be a slippery slope into groupie-ism.

She could hear him in the front room, moving around in the kitchen, getting ready for his day. She didn't have any experience with "morning-afters" and didn't know how to navigate them. Should she walk out and wrap her arms around his waist with a little kiss on the cheek? Or was she supposed to walk out and act casual, no strings attached, since that was their agreement? She tried to figure out what Veronica would do in this scenario. She might have to get a bracelet: What Would Veronica Do? Although WWVD had the sound of a venereal disease.

As she continued brushing her hair, something on the windowsill caught her eye.

She sucked in some air.

Next to a tan-colored soapstone was Coco's broken abalone shell.

She'd thought he was fibbing when he'd told Coco he kept it.
But there it was—right where he'd said. Of course, he wasn't
keeping it in his pocket, as Coco had suggested. Men like Fin
didn't need help being princes—men like him probably weren't
in the least bit interested. But she ran her fingers across the iri-
descent blue and lavender of the shell, feeling its broken smooth-
ness under her skin. She wasn't sure whether it was the sudden
realization of Fin's honesty, or the sweetness that he'd kept a little
girl's gift, or the idea that he saw this broken thing as something
beautiful and worth keeping, but a balloon of warm air settled in
her chest, and she went back to slowly brushing her hair.

She was in trouble. She was feeling much too much.

Giselle settled into Fin's bucket seats as he drove her home.
The masculine scent of sandalwood soap and toothpaste mingled with the leather interior.

Fin had hardly said a word since they'd left. Maybe he'd
already moved on. She reminded herself again of his multiple
warnings: no thoughts of long-term. He'd wanted her to feel
desired. And she had. End of story.

Giselle forced herself to stop stealing furtive glances at his
profile and instead watched the bougainvillea and palm trees
speed past her window. This might be the last time she'd see
him. He'd drop her off; she'd say good-bye. He'd wave as he
pulled out of the lot. She'd keep his photos, of course, and
scan them and send them back, as she'd promised. She shuffled the edges together carefully in her lap.

In the future, he might ask Lia about her. Or maybe not.
Maybe he'd never wonder about her again. Maybe this was
how things went once you slept with Fin Hensen.

"Do you have a busy day today?" She forced a conversation just to avoid the silence that was starting to feel awkward.
WWVD?

"I have to train," he said, glancing in her direction. "Run a
little. Pack for a couple of weeks."

She nodded and forced herself to turn toward the window
again. Fin had given her what she'd thought she'd wanted—

being desired—but he was right: It wasn't what she wanted at all. She wanted to *matter*. She wanted to be his favorite. She wanted to be remembered. . . .

"Are you trying to figure out how this works?" he asked.

"What?"

He was smirking. "You're wondering how to talk to this guy who had you bent over the side of his bed last night, and his hand running up the inside of your leg—"

"*Fin*, stop." Giselle rearranged the photos in her lap.

Fin's low chuckle drifted through the car.

She pretended she was studying the soul-arch photo. "So . . . okay. Yes. I'm wondering. Are there rules?"

Another smile slid her way. "Sometimes."

She bounced sideways in the seat to face him. "Tell me." She was actually curious.

The greenery off the side of the freeway sped past his profile as Giselle studied him. She was always going to remember Fin in profile, with bougainvillea behind him.

"What do you want to know?" he asked.

"What am I supposed to say during a 'morning-after'?"

"You sound like you're taking notes. You're not going to make this into a habit in Indiana, are you?"

"Maybe," she joked.

He stared out the window, but the amusement slid off his face.

"So do I say, 'I'll call you later,' or do I wait for *you* not to say that, or what?"

His cheeks grew ruddy. "I usually just grunt in my caveman language. She figures things out."

"I don't suppose we become Facebook friends?" She smiled sweetly.

He cut her a sidelong glance that bordered on a glare.

"Do we—"

"All right, all right, let's change the subject. What are you doing this evening after you pick up Coco?"

Giselle raised her eyebrows. She didn't see that one coming. "I . . . uh . . . don't know. I'm not sure if Roy is going to be there, or if we're going to talk, or how late that might go."

"Will you be okay? With him?"

"Of course."

Fin didn't seem appeased. "Why don't you and Coco swing by afterward? If you haven't had dinner, we can do that. And if you have, we could . . . get ice cream . . . or something."

"Is this typical of morning-afters?"

"Not usually."

"Is this a *date*, Fin Hensen?"

"Does it involve *sex*, Giselle?" She'd been kidding, but his voice had taken on an edge. He actually looked angry. Maybe she'd taken the questioning a little too far.

"No," she admitted. "Not when I have Coco."

Another two blocks of palm trees went by. Giselle watched a cluster of kids getting off a city bus with towels over their shoulders. Fin's breathing slowed.

After the next stop sign, his palm reached across the console and squeezed her thigh. "Sorry," he said. "I know that. I just . . . I don't know why I'm inviting you, honestly. I want to make sure everything goes okay with your ex. And I . . . just want to see you again, I guess. It's not typical."

Giselle allowed herself three seconds of joy from the tiny flutter of hope that rose in her chest.

But then his hands were back on the steering wheel; his attention was back to dropping her off; and she tamped the flutter down and focused on reality.

That was what Veronica would probably do.

Giselle approached the well-manicured flagstone walkway of Joe and Lovey's house. She couldn't wait to see Coco again. She could feel the tiny weight her little girl would throw into her arms—her silky hair against Giselle's shoulder, the smell of waffles coming off her like a cloud.

"Darling," said Lovey, opening the door before Giselle had even knocked. Lovey gave her a weak smile, one that hinted at too many days of excessive emotion.

Giselle glanced over Lovey's shoulder, then around her hips. Coco wasn't running to meet her. "Good morning," she said hesitantly.

"Oh, you remembered," Lovey said, taking the pink baker's box from Giselle's hand. She peered inside at the glazed old-fashioneds. "You're so thoughtful, dear. Come in."

Giselle closed the massive door behind her and followed Lovey's clicking kitten-heeled slippers through the entryway.

"Coco went out with Roy," Lovey called over her shoulder. "They'll be back in a bit."

Giselle tiptoed past the doorway where Fin's nose had bled and stepped around the corner into the empty massiveness of the house. The marble emptiness had the feeling of a tomb. Giselle wondered whether Lovey would stay here, all alone, now that Joe was gone. She knew she wouldn't.

"Where did they go?" she asked. She didn't know why it should bother her so much. She welcomed any moment Roy could act like a father—she knew it meant a lot to Coco, and she had always wished Roy would be more like her father had been: playful, fun, full of surprises, full of love and life.

"They went to the park," Lovey said from the kitchen. "Coco wanted to show him how she can cross the monkey bars. Coffee?"

"Sure." She'd welcome having something to do with her hands. She put her purse down and pressed her palms into the cool granite countertop so they would stop shaking.

"So your friend Fin? How did you meet him?" Lovey whirled into the center of the kitchen with the coffeepot.

Giselle felt a sudden catch in her throat at the unpredictable mention of Fin's name. Or maybe the idea that Lovey called him her friend.

She took a deep breath. She wondered how horrified Lovey would be if she knew that Giselle, scrapbook mom extraordinaire, had just had a one-night stand of acrobatic, meaningless sex with a man she barely knew, simply because that man had agreed to, and he'd had the most amazing blue eyes, and a body to die for, and made her heart pound when he stood too close.

"I . . . um . . . met him through Lia," Giselle said, staring at the countertop.

Lovey arranged the doughnuts on a china plate.

"We're just . . . *friends*."

Giselle felt the need to add the last part, despite the fact she knew Lovey wouldn't judge. Lovey had always seemed embarrassed by what her son had done and seemed sensible enough to know that any blame that might get slung around would have to begin with him.

"Fin Hensen's pretty famous around here." Lovey reached for two gold-rimmed mugs. "Shame what happened to that girl."

Giselle cast her eyes down again at the granite. Yes, very much. And yes, Fin was right. This was going to end up being what he'd be known for—not his beautiful shape, not his skill in the ocean, not his soul arch. But this—this terrible, ugly thing.

"I'm sure he had nothing to do with it," Lovey added. "He seems like a nice young man. But it's still such a shame. She was a beautiful girl. She came here for dinner once."

Giselle's head shot up. Lovey rummaged for creamer in the fridge. *Came here for dinner?* Her mind stalled, trying to put it in the right context, trying to connect it to the right people.

"Why did she come here for dinner?"

"Joe knew her," said Lovey, shrugging. "He was friends with her father, and Jennifer and a few of the other surfers used to do some safety benefits with the children's hospital down the street. She came here a few times. Roy met her."

Giselle raised her eyebrows. No wonder Roy was so upset about the whole thing, or Fin's possible involvement. It softened her a little toward Roy—maybe he had been sincerely worried—but it also bothered her that this went on without her: dinners with surfers, here in California, and the fact that he never told her about this tragic death of a family friend. What kind of a charade had she been living all these years?

"What was she like?" Giselle asked.

Lovey tilted her head. "Beautiful. Dark. Hawaiian influence in her family—dark skin, long black hair. She spoke with her hands a lot. She had a charming laugh. . . ."

The women both stood there in silence for a moment, sipping their coffee, paying homage to a beautiful girl whose life was cut short. Giselle remembered the online images she saw of Jennifer on her surfboard, with her Hawaiian good looks and silky hair. Giselle let her mind drift to the fact that Fin had known her, and taught her to surf, and traveled with her. She wondered whether he'd called her "wahine." She wondered whether he'd slept with her. . . .

Of course, he'd said they were just friends and didn't have a relationship, but he could say that about Giselle, too. The thought of him sleeping with Jennifer just for fun twisted a knot in her stomach, taking her by surprise. First she felt guilty for begrudging a dead girl any joy, and then she felt guilty for feeling a twinge of jealousy about a man who never claimed to be hers in any way. Guilt was followed in short order by sadness, though. Giselle must have been crazy to have thought being with Fin for one night would make her feel better. It just intensified her feelings—made her realize what she'd been missing all these years—and made her feel about a hundred times worse that she'd continue to miss it, possibly for the rest of her life.

"How are *you* doing, Lovey?" she asked, forcing herself to stop thinking about Fin. With the idea of loss still hovering in the air, Giselle thought it would be a good time to find out how Lovey was holding up.

"I'm okay. It helped to have Coco here. It gave me other things to focus on, and reminded me how life goes on. I'm so glad you let her stay."

The women leaned into the kitchen counter and sipped their steaming coffee and shared the little they had left in common.

Fin wandered along the patio beneath the extinguished tiki torches, coffee mug in hand, and inspected the surf. He was surprised he'd missed his morning session. Especially right before a contest. According to the tide charts, the surf was supposed to have been great at seven this morning, but he could catch some good lefts later today at Trestles, if he could make it down there in time.

But his mind was wandering.

Which bothered him to no end.

It was wandering to Giselle's lower back, and how she had those two sexy dimples there that became more pronounced when she lay on her stomach on his sheets. He thought about her crazy golden-strawberry-reddish-blondish hair, and how it felt sliding through his fingertips this morning as they lay against his starched pillows and stared up at the ceiling fan. He thought about her languid smile when she woke up, and how she ran the back of her hand across her eyelids like a child and laughed. He thought about what a relief it had been in his chest when he'd told her about Jennifer, how he'd felt an enormous weight lifted when she'd told him she didn't see it as his fault. He thought about how she'd defended him to Fox, called him a "hero." He thought about that strange stab of jealousy when she'd joked that she might continue having casual sex in Indiana. . . . At least, he hoped she'd been joking.

And did he just ask her and Coco over tonight?

He groaned and rubbed his face. He didn't know why he'd done that.

Of course, it beat the alternative. It beat leaving her standing on the curb in front of her apartment. It beat feeling like a cad, who'd played the singular role of unlocking a gate for a sweet woman to start living a life of meaningless sex. It beat knowing Lia was never going to speak to him again.

But he knew that was not why he'd invited her.

He just wanted to see her.

And yet no sex would be involved, since she'd have her little girl. . . .

He took another sip from his mug and wondered what was happening here. He tried to think of another situation— another woman—he could compare this to, but came up with no one. He *liked* Lia and Jennifer the same way—always respected them and cared about them. But they never turned him on every moment he was in their presence. And Veronica and Catalina were just the opposite—he was attracted to them, and the feeling seemed to be mutual, which was a turn-on—but he didn't worry about them or concern himself with what they did when they weren't with him.

But Giselle . . . she was a mixture of both. He liked her *and* respected her *and* was turned on by her. She was really everything he loved about every woman he'd ever known. . . .

He took another sip. It was a good thing he was leaving in two days. If he stayed, he might find himself actually chasing her. But he'd be chasing a woman he couldn't have: She had a sophisticated life in Indiana that she wasn't interested in leaving, and was much too smart for a guy with barely a GED. And he, of course, had a career that took him around the world.

A career he was going to lose, in fact, if he didn't get his mind in the right fucking place . . .

Concentrate, man.

The swells weren't great. They looked a little mushy out there. But there were a few good lefts. Trestles was a long drive. And he had to pick out the boards he'd be bringing. Definitely the new Channel Islands Red Beauty . . .

His mind drifted to what Coco might like for dinner. Maybe he could borrow his neighbor's fire pit and let Coco roast marshmallows after dinner. Kids still liked s'mores, didn't they?

He rubbed his forehead and forced his thoughts back: The Red Beauty would fit in the same bag as his shortboard, if he detached the fins. Maybe he could bring five boards. . . .

He took another sip of coffee and counted his patio chairs. Coco could hang out on the patio with him and Giselle. He suddenly realized the situation he'd just put himself in: He was going to have Giselle in front of him all evening; he was going to be lusting after her; and she was going to be 100 percent off-limits. . . . This was going to be a rough night.

Maybe, in the back of his mind, he'd invited her over thinking he could get one more night of awesome sex—Coco had to fall asleep sometime, after all.

But that would be slimy. He needed to behave.

He would simply enjoy Giselle's company. He liked laughing with her. He liked talking to her. He liked seeing her with Coco. He liked how she smelled, how she smiled, and how she left him feeling whole, and absolved, and smart, and . . . like he *mattered*, somehow. He wanted Coco to like him. For whatever reason. And, despite all he'd told Giselle about himself—which was embarrassingly a lot—she hadn't left. Or died. Or abandoned him.

The last two thoughts took him by surprise.

Damn.

He scrutinized the day's waves, took a long sip of coffee, then pushed the thoughts away and walked into the garage to find the Red Beauty.

From the kitchen, Giselle heard the *whoosh* of the entryway door. As excited as she was to see her little girl, her stomach constricted as she waited to hear Roy's footsteps. She brushed her palms along her slacks and pushed her coffee mug forward.

"Mommy!" Coco threw her arms around Giselle's waist.

"Hey, baby." Giselle stroked Coco's hair and kissed her

part. Someone had brushed it into cute ponytails this morning. Giselle wondered whether it had been Roy in a sweet act of fathering, but then she thought of Kimber. Her stomach clenched as her eyes swept the entryway for oversized sunglasses and oversized breasts.

"Did you have fun at the park?" she asked shakily.

"Yes, I showed Daddy the monkey bars. I can go all the way across now!"

Giselle continued to stare at the marble entrance but no one else emerged. "Where's Daddy?"

"He dropped me off. He had to go see Kimber."

She said it so matter-of-factly, like this was her new world, that Giselle was taken aback. She couldn't quite believe her little girl was stating the name of her husband's mistress with such nonchalance. She couldn't believe Roy was moving on. Couldn't believe there would be another child, and another mother, sitting here in Lovey's kitchen, taking their place.

She glanced up at Lovey, but Lovey didn't seem to notice anything amiss. She was, instead, gazing at Coco adoringly.

"Why don't you get your things, sweetie?" Lovey prompted. "Show Mommy the new stuffed animal we bought you."

"Oh! Ninja Zebra!" Coco galloped up the stairs.

Giselle allowed a shaky breath to escape.

As the kitchen clock ticked away the silence, Giselle tried to wrap her mind around her new circumstances. She was overcome with gratitude for Lovey—how much she loved Coco, how much she would help them make things work, how she would not abandon Coco like Roy might, with the new baby.

"Thank you for everything," she blurted.

Lovey gazed at her for half a minute; then her silky robe sleeves brushed the countertop as she reached over and cupped Giselle's hand. "It'll be fine, sweetheart."

Giselle nodded as tears pricked her eyes. She hoped so.

Twenty-one

As Giselle's tires made the rumble over the railroad tracks again, she wasn't sure what she was doing.

She didn't feel easy in the new jeans she'd slipped on—a pair of Lia's, from the bottom drawer, a much lower cut than she was used to. She didn't feel easy parking near the piano-key row of white trailer homes, or grabbing Coco's hand and hustling across the street with the Tupperware in her arms. She didn't feel easy walking up Fin's sidewalk as the sun began to set behind his house, or as she listened to the rush of the crashing waves come down between the homes. She didn't know why he'd invited her, or whether it was strange to bring Coco, or what the rules were for morning-afters, afternoon-afters, evening-afters. . . .

But when Fin opened the door—rubbing his jaw and grinning down at her, wearing faded blue jeans—she felt instantly, completely at ease, as if he'd been waiting like this forever.

"Come in," he said.

Giselle drew a relieved breath and stepped inside the warmth.

"We brought you a cake!" Coco bounced up and down on the patio. "For your birthday!"

"Coco!" Giselle exclaimed.

Coco giggled and pressed her hand against her mouth. "It was supposed to be a surprise," she said in a stage whisper.

Fin laughed, but his eyes cut to the covered bakery plate with a degree of nervousness.

"Seriously?" he asked, following her into the kitchen.

"I did." She unsnapped the Tupperware lid and unveiled the simple two-layer round that she and Coco had frosted. Across the top, they had piped "*Happy Birthday, Fin!*" in blue cursive. Coco had sprinkled the whole thing with confetti candies.

Fin stared at the cake for an unreasonable amount of time, a sense of wonder and confusion etching his features.

"Do you not like cake?" Giselle asked, bewildered at his reaction.

"How did you know it was my birthday?"

"You told me. You said you were turning twenty-nine this weekend. . . . Right?"

"Yeah. I just . . . didn't think you'd remember, I guess."

"You look like you've never seen a cake before."

"Not with my name on it. More used to beers and bongs, I guess." He glanced at Coco and cleared his throat. "But this . . . this is . . . really nice."

"You've never had a birthday cake with your name on it?" Giselle couldn't keep the incredulousness out of her voice.

"Surfing bros aren't really the type."

"Your mom?"

"Ronny's mom might have once." He frowned, as if he were trying to remember. He threw her a little smile, seemingly wanting to console her, but he couldn't keep his gaze off the homemade confection.

"I put the sprinkles on!" Coco bounded up beside him. "See? I put a lot right by your name, because Mommy always lets us eat that piece—the piece with our name, that's what we always do—and then you get a *lot* of sprinkles." Her eyes widened. "You like sprinkles?"

"I love sprinkles, Coco. Thank you."

"See, I put *those* by your name." Coco pointed dangerously near the frosting.

"Coco," Giselle warned. "I know you're trying to get some on your finger."

Coco giggled and leaned in toward Fin's arm.

He smiled, still staring. Giselle thought she saw his eyes dampen, but he looked away before she could tell. He turned toward the elaborate telescope that stood in the center of the room.

"Do you know what this is, Coco?" he asked gruffly, rubbing the side of his nose.

"A . . ." Coco put her finger to her lips, as if thinking. "A tever-scope?" She knew it wasn't quite right.

"Telescope. Good! Do you want to look through it? This is the best time—while the sun is low in the sky. But don't look at the sun, just the reflection in the water."

He hauled a dining chair toward it, and helped Coco balance on the chair as he adjusted the viewfinder to her height.

Giselle covered the cake and put it away, trying not to dwell on this latest fact of Fin's isolation. Although his life seemed glamorous and exciting, she could see how he'd missed out on some of the warmer parts, the parts that made you feel part of a family.

She listened distractedly as he instructed Coco to focus on a point on the horizon, and how sometimes you could see dolphins.

"You see *dolphins*?" Coco gasped.

"Almost every day," he said.

Giselle wandered toward them, crossing her arms and leaning against the dining table, watching the two of them look excitedly for pods. The setting sun threw its rays through the windows, bathing her baby and Fin in shades of copper. It was fun to see Fin acting almost like a child himself, giddy at each discovery. As they took turns looking at sailboats, ships, and surfers, it was as if they'd forgotten she was there.

"I see them!" Coco finally squealed. "Dolphins!"

He showed Coco how to keep them in the viewfinder without holding on to the telescope, then stepped back and crossed his arms, smiling as if he'd just presented the ocean to her as a gift. After a few moments, he threw Giselle a look over his shoulder, then backed toward her, leaving Coco to her dolphins.

He scooted Giselle back into the kitchen.

"How did it go today?" he whispered.

"With Roy?"

He nodded.

"He wasn't there."

"Good."

A liquid heat ran through her, to all her extremities, as he stared down at her. She wanted nothing more than to melt into that baritone voice of his right now, let his hands slip around her, let him stroke her, let him take her against the glass like he'd done last night. . . . But they were following some strange set of rules she didn't understand now. Instead, he stood too close, staring at her intently through a lock of hair falling down his forehead, but hooked his thumbs on his pockets.

"Did you two have dinner yet?" he asked.

"Yeah."

"Already?"

Giselle smiled. "She's a child. She eats at six."

"Oh . . . yeah." He glanced over his shoulder and peered at Coco as if she were a strange zoo animal. "Does she like dessert? I bought stuff for s'mores."

"Oh, Fin, that was sweet. You didn't have to—"

"And I borrowed a fire pit. Outside." He ran his hand over the back of his neck. "I didn't know what to get her to drink, though. Does she drink milk? Or I could—"

"*Fin.*" Without thinking, she rested her hand on his arm to stop him. He stared at it until she removed it quickly.

"She'll be fine," she uttered quickly, stepping away. "Do you need to eat? You can go ahead. Don't let us interrupt your dinner."

"I can eat later."

"We won't stay long. I just wanted to bring you the cake."

"No, stay."

An awkward silence fell as he stared at her intently.

"I'm not sure what to do, though," he said.

"What do you mean?"

He glanced at Coco, who was holding Ninja Kitty up to see the dolphins.

"Am I allowed to touch you?" he whispered.

Her body responded before her brain. Tingles shot straight through her arms, her legs, at the memory of what exactly that meant, and—like her life flashing before her eyes—a series of vignettes floated behind her eyelids of Fin's naked body in the sheets last night. She bit her lip against the betrayal of her own body. A quick glance around Fin's shoulder at Coco served as a needed bucket of cold water.

"I don't think so," she choked out on a whisper. "But I don't know. I've never done this before. You're the one who knows the rules. What would Veronica do?"

He frowned. "Veronica?"

"I'm always thinking of what Veronica would do—what are your rules with her?"

His frown darkened. "This has nothing to do with Veronica."

"I'm just saying I know there are rules to this kind of thing—you said so yourself—and Rabbit mentioned you have some kind of arrangement with Veronica, so I thought maybe you two had . . ."

Fin ran his hand down his face and seemed to reset his jaw. "Giselle, this isn't even the same—"

"Mommy? Come see!" Coco called.

Giselle whipped her head toward Coco, snapped back into reality. The bucket of water emptied: She was here with her little girl. She did not have a relationship with Fin. They had had a one-night stand. It was over. End of bucket.

With a brief apologetic glance at Fin, who was staring at the kitchen floor, Giselle slid out of the kitchen to see the dolphins.

Fin lit the tiki torches and got to work on the fire pit. After rummaging through his coat closet, he came back with three wire coat hangers, which he twisted into sticks with handles. Giselle watched his forearm muscles dance under his skin.

"Giselle? You okay?"

"Yes. Yes. Fine." She snatched the wire hanger he was holding out and tried to focus on what he was instructing them to do.

"You can do two at a time," he told Coco, stringing a second marshmallow on her hanger and handing it over. "Okay, I've got one: Knock, knock."

"Who's there?" Coco dipped her head dramatically.

"Who."

"Who who?"

"Is there an owl in here?"

Coco collapsed into a fit of giggles, and Fin seemed as if
he couldn't keep from laughing from her delight. He ran
through "Orange you going to open the door," "Lettuce in,"
and "Water you doing here" while they dipped their marshmallows into the flames and blew out any mini fires. By the
time they got to "Turnip the volume," he told Coco he was
going to get something and asked her to hold his hanger until
he emerged from his bedroom with a small wooden game,
along with her Boo Boo Buddy.

"I owe you this, little grommet." He traded her the hanger
for the Boo Boo Buddy, taking his seat back near the fire pit.

"How did you get it?" she asked.

"Your mom let me borrow it. When I hurt my nose." He
motioned toward the cut that had mostly healed.

Coco laid her hanger on the paper plate, the way Fin had,
then stepped up closer and leaned against his knee for a better
look at his nose. He looked briefly startled by her nearness,
then simply stared at her, a wave of compassion sweeping
across his face. The light of the flickering shadows danced
across their matching old souls' eyes.

Coco touched the light line shimmering across the bridge
of his nose with her forefinger.

"Mommy healed it. It looks good now." She leaned back to
give him another few inches of breathing space.

He seemed to still until she'd moved, staring at her as if
she were something he'd lost and then found again. He
frowned as the waves crashed behind them, then rubbed his
face. "Let's play this game," he said.

Giselle looked away. It was almost painful to see how easily Fin was moved by simple acts of connection. She wondered whether all his years alone made him further isolate
himself, or if he simply isolated himself because it was all he
knew.

"You're going to have some cake, right, Fin?" Coco asked.

"Will your mom let you have s'mores *and* birthday cake?"
The smile returned to his face as they both looked at Giselle.

"Just a *small* piece," she acquiesced.

He and Coco raised their eyebrows at each other in joy and surprise.

As their plates sat empty on the patio concrete, and the fire became just a glowing ember, Giselle ran her fingers along Coco's sleeping profile and snuck glances at Fin's lazy smile. She thought about how she could spend every evening like this, lounging with a man who could surf near sharks, swim against tides, haul a drowning woman out of a midnight rip-tide with one arm, but whose eyes could soften at Coco's tales of Christmas mornings, or turn moist at the simple gesture of two females singing "Happy Birthday" off-key. He wanted to know all about Coco's class, what the "Teddy Bear Journal" was, and all about her and Coco's Friday night ritual of fish sticks and swimming lessons.

She sighed. Fin would've made a perfect husband. Too bad he wasn't interested. Too bad he lived a life that took him around the world most of the year, keeping him from claiming a real home. Too bad he chose a life of isolation.

She shifted, plates in hand. She needed to leave. Staying here a minute longer was just reminding her of what she couldn't have. As she stood, Fin looked panicked. He grabbed her hand and stared at her, as if memorizing her face. With a brief glance at Coco, he nodded Giselle into the kitchen, following behind her with the mugs and mismatched forks.

In the darkened kitchen, he took the cake knife out of her hand, then backed her against the wall and covered her mouth with his, kissing her until her knees were going to buckle.

"I've wanted to do that all night," he said huskily. "Damn, Giselle, I don't know what the rules are to this."

She gripped his biceps—they were helping to hold her up—as he made his way down her neck and toward her breasts. She'd thought she would escape this evening, her heart cracked a bit at what she couldn't have but at least in one piece. But his kisses were shattering her. He managed to make her feel sexy and seductive, but cherished, upon a pedestal, all at once. And this was exactly what she needed. But couldn't have . . .

Except . . .

Maybe, just once more . . .

She threw herself into his arms, knocking him back

against the refrigerator, and kissed him with every ounce of energy she had in her body. She couldn't get close enough—she wanted to be in him, absorbed by him, wrapped into the center of his attention and care and passion. . . .

"Damn, Giselle," he breathed, but he met her, pulse for pulse, and flipped her around so she was against the narrow kitchen wall and he had better access to her breasts, her hips, her thighs. She knocked over a board that was hanging on the wall, and it crashed to the floor as he nudged her legs apart, breathing heavily into her cleavage.

"Do you want to stay?" he asked, his lips against her left breast, where he was fumbling with the buttons of her blouse. "We can set her up in the guest room."

"Mommy?"

They froze.

Fin moved first, meeting Giselle's eyes with something of an apology in them, then made a brief attempt to straighten her blouse as he blocked Coco from any dishevelment.

"Baby, what do you need?" Giselle squeaked out, helping Fin with her top button.

"What are you doing?" Coco asked sleepily.

"Nothing, nothing, baby. . . . Fin is just . . . *kissing* me. We're friends, and he's saying good-bye. . . ."

Fin glanced up at that comment, then cleared his throat and turned toward Coco, nodding once.

Coco just stared at them, a little frown puckering her eyebrows, Ninja Kitty hanging by her side. "Is that what princes do?" She directed the question at Fin.

"Uh . . . well, sort of, Coco. I, um . . . I could have been more princely about it, I think. What do your books say?"

"They dance first." Coco frowned sternly.

"Of course." Fin smirked. "I think I need to work on some of this."

Coco gave him another frown and sharp nod, then stretched her arms. "Are we going, Mommy?"

"Yes, yes, we are."

Giselle moved swiftly around Fin, into the kitchen, to gather the Tupperware lid and rinse the cake knife.

Fin got back into Coco's good graces with a few more knock-knock jokes as he helped them load the car with the

Boo Boo Buddy, Coco's jacket, the leftover graham crackers, marshmallows, chocolate bars, and birthday cake. He finally closed Coco's car door, quickly cupping Giselle's neck once they were out of eyeshot and drawing her toward him for a quick kiss to the part in her hair. "That was the best birthday I ever had," he whispered. "Can you come over again tomorrow night?"

"I thought you were flying out."

"I can postpone."

"You would . . . you would *do* that for me?"

"I would."

He looked almost confused about that, but her pulse quickened at the thought of seeing him one more time—and that he wanted to see her.

"That would be great," she finally said.

He nodded once and got her into the car, closing her door behind her.

She watched him in her rearview mirror, thumbs hanging off his jeans pockets, and sighed into the darkness of the rental car.

Darn.

Fin *was* a prince. And she was falling in love.

Twenty-two

The gulls began their morning cry through Giselle's window. She turned her head to see her little girl. She reached out and stroked Coco's hair. No matter where they were, where Roy was, she and Coco would have each other.

The thought filled her with warmth as she stared at Coco's little eyelashes, but her thoughts then turned to Fin, wondering whether he'd ever find anyone he could love. It was a strange turn. She even tried to push the thought away. But then she let it settle, and wondered whether Fin could fall in love with her. For the first time she saw how her own happiness could have its place in her life with Coco. For the first time she saw that finding her own joy was not so selfish when she was able to bring that joy to being a better mother.

She kissed Coco on the nose and climbed out of bed.

The smell of eggs filled her kitchen as she whipped up a quick breakfast, then gathered towels and bathing suits for surf camp. Coco was excited to return—she'd made Giselle promise five times they'd go.

"Coco!" Rabbit exclaimed when they arrived.

"I'm back!" she yelled, running down the dune and throwing her arms out like she'd just announced she was the Queen of England.

He laughed and extracted himself from her hug to pull a foam board for her. "Do you need to practice?"

She nodded, and he got her settled into some catch-up practice while he turned to meet the other parents.

"Glad she's back," he said to Giselle. "You can leave her here for a couple of hours, you know. Most parents do."

Giselle spread her towel. "I'll stay."

"You can have a whole few hours alone, you know."

"That's okay." She settled herself on her towel and pulled out her laptop. She still wasn't in a place where she could leave Coco all by herself. She'd brought her camera again in case she needed a few more shots, but she was pretty sure she had what she needed. She planned to finish the brochure today.

As she shuffled granules of sand off her laptop, she saw Callie Sandoval arrive and drop off Jordan. Rabbit stumbled to greet her, and his face went red as he made small talk. Giselle smiled. She really needed to get those two together.

Surfing camp went smoothly. Although pangs of nervous terror still jolted through her every time Coco's head disappeared underwater, she had to admit her day in the ocean with Fin had helped. She watched Coco doing the same tactics Fin had taught—how to go under the waves, how to count underwater, how to watch the beach and not drift too far.

Coco was giggling as she ran up, dripping, to Giselle's wide-open towel. "Did you see me, Mommy?"

"Of course—I've been watching you the whole time. You're something else out there."

"Will you come out with me?"

"After camp."

Coco's eyes went wide. "Mommy's coming out with me!" she squealed to Rabbit, who was handing out juice boxes to each of the kids. He winked at Giselle and kept moving.

Giselle settled Coco in her lap and let her drink the ridiculously sugared drink.

But mostly she thought about how loosening your grip on things often did bring them closer.

* * *

As grommet camp wrapped up, Giselle heard Coco squeal: "Fin's here!"

Giselle felt a panic spike, but then she continued folding her towels, pretending she didn't notice Fin's eyes on her the whole time, pretending she wasn't going to miss feeling this exhilaration every day, pretending her heart wasn't already breaking at the idea she'd have to say good-bye. To him. To this. To this new life that was feeling better and better every day.

He talked with Rabbit and Corky about onshore swells in Trestles and whether there was too much coral in Ballito. His eyes kept drifting toward her, as if to make sure she wasn't leaving. A few of the dads noticed Fin and asked for an autograph.

As Giselle turned her back, trying to act casual and packing her towels neatly, Callie caught her attention. She was one parent who didn't notice Fin at all. She, instead, cast furtive glances at Rabbit, who zeroed in on her about the same time and broke his conversation to walk over and say good-bye. Giselle was proud of him.

"I forgot we needed to finish our surfing lesson." Fin's voice came over her shoulder.

She whirled and almost bumped right into his golden chest. "Oh—gosh, I . . . I don't know if I can go out today." She'd wanted to go out with Coco, but she planned on only going to her knees—wading all the way out again would take an emotional commitment she felt too drained for, after last night and this whole darned week. But man, she wanted to look at Fin . . . and be near him . . . and have him looking at her, like he was right now. . . .

"Mommy's coming *out to the ocean*!" Coco punctuated the celebration with a cartwheel.

"I can take Coco," Rabbit announced.

"Hey, Coco," Fin called, "is it okay if your mom comes out with me?"

Coco nodded. "She might need help."

Fin laughed. "I'll remember that." He clapped Rabbit's shoulder. "Thanks, man."

Before Giselle could think it through, Fin caught her hand and began dragging her down to the water.

"I don't know, Fin." She couldn't help leaning back to slow him down. "I had a long time to get used to the water before."

"I can throw you in if it's easier. But you'll need to get rid of some of those clothes first." The grin that followed made it clear he was pleased with that fact.

She hesitated. She'd timidly put the red bikini on this morning, not expecting to unveil herself—or at least knowing she'd have the option to change her mind if she wanted to. But now she panicked. She hadn't expected him to see her in it.

While he stared at the ocean with a pretend nonchalance, she forced the thoughts that had gone through her head this morning when she'd pulled the bikini out of the drawer: *I'm beautiful. I'm sexy. I'm an imperfect leaf. I'm desired. . . .*

As the waves crashed chaotically, she wriggled out of her new jeans and threw her sweatshirt aside, leaving them right there in the sand.

Fin's head turned. "*Damn*, Giselle." His jaw went slack.

She walked past him, down to the water, her confidence soaring at every step.

He ran to keep up with her. "You're killin' me," he said. "Not sure I can maintain princely thoughts."

It was just as cold as the other day, but Giselle met the first few waves with intakes of breath and much less fear.

"Sorry about last night," he added out of the side of his mouth. "Has she forgiven me?"

"You might have to learn to dance."

Fin held her hand. She squeezed his.

"We're here," he said when they were in about to their waist. He tore his gaze away from her body for about the twentieth time and threw the board down, resting his palm on it. "This is where I'd paddle out, but we'll keep you close here on these baby waves."

She followed his instructions on everything. They leaned on the board together, so she could feel how it would hold their weight. He helped her climb on, balancing on her stomach, and stood beside her to hold the board until he found a wave he liked. His biceps strained against the power of the ocean,

holding back her entire weight, one hand gripping each side of
the board near her hip. His arm leaned across her thigh, near
her bottom, shooting a tingle of awareness through her body.

"Fin!"

He laughed, as if embarrassed at being caught, and they
both watched the ocean.

"Look behind you," he instructed. "You're waiting for
some lift, waiting for just the right rise."

She glanced over her shoulder and caught him taking a
peek himself—staring again at her bottom.

"You don't have to move your body like that, Giselle."

"Oh." She shifted again. "Am I changing the balance of
the board?"

"No, you're turning me on," he said, staring out at the waves.

She tried to stay still.

"Okay, here's one. See that peak?" He stepped forward,
moving as if he were one with the ocean. The water lifted
them up, up, up, and he let go of the board, giving her a push.

She "rode" all the way in, on her stomach, feeling the
wind against her face and the rush of water and foam all
around her.

"Stay on!" Fin yelled.

She did as he said—gripping the edge and flying through
the air like Neptune until the wave wedged her into the sand.
She pushed up before the water rushed back into her face.

"You did it!" Fin was sloshing through the water toward
her, grinning. "Stoked?"

"Oh yeah!" She was breathless. And, most surprisingly of
all, not scared.

"Want to go again?"

"Yeah!"

He laughed and helped her up. And they began all over
again.

Giselle rode about fifteen tiny waves—a few on her stomach,
several on her knees, and then one in a wobbly stance. She
could see how addicting it was—each time she fell off, she
wanted to get right back on.

They checked in with Rabbit and Coco a few times, but the two of them were having their own fun. Coco was already standing on the foam board. Eventually, Coco wanted to return to shore and have a snack. Rabbit said he had some extra cheese and crackers and juice from the lessons, so he nodded for Fin and Giselle to take off if they wanted.

Fin set Giselle on a couple more waves on her stomach, then helped her get way out into the water where they might find bigger waves. Although "bigger" on that day simply meant higher than a kneecap. It was a quiet day for the Pacific.

Out in the deep water, waiting for anything with lift, Fin and Giselle faced each other over the board, her toes no longer touching the sandy floor. Out there, it felt as if they were floating in a giant swimming pool, the water lifting them about two feet, then gently dropping them again. Fin kept glancing toward the horizon, but there were no peaks at all.

"Want to get on?" he asked. "We usually straddle the boards out here."

"In a second—I'm kind of tired."

He nodded and dropped under the water a moment, coming up and then stretching his arms to grip the other side. Water dripped from his eyelashes, his hair, his neck. He was hardly even breathing heavily.

"I want to see *you* surf," she said, gripping the opposite side of the board and letting her legs kick loose underwater. She had been stealing glances at his abs and trunk-clad thighs all afternoon, the same ones that had given her so much pleasure just two nights before. The memory shot a tingle through her.

He chuckled. "Not much to ride."

"Maybe another day?"

He lowered his watery eyelashes and didn't answer. They both knew this was the end of the line for them.

His arms pulled across the board, parallel with hers. Water lapped against the fiberglass, and the gulls cawed. Only three other surfers were out.

As she caught her breath, kicking her legs underneath and staring at the board between them, he rested his chin on his arm and touched her shoulder with his knuckle, as if he were wiping away the drips. The gesture was so intimate, protect-

ive, yet suggestive, all at once—amplified, perhaps, by the
fact that he refused to meet her eyes—that she almost stopped
breathing.

"You did great," he said. "I think you can check surfing off
your short-term list."

"That and the danged swearing?"

He smiled. "You might need to work on the swearing."

His knuckle skimmed her shoulder again.

"Thank you, Fin."

The smile left his face. "What you said about Veronica last
night, though . . . It bothered me."

Giselle blinked back ocean water and surprise. "Why?"

"I don't want you to think I regard you that way, or regard
our night that way. It was . . . different. Completely."

Giselle stilled. "How?" she dared ask.

"I don't think about Veronica the next day," he said. "Or
count the minutes until I'm going to see her again. But with
you, I have been."

Even as a crease formed between his brows, even as he
seemed to hesitate while a million considerations raced through
his head, he reached for her and secured his fingers at the base
of her ponytail, pulling her toward him.

His lips met hers in a salty softness, causing everything
around her to fall away, even the cold, even the fear that she
couldn't touch her toes to the sand. Her body floated forward
as he slid his lips across hers once, then twice—as if still
deciding whether he should do this or not. They leaned into
the board, dipping it down enough for a rush of water to
sweep past her breasts. His hand behind her head secured her
to him, his mouth exploring with a sense of desperation that
felt like a man remembering something he'd always wanted.

With that, he pulled away and leaned his forehead against
hers. It was the first time she heard him trying to catch his
breath.

"I told myself I wasn't going to do that," he said huskily.

"Coco got you scared?"

He smiled. "Well, you know, she *is* right. You deserve the
whole dance." A larger swell lifted them and dropped them
slowly. "I wish I could give it to you." He held her there for a
second longer, then lifted his head. "We have today, though,"

he finally said, letting go of her. "Want to grab lunch and take Coco somewhere this afternoon before you come over tonight?"

"I need to see Roy, actually. This is the evening we're supposed to talk."

"You'll be all right? Do you want me to come with you?"

"No, no." A slight panic rose at how angry Roy would be if Fin showed up.

"Do you feel comfortable with him? You can tell him off, you know. Anyone who can hold off those waves when she's scared of them can hold her own, as far as I'm concerned."

"Maybe I should have taken the swearing more seriously."

"You can tell him to fuck off."

She couldn't help but laugh, but shook her head.

"Try it," he implored.

She shook her head—it was too vulgar for her own sensibility. "I can't," she admitted.

He smiled and shook his head. "I love you, Giselle."

He looked away, but, as if he realized what had just slipped out of his mouth, he glanced back at her. Rather than correct himself, he dipped his head underwater and watched the horizon while he sluiced water off his face.

Although she knew he didn't mean it the way she wanted him to, her heart kept an out-of-control rhythm for the next several seconds. Even just hearing the words from his lips—however unintended—was thrilling in a way she couldn't give credence to.

While she closed her mouth, he studied her intently.

"Come with me," he said.

She frowned.

"To South Africa."

He met her eyes as a silence welled between them. Giselle caught her breath and studied the blues in his eyes. She would love to spend time in South Africa staring into eyes like this—over sand, over ocean, over sheets, over some exotic beach drink. She would love to have Fin's hands on her every night in a hotel, would love to wake with him every morning, would love to hear him laugh, and get him to open up more.

But of course she couldn't. She was a mother. She couldn't just pick up her child and traipse off to South Africa like some kind of eighteen-year-old groupie. Coco didn't have a passport. Giselle had no clothes for a trip like that. Plus, she had a job here in Sandy Cove that she had to finish for Lia and Rabbit. And she had her life back in Indiana, including the first day of school and Daisy Scouts, that she had to get her and Coco back to. . . .

Fin's life was enviable, but it wasn't something she could ever be part of. The reality settled like a yoke around her shoulders.

"Wouldn't that be something?" she said, laughing it off—laughing off the fact that she felt old. Heavy. Tied down. And that the chasm between her and this sexy man just seemed to elongate about another ten years. . . .

He brought his chin close to the board. "I could picture you in South Africa. In this bikini, particularly. And, of course, out of this bikini."

Giselle would never do it in a million years—would never leave Coco—but this fantasy, and the way Fin was looking at her bikini strings right now, would fuel her for the next several years. Like the kissing hand.

"I can't," she admitted. "I have Coco, and . . . I have to get her home, and . . . Well, you know, school will be starting. . . ."

He nodded. She could see the exact moment he reeled it all back in and shut down.

"Up." He patted the center of the board.

She struggled to get on the board on her stomach—it couldn't have appeared graceful—but Fin didn't seem to notice. He already seemed a million miles away.

They paddled forward, found a wave closer to shore, and Fin found his footing and gave her a gentle push. "Last one!"

She struggled to pop up, holding the sides of the board until the last possible minute, then brought her feet underneath her and tried to balance. She wobbled like crazy, but managed to finish the wave all the way onto shore. She was only about two feet off the sand, but it still felt exciting.

Fin was laughing when he caught up with her.

They met up with Rabbit and Coco, and called it a day. Fin didn't bring up the "L-word," or South Africa, again.

Twenty-three

Giselle sat in Lovey's kitchen, waiting again for Roy.

Coco splashed in the backyard pool with Lovey. At each giggle, Giselle glanced in their direction, then twisted her china cup in another three-sixty.

When she heard the door open, her stomach fell. She waited with trepidation until Roy emerged from the entryway.

"You're here," he said, tossing his keys on the countertop. He railroaded into the kitchen to get a glass of water. "I was expecting you to be late. Do you want to go to dinner?"

She'd been waiting for words from him for so long now—wanting to talk, wanting to hear his reasons why he'd left. She was excited to get answers, but half-horrified they wouldn't be what she wanted to hear. Although she didn't even know what she wanted to hear. That he'd made a mistake? That was it, in a nutshell. But now she realized hearing that from Fin was even more satisfying.

She regarded Roy's thin frame, his beady eyes as they watched out the kitchen window, and was struck with how much he looked like a stranger. For the first two months, all she wanted, all she cried about every night, was getting her old life back. And she'd assumed that meant him, too. But now—now she could see that she wanted her old *life*, but not him in it. She wanted to be married. She wanted a father for Coco. She wanted basil on the windowsill, and neighbors who would come by for coffee. But she didn't need Roy specifically. He'd failed.

"We don't have to go to dinner. We can just talk here," she said.

He nodded. "Good. Let's go out front."

Outside, Roy motioned toward a gazebo that sat on a green knoll in the center of Lovey and Joe's front yard. A comfortable heat hung in the air between gentle breezes, warming up the jasmine that surrounded the yard and sending the sweet scent drifting toward Giselle in waves. Roy shoved his hands in his trouser pockets as they walked in silence across the lawn.

"Your hair looks interesting," he said.

She sighed. She was tired of Roy's non-compliments. She dismissed the comment and headed up the gazebo's wood stairs. The planks creaked as Giselle took a few steps into the center and circled it. As romantic and pretty as it was from the outside, the floor was scuffed and rotting at the edges.

Roy leaned against the pillar next to hers. The paint was peeling, revealing exposed brown stripes. He crossed his arms.

"So where is this coming from?" he asked.

"Where is what coming from?"

"This new"—he waved his hand toward her—"you."

She wasn't sure what to make of that. Was he referring to her hair? Her minimalist makeup? Her more casual clothes? She'd found another pair of Lia's jeans in a bottom drawer and had tugged them on today, remembering how Fin had checked her out when she'd worn a similar pair yesterday.

She shivered at the memory and decided not to answer Roy. It made her feel stronger.

"Perhaps . . ." he said, shifting against the railing, "this 'new you' is courtesy of Fin Hensen. Does he inspire this?" Contempt crawled across his face.

Giselle resisted the urge to feel ashamed. She hooked her thumbs in the pockets of the jeans and threw her shoulders back, knowing she looked kind of hot doing it. "I don't think you, of all people, should be contemptuous about such a thing. I don't imagine I need to remind you that you've had plenty of 'friends' who have 'inspired' you in a variety of ways. And you had them while we were married. At least I had the decency to wait until I was single again."

"You're not single."

"Of course I am."

"I mean, you're not . . ." He frowned, studying the neighbors' yards, trying to rephrase it. "I mean you're a *mother*. You're not like some single girl again. You have responsibilities."

A laugh escaped her. "I don't think *you* need to lecture *me* on responsibilities, Roy. Would these be the same responsibilities you've had for the last five years? They didn't seem to stop you from acting 'single' even when you weren't."

He glanced up, seemingly surprised at her response. Or maybe just that she had one. He shifted against the pillar. "Giselle, you're the one who wanted full custody of Coco."

She frowned at the turn in the conversation. "Yes."

"So if I'm going to grant you that, I need to know that you're not going to have her around dangerous men."

Giselle's casual demeanor evaporated. She stiffened against the peeling paint. "Are you saying you don't want me to *date*?"

"I'm saying I don't want you to date anyone *dangerous*."

"And you're going to be the judge of that?"

"I think I can tell."

Her mouth dropped open. While she was trying to formulate a sane response to a clearly insane train of thought, he shook his head.

"Listen," he said, shifting uncomfortably. "Let's not make this a crazy conversation. I'm just saying I don't want you to date Fin Hensen. And after this, back home, you need to be more careful about who you choose."

"Or what?"

"Or I won't give you full custody."

Giselle gasped. He was *blackmailing* her? And over *Fin*? What was his strange obsession with Fin? And would he really inspect her dates? Was he *crazy*?

She pressed her shaking hands against the rail so Roy wouldn't see. Was this her life now? Negotiating with a man who used to be her loving husband but was now some shell of a man with beady eyes who was emotionally blackmailing her?

Even though it shouldn't be a difficult decision to agree to not see a man she wasn't going to see anyway after his plane took off for South Africa, she still hesitated. It was the principle of the thing. She hated that Roy was still controlling her.

Yet if all she did was agree, she'd have full custody of Coco, and Roy out of her hair. Without the shared custody, she wouldn't have to run things by him, like moving or switching Coco's schools. She could even come back to California and be near her family again.

She peered at him from under her new bangs. "I'll consider your offer."

Roy took a deep breath and loosened his shoulders. He just wanted to make this easy on himself. And maybe she wanted it to be easy, too. But this wasn't what she came to talk about.

"I need a few answers, though," she said.

His spine straightened. He shifted against the rail and crossed his arms. "I thought you might."

"I need to know why you left."

He nodded. The cypress trees across the lawn demanded his attention while he seemed to think that over.

"I know this isn't helpful," he said, "but I don't have a firm answer for you. I was just feeling . . . like my needs weren't being met. . . ."

"Are you talking about sex?"

"Among other things."

"What are you talking about, Roy? I was by your side for every—"

He held up his hand. "Listen. I don't want to get into a big discussion about it, Giselle. It's not going to change anything. That's why I didn't want to talk to you these months. I feel how I feel. It's not going to change."

She shook her head. "That's not good enough for me."

"I'm not in love with you anymore." He peered up at her through his eyeglasses, over the top of his birdlike nose.

She let out an expulsion of breath and searched his hollow eyes, his set eyebrows, his stranger's face. And, much to her surprise, she realized she didn't care.

After four months of wanting to talk to him, wanting to catch him on the phone, wanting to hear four simple words, she realized—as she stared at this stranger—that the words she'd wanted to hear weren't "*I still love you*." The words she wanted to hear were "*It's not your fault*."

"But why?" she tried again. Her voice was strangely strong.

"It doesn't matter."

"It does to me."

He shook his head. Roy was not interested in making her feel better. That much was clear. The most she could hope for was to step around the rubble they'd left and get to the other side. Maybe just find a path of civility that would at least help Coco.

"Even if I have full custody, I need you to visit with Coco," she added. "She misses you. She needs to know you love her."

"I can do that."

She stared at him and was struck by how much she just wanted to be away from him now. This strange new man was not her Roy. But her Roy was not coming back. There was no going back. This was her new reality. He was just Coco's father now; there would never be any good answers.

She pushed up from the pillar. "I'm going to go."

"Do we have a deal, then?"

His question was laced with enough nervousness that Giselle peered at him. Maybe he didn't want custody of Coco at all—it would be very difficult for him, given how much he traveled—and maybe this thing with Fin was just a perk for him that he knew he could work into the deal.

"I'll think it over," she said.

"No seeing Hensen."

"I said I'd think about it." She was surprised at the snap in her voice.

His neck jerked back, as surprised as she was. "Did you sleep with him? Wait. Never mind." He shook his head. "I don't think I want to know. Or . . . yeah, I do."

"Roy, stop."

"I think I want to know."

"No, you don't."

He squinted at her. When she looked away, not planning on answering such ridiculousness, his frown became sharper. A vein appeared in his forehead. "*Damn* him," he whispered.

"First of all, this is very hypocritical of you, I hope you can see. And second of all, you and I were divorced when I made my decisions. We weren't when you made yours. Yours was out of disrespect. Mine was moving on."

"He's dangerous, Giselle."

"He's not dangerous."

"You know he was accused of all sorts of things around here—drugs; abandoning his own lover in the ocean. Her name was Jennifer Andre."

She let out a breath of agitation. "I know about Jennifer, and he doesn't do drugs."

"Not what I heard."

"And she wasn't his lover."

Roy's head jerked up. As confident as he'd seemed about everything else, his eyebrow raised in uncertainty on that one.

"Of course that's what he told you," he said.

"He was a friend of hers. And—speaking of whom—why didn't you tell me you knew her?"

"That has nothing to do with anything. She was a friend of my father's. But the issue is, Giselle, she was drugged with a kind of date-rape drug. He was *with* her at the time. He's bad news."

Giselle's thumb slipped to the space where her wedding ring usually was. And where the turquoise ring had been those two nights.

"He said it was Xanax," she said, despite the clenching in her gut.

"He lied."

"He wouldn't lie about that." Her voice, however, was dropping to almost a whisper. Did she really know that for sure?

She shook her head. She'd try another tactic. She wasn't here to defend Fin. She was here to get answers from Roy. And he'd given all he was going to give.

Without another word, she pushed up and headed down the gazebo steps, across the lawn, and into the house to get Coco. She could feel tears prickling the backs of her eyes—tears for the life she was leaving behind. She had thought she was giving Coco everything she needed—an ideal life, an ideal childhood—but now, at this glimpse of all the rubble at her feet, these concrete blocks she was now forced to step over, she knew she'd been a fool. It had all been a sham. *She* had been a sham. She wasn't a perfect wife, or a perfect mother. And she never would be.

She wiped an errant tear and glanced around the kitchen for Coco and Lovey. She couldn't get out of here fast enough.

As she was pulling away from the curb in her rental car, Coco finally in her seat belt and Lovey waving from the curb, Roy leaned into the driver's window.

"If you see him again, no full custody," he said.

Giselle squealed away from the curb. She was exasperated and exhausted and wanted to take Coco away forever. She hated having to plead, hated having to defend herself against something she shouldn't have to, hated feeling like she'd found something she'd wanted—although it was still elusive, but vaguely in the shape of Fin—and Roy was managing to take one more thing away from her.

She sped out of the neighborhood and took a long, deep breath. But her mind wandered, immediately, to the uncertainty of what she had been doing, and what she wanted, and what she would do from now on. Instead of feeling like she'd pulled herself together by coming out to Sandy Cove, her life felt ever more in shambles.

"Mommy, what's black and white and goes 'round and 'round?" Coco asked.

"Um . . ." Giselle sniffed and wiped the back of her hand across her eyes. "I don't know, baby. I give up."

"A penguin in a revolving door," Coco said, giggling before she could even finish the entire line.

Giselle tried to smile, but she was concentrating on her life falling apart instead.

As soon as Giselle got home, and got Coco settled into a coloring book, she called Fin.

"Did Jennifer die from Xanax or a date-rape drug?" she whispered.

A long silence stretched on his end. "Xanax."

"Roy said it was a date-rape drug."

"Roy is wrong."

Another silence. Maybe she should have looked it up online

first, but she wanted to hear Fin's answer straight from him, give him a chance to correct it.

"You can look it up," he said quietly.

Guilt swept over her. . . . *What had she just done?* Had she just brought this up to throw it back at him like everyone else in his life?

"It's online," he said, quieter still.

She could hear the disappointment and heartache seeping from his voice. But she needed to cut things off. "I'm not going to be able to make it tonight, Fin."

The silence elongated.

"What did he say?" Fin asked tightly.

"It's not because of that. I believe you. But he thinks you're unsafe, somehow, and . . . I don't believe that at all, Fin, but he said he won't grant me full custody if I continue to see you."

Eventually, she heard a knife start up against a cutting board. "It doesn't seem like he should be able to do that."

"He probably can't. And shouldn't. But it just seems like it could make everything complicated. And you said yourself that you and I have no business continuing this. And I'm . . . I'm just tired of fighting him."

"It's not worth it to you." He said it more as a statement than a question. Almost as if it answered a question he'd had.

Neither of them said anything for a long time. Giselle could hear the knife making its rhythmic cuts against the wood. The possibility of a new life, especially one with Fin, was so tantalizing. Living with the joy he brought her, the rapid heartbeat, the feeling of being whole and sexy and cherished, was beyond what she had ever dreamed. But she was a mother first. Just as Roy reminded her. And Roy was too much to fight.

Finally, Fin came back: "I understand. I don't want to make trouble for you. If you think it's best to stay away, you should."

"I hope you didn't change your flight yet."

"It's okay."

She winced. She'd been making waves since the moment she met him—and not the good kind. But she hoped she'd leave him with good memories, too.

"I hope you do well in Ballito." A lump formed in her throat. "I know you'll get your contract."

"Yeah," he answered. He didn't say anything further.

Giselle forced herself to stop. She was just messing things up now. She needed to let him go.

"I never got to see you surf," she announced anyway, seemingly unable to stop herself. "Are these competitions televised?"

"Ballito should be on Fuel TV. Or you can look it up on-line." His voice was sounding more and more distant.

"Okay. Well . . . thank you. For everything. I had an amazing time with you while I was here." She bit her cheek so as not to cry. "The art show, and the gallery, and the photos, and just . . . *everything*."

"I enjoyed the 'everything,' too," he said. She could hear the smile in his voice, but it was still tinged with sadness. "If you're ever in town again, and I'm in town at the same time, maybe we can have dinner or something."

The lump in her throat lodged more securely, and all she could do was nod. What she was really thankful for was the way he made her feel—the confidence he'd given her to step back into the world after Roy. She tried to find the words to say it, but her head was pounding with the effort to hold back tears.

"Take care," he said when they let the silence linger too long. "And thank you, too, Giselle."

Before she could say another word, he hung up.

Giselle clicked the receiver off and felt a crushing in her chest.

Fin tossed his cell phone onto the breakfast bar and hung his hands on his hips, surveying the ridiculousness he'd just created.

He collected the plates he'd just bought, the first set of four matching glasses he'd ever owned, and the Disney Princess glass he'd bought Coco, and shoved them into his cupboard.

Slamming the doors closed, he grabbed a bottled water and snapped off the burners for the tilapia and the green beans. He threw the fish back into the freezer.

He was a fool.

He collected the tickets off the dining table that he'd bought for the three of them—day passes to Disneyland, since he thought maybe Coco would want to see her princesses in real life—and shoved them under his phone. Maybe he'd just drop them off at Lia's. He'd leave them on the doorstep when Giselle and Coco were at Rabbit's surf camp. They could take Rabbit, in fact. Or maybe wait for Lia to come back. Or maybe they'd even go with Dan the Man.

Fin ground his teeth at that thought, but it was up to her. And something like that would probably be best for her and Coco. They needed someone who might be able to stay, someone who was considered stable, someone she wouldn't have to question about drugs, someone who didn't have riptides outside his door.

His chest was killing him. He thought he was going to throw up. He glanced at the garage door and told himself he needed to get in there and move those board bags.

He leaned against the cupboard doors for another two minutes and tried to get some air in his lungs. He'd endured many losses in his life—from heats, to meets, to Jennifer, to his parents—but this one felt different.

This one felt like the perfect wave—the last wave he ever needed—and he'd just let it go.

The next day at surf camp, Rabbit repeated his offer to Giselle for leaving Coco, in case she wanted to do something for herself for a couple of hours. But she declined again, hiding her puffy eyelids behind a pair of sunglasses.

She'd cried after Coco had fallen asleep, feeling like a silly teenager with her tears soaking the living room pillow, but it made her feel better. She was tired of keeping her feelings all bottled up.

"Are you sure?" Rabbit said, selecting a foam board for Coco.

The other parents hadn't arrived yet. Giselle scouted her favorite spot and laid her beach blanket territorially. "I'm sure."

Rabbit glanced up the hill toward their apartment complex. "You could have a hella cool little hookup with Fin," he offered, low. "Can't be easy with the little grommet around."

Giselle felt her face flush. She smoothed the blanket and sat on the edge. "Um . . . Well, we—Fin and I—we're over with, Rabbit."

"No kidding?" He frowned, sitting next to her. "What happened? Or—oh, wait. He's leaving today, right? Ballito?"

Giselle nodded.

"Well, all the more reason to see him."

"It's not like that, Rabbit. It's just . . . We're done."

"You shouldn't give up that fast."

"No, it's . . . complicated." She didn't want to think about this anymore. She could already feel the lump in her throat again. "How are you doing with Callie?"

He paused, squinting at her transparent change of subject, and threw a piece of driftwood. "That's ending before it ever began."

"No! Why?" It was Giselle's turn to be shocked.

"She probably won't go for me, Giselle. She's all responsible and crap. She's a mom of a five-year-old *kid*. I'm like a kid myself."

"Rabbit! You take care of kids every day."

He shook his head as if that were irrelevant.

They both watched the surf for a minute, watching the white foam marble across the water.

"Rabbit." Giselle shifted on the towel to look at him closer. She wished she could take her sunglasses off but she didn't want him to see the evidence of her own pain. She settled on gripping his elbow to make him understand. "You are smart, and funny, and responsible, and a caring man." She gave him a small shake with each compliment. "You could make someone like Callie feel very secure."

"You think I'm responsible?"

"Yes! I think you're wonderful, and caring, and you have those beautiful eyes."

He peered at her sideways. "You're not flirting with me, are you, Ms. Underwood?"

"I wouldn't dare. But I think you should go for Callie. You'll never know what could happen if you don't try."

"Maybe you should take your own advice."

The waves crashed right then, along with a dousing of guilt in her chest. She had tried. Had opened up, just a little. Had let out her gasps of joy. Had allowed herself those pleasures. But she needed to decide between motherhood and love now. And love held no guarantees.

"It's different for me, Rabbit."

"No, it isn't."

"We live in different worlds. And different states. Trying

to make something work for Fin and me would be like trying to get a sea horse to live on a prairie."

He looked at her plaintively and then pulled off her glasses. He took in her swollen eyes, then dropped his gaze. "Thought so."

He set her glasses on the blanket. "Listen, Giselle, I know this isn't any of my business, but I haven't seen Fin this happy in the five years I've known him. His face has 'ga-ga' written all over it every time he sees you. And, based on your puffy peepers there, you've been cryin' a river yourself at the idea of him leaving. So I think the two of you need to have a long look at what you're doing. Because, from where I sit, it looks like you've both been looking for something, and you've both found it. But for false reasons, you're both afraid to dive in."

"Hi, Rabbit!" A parent snuck up behind them, and Rabbit leaped to his feet. He shook hands with the mom and gave the six-year-old a low five. "Tanner. Put it there."

Giselle closed her mouth at Rabbit's lecture and shoved her glasses back on. She was glad he turned away and went to greet the other parents.

Mostly because she worried he might be right.

When Giselle and Coco trudged up the pebbled-concrete stairs to her apartment—Coco still bubbling with enthusiasm about how well she surfed—they came upon an envelope taped to Lia's front door with Giselle's name on the front. She didn't recognize the handwriting.

Inside were three gift-card passes to Disneyland wrapped in a piece of notebook paper.

"So Coco can meet her Disney princesses.—Fin"

She took in the handwritten words five or six times.

There were *three* passes. He must have intended to go. The idea of Fin wanting to spend the day at Disneyland with her and Coco was a little much for her to handle. She sniffed and focused on unlocking the door while Coco kept yanking at her cover-up and asking what it was.

"A generous gift for us, baby," she said.

When they got inside, Giselle told Coco to clean her hands and face for lunch. She grabbed her cell phone and glanced at the clock. He was probably already on his twenty-hour flight.

"Fin, I got the tickets," she said into his voice mail. "Thank you. That was . . . *too* generous. I can't thank you enough. . . . Coco's going to love it. We'll take Lia. I . . . just . . . want to say thanks. Again. And I miss you already."

She hung up hurriedly, before she could gush. She didn't want to sound like one of his groupies. But she did. Miss him, that was. And she wanted him to know.

And maybe a tiny bit of Rabbit's speech had lodged into her consciousness like hope.

"Lia!" Giselle exclaimed, rushing to hug her as soon as her sister came bumping through the doorway with her suitcases.

She hadn't seen her sister in about two years—except random photos in e-mails—and it was so good to see her in person, to feel her strong hug, to jump up and down with her, to touch her hair. She still smelled like apple shampoo.

"I canceled my last two appointments so I could catch you. Where's Coco?"

"Surprise!" Coco squeaked, bursting out from under a blanket.

Lia laughed and rushed for a big hug.

The three of them jumped around in a hug circle, then made potato au gratin for dinner, along with three large salads.

Giselle nervously served everyone while she wondered how to broach the topic of Fin with Lia.

"So," she began, "I've been meeting your friends." They all sat down at Lia's dining table. Giselle had put a vase of fresh flowers in the center of the table—beautiful sunflowers from the farmers' market on Main Street—and Lia eyed them appreciatively.

"Rabbit?" Lia asked.

"Yes. And Corky, and Jezzy, and Brent and Kino . . ."

"Did you get them all in the brochure? They're amazing up-and-comers. Jezzy is up for the Junior World Title already— did they tell you that? He's—"

"And Fin!" Coco exclaimed.

Lia halted her first bite of salad midair and turned a large set of eyes toward Giselle. "You met *Fin*? I thought he was going to South Africa?"

"He postponed a little, I guess."

Lia raised an eyebrow.

"We brought him a birthday cake!" Coco added.

Lia's eyes widened farther.

"And his nose got a boo-boo, but Mommy made it better."

A million telepathic questions seemed to shoot Giselle's way as Lia wiped her mouth with her napkin. Her expression was vacillating between shock and worry. "What else, Coco?"

"He kissed Mommy at the funeral."

Giselle's face went hot. She became determined to stab a crouton with her fork.

Lia sighed. "Can't wait to hear all about this. . . . But I think I'll wait until you're in bed, my dear. Tell me about surf camp with Rabbit."

Once Coco was snuggled into her Polly Pocket blanket on Lia's bed, and Lia had a chance to read *Stellaluna* to her twice, Lia sauntered back through the living room and joined Giselle in the kitchen. She leaned against the countertop, watching Giselle load the dishes into the dishwasher.

"So," she said, "why don't you start at the beginning?"

Giselle felt a wave of rebellion against Lia's accusatory tone—like a teenager who'd come home late for curfew. Maybe Roy had been right. Maybe he and Lia knew something about Fin she couldn't see. Maybe she wasn't the responsible, capable mother she'd always thought she was. Maybe she'd put Coco in some kind of danger because of her own lust. . . . She slammed the next two plates into the dishwasher.

"I tried to call you," Giselle said. "I was asking on the phone what you thought of him."

"What *happened*?"

"I just . . . *met* him."

"Doesn't sound like that's all that happened."

"I . . . Well, Rabbit took us to a party, and Fin was there, and . . . he asked me to an event with him, and I asked him to go to Joe's funeral with me."

"You asked him to Joe's *funeral*?"

When she heard it laid out like this, it did sound a little crazy. Giselle shoved the forks into the basket holder.

"So what happened then? How did he kiss you at the funeral?"

"Why don't you tell me why you're interrogating me first?" Giselle snapped. "What should you have told me after my *many* phone calls to you?"

"I told you I lost my phone."

"Duly noted. But what *would* you have told me? What should I know about Fin?"

Lia sighed. Her shoulders slumped. "He's hot. No question. You have good taste. But he's . . . kind of a *player*. Did he sleep with you?"

All of Giselle's old insecurities came crashing down like a velvet play curtain. She remembered Fin at the party, hand across Veronica's abdomen like it had a home there; all the women at the party who were touching his shoulder, leaning in toward him; the waitress asking for his autograph, looking at him adoringly. . . . Maybe he *was* just a player, and she'd just caught him on a few dull nights when his calendar happened to be empty. Maybe he'd just been giving her his usual lines. . . .

"Yes, I slept with him." She could hardly get the words out of her mouth.

"Damn him!" Lia pushed up from the counter. "I sure hope you used a condom." She marched into the living room, throwing pillows aside as if she were looking for something.

"What are you looking for?"

"I already can't find my new phone. Did you move it? I need to call Fin."

"Lia! You are *in no way* calling Fin about this."

She did, in fact, know where Lia's phone was. She'd seen it charging in Lia's bedroom when she'd gone to get Coco's pajamas. Lia seemed to remember it at the same time, and whirled toward the bedroom.

Giselle galloped in front of her and threw herself across the door. "No! Mother-of-pearl, I'm serious, Lia. This is *not* going to happen."

Lia reeled back, surprise in her eyes, but then a grin stole across her face. "Nice. I see you're getting a backbone. I like the forceful body against the door. Your swearing needs a little work, though."

"Lia, please. Let's sit down." She whispered the last part, hoping they wouldn't wake Coco.

Lia backed off. "Okay. But you need to tell me what happened. Everything. I'm pissed. Do you *know* how many women he sleeps with a year? He's got seventeen-year-old girls lined up at his hotel room wherever he competes, you know. Brazil, Australia, Hawaii . . . He couldn't have left *you* alone?"

"He said you would be mad."

"I am. So spill it. And tell me when you became such a hussy."

Giselle groaned but Lia threw a pillow at her. "Kidding. Just tell me. If you say enough nice things, maybe I'll spare him his balls next time he shows up."

Giselle told Lia most of the story, leaving out some of the more embarrassing parts about her own giddy feelings toward Fin. But she told her about the sex in pretty graphic detail. Lia's eyes widened.

"All right," Lia said, shifting her legs underneath her on the couch. "I probably don't need to know this much about him. . . . But, well, maybe I want to."

Lia collapsed into a fit of giggles, hitting Giselle with a couch pillow she'd been clutching at her stomach. Giselle leaned her head back on the cushions and sighed. The grin on Lia's face slipped away, and she touched Giselle's hair.

"I missed you, G."

"I know. I missed you, too."

"I'm glad you're over Roy."

"I didn't say that." She frowned. *Did* she say that?

"You don't have to. You're here. You're laughing. You're relaxed. You look smokin' in my jeans, and you seem ten years younger with that cute hair. And you had what appears to be amazing sex with the Gigolo of Sandy Cove."

"Lia!" Giselle's face flushed again. She plucked at the fringe on the pillow.

"But, I have to admit . . ." Lia leaned back in the same manner and stared up at the ceiling.

"What?"

"It does sound like he *did* spend more time with you than I ever recall him spending with anyone. Maybe he actually fell for you a little." She looked at Giselle with something that hinted of admiration.

"Too far-fetched?"

"No, not at all. If he *were* going to fall for someone, it would be someone like you."

"What do you mean?"

She seemed to think that over, bobbing her head to one side as if making friends with the idea. "You're very beautiful, Giselle. I don't know why you never believed that. But you're beautiful on the inside, too. I think that's what he's been missing in the floozies he dates. And you're smart. He loves that. And you're . . . *stable*. I think Fin needs that especially."

"Stable sounds boring."

"Stable can be a lifesaver to someone who's looking for it."

"And you think he is?"

"I know he is. *He* doesn't seem to know it, but it's obvious to the rest of us."

Giselle nodded. It even seemed obvious to her and she hadn't known him long.

"You think I'm stable?" she asked.

"Of course. I've always admired that about you. You always do the right thing."

"But . . . not recently. I thought you and Mom and Noelle were giving up on me, thinking I'd made such a bad decision with Roy. And now"—she flung her hand—"with Fin. You think he was an irresponsible decision."

"No, not at all!" Lia sat up. "We love you, Giselle. We just want you to be happy. Roy was too controlling. He was turning you into a robot. I can't tell you how happy it makes us to see you out in the world, making your own decisions and not walking around like a Stepford Wife. And Fin was, maybe, a good decision after all—for good sex. Maybe you needed someone like him, to loosen you up a bit. But just don't let him hurt you. Don't count on him to send you a Christmas card or anything." She cupped Giselle's hand. "You're going to be fine, G. You're the best mom ever, and the nicest person, and you always land on your feet. You and Coco are going to thrive."

Giselle felt tears stinging her eyes again, and this time let them fall. She leaned over and gave Lia a big hug. "You don't know how much I needed to hear that."

"You're welcome," Lia said in a strangled voice. "Now let's break into the wine. We haven't had a sisterly 'whine-fest' in a long time. I wish Noelle were here. I've got a lot to tell you about New York. . . ."

Twenty-five

Giselle wrapped up the brochure, and it came out better than she expected. She got releases from all the parents she needed, and her photos were stunning. At the last minute, however, Rabbit decided to change the name. He wanted to call it the Jennifer Andre Grommet School.

"For Fin," Rabbit told her over coffee at Lia's dining table. "We'll give a Jennifer Andre scholarship to a former camper when he or she goes to college anywhere in the country. I think this might help him. He funds the school, you know."

"No. I didn't know."

"The scholarship'll be perfect. He's always telling us we should go to college, even when the big sponsors come sniffing around." He blew the steam from his mug. "I think he'd like that he could do something for Jennifer."

Giselle's chest filled with gratitude. These boys loved Fin so much. They were good people. Although Fin hadn't called once in two days, and Giselle was starting to wonder whether Lia was right after all, she wanted nothing but the best for him. He had a good heart. And he'd loved Jennifer. All he needed was a chance to move on.

"Hey, your photos were slick," Rabbit announced. "Jezzy's

agent wants to buy a few. And Corky's manager wants some, too."

"Oh! Yes, certainly." She knew she'd done a good job. As well as Fin had helped her feel like a desirable woman again, Rabbit and the boys had helped her feel like she could forge forward with whatever career she set her mind to. "Should we do a focus group?" she joked.

"What do you mean?"

"I have a couple of friends stopping by to say good-bye, and we can ask them which brochure they like better." She pointed to the two versions she couldn't decide between.

As if on cue, the doorbell rang, and she welcomed Tamara, Fox, and Toni. Tamara looked completely overdressed for Lia's little apartment—her huge copper earrings brushing against a silk blouse that probably cost more than a month's worth of rent here—but Tamara didn't seem uncomfortable at all, flinging herself onto the couch and making herself at home with Rabbit.

The three of them stayed for about an hour, helping her select a brochure, discussing whether Toni might sign up for Rabbit's camp next session, and reminiscing over the Pageant of the Masters show. Giselle was going to miss them all.

"Can Toni spend the night, Mommy?"

"Oh, darling, no. This isn't our house. And besides—we're flying home tonight."

"Home?"

Coco knew this, but it seemed like it was hitting her again, anew.

Giselle nodded, and Coco burst into tears, running into the bedroom. Toni stood, looking perplexed.

"Sweet, why don't you go cheer her up?" Tamara asked her.

Toni nodded and went to find Coco.

"She doesn't want to go?" Tamara asked.

Giselle shook her head.

"We wish you could stay, too."

Fox came to life and leaned forward. "I've never seen Fin quite as happy as he was when you were here, Giselle. I think you were good for him. I hope you'll visit soon."

"I still can't believe you two weren't really dating," Tamara said. "The affection in both your eyes . . ." She shook her head.

Giselle wished Lia weren't at work so she could hear these assessments from others about Fin's reaction to her. It was confusing her now, and she wished Lia could help her sort it out.

"I'll visit as often as I can," she promised, although she wondered how possible that would really be until she could secure custody. Who knew how long that took?

She walked the Foxes to the door, under dramatic protest from Coco, and was met with Roy on the other side of the threshold.

"What are you doing here?" she whispered.

"Wanted to say good-bye to Coco." He and Fox eyed each other uneasily.

"Davis Fox." Fox thrust his hand forward.

"Roy Underwood."

"This is my wife, Tamara. And my daughter, Toni, is back there."

"Roy is my ex," Giselle blurted. She was starting to get used to the line.

Fox nodded, still studying Roy strangely, while Roy peered past Giselle's shoulder to try to spot Coco.

"Is she inside?" he asked.

"Yes." Giselle stepped to the side and let him through. Although she wasn't crazy about being around him anymore, she was glad he was coming to say good-bye. She never wanted Coco to feel anything but adored.

"Mom's right behind me," he notified her, stepping inside.

Giselle greeted Lovey with a big hug, then excused herself to say good-bye to Tamara and Fox on the street.

Once Toni was buckled into the backseat, and Coco and Toni exchanged good-byes and Polly Pocket dolls, Giselle waved to the Foxes as they pulled into the palm-tree-lined streets of Sandy Cove.

She would never forget these two weeks.

Or these wonderful people.

Or Fin.

Rabbit stood behind Giselle with his hands in his cargo pockets, watching the planes fly in.

"I have a date," he whispered when Lia and Coco were out of earshot.

"With *Callie*?"

He winked. "I listened to what you said."

"Flight 258, now boarding."

Lia rushed over from the window where she'd been watching the planes with Coco and threw her arms around Giselle.

Giselle was going to miss Lia again. She hadn't gotten nearly enough time with her. "I'll try to come back soon," she promised.

Lia nodded. "Mom's mad we didn't drive up there. We can meet in L.A. next time. Noelle will meet us, too."

Giselle agreed, but she wanted to come back here. She would always want to see Fin now, although matching up with a week he happened to be in town would be miraculous.

"Thanks for everything," said Rabbit, yanking her into a hug. "You were great for all of us here. And thanks for your advice about . . . you know."

Giselle hugged Rabbit back. "You were great, too, Rabbit. You did a great job watching over me, even though I didn't want you to. And good luck with 'you know.' "

He dropped to one knee to give Coco a big hug, along with some last-minute advice about how to practice pop-ups as a goofy-footer; then Lia wriggled Coco into a huge bear hug.

Soon, Giselle and Coco were buckled into seats 8A and 8B, Coco crying and looking out the window.

"I'm gonna miss it here," she whispered to no one in particular.

Giselle sat back in her seat and swiped at her own eyes.

She would, too. . . .

They arrived home close to midnight, Coco asleep on Giselle's shoulder.

The house felt strange and tomblike, sort of like Lovey's house, only without the death. Or maybe there was.

She set her purse down, and her tote bag, and Coco, then spotted a package on the backyard deck in front of the slider. She opened the door with a *whoosh* of summer humidity and drew the heavy box inside. It had a note attached from her neighbor: *"Thought you'd want this when you got home."*

Giselle tore into the brown wrapping. Amid the tufts of paper and Styrofoam popcorn was a miniature bronze statue of Camille Claudel's "La Valse." It was a replica of the bronzed man, shirtless, clinging to the woman in the hold of being cherished, or maybe being saved.

A note accompanied the package.

"This is the one that really reminded me of you," it said. *"Fin."*

Giselle walked through the dark house to set the statue on her living room mantel.

She touched the man's legs, his face, his protective arms. She would never forget these two weeks, or the man who'd saved her, even temporarily.

She swept Coco off the couch, turned off the hallway lights, and carried her little girl through their house of loneliness.

The waves broke hard and to the left.

Fin stood in the sand with his competition jersey on and studied the next set.

The contest had gone from ninety-six competitors to forty-eight, then to twenty-four, then to sixteen, and now he was one of the eight left going into the quarterfinals.

"Good luck, mate."

Fin nodded back to Jess Casper of Australia.

"I hope you beat Caleb," Jess went on. "I feel like he stole that heat from Winny yesterday."

"I'll do my best." Fin smirked at him.

The competition had been more heated than he'd imagined. He tried to distance himself from most of the crap—he stayed in his own hotel, as he had for years, rather than in the luxury homes that housed tour surfers together.

But he was here.

And he had the nagging feeling Giselle might be watching him on television.

He blew out a breath and inspected the swells again.

He didn't know, of course. For all he knew, she could have forgotten about him the second she hung up the phone that night. It sure didn't seem hard for her to cancel. Her lying ass-hole ex was able to sway her pretty easily. He rubbed his neck and tried to tamp down the anger that surfaced every time he thought about it.

But the thought that she *might* watch him made him perform. He'd pulled off airs in these last few days that he'd never tried before: flying above the lip of the wave with one-handed grips on the board; doing one-eighties on the board in midair; and even some cutbacks he hadn't done since he was a teenager.

And now here he was in the quarterfinals.

He couldn't believe it.

Giselle had, in essence, become his muse. . . .

He ran his hand down his face. The winds had been vari-able all week, and storm clouds moved in now, casting Balli-to's waters in a gray-blue. The surf kicked up, throwing some angry backlash.

He watched the next two surfers—Jose Manilla from Mex-ico, who was dominating Pierre Petrone from France. The bad set didn't seem to stop Jose from scoring twelve points com-pared to Petrone's nine-point-six. Jose moved easily to the semifinals.

Fin looked for Caleb while the next pair of surfers went out. It was only four heats today, and he and Caleb would be head-to-head. With his new comfort level for the airs—and his knowledge that thoughts of Giselle fueled him—he knew he could take Caleb.

When his heat was called, he hustled into the cool waters of the Indian Ocean and threw his board down, paddling out hard with sweeping rotations of his shoulders. Caleb was right behind him.

The storm clouds drew the water into riotous ridges, rather than the smooth glassy waves that barrellers like him favored. He glanced at the yellow buoy that noted where shark waters were, and pulled to the left. A nice eight-foot lift rose ahead of him.

He took it with confidence, and Giselle popped into his head. He showed her what he could do: He rode straight up the wall, hitched his board back, and rode it down, then repeated the action four times on a long, wild wave. On the last ride up, when the wave had more face, he gripped the board with one hand and pulled it into the air, spinning once and landing with a splash back into the white water. He bent low and looked for whatever barrel was left, then let it curl over him and rode it out, dragging his hand along the wall. He came out the other side to wild applause from the sweatshirt-clad beachgoers on Willards Beach.

Damn.

He loved showing off for Giselle.

Caleb took the next wave, which was—admittedly—shitty. Bad luck of the draw. Fin straddled his board, sluicing the water off his face and watching Caleb barely make it out of his tube. The wave had given Caleb such crappy lift that he hadn't caught any air or done a single trick. Fin could see him swearing under his breath.

Fin paddled out for the next one and managed four awesome maneuvers. The crowd went wild.

Caleb followed up, paddling past Fin with a glare, then went into a few simple turns before his wave turned to mush. The crowd didn't love him, and obviously he'd pissed Mother Nature off, too, because she was delivering some crappy white water that gave him nothing to ride.

Fin took his last wave with ease. He knew he'd already won, and knew he'd drive his score up even further with the beautiful gray waves Mother Nature was handing him. He pretended Giselle was watching his rolls, his twists, and one last spin, when he rode way up over the lip like an acrobat.

At the end of the day, Fin had scored an impressive fifteen to Caleb's nine-point-two.

He was going to the semifinals.

"Thanks, Giselle," he whispered under his breath as he trudged back up onshore.

In the tented locker room, amid the backslaps of the other competitors who would be joining him tomorrow, Fin peeled his jersey off, changed out of his wet-suit pants, and pulled on dry shorts and a T-shirt. He asked around to see whether any of the Americans had an extra voltage converter. It had been out of character for him to forget—his mind must have been drifting as he was packing—but he found himself stuck in an out-of-the-way hotel room last night, separated from his fellow teammates, with a dead phone.

But damn, he wanted to call.

He wanted to call *her*.

He'd never had anyone "back home" to reach right after a heat, except managers and agents. When he was a kid, he'd called his parents, but when his dad started letting in with how much Fin was selling out, he'd stopped. Sometime around sixteen. And now . . . Well, now no one cared.

Except Giselle. She might be happy for him.

"I have one, bro," said R.J. Williams from the other side of the tent. He was a young mop-topped kid—his mom had probably packed his converter for him. The kid dug into his backpack and threw it to Fin.

"I'll return it in an hour," Fin said, lifting it in his fist and charging out of the tent.

He'd just mastered five-foot storm swells and shark-infested waters. But right this minute he'd have to contemplate whether he was brave enough to call a woman.

Once inside his off-the-beaten-path hotel, he plugged in R.J.'s converter.

When his phone had enough juice, he logged on to hear his messages, his chest constricting when he heard the two from Giselle—one thanking him for the Disney passes and another thanking him for the bronze statue of "La Valse."

He sat on the edge of the bed and listened to them another four times. She hadn't said much else beyond thanks, although she did say she missed him. He wasn't sure what that meant. And when had he become such a love-struck fool, listening between the lines on a voice mail for anything he could work with?

He rubbed his face and looked around his hotel room. There was someone else he needed to talk to.

"Hey," he said into the receiver.

"How's it goin'?"

"I'm in the semifinals."

"Damn! That's great!" Fox's voice was jubilant.

In the last week, Fin had realized how much he liked Fox.

Giselle had opened his eyes to how good it felt when you let someone in a little—opened up, told them what was on your mind. And Fox was not letting him down. Fox had *never* let him down, in fact.

"I got some crazy airs on Caleb," he said.

"I'll watch it on Fuel tonight. Damn, Fin. All you need is this, and it could hoist you into the tour next year."

"Yeah, but here's the thing. . . ." Fin wandered to his window, trying to phrase this in his head. The clouds had parted in the last two minutes, and rays of sun were peeking through the dark clouds, casting columns of light all over the white-walled city of Ballito.

"*What*, man?" Fox prompted.

"I don't know if I want to do the tour next year."

"*What?*"

"I think I might be ready to retire."

A silence fell.

Fin knew he was blindsiding Fox with this. He let the last sentence sink in. All this work they'd done together, all these months of planning and plotting for this contract, all the negotiating Fox had done on his behalf . . . Fox was probably figuring out how to beat him over the head with a shortboard.

"I figured," Fox said.

Fin wasn't sure he'd heard him correctly. "You did?"

"Yeah. There's a moment a man reaches, when he's been chasing success all his life, when he either achieves the success and moves on, or realizes he's been chasing the wrong thing all these years."

Fin watched the clouds open up over the city as a spire of heat coiled in his gut. "And which category do I fall into?"

"Maybe a little of both."

"You think I've been chasing the wrong *thing*?"

Fin ground his teeth. Fuck *that*. He thought of the medals, the money, the champagne sprayed over his head on the dais all those years. Fox was sounding like his dad now. Fuck if that had been the wrong thing. . . .

But, he had to admit, he *was* still searching. As if the perfect wave were still out there—he kept going back, as if he would eventually feel what he was supposed to feel and know he'd "made it." But that feeling wasn't happening.

"I think it was the right thing for you at the time," Fox said in the voice you use for mental patients. "But now, I think you found what you were really looking for."

Fin frowned, confused for a minute. What did Fox think he was *really looking for*? Did Fox mean the longer-term contract? Not competing? Beating Caleb with airs?

"And that would be . . ." He left the bitter words hanging, daring Fox to fill them in.

"That would be *Giselle*, you idiot."

The floor shifted under Fin as he watched the rays of sun open up and spread like spotlights over daytime Ballito.

"I'm talking about *love*, you asshole," Fox went on. "I asked you to bring someone to the gallery who looked sophisticated to you, who you could be photographed with, because I knew you'd zero in on someone you thought you couldn't have. But that's what you needed, Fin. You don't think you deserve what you *do* deserve. You want someone smart. Sophisticated. Someone you respect. You want a home. A family . . . And that's exactly who you brought."

Fin steadied himself against the hotel dresser and sucked some air into his lungs. It all seemed so obvious now. He was obsessed with Giselle because she represented everything he *ever wanted*: home, normalcy, tradition, peace, a place to come back to, a place you could be yourself and fall softly at the end of each day. He'd been searching for perfect waves all his life—there was, truly, always a next one. But with Giselle there wasn't a "next one." She was it. She was his perfect wave. She was his perfect moment.

A ray outside caught a metal scroll on top of a white-washed steeple and bounced the light back into his face.

"I don't suppose you have contracts for Indiana." His voice came out as a wheeze as he pushed the words through his airway. He doubled over and pressed his palm on the dresser top.

"No." Fox chuckled. "But let me think on this. I might have an idea. . . . And I saw your girl, by the way."

Fin concentrated on breathing. "What?"

"The day she caught her plane. I met her ex, too. So he knew Jennifer?"

Fin kept trying to assemble the shards that Fox seemed to keep throwing. "What do you mean?"

"He was at Jennifer's funeral."

"Roy was?" It was as if the shards were all supposed to line up, like a puzzle, but too many pieces were mismatched.

"In the back. I thought you remembered him."

"He was *there*?"

"Yeah. It took me about an hour after I met him, but then I remembered that's how I knew him. I was standing right next to him in the back of the church that day. We both came in late. He left before the service ended, I remember. He must've known Jenn. Maybe that's why he's so wrought up about you?"

Fin stared at the rays dancing through the city. *Roy?* At Jennifer's funeral? A sickening thud fell into his stomach that Giselle might have known her, too, but why would she have kept it a secret?

"Maybe," was all he said.

"Anyway, do well tomorrow," Fox said. "Even if you're retiring, you can go out on a high note. What boards are you using? Use something that'll show up on camera and might garner you a contract even after you retire."

"Are you advising me as my agent now, Fox?"

"Thinking about it."

"Seriously?"

"Just thinking. Tamara's tired of all the traveling and drama with Mahina. I thought maybe you could use someone. Make your woman happy—that's smart, Fin. It'll make you happy, too."

All Fin could do was nod. "I'll call you after my heat."

"Good luck, man."

After five or six deep breaths—to put the world back on its axis—Fin unpacked his laptop and fired it up with R.J.'s converter.

He steadied himself into the hotel desk chair and began clicking through some old e-mails. A niggling thought kept itching the back of his brain.

Fin found some of Jennifer's old e-mails, when she'd been traveling in Costa Rica a couple years ago and had sent him a flurry of correspondence to tell him about the trip. She had tried to convince him that her affair wasn't so terrible—that this married man planned to leave his family, truly wanted her—so she'd sent photos about the great time they were having as "proof."

Fin, of course, had felt compelled to argue with her. This man would never leave his family. They never do. And Jennifer had told Fin, in no uncertain terms, that she respected his opinion, but she believed otherwise. That was the last time she'd talked about it.

Fin clicked through his folders. He kept pictures his acquaintances sent of good surf—Barritz in the south of France, Jay Bay in Australia, Cape St. Francis in South Africa. He scrolled through all of them until he came to Costa Rica.

He ran the curser down until he found the one he wanted: "Me and Mystery Man, Costa Rica."

He blinked back the shot of pain that coursed through his veins whenever he saw Jennifer's smiling face again. But then, as he took in the rest of the picture he'd barely recalled, he felt the blood drain from his head.

Jennifer was standing next to Roy.

The orders rolled in.

Giselle couldn't believe it, but she was able to sell fifty individual photos she'd taken of Jezzy, Corky, and the boys as packages to their agents and managers. They used them for press releases, websites, social media avatars, and more, and a couple asked whether she could take photos of their other athletes, most of whom were surfers but a few tennis players and race-car drivers. Jezzy's agent was so insistent he wanted to fly her to Florida that week to capture an athlete in his hometown.

She sighed and told him no. She couldn't leave Coco right now. She'd just signed her up for a Daisy Scout troop that had a few "adventures" that week. She could comfortably leave Coco with a grandparent or aunt, but she didn't feel right leaving her with a babysitter overnight. It was one of the 800 times this week she thought about living in Sandy Cove, near Lia and Lovey.

And, of course, Fin.

When he was home. Which wouldn't be often.

She sighed and glanced at the statue on the mantelpiece. He hadn't called her once. Of course, he'd sent her the beautiful statue. She'd called to thank him again, but got his voice mail. She'd stuttered through the thanks and hung up quickly,

afraid again to sound like a groupie. She couldn't stop thinking about what Lia had said.

But that didn't stop her from watching him compete all
week. She'd found daily video coverage from Fuel TV on her
computer, and had tuned in every night. She'd watched Fin
flying through the air in incredible feats of athleticism, coast-
ing through barrels, pushing his board into the walls of the
wave, pumping his legs into acrobatic turns, and smiling back
at the crowd as they roared for him. Coco came to watch, too,
and they clapped and hugged at the end of every set. Giselle
closed her laptop every night with a smile on her face.

The smell of furniture polish wafted up now from the old
antique desk in the living room as she settled into its wooden
seat in front of the computer. It was a desk from Roy's family
that neither of them had used much, mostly because it had an
uncomfortable formality about it, but for now it was better
than using Roy's old office.

She fired up the computer, although she had an hour before
she could catch the next competition. In the meantime, she'd toy
around with Photoshop. She might start using it for some of her
new projects. She opened old photo files—most of which were
Roy's from heart conferences—and thought about trashing
them all to start clean. He probably had backups already. But,
just to be nice, she grouped them into one folder, and she'd ask
him. They were labeled Austria, Heart and Health Convention;
Singapore, Cardiovascular Institute Convention; Seattle, Heart-
Beat Convention—and they all went into a new folder she enti-
tled "Roy's Crap." She giggled at her curse word.

As she dragged folder upon folder, a strange one caught her
eye. It was labeled "Costa Rica" but didn't have a conference
name. She hadn't remembered him ever going there. She opened
the first photo and saw a beautiful beach hut—hammocks strewn
between poles, hibiscus in vases. It was gorgeous, but she couldn't
place what the photo was, or what it was doing there. She clicked
through the remaining photos: They looked like resort pictures.
Roy's suitcase was in one of them, and some of his clothes were
on one of the beds. No people were in any of them. When she got
to the last photo, however, her hand froze.

Roy was in that one, a goofy grin over his hibiscus shirt.
But that was not what made her heart stop.

What made her heart stop was that his arm was wrapped possessively around Jennifer Andre.

The Ballito skies opened to the morning sun, casting the water in a turquoise blue and sending long, glassy tubes of surf to race parallel with the shoreline.

Fin glanced at his other competitors in the tent—they were down to four now. He was pitted against Jose Manilla.

He tugged his competition jersey over his head.

He couldn't stop thinking about what Fox had said. It was what his dad always spouted. His dad had given up professional surfing when he was about Fin's age, claiming the competition took the love out of the sport, and it was better to get your money somewhere else so you didn't have to confuse your love for surfing with your need to earn a living. That way you could hold on to that joy that overcame you when you rode out of a barrel after a two-minute ride with the universe. All his dad needed, he'd said time and time again, was "his good woman, his good love, and three meals a day."

For the first time, after talking with Fox yesterday, Fin's dad's words made sense. What he was feeling with Giselle was a connection he'd never felt before—a moment of opening his heart to the universe, or at least to this one person, and letting her in. He wanted Giselle. And Coco. And a feeling of family. And Thanksgiving at Giselle's mom's house, and crazy relatives around the table. He wanted Giselle in his bed every morning, and more of those mornings where something was more important than surfing. He wanted Coco's knock-knock jokes in the evening out on the lounge chairs, and more of those moments when she'd touch the bridge of his nose with concern and pucker her little eyebrows with satisfaction that his boo-boo was healed. He wanted Giselle's vanilla scent, and her grateful smile when her eyes lit upon a work of art or anything she found gorgeous. He wanted birthday cakes and birthday songs sung by a motley chorus of people who seemed to love you. Unconditionally. In that moment. Or forever. He wanted family that would stick.

The announcer called his and Jose's names, and Fin jogged out into the surf. He glanced at Jose. The kid reminded Fin of himself at that age—hungry, not sure of his place in the world, focused on the surf and nothing else because it seemed like the only thing you had. Fin threw his board down into the water, leaped onto his stomach, and began paddling out. He nodded for Jose to go first.

As a beautiful rise came, Fin straddled his board, pushed the water out of his face, and watched Jose take it like an aerial artist in the new-school moves the judges loved. He couldn't help but grin for him.

Fin scanned the horizon for his wave. He passed on the next two, and took the third, his heart thudding when he saw the curl of the tube. He pictured Giselle watching and thought he'd show her what pure joy looked like, pure love. Sticking to what he did well, he showcased one of his old-school specialties: ducking to ride through the barrel, his hand dragging along the water wall. He wouldn't score high for this. The judges were focused on aerials. But Fin didn't care.

It was, truly, a perfect moment.

Because he'd just realized he was in love.

And he was about to go—for the first time in his life—home.

Giselle's hand shook as she picked up the old-style landline from the antique desk. She wanted to be looking at the pictures when she made this call.

She waited until Coco was playing in the backyard, creating a campsite for her Polly Pockets in a terra-cotta planter whose geraniums had died.

When Roy answered, she cut right to the chase: "Were you having an affair with Jennifer Andre in Costa Rica?"

The silence on his end lengthened into oblivion. After a moment, she wasn't sure he'd even picked up the phone. "Roy?"

"Yes."

"'Yes' you're there, or 'yes' you had an affair with Jennifer Andre?"

"Both."

She felt as though a diesel truck ran over her stomach. She'd known he'd had the two affairs, but this made a third. And this one had obviously lasted for years, overlapping the others. And this one was *Jennifer Andre*. With beautiful eyes, and a long life ahead of her. With parents and friends who wanted the best for her. And who was now dead.

"Were you the married man she was seeing when she died?"

"Yes." His voice was small.

"Did you promise her you were going to leave your wife?"

"Giselle, please."

"Did you promise, Roy?"

"It doesn't matter anymore, does it? It—"

"It matters to me."

"Why? What good does it do you?"

"I want to know how much of a slime you are."

He paused.

"The more I learn what a weasel you were, the less I feel guilty about our marriage breaking up. I'm realizing, more and more, that it was all *you*. There was nothing wrong with me, Roy: There's something wrong with *you*."

He sighed into the phone, apparently not planning to argue that.

"Is this why you were so adamant that I not see Fin? It wasn't about Fin not being safe for me and Coco, was it? You didn't want him to recognize you."

"He didn't, by the way. You didn't find the sharpest knife in the drawer, Giselle."

"Damn you, Roy!" The swearword came out of nowhere, along with a heat around her ears, as well as a protectiveness for Fin and even Jennifer. She didn't know how to process all of her emotions, but she was determined to speak them, even determined to feel them fully.

"Did you give her those drugs?" she whispered, reality dawning.

"Giselle, I wasn't anywhere near Tahiti when that happened."

"But you could have prescribed them."

He didn't respond.

"Roy? Did you prescribe her those Xanax?"

"Listen, Jennifer Andre was a grown woman. She could make her own decisions. I wasn't responsible for what she did."

Giselle recoiled at the words, almost exactly what she'd told Fin. But Fin had taken on the responsibility, knowing that when you loved someone, you were responsible for their heart, and their emotions, and where their emotions were going. Apparently, Roy hadn't gotten that memo in medical school.

And it made her love Fin all the more.

"You're despicable," she whispered.

Her mind was whirling, trying to put all the pieces together. "Did your parents know you were seeing her?"

"My dad knew."

Another spear of pain shot through her. "Did your mom?"

"No."

"Is this why you never wanted me in California?" The idea that he'd kept her away from her family because of his own secretive, despicable life—and that she'd allowed it—shot another dagger into her soul.

"Listen, Giselle—"

"No, *you* listen, Roy." She was trembling. She'd never felt her rage before. She'd always tamped down her anger, looked the other way at things that were obvious, to keep a perfect façade of a perfect life. But no more. She was facing the rubble head-on.

"You've ruined their lives," she went on. "Not only Jennifer's, of course—stringing her along when all she wanted was love. You denied that girl the experience of true, honest love in her short life. And you've ruined her family's lives—they have no answers; they don't know what drove their daughter to sadness. They could be blaming themselves. And you've ruined Fin's life. He's the most decent man I've met in ages—trying to love properly, trying to take care of the people in his life—and he feels guilty for Jennifer's death. He blames himself when he should blame you. And the public blames him—and has almost destroyed his career—when it was *you*, Roy. You're responsible for *so much destruction. . . .*"

Giselle's head began to pound. She gripped the edge of the desk. "I want you to fund a scholarship for her in Fin's name."

"What?"

After she blurted it out, she wasn't sure where it had come from, but the idea crystallized right in front of her: "The scholarship was just started, but I want you to donate fifty thousand a year for the next forty years—I'll get you the address."

"Giselle, you can't—"

"If you don't want me to go through the press, and drag your name through the mud, and point someone in the direction of your prescription pad, you'll do this, Roy. You'll do it for me. And for Fin."

"Are you *blackmailing* me?"

"Think of it as a friendly persuasion. It's the least you could do."

She glanced at the sculpture of "La Valse" on her mantel, of the man dancing with the woman—or perhaps saving her.

"I already have the ideal logo," she added.

Still shaking, Giselle drove Coco to her first Daisy Scout meeting, then came home to her empty house.

She took out the trash, straightened her new desk, tried to forget about Roy, and dusted the dining table, glancing at the clock and hoping the next hour would go by so she could go get her daughter.

A knock sounded on the door.

Surprised, she shuttled through the entryway, hauled the door open, and was stunned to see . . . Well, it took a moment to coordinate the image. She struggled to put together his sun-kissed hair, his gray-and-white board shorts, and his tanned wrist leaning near her brick-lined Indiana doorbell— all with her suburban summer lawn behind him, and Mrs. O'Dell out there in her front yard, selecting roses. He was a sea horse on a prairie.

"Fin, what . . . what are you doing here?" she breathed out.

"I came to get you."

"*Get* me?"

"To bring you home."

There didn't seem to be enough air. Giselle glanced around, as if other images from this mirage might appear. A surfboard, maybe. Rabbit, even.

The mirage moved. The corded bracelet moved down his wrist as he shoved his right hand into his pocket.

"Home," he repeated.

The mirage shifted again, glancing down once at his shoes.

"Giselle, I think we've both been searching for home for a long time. I didn't even know that's what I was looking for. But meeting you . . . being with you . . . That's the closest thing I ever felt to home. I've never been as happy as I was in those days I spent with you. You asked me that night while we were watching the water if I'd been in love before, and I hadn't, but I couldn't help but stare at you and wonder if it was like what I was feeling right then for you. From now on, I'd have to say yes. I've been in love. With you."

Giselle's breath was coming faster, not sure she was hearing this correctly, not sure it was really happening, not sure this tanned, handsome man with the powerful forearms and golden hair was even real at all.

"I know you probably never saw yourself with a beach bum, a guy who barely got his GED, and you're way out of my league. I know you deserve to be with doctors and rich real estate gurus. But if you give me a chance, I want to do my best for you and Coco. I need you, Giselle. I need you *with* me. Will you come back to Sandy Cove? Live with me? You and Coco?"

As she opened her mouth, Fin held his hand up.

"I know you're going to say your ex won't allow it," he went on. "But I have a feeling I can convince him. I need a few words with him anyway."

Giselle thought again of Roy and his part in Fin's misery. She knew she needed to tell him.

"Before you say no, let me throw in a few more things: I won't travel. I know your ex was always gone. And I don't want that for you. Or Coco. I've already talked to Fox. I made it to the semifinals in Ballito, but I threw the last heat because I don't want to compete anymore. I love surfing because it's surfing, but I don't want to compete. I told Fox, and he agreed. He said they can use me in Sandy Cove—I'm going to help them design boards and fins with my name on them. They'll name them after the competitions I've won, and I'll just travel a bit for exhibitions, but it's up to me. We can travel when it suits us, and when I can bring you and Coco. In fact, Fox wants to come along, with Tamara and Toni. I think we've got traveling companions." He grinned. "I just want to surf in peace. And pursue the things that are missing in my life."

Giselle frowned and shook her head. "What's missing?"

"You."

He paused for what seemed like a lifetime, then pulled her toward him—as if uncertain whether she wanted to come. But his body was looking like a shelter to her now, his arms a circle of strength, his chest a rock-solid wall. She wanted nothing more than to be wrapped with him, absorbed in him. She stepped into his chest, pressing against him, wishing she could somehow be even closer, and looped her arms around his neck.

"There's one thing that's keeping us from giving this a whirl," he said.

"What?"

"I don't know if you feel the same way."

Giselle threw herself forward, kissing him until he staggered against the porch and caught himself against the bricks. She ran her fingers through his hair and tugged, meeting the insistence of his lips with her own promises, promising more of this, more of her. . . .

"Is that a yes?"

"Yes!"

"I'm not too uneducated for you?"

"You're world-wise."

"I'm not too much of a loner?"

"I like iguanas."

"What?"

She shook her head and kissed him harder.

"God, Giselle, have I mentioned you're the hottest kisser?" He tugged on her bottom lip, shooting a longing straight through her that she felt pull throughout her body. . . .

"Coco here?" he mumbled against her mouth.

"I have to pick her up in about fifteen minutes."

He ran his hands up her body, pushing her back through the doorway on a kiss and closing the door behind them.

As Giselle felt his hand slip under the lace of her bra band, she pushed him against the couch, and her hand drifted to his waistband. "*This* is what I've been missing," she whispered to him.

Passion wasn't just something in Humphrey Bogart movies. It was real. And possible between two people who loved each other, and respected each other, and maybe thought they weren't quite good enough for each other. And two people who only wanted the best for each other.

"We . . ." He snapped his hand around her wrist as she got his zipper down. "We have to get Coco, Giselle."

"Fast, maybe . . ." Her words came out in a rush.

He laughed. "We have all the time in the world. Every day. For the rest of your life. If you'll have me . . ."

Giselle stared at him. This was real. *This* was what she wanted.

Unable to adequately respond to every one of her dreams coming true, she simply nodded.

"You'll come to Sandy Cove?"

She nodded again.

"Let's get Coco. Then we're continuing this. Tonight."

After Coco was in bed, Giselle removed the cookie plates from the coffee table, sauntered back to where Fin sat on the couch, and drew him into the bedroom.

"Sex always has to take place behind locked doors when you have kids, you know," she whispered over her shoulder.

He turned when they got inside the room and locked hers. Then he whipped his T-shirt over his head in one deft movement. "I can live with that." He paced toward her.

"And you have to be kind of quiet."

"Duly noted," he whispered.

"And it might start to feel 'routine.' "

He wrapped his arms around her. "I doubt that."

"And it can be kind of predictable."

"I'll look forward to it predictably, then." He nibbled on her neck, moving her back toward the bed.

"And it might—"

"Giselle." He silenced her gently. "I don't care. We're going to have great sex. Being the passionate woman you are, and all." He followed that comment with a grin and a fingertip down her front. "And I'm going to thank my lucky stars every day that I found you." He kissed her collarbone. "Every single star." He unbuttoned the top of her blouse and landed another kiss to the top of her breast. "Every single night." Another button . . .

And Giselle moaned with pleasure as all her buttons came undone.

Her new life had truly begun.

* * *

On the flight home, Fin sat between his two new women. Giselle fell asleep on the aisle seat. She'd had a hectic few weeks, packing up most of what they owned and handing it to him to box up in the garage. They planned to get the last of it later, after she'd wrapped things up with Roy and decided on a sale date. Roy was happy to oblige. Fin had had a private phone conversation with him, in tones he hadn't wanted to move into threats.

Fin glanced over at Coco. "Are you happy?"

She grinned and nodded.

He smiled back. He'd never been happier. "You gonna surf with me every morning?"

She nodded again, emphasizing her point by bouncing in her airline seat.

"Hey, little grommet, I've got to thank you, you know."

"For what?"

"It worked."

"What worked?"

Fin wriggled to the side to access his pocket. When he felt the smooth surface, he pulled the shell out of his pocket and held the abalone out in his flat palm. "It made me a prince, just like you said."

Coco touched her fingertips to her lips and giggled. "You carried it with you?"

"I needed to."

"You're a good prince."

"Thanks, Coco."

"Mommy needed one."

"She deserved one."

"You'll be just right."

Fin nodded around the lump in the back of his throat. "I plan to spend the rest of my life making sure of that."

He laid his head back, feeling content on a plane for the first time in his life, not chasing anything, not searching for the perfect wave.

He'd found it.

And he was ready to make it last a lifetime.

Read on for a preview of
Lauren Christopher's next

Sandy Cove Romance

Coming Spring 2015 from
Berkley Sensation

Lia's rolling briefcase bumped over the wooden dock slats as she rushed down the ramp in her high heels toward Drew's boat. The rhythmic thumping of the slightly broken left wheel echoed the relentless thump in her chest, especially when she saw the empty wheelchair parked at the end of the dock, a seagull perched haughtily on the handle in the late-winter sun.

"Drew?" She pulled her case toward her and peered up and down Drew's enormous white catamaran deck. Long shadows darkened the entire back end.

When she was met with only the quiet laps of the harbor water splashing against the hull, she mentally measured the leap from the dock to the three small steps at the back of the boat, then eyed the deep Pacific below. She took a tentative step with her toe, but the catamaran pitched a little too wide for her pencil skirt.

"Lia!" Douglas's gruff voice, rasped from at least five decades of smoking, preceded him as he hoisted his bearlike body through the narrow cabin door.

"Douglas! Glad to see you. How is he?"

"Churlish."

Douglas wiped some kind of potato chip grease from his fingers onto the belly portion of his T-shirt, took the steps down to the catamaran's low stern, and hauled Lia's briefcase into the boat. He reached out his weathered hand to help her make the leap, but his eyes slid to her shoes.

"Where are your boat shoes, sunshine?"

"I came straight from my last client when you called."

"On a Saturday?"

"No rest for the promotion-bound." She threw him a tired smile for proof. Her boss, whom she not-so-affectionately thought of as The Vampiress, and who regularly used phrases like "I'll hold your feet to the fire," had been running her ragged.

"Here." Lia undid the dainty straps of her shoes and handed them, one at a time, to Douglas, who stared at them curiously before chucking them onto the bench seat that ran along the edge of the boat.

He jutted his chin toward the main hull. "Enter at your own risk."

Drew's galley was clean and sparse, mostly bright white with splashes of nautical blue and meticulously shined stainless steel. Lia was always surprised at how spacious it seemed, even when the catamaran was filled with the forty-five guests he usually had on a whale-watching trip. But today it was eerily empty, with just Drew sitting at the small galley table, twisted so he could unload a tiny cupboard that was part of the curved bench seat. He slammed paperwork and small canisters onto the tabletop, then hauled out three or four folded plastic tablecloth items that looked like some type of covers. Beneath the table, two bright white, slightly bent casts covered both his legs, toes poking helplessly toward the narrow walkway.

She stifled a gasp. "Drew, I'm so—"

"Save it, Lia." Without a glance back at her, he continued slamming things onto the table. "I know you're sorry. Everyone's sorry. I'm sorry. But I just don't want to talk about it right now."

She pressed her lips together and tore her eyes away from the casts, then sidled in toward the table, lugging her briefcase behind her. The case was filled with two hundred new color brochures, plus two hundred colored tickets and passes she'd had made up for his new whale-watching business. She really wasn't supposed to be doing free marketing work on the side for her friends—The Vampiress would screech into her twenty-third-floor ceiling tiles if she found out—but Lia's friends had terrific businesses, and Lia always had marketing ideas for them.

"Drew, I think we need to talk about this and come up with a plan for what you're going to—"

"I don't *know*, Lia." A small vinyl bag landed on the table next to the canisters. It seemed to be the main thing he was looking for. He turned slightly in the dinette seat. "I guess you didn't understand the part about 'don't want to talk about this right now.'"

She tugged her briefcase closer to the table and edged around his casted feet to take a seat. "Drew, as your friend, I would honor that one-hundred percent. And I would come here and make you soup in your lucky bowl from college and pour you a nice, neat scotch and we'd sit here and get plastered. But, buddy—" She put her hand on his wrist. "I have to come to you today as a marketing manager. Because I just booked The Vampiress's most important client on *your boat*. Because you needed the business. You need to come through for me on this, Drew. *Please*."

Drew stared at the table. "I don't see how I can make that happen."

Images of The Vampiress and her rage floated through Lia's head. Lia was not much more than a glorified administrative assistant right now, and had been for the last four years. But she was on the cusp of a promotion—a huge promotion—if she could pull this off. She could feel it. It had been a dangling carrot for the last three years, but now, finally, it looked like it could happen. And just in time, too. Turning twenty-nine and still hoping she got the coffee right for her boss was not exactly what she'd had in mind for herself when she'd stepped into the hallowed glass walls of the most famous ad agency in Southern California.

"Drew," she started again. She kept her voice calm. "I just spent two whole vacation days helping you sell a hundred freaking tickets for excursions over the next six weeks, and you launch Monday. I know you're feeling frustrated. And I know you're feeling desperate. But you need a plan. Quickly. And I need that client charter next weekend. So let me be your free PR person and help you come up with something. And then let me be the friend who's going to help you through all this." She stole another glance at the casts.

"I need the friend who will sit quietly and let me brood."

"Then you should have called Xavier."

Drew smirked and stared at the table. They both stilled, listening to the gentle marina waters lapping the sides of the boat and Douglas's distant whistling of "(Sittin' on) The Dock of the Bay."

"I wanted you to come," he said quietly. "I knew you'd know what to do. I just don't want to keep rehashing the accident."

Lia nodded. She knew her friendship with Drew was strong. And she knew he'd come through for her. Their friendship had undergone a subtle shift in the last six months, when she'd become his free public relations manager in addition to his friend. He was about the fourth friend she'd started helping with marketing. She knew it probably wasn't smart to give up her measly leftover time off to help friends on the weekends, but she enjoyed it. She helped Drew and their friend Vivi, who ran the cute little vintage clothing store on Main Street, plus her landlord, plus Mr. Brimmer, who'd just opened his own wine-and-cheese shop on Main. She was really proud of the campaigns she'd launched for them, and proud of all her friends for starting such brilliant businesses. Until today anyway.

Drew was flexing his hands, staring at them on the table. "We need to find someone for at least the first week," he finally said.

"Yes." A breath of relief escaped Lia's throat. "Do you know any other captains we can call?"

"No one I can trust."

Lia listened to the waves lapping. "What about Douglas?" she finally asked.

"He doesn't have a commercial captain's license."

She figured as much. Otherwise he'd have been the clear choice. Her mind raced. "Kelly from the marina?"

"He's fishing boat only."

"What about want ads?"

Drew scowled further. "This is an expensive boat, Lia."

She nodded and touched his arm again. Drew was more of a control freak than she was, with touches of OCD to boot. She couldn't imagine him giving up his boat to anyone. It cost more than his house.

He gingerly began putting the items from the table into a box that was wedged onto the seat next to him.

She wanted to stay focused on business, but her mind kept drifting to the motorcycle accident, imagining it again and again. This morning she'd flown in from a trade show in New York that The Vampiress had sent her to, gotten dressed for work, thrown everything into her car to start visiting the San Clemente clients she'd missed this week, then received the call from Douglas. The horror of the accident—Drew sliding across the freeway off his motorcycle—and the fact that they could have lost him, played over and over in her mind all the way here.

"Does it hurt?" she asked.

"I'll be okay. Painkillers help. No talking about it right now."

Lia nodded again and eyed the neat stacks in the box. "Need help?"

"I got it."

They sat in silence again, Drew organizing the items in the box in his fastidious way, his movements slowing as he thought.

"I considered calling my dad out here from Virginia," he said. "But his heart's been bad. My mom thought it best we not tell him just yet."

Lia nodded, her mind racing back through everything she knew about Drew. They'd been friends for six years, part of a small circle of really cool people she rallied with once a week at The Shore Thing bar, and they'd all become like family, really. Until recently, anyway, when she'd started working eighty-hour weeks. She and Drew had even tried to date once, eons ago—he'd picked her up to take her to a nice restaurant near the pier, but when he'd leaned over to try to kiss her, they'd both burst out laughing.

"Oh! What about your old first mate, Colleen?"

"Maternity leave."

Lia slumped back. Colleen would have been perfect.

"There is . . ." He stared at the table, as if trying to decide whether to mention it or not, but then he turned his focus back to the box.

"Who?"

"Never mind. Maybe not. It's too risky . . ."

"Who?"

Drew shook his head.

"Look, if this person can sail and knows anything about whales—whoever this is—let's think about it. This is thousands of dollars we're talking about . . ."

"My brother."

Lia frowned. "I didn't know you had a brother, Drew."

"He just . . . showed up."

Behind her, Douglas took a step down into the cabin. "He just washed up on shore, is what you mean. Need anything more, boss? Want me to get you loaded up?"

"In a minute. Here, take this." He shoved the box across the small galley table.

When Douglas stepped back into the sunshine, Drew glanced up at Lia. "My brother's a wild card."

"Where is he? Why haven't I heard you mention him in all these years?"

"Well, 'just washed up on shore' is about right. He sailed in yesterday. He's a little messed up. Been sailing the world."

"Well, that . . . that sounds *fortuitous*. Sounds like perfect timing." Lia's heart began racing. Maybe this was an easier solution than she thought.

"Did you not hear the 'messed up' part?"

"What do you mean, 'messed up'? If he can sail the world, he can certainly sail in and out of the harbor. Does he know anything about marine life?"

"Oh, yeah. Former U.S. Coast Guard. Naturalist. Environmentalism degree."

"What are you waiting for?" Lia scooted her hips out of the bench to reach into the briefcase for her cell. "He sounds perfect. Let's call him."

"Lia." Drew grabbed her wrist. He looked up at her through the bangs that fell across his forehead. *"Messed up."*

"How messed up? You mean on drugs?"

"No, not drugs."

"You mean, like, crazy?"

Drew shrugged.

Lia sat back and leaned in toward him. He looked miserable. In addition to the scraggly hair, dark circles ringed his eyes and his normally tan skin had a strange sallow color. Beads of perspiration lined his forehead. He winced, as if in pain again. Lia lifted her hand off his forearm.

"He went through a lot of tragedy over the years," Drew said, low. "He's just kind of . . . on his own. Just stays on that boat and anchors wherever the winds take him. He rarely even talks. He won't agree to a tourist boat, no way."

"Can't you ask?"

"He won't agree."

"Drew!" Lia brought her head down to try to get him to look at her again. "You *need* him. You don't have many options to keep your business alive in this most important week, and I *really* need that charter. He's family. He'll do it for you. Just ask."

Drew looked away without answering, clearly unconvinced. He scanned the cabin, as if searching for something else he needed.

"Drew!" Lia couldn't believe he wouldn't consider this. It was an easy solution to a problem they needed to solve by Monday. Family would do anything for you, right? Granted, she had purposely put miles between herself and her own mother—and even one of her sisters—but if they really needed her, she'd be there.

Drew hollered for Douglas.

"I think we need to come up with a plan," she said softly.

"Let's talk about it tomorrow. I need another painkiller. Douglas! So how's your boyfriend, anyway?"

"He's fine. But Drew, let's talk about this. I booked some really impor—"

"Did he leave for Bora Bora?"

"Yes, but let's stay on task, here. I think—"

"I thought you guys were getting serious. I can't believe you let him go to Bora Bora without you."

"It's not serious, and I don't think 'let' should be a phrase in any healthy relationship . . ."

Drew threw a grin at that—an argument they'd had time and time again—but he looked frantically for Douglas.

". . . but I think we need to come up with a plan, Drew, for who's going to sail your boat Monday. It's booked solid for the first three weeks, and my client wants to show up to inspect it before the big charter on Saturday, and—"

"Tomorrow, Lia. Doug!" His yell had a twinge of desperation.

"Let's just ask your brother. It would be a simple solution, and you trust him, and—"

"Asking my brother would *not* be a simple solution. In fact, the more I think about it, the more disastrous it seems. So let's get that idea off the table. Let me think of another plan overnight, and we'll talk about it tomorrow."

"But we're running out of time."

"Give me until tomorrow. Maybe Doug and I can handle it—he can lift me into the captain's chair every day." At the sight of Douglas lunging down into the cabin, Drew gave a weak smile and began maneuvering to the side of the dinette, his casts clunking along the deck floor.

Doug lifted him with a loud grunt—about two hundred forty pounds of man lifting about a hundred and sixty—then lumbered back up the four narrow stairs, somehow managing to twist Drew's casts and a combined four hundred pounds through the cabin door and onto the deck. Douglas staggered down the stern stairs and hoisted them both back up onto the dock. The wheelchair was waiting, set up with its brakes on, now with three boxes next to its wheels and the seagulls scared away. Douglas dropped Drew into the chair with a hiss, then straightened and wiped his brow. Both men were drenched in sweat and their faces had gone white.

At the sight of Drew's pain, and then the boxes, Lia felt the color drain from her own face. Drew's pale, crumpled forehead registered his dismissal of that last idea.

What were they going to do?

Drew made 80 percent of his annual income in the six weeks of whale-watching season. He and his new girlfriend, Sharon, were struggling as it was, trying to launch this business, trying to make ends meet. And Sharon had a special-needs child that Drew said he didn't pay for, but Lia knew he did. And now these new medical bills . . .

And man, Lia hadn't even told him the part about the first two clients she'd booked for Monday and Tuesday—she didn't want to make him feel guiltier than he already did, or cause more worry to spike with his pain. In addition to the client she'd booked for The Vampiress, she'd found two potential investors for Drew, which he'd said he really needed. And both were showing up this week. If they showed up to a boat that was inoperable . . . well, not only would they run from investing in such a thing, but Lia's reputation would be shot.

She quietly gathered her shoes from the blue-cushioned bench seat and tugged her rolling briefcase against her side. Douglas lumbered back onboard to secure the cabin door.

"Douglas, wait." She jerked her case back toward the galley. "Let me leave this here."

As he unlocked the cabin door again and helped her move it inside, she moved closer to his shoulder. "What about his brother?" she whispered. "Could he operate this thing?"

Douglas gave her a sympathetic glance, but then his allegiance shifted back toward the dock. "His brother's trouble, sunshine."

"We need someone, Douglas. Full tours start Monday."

"Can't you refund them?"

"For *six weeks*?" Her whisper rose to a panic. "These are really important clients. And Drew's already spent half that money, I imagine. And the other half is probably going to new bills after this accident."

Douglas's silence gave her the answer she didn't really need.

"Where does his brother live?"

Douglas ushered them back out into the harsh February sunshine and fiddled with the lock. When his silence lengthened, Lia let her shoulders fall. He wasn't going to answer. She turned away from his weathered hands.

"Slip ninety-two," Douglas finally mumbled under his breath.

"What?" She turned her head slightly. Drew was staring at them intently.

"Guest slip. Ninety-two. Far north end," Douglas said without moving his lips.

He turned into the sunlight, heading back toward the stern,

and Lia followed. As they stepped back ashore under Drew's watchful gaze, Drew shot them both a suspicious look.

But Lia was going to have to betray him.

Drew wasn't thinking clearly, and she was going to have to make this right.

For him.

For her.

For this promotion.

And for about five other relationships she couldn't seem to get right lately.

Guest slip ninety-two was nearly at the end of the marina, at the end of the dock. A lamp sputtered as she passed, and dusk fell in light purple. There were no liveaboards allowed at this end of the marina and, with a cool February night that threatened rain, there weren't many people out, even on a Saturday. Lavender water lapped against the empty boats that lay still and quiet at day's end, all packed together like sleeping sardines.

Lia glanced again at the piece of paper where she'd written the number, pulling it back from the breeze that tried to curl it, then slid it into the pocket of her skirt with the dock key Douglas had slipped her. She concentrated on not getting her heels caught in the weathered wooden planks.

When she reached ninety-two, she pushed her wind-strewn hair out of her face and peered around the deck. It was a small sailboat, about a twenty-footer, dark and closed up for the night. The sails were covered, the ties set, the cabin lights seemingly off.

"Hello?" she called anyway.

Nothing.

Her footsteps sounded obnoxious in the otherwise peaceful night as she headed slowly down the side dock along the boat's starboard side.

"Hello?" she tried again. "Drew's brother?"

Dang. She didn't even know his name. Her heels rang out as she wandered farther. The only other sound was the familiar creaking of the boat's wood against water, and one rope hanging off a mast that thumped lightly as the boat pitched and rolled slightly. The sailboat didn't have the gleaming OCD-ness of Drew's catamaran, but was relatively neat, the teak floors swept, the sails snapped up firmly, the ropes in perfect twists. A jacket and an empty bucket sat on a faded deck bench.

"Hello? Mr. Betancourt?"

A slight shiver ran through her. Maybe she'd rushed into this too quickly. She should have asked more questions—at least his name—and maybe pressed for more information about what, exactly, "messed up" meant. As an image began to take shape in her head—ex-military, maybe post-traumatic, older, bigger, bearded, crazy, loner—the light on the dock snapped and buzzed, threatening total darkness. Her pulse picked up and she turned on her heel. She wasn't one to scare easily, but this probably wasn't one of her brightest moves.

But then . . . a flicker of light in the cabin.

She turned nervously.

The cabin door creaked and a man's shadow emerged, buttoning a shirt as the tails flapped in the night wind, as if trying to get away from him.

He twisted his shoulders to clear the cabin door and stepped slowly toward her while the boat pitched, moving across the deck with all the assurance of a man who is used to the sea.

He was bigger than Drew—nearly half a foot taller, and broader in the shoulders. He had the same dark hair, but his was much too long, and he swiped at it as he looked up at her on the dock. Although his face was in shadow, she could see that about a week's worth of facial hair darkened his jaw. His eyes narrowed as he studied her and finished the last two buttons. "Whadoyouwant?" His voice was like gravel.

"I'm, um . . . a friend of Drew's."

His eyes made a quick sweep of her—not out of interest, seemingly, but in the way you'd assess a dirty floor, deciding how much work it was going to be to get rid of.

While he continued to wait—probably for a better answer—Lia fumbled with her purse. "I, um . . ." For some reason, she checked the piece of paper again. Ninety-two, right? But certainly this was him. She could see a vague family similarity in the straight, narrow nose, the hard-edged jaw, the dark eyebrows. Though this man's brows seemed much more sinister than Drew's, pulled into a deep *V* beneath a lined forehead as he waited for her to say something.

"I . . . I came for Drew. He needs . . . um . . . well, he needs a favor."

The boat creaked and rolled under the man's spread legs, his knees giving way in the slightest movement to make him as sturdy as the mast.

"Doesn't seem like Drew would send you to tell me that."

Lia licked her lips. He had her there. She tried to give him one of her friendliest smiles—it worked on everyone—but he seemed unfazed. He simply narrowed his eyes even farther and waited for her to go on.

"I, um . . . well, yes, that's true. You're *absolutely* right about that." She laughed just a little, flashed another smile. Normally men didn't make her nervous at all. She'd learned a long time ago that an optimistic attitude, a great smile, and a positive view on the world could do wonders and get her almost anything she wanted, with men or women. Or hide anything she wanted.

But this man seemed too robotic to care.

"He's, uh . . . well, you know about the motorcycle accident, right?"

Nothing.

"Well, after his accident, he's a little stuck. He's got whale-watching season right ahead of him, and he needs to run his business. This is *his* season. It's the biggest season. I mean, from February to April, it's—"

"I know when whale-watching season is."

"Yes, of course. Then you know. It's huge. And he's booked every single day for the next four weeks, and I could easily book the additional two, and—"

"*You're* booking him?"

"Well, I help, yes."

He didn't seem to like that for some reason, but he gave a slight shift on his leg that somehow indicated she should go on.

"So I'm . . . I'm just so worried for him, and he needs a captain, since the accident and everything, and he just needs someone to sail his cat, and who knows about whales, and who can take on the business for him for just a few weeks, and—"

"Sounds like this is your problem, not his."

"Oh, no, it's *his*."

Well, *too*. But Lia's own personal problems didn't need to be part of this discussion. "He's . . . the *money* . . . you know. This is the majority of his income. And medical expenses now. He's . . . he's in trouble, Mr. Betancourt."

He scanned her again—some kind of assessment—and blinked, the slow blink of a man unimpressed. "I'm not your guy."

"What do you mean?"

He turned and started back into the galley.

Lia found herself stumbling toward him across the dock, although she didn't know where she intended to go or what she intended to do once she got there. "Wait, Mr. Betancourt. You can't help?" She couldn't control the incredulousness in her voice.

"No." His deep voice gave the word a feeling of cement. He wandered toward the jacket and snatched it up.

"But you . . . you *have* to."

"No." He turned back, giving her high heels a strange glance. "I don't."

He scanned the deck again, seemingly to see if anything else needed to be crushed in his fist the way the jacket was. "If Drew wants to talk to me about this, tell him to come tomorrow. But I have a hard time believing he sent you."

He lumbered across the deck, and the brass rails of the galley door glinted as the door slammed shut.

Stunned, Lia closed her mouth, her protest swallowed.

The dock light flickered again behind her with a loud pop, sending her into an embarrassing jump, then began an ominous hum and flutter. She glared at it, trying to figure out what to do as darkness fell. She'd thought she'd be able to simply solve this problem, but apparently she was losing her touch.

Not that this guy was an ideal solution. Drew was right. He'd be a nightmare with the guests, especially The Vampiress's client. He looked more like he was going to slit their throats and steal their bounty than tell them the gentle breaching habits of blue and gray whales.

But at least he'd be a Band-Aid on the problem, and a start to a better solution.

As the lamp began its death hum, she glanced down the

long dock toward the main part of the marina. She only had about one minute left of any kind of light at all, then she'd have to find her way back in a sliver of moonlight, now shadowed by black-tinged rain clouds.

With one last glance at the now-darkened cabin, apparently closed up to fool the harbormaster into thinking there were no liveaboards here, she headed back along the dark, narrow planks.